NOMADIN

Shawn P. Cormier

Pine View Press

Nomadin

Visit us on the Web! www.pineviewpress.com

ISBN: 0-9740151-0-5
Library of Congress Control Number: 2003094497

Published by:

Pine View Press
42 Central Street
Southbridge, Ma 01550

Printed in Canada

A BOY AND HIS DOG

P ile it there—in that clear spot!" barked the dog, running back and forth between the trees. "A fire may keep them at bay!"

Ilien stacked all the branches and logs he could find in the center of the clearing. The pile of wood grew taller than him.

Thessien's black steed suddenly screamed. It threw its head and stomped about, the heavy scent of the wolves finally driving it mad. Ilien thought of unbridling it—freeing the big black of encumbrances in case of trouble, but the giant dog shouted out, "We need more wood than that! Follow me!" and Ilien left the horse to fend for itself. He had no doubt that it could.

"Move!" shouted the dog.

Ilien grabbed the Illwood sword where he'd left it, propped against a tree. He eyed the three sharp thorns on its end. It would make a deadly weapon in a pinch. He shuddered at the thought, then moved down the hill after the dog.

They traveled only as far as they needed to fill Ilien's arms heaping with wood, then returned up the hill. The dog led the way, and thankfully so. Night had fallen quickly. But when they reached the woodpile, Ilien gasped and stumbled forward, dropping his armful of wood.

The pile was gone. So too was Thessien's steed.

The dog let out a low growl, and Ilien spun around. They stood surrounded by a jury of shining yellow eyes, peering at them from between the trees. The dog lifted its head to the deepening dusk. Its long howl shuddered the forest. The wolves stood unfazed, their grins only widening.

Acknowledgments

The following is a chronological listing of those special few who helped make this book possible:

1. My parents, John and Emily, for their support.
2. Mr. David Yacavace, for his love of words.
3. Joe Romano, for his belief in dreams.
4. Steve Westcott, for leading the way.
5. Paul Cormier, for his constant encouragement.
6. Nancy Holder, for her keen eye and red pen.
7. Robert Holland, for his help with the 'technicals'.
8. Jeff and Kelly Maraska, for my wonderful cover.
9. My children, Tom and Nicole, for keeping me young at heart.

But most of all, I would like to thank my wife, Lynn, for without her there would be no book.

For Glenn,
who I will always remember.
And for Keith,
who I will never forget.

CONTENTS

I	The Map in the Hall	1
II	Of Witches and Wands	18
III	Whispers and Warnings	34
IV	The Illwood Tree	44
V	The Bark and the Bite	53
VI	Evernden	63
VII	The Groll	75
VIII	The Drowsy Wood	94
IX	Kink and Crank	104
X	Into the Dog House	114
XI	A Shadow in the Dark	124
XII	The Swan	135
XIII	The Test	148
XIV	Runner	163
XV	The Best Laid Plans	172
XVI	The Giant's Tale	182
XVII	Kink's Revenge	192
XVIII	Herman the Heretic	203
XIX	The Giant's Encampment	215
XX	Alone in the Night	229
XXI	Greattower	244
XXII	NiDemon	257
XXIII	Nomadin	272

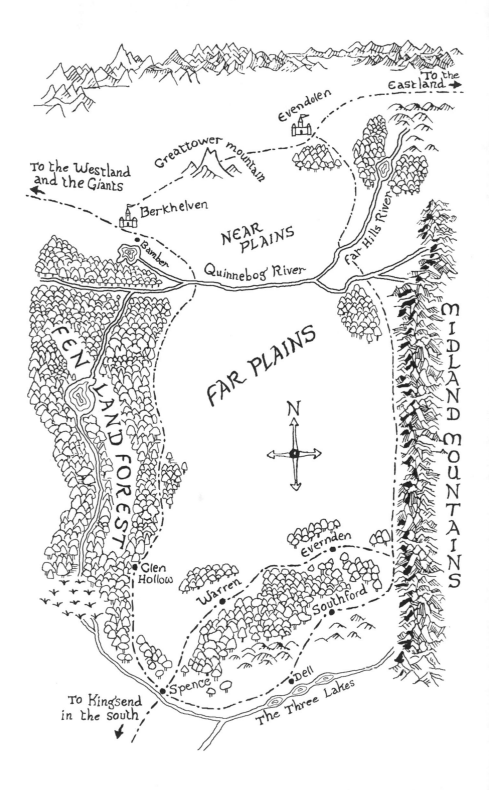

Chapter I

The Map in the Hall

He was dead for sure.

Twice before he had foiled their attacks. Once by hiding in a thicket of brambles at daybreak whose prickers left claw marks down his face, next through sheer luck, overhearing their whispers of revenge as he hid behind a tree at dusk. Then he was able to avoid their trouble. But now, this third time . . . three times was a charm, but not always a lucky one. He braced himself as his enemies approached.

The two figures moved from behind the trees and stopped a dozen paces away. Their leader, small and thin, dug a finger up his nose. "Get him!" he commanded, wiping snot onto his dirty overalls. "Get him, and that pencil too!"

The other boy lumbered forward, his wide face creased in delight. There was nothing to fear here, that much he knew. After all, he was the biggest twelve-year-old in town, and taller than most thirteen-year-olds as well. Heck, he'd even made a few high schoolers cry. This little one would go down easy.

"Give it to me or else," he said, advancing and raising a meaty fist.

Ilien looked up the dirt road, hoping to spot the plume of dust in the distance that would signal help was on its way. A lone hawk circled above the flat, surrounding fields, a black spot in the sky above. He was on his own, as usual. He clutched his pencil tight, poised between rabbit and rain—in his fright he couldn't decide whether to run or fall down.

"Or else what?" piped a voice that sounded, oddly enough, just like Ilien's.

Ilien moaned. He knew he should've left the pencil at home. An "A" in math was little consolation for a beating.

The boy left the fist in the air and turned to look back at his impish leader, who was in the middle of mining another booger for his pant-leg collection. "Did you hear that, Peaty? Now I'll hafta hurt him."

Peaty laughed him on, his lips drawn back in a sneer, his finger still up his nose. "Do it, Stanley," he said in a nasally voice. "Do it."

Ilien held the pencil at his side, his feet frozen to the ground. He might still escape unharmed. There was still a chance. If only . . .

The pencil cleared its throat to speak again.

"Shut up! Shut up! Won't you ever shut up?" cried Ilien.

Stanley's fist streaked forward. Ilien tumbled to the ground, clutching the stinging wound beneath his eye. His head hummed like a broken beehive.

"Don't tell me to shut up," said Stanley. "Now give me the pencil!"

"Why?" piped the pencil, mimicking Ilien again. "I bet you don't even know how to use it. Besides, I'd be afraid you'd poke yourself and pop. Someone in your condition should be careful around sharp objects."

Stanley charged, leaping on top of Ilien like a marauding pig, pudgy pink fists raining blows. Ilien threw his arms across his face. Pinned beneath the sweating Stanley he could do little more than shield his wounded eye, but his thoughts were racing.

"Let the wimp up!" barked Peaty. "Let him have his precious pencil. Geek!"

Ilien gasped for air as his attacker climbed off. Both eyes

stung now, and a small tear of blood trickled from his nose.

"It's his only friend anyhow," said Peaty. "I bet his deadbeat daddy gave it to him right before he ran out on him."

Ilien squeezed his pencil in fury. It didn't matter that he never knew his father. No one talked about his dad like that. A few choice words of his own came to mind as anger swept through him, words that would do more than just sting.

"Ilien Woodhill! Don't you dare!" cried a voice behind him.

The two boys backed away, as boys often do when confronted by the dog who guards the yard they're meddling in. "It's that crazy old man. Let's get out of here!" yelled Peaty. Ilien watched from the ground as the two boys ran off, casting back menacing looks. "Look! It's freak and geek!" they called, laughing. Then they were gone.

Ilien climbed to his feet and wiped the blood from his nose. "I'm okay, Gallund," he said. Deep inside he felt like crying, but deeper still he wished Gallund had never showed up.

The old man leaned on a thin, wooden cane. His cheeks flushed bright red. His pale, silver hair stuck out at the sides, but he smiled as he surveyed the boy before him. He squinted one eye, scratched the stubble on his chin, then tugged up his pants till his socks showed beneath. "It wasn't you I was worried about," he said.

Ilien summoned tears and hid the pencil by his side. He'd learned to summon tears on cue since Gallund had come to stay at the house. A most useful skill.

"You know what I mean," said Gallund, and he reached into his pocket and pulled out a handful of peanuts. "I'd say it's a good thing I got here when I did, wouldn't you?" He popped a peanut into his mouth and began to chew.

What luck! It seemed he was safe after all. Gallund hadn't noticed the pencil. "Why yes. I guess you're right," said Ilien, smiling and puffing out his chest.

3

"They obviously didn't know who they were dealing with," continued Gallund, popping in another peanut. "If they had, they surely would've run long before I showed up."

"You can say that again," said Ilien. "Why, I could've taken them easy. In fact, I was just about to cast—"

Ilien marveled for a moment at his own stupidity.

"Ilien Vorasius Woodhill!" Dust swirled around Gallund, the product of an angry foot upon the road. His hands were at his hips, but he still held his fistful of peanuts. "What is rule number one?"

Ilien's shoulders resumed their usual droop. "No spells whatsoever outside the house," he muttered, "unless confronted by dark magic of the worse sort."

"And it seems I can't stress that enough, can I?"

"But you didn't hear what they said."

"I hear more than you think," said Gallund. "And if you're talking about what mister Peter Wilson said concerning your father, he should be as lucky. His father's a lying, cheating drunk. He beats the boy, I know. Better to have no father at all than one like his."

Ilien doubted that, but he kept his arguments to himself. He was in enough trouble already. Besides, he suddenly didn't feel like talking about it. He cast a glance up the road where Peaty had fled.

"Now back to the point at hand," said Gallund, tapping his cane on the road to garner Ilien's attention. "You know better than to use magic outside the house."

"But I wasn't really going to electrocute them."

"Electrocute them?" cried Gallund. "Electrocute them? You can't be serious!" He wagged a finger at Ilien as he yelled, and peanuts flew everywhere. "Not only have I been careful not to teach you offensive spells, but I am quite sure I have never taught you anything as low-down as electrocution. Surely you know that I myself would never consider using such a crass, and frankly, low class spell when Flaming Fingers would do a much better, and might I add, more impressive job. And let me remind you that Lightning spells are about as predictable as the weather. For all you know you might have electrocuted yourself."

Ilien kicked at the ground in front of him, scattering dropped nuts. "Well, I think Lightning spells jam," he mumbled.

"Jam? Jam? What is that language you're speaking? Where in the world did you ever think that one up? Jam indeed. I never will understand you kids. Jam. Jelly. Marmalade. Really!"

Gallund turned and walked up the dusty road, carrying his cane like a sword and ranting under his breath about everything, from what kids say to what kids smell like. "And how your mother ever gets your britches clean after god knows what you've been rolling in. If she wasn't away visiting your uncle— How I ever let you convince me to teach you magic behind her back, I'll never know!"

He spun and pinned his pupil with a look that could have tacked paper to the wall. "And don't you think I didn't see that pencil in your hand," he said, dropping more peanuts as he pointed in accusation. "I didn't give you an enchanted pencil so you could cheat on your geometry test. It's for spellwork, not schoolwork. Once more, just once more, and you'll lose it for good. Now let's go. If you can't play nice then you won't play at all. Study. That's what you'll do. Study!"

As Gallund turned to go he looked into his hand. "Nuts!" he cried, and threw the remaining crumbs to the ground.

To Ilien, the short walk back to the house felt as long as a forced march to certain death. He trailed behind his teacher, kicking along a small rock that had been unfortunate enough to get in his way. His small town of Southford stretched out around him like a taut, green blanket with occasional wrinkles where the sudden hills dropped down to flooded gullies and trickling streams. Luckily, he had to pass only one house along the winding road, Farmer Parson's, and no one there was home to witness his humiliation. Study. On a Friday, no less! He shoved his hands to the bottom of his pockets in disgust.

So it was that Ilien found himself imprisoned on a sunny, green April day while the rest of the world fished and climbed trees and chased dogs. Even his house, a small, two story farmhouse with no trees nearby to speak of, got to bask lazily in the warm afternoon sun, and Ilien desperately wished he could join it, lying half-asleep in the backyard out by the small, meandering stream that snaked away into the surrounding fields. Instead, he sat in a small, hard chair poring over a textbook big enough to choke a dragon. It wouldn't have been so bad, after all he was studying magic, if it hadn't been for the eyes he accidentally conjured up.

All seventeen of them. The size of dinner plates.

Fortunately, they weren't sword-wielding arms, or fang-filled jaws. Just eyes. A mob of them, huddled together in the far corner by the window, their lids flapping up and down in unison like tiny window shades. They hovered above the floor, squinting in the sunlight as if woken from a nap, thankfully taking no notice of the boy who sat frozen ten feet away.

Ilien eased his chair back and inched from his seat, keeping his two small eyes on the seventeen big ones across the room. He hoped to make it at least halfway to the door before they saw him. No small feat considering their number.

He turned and crept away. Then something caught his eye and he looked back in disbelief. His pencil was rolling across the table! He knew he shouldn't have choked the blasted thing. Now it was going pay him back. Magical pencils were so vindictive.

6

He held his breath as it neared the edge. If it fell he would be caught for sure. Magical pencils could make quite a racket when they wanted. Once, he accidentally broke its tip and it screamed so loud it woke his mother out of bed. He had to do some quick thinking to explain that one.

The pencil continued its vengeful march. Ilien pleaded silently for it to stop. It teetered on the brink.

"Over here! Over here!" it screeched as it hit the floor.

Seventeen black pupils narrowed to angry slits, and Ilien ran for the door. The eyes flew after him, flapping and hissing. Ilien's feet barely touched the floor, but the eyes were too quick. They reached the door before him and turned with an angry leer. Ilien was about to do the only thing he could think of, apologize profusely then run the other way, when the eyes sprang open wide. They retreated. They backed into the door, wincing in fear. One eye opened wide, peering at him through a pool of shimmering tears.

"Forgive us," it said. Its pupil formed the words like a mouth with no tongue. "Forgive us, Master. We had no idea it was you. Please forgive us."

Ilien forced a smile and shuffled back toward the table. "I forgive you," he said, secretly wondering how much his fall from the second story window would hurt.

At that the other eyes joined the first in blinking away their tears. The whole sopping cluster moved toward him, laying a watery trail behind. They seemed relieved, almost grateful—

—until Gallund stepped through the door.

In the blink of sixteen eyes (one remained shut in fear) they spun on the new intruder.

"*Ilustus bregun, ilustus bregar!*" cried the wizard as the eyes volleyed toward him. No sooner was the last '*bregar!*' out of Gallund's mouth when the eyes burst and disappeared, soaking him nose to knees in a deluge of warm tears.

"Ilien Woodhill!" Gallund's cheeks glowed red, and his hands at his hips framed a thoroughly wet mid-section. "What have I told you about jumping ahead? If I've said it a thousand times I've said it once, just because you can read a spell doesn't mean you're ready to cast it!" He rapped his cane on the floor. His clothes dried in an instant. "It's a good thing your mother's not here, that's all I can say. I don't know how I would have explained that one."

Ilien tugged at his shirt. He was a small boy for his age, and seemed to shrink even smaller before the angry wizard.

"I had no idea it was a Conjuring spell," he said.

"It most certainly wasn't!" exclaimed Gallund. "Conjuring spell indeed! It was merely an illusion, as were your delusions of grandeur, I might add. Master? Bah!" Gallund studied him silently for a moment, then said, "Now pick up your book and please sit down. It's time to go over your homework."

Ilien picked up the spell book. He snatched up the magical pencil as well, putting it in his pocket to keep it quiet. With a nervous glance at the wizard, he sat back down, turning his attention to the book in front of him. A curving, black symbol emblazoned its faded cover, like two cast iron horseshoes stuck belly to belly. He set it open to its first page.

Beside him on the table sat a tall, unlit candle in a holder of tarnished brass. Ilien read a short passage from his spell book in silence, took a deep breath and pulled the candle close. At a glance, a thin wisp of smoke curled upwards from the wick. A small flame jumped up, flickering as if a breeze blew in the room. He furrowed his brow in concentration and the pale flame grew steady. He breathed a sigh of relief as he watched it dance atop the candle. He turned to Gallund with a smile.

But suddenly the tiny flame flared angrily. It blazed upward. In a sizzling flash it burned the candle down to its end, leaving behind a pile of hot drippings and the smell of scorched wax.

Gallund's cane beat a steady tap tap tap on the floor. "Control," he said. "Control. Always say the spell aloud, It's much easier to tame your voice than it is to master your thoughts. And remember, the language of magic is no different than your own. Don't massacre it. Watch your tenses, avoid incomplete sentences, no unnecessary adverbs and please, oh please, use the proper words! Slang in a Flaming Fingers spell will get you just that."

Ilien nodded and tried to ignore the cane's impatient tapping as he studied the next passage.

"*Kinul*—" he began.

"Tut tut! Tenses! Watch your tenses!"

Ilien eyed Gallund's cane with wishes for a saw. "*Kinil ubid, illubid kinar*," he said aloud.

He held up his hand and a small globe of light, like a tiny full moon, appeared in his palm. It grew to the size of an apple, glowing pale gold. He removed his hand and the spot of light hovered where he left it. Upon his command he sent it flying about the room. Finally it came to rest like a halo above the wizard's head.

"Better," said Gallund, his eyes tempered with good humor. "Keep reading, but remember, no jumping ahead. I'll be downstairs. When you're through you can come down and eat. We wouldn't want you wasting away to nothing while your mother's in Dell, now would we?"

Ilien went back to studying the Kindle Candle spell as Gallund closed the door behind him. But as soon as he heard the wizard's footsteps descending the stairs he flipped the page.

One page isn't really jumping ahead, he thought. *It's really more like creeping than jumping.*

Creeping sounded more cautious, and thus more responsible. He had just begun reading about the dangers of lightning bolts—"*Caution! Be sure to avoid the future tense of the verb*

9

Involt for risk of being struck next Monday"—when . . .

"Ilien!" The wizard stood in the doorway, his eyes flashing with annoyance.

Caught!

Ilien slammed the giant book shut—on the fingertips of his left hand! He bit back a startled cry and looked up at Gallund, forcing a smile across his grimace of pain.

The wizard merely pointed to the space above his head where the tiny globe of light still hovered. "Would you mind?"

Ilien stifled a laugh and called the light back to his side where it floated lazily above the table.

As the late afternoon faded into early evening and the sun sank below the hills, Ilien was forced to abandon his studies. Even after he had brightened the magical light so he could see, he just couldn't keep it from wandering away. Whenever he tried to concentrate on the lightning bolt passage he lost control and the light drifted off, making it impossible to read. He thought of lighting a lamp, but he was tired and hungry and decided to quit for the night. Besides, he had only managed to shock himself twice while trying to learn the blasted spell, and only hoped the beginning of the week didn't bring any unexpected storms.

"Control," he mumbled, lamenting his lack of it. He spoke a few words to the magical light and it dimmed, but didn't go out. A few more words spoken sternly and it reluctantly faded to darkness, leaving the room steeped in shadows.

The clatter of hooves outside sent Ilien rushing to the window, tripping over his chair on the way. The western horizon glimmered purple and grey, and a few bright stars shone in the black sky to the east. Down below a single rider sat astride a black horse. Gallund went out to greet him, and from the way they acted it was apparent they knew each other. The rider dismounted and hitched his horse to the fence surrounding the front yard. The two talked briefly in the gloom, then Gallund motioned toward the door and they walked inside.

Who in the world would come to visit Gallund? wondered Ilien. Surely the crusty old wizard didn't actually have friends. Well, he'd just have to find out. Besides, it was time for supper anyhow.

"Wouldn't want you wasting away to nothing while your mother's in Dell," he said in his best wizard's voice. At that, the tiny globe of light flickered to life behind him and Ilien nearly fell back over his chair.

"Go away," he said. "Didn't I tell you to fade? Now fade!"

Again the little light dimmed but didn't go out. Instead, it flew under the table and hid. Ilien sighed. He shut the door behind him, locking the magical globe of light in the study.

Ilien tiptoed his way along the darkened hallway. The pictures on the wall looked like square, black patches in the gloom. As he neared the stairs he heard Gallund down below invite the rider to sit, then the wizard must have lit a lamp for the bottom of the stairs grew brighter. Ilien crept quietly down, avoiding the creaky fifth step, and hid in the shadows to hear their conversation and see who it was.

The rider sat in one of the high-backed chairs by the hearth. Ilien saw then that Gallund hadn't lit a lamp, but rather had stoked the fire, and was throwing more wood into the flames even then. Soon a large blaze hissed and crackled in the fireplace, casting its orange light upon the stranger.

Week-old whiskers stained a weather-beaten face. Bright green eyes canvassed the room. That was all Ilien saw before the man looked away and stretched his muddy boots out toward the fire. As he did so the glint of chain mail flashed beneath his cloak, and Ilien's heart suddenly jumped with thoughts of adventure and knights and swords. But what Ilien found most curious was not the armor. What stuck with him were the piercing eyes that had searched the room. And though they never fell his way, Ilien felt somehow certain that the man knew he was there, crouching like a cat upon the stairs. As Gallund left to fetch some hot ale, Ilien shrank back further into the shadows.

Just then the magical globe of light appeared beside him, trying its best to be as dim as an ember. The stranger flew to his feet. The tiny light disappeared, but it was too late for Ilien. The man seized him quickly by the collar.

"And what do I have here, lurking in the dark like an overgrown rat?" He looked Ilien up and down. "Or should I say mouse?"

Ilien struggled to free himself. "Let go of me!"

At that moment, Gallund returned from the kitchen with two steaming mugs. When he saw Ilien suspended off the floor in the other's rude grasp he burst into laughter, nearly spilling the piping hot ale.

"Put him down, Thessien. That's no way to treat my new apprentice."

The rider looked at Ilien in surprise, then set him down, bowing low in apology. "My pardons, young master. It has been a long time since I've been in a respectable place where people can be trusted." He bowed again.

Ilien stood dumbfounded. The magical globe of light reappeared, hovering above his head, but he didn't notice. He was transfixed by the tall stranger before him.

"Were you spying on us?" asked the wizard.

Ilien swallowed hard and looked at his teacher. "I just wanted to—" but he stopped. The magical globe dimmed as if suddenly ashamed as well. Gallund handed Thessien his mug and they both sat down.

"Well, are you just going to stand there all night and tire your legs?" asked the wizard. "Please, sit down."

Globe tried to follow, but Gallund pointed a long finger in its direction. "Not you! It's back upstairs for you." When Globe refused to move, Gallund reached for his cane. The tiny light disappeared.

Gallund and Thessien talked long into the night, many times sending Ilien to stoke the fire and fetch more hot ale. Ilien was beginning to wish he had stayed upstairs with his nose in his spell book; the man's thirst had no end! But in between trips to the kitchen he listened to their conversation and soon changed his mind.

"Tensions rage anew," said Thessien, gesturing with his mug and spilling ale in the process. "Berkhelven has raised an army, if you can call it that, and Evendolen has been training its archers and footmen."

"I do hope this story has an ending," interrupted Gallund. "Preferably one that will tell me why *you* are here. It seems unlikely that you would travel so far from the Eastland simply to request help with some ridiculous land spat. Surely this mountain they're fighting over can't hold that much gold." He reached into his pocket. "Nut?"

Thessien smiled and took a long pull of his ale. "I see you're still as impatient as ever." He wiped his mouth with a grimy hand. "Yes, my story does have an ending, even one worthy of a Nomadin's ear, though I'm not sure it's one you'd choose to hear."

"A Nomadin? What's a Nomadin?" asked Ilien as he threw yet another log onto the fire.

"I am Nomadin," answered Gallund, settling back in his chair with a handful of peanuts. He stretched out his long legs and tapped his boots together as he ate. His cane lay on his lap.

"But I thought you were a wizard."

"I'm called a great many things, Ilien. Whatever the name, rest assured, I'm still the same."

Thessien leaned forward in his chair. "May I finish?"

"Please do," said Gallund.

"Both sides in the dispute claim their miners have been disappearing. Each blames the other. Each denies the accusation." Thessien turned silent.

"And?" prodded Gallund, looking up.

"We believe a NiDemon has crossed."

"What are NiDemons?" asked Ilien.

Gallund gazed at the hissing fire and sighed. He stroked the handle of his cane, his eyes soft and polished in the flame light.

"What's your proof?" he asked.

"This." Thessien reached beneath his cloak and withdrew a small leather pouch tied fast with heavy string. He opened it carefully, producing a small, smooth stone. *A perfect skipping stone*, thought Ilien. It fit easily in Thessien's palm. He held it out for Gallund to see. As he did the room filled with a foul stench. The fire in the hearth sputtered and crackled. Ilien grabbed his nose. He hadn't smelled anything so awful since coming across the remains of one of Farmer Parson's calves after the wolves had taken their fill last July.

"Put it away," bade the wizard, as if pained by more than just the sickening odor.

Thessien placed it back in the leather pouch, cinching it tight. "It was found deep in the mountain where the mining tunnels end and the natural ones begin. There were others."

"What is it?" asked Ilien, still holding his nose.

Gallund sat slumped in his chair, and Ilien thought his face looked suddenly pale. "It's spanstone," said the wizard. "It's proof of a crossing."

"A crossing?"

The room fell silent save for the hiss of the fire. Ilien had no idea what it meant but he knew he'd get no further explanation.

Gallund stood up and waved his cane through the air. The

putrid smell of the spanstone disappeared. The color returned to his face, and he turned to Thessien.

"We leave in the morning." He tossed the remainder of his peanuts into the fire, where they sputtered and smoked.

"Leave?" asked Ilien. "Leave where?"

"Why, to Berkhelven," said the wizard. "Where else?"

Thessien fingered the chain mail near his collar. "We had better not take the road."

Ilien froze by the fire, a log poised over the flames. "Why is that?" he asked.

Thessien's eyes danced with reflected flames. "I stole across a dozen men camped near the East Road. Amber-eyed, every one of them."

"This far south?" said Gallund. "Ilien, fetch me the map in the hall."

The log Ilien held began to smoke. "Amber-eyed men?"

"Move, boy!" cried the wizard. "We don't have all night."

The map that hung in the hall revealed in detail the hilly land south to Clearwater River, north to the outskirt kingdom of Evernden, and east to the Midland Mountains. The western edge of the map lay blank. It was said that Giants roamed the west, so it was no mystery to Ilien why that side of the map remained unfinished. The map had been drawn by Ilien's father, who had been quite an adventurer in his youth, rumored to have even crossed the Midland Mountains, or so Ilien had been told.

Ilien returned with the map and handed the parchment to Gallund, who spread it open on his lap.

"Camped by the East Road, eh?" Gallund's cane tap danced on the floor. "Then we'll ride due north, over the hills behind us and through the outlying forests to Evernden, avoiding the road completely." He traced the route on the map with his finger. "Then from there, hmm, this map fails us there. No matter. I know the land north of Evernden well enough, and a relatively safe path through the Far Plains."

Ilien looked on with excitement. Often he had studied the map as it hung on the wall, imagining the land beyond the hills he hunted. More often still, he wondered about the world outside the edges of the map, beyond the Clearwater, past Evernden or especially over the mountains to the east, the mountains his father had once crossed. Perhaps soon he would know.

"What about the boy?" asked Thessien. "Surely we can't take him with us."

Ilien's face must have wilted to the floor for Gallund looked at him queerly. "This is not a game, boy."

"I know," said Ilien.

"You'll have to carry your own weight."

"I will."

"And keep up."

"Yes, of course!"

"And keep quiet!"

Ilien nodded.

Gallund shrugged and looked at Thessien. "I can't leave him here alone, that's for sure. And leaving him with the neighbors will only raise questions best left unasked."

Thessien stared into his mug.

Ilien stood as rigid as a sign post.

"Okay then," said the wizard. "You'll come as far as Evernden. I have a friend there who can watch over you until your mother returns from Dell. In fact, I believe he has a daughter to keep you company. When you do return home, tell your mother I was called away on important family business."

Ilien bit back his disappointment. As far as he knew, Evernden was only slightly farther away than Dell, and he had been to Dell before. And a girl? That was the last thing he wanted to keep company with. So much for his plans to see the world. He sighed and glanced at the map in Gallund's lap. *Evernden. Humph! Probably doesn't even have a castle,* he thought.

"Up to bed now," said Gallund. "And wash your face. You look like a raccoon."

Ilien touched his right eye. It still smarted from his scrabble with the bullies, but he did as he was told. He learned long ago, there was no sense in arguing with a wizard.

"So that's him," said Thessien after Ilien had gone upstairs. His speech was thick from too much ale, and he picked up his mug for more. "Doesn't look like much to me, even for an apprentice, let alone what you claim he is."

Gallund snatched the empty mug from Thessien's hand. "Looks are deceiving," he said, and rose to go into the kitchen. "Not all appearances are what they seem, oh brat of Ashevery. You, of all people, should know that."

"You haven't even tried to kill him yet, have you?" Thessien called after him.

Gallund spun around. "Shut up, you fool!" His eyes strayed to the staircase. He continued in a hushed voice. "We all deserve a life of our own choosing. Should it be any different for him?"

Thessien smiled. "Some would say yes, my friend. Some would say yes."

Upstairs, Ilien lay awake under his covers thinking about the mysterious visitor and the adventure he'd brought with him—the adventure he would miss. He imagined amber-eyed men laying wait for them upon the road, fearsome NiDemon haunting darkened caverns. And in the darkness of his room he thought of his father too. When at last he fell asleep, he dreamed of mountains.

17

Chapter II

Of Witches and Wands

In the stable yard behind the house, the horses were blowing steam and stamping the cold from their shoes. Their packs bulged with food, clothing and blankets.

Ilien's pack was especially full. Gallund had made him re-pack it three times already. He really didn't understand why. He had only packed the essentials. Still, the wizard had insisted and he finally had to leave his rock collection, marbles and lucky slingshot behind. He did manage to sneak in his pet frog, thus the small shifting bulge on the side of his pack. He just hoped it kept quiet.

The stars peeped above, bright white in the pitch of night. The sun wouldn't rise for another hour, and Ilien was tired. His dreams had been full of mountains and caves and the terrible things that lurked around in them. He had hardly gotten any sleep at all.

Off to his left sat Thessien astride his tall black horse, taller even than Gallund's grey one. Ilien's brown horse was smaller than both, pony-sized really. Why Gallund wouldn't let him take old Winnie, he didn't know. Granted the horse was old, ancient more like it, but at least on Winnie his feet wouldn't drag all the way to Evernden.

Ilien shook his head and yawned, wrapping his heavy riding cloak more tightly around himself. Secreted beneath it lay his bow and quiver. Gallund nearly made him leave that behind too. "You won't be shooting anything where you're going,"

he'd said. "Best you leave it in your room where it'll be safe."
Safe. Right. He still couldn't believe he was going to miss out
on all the adventure. Typical, really. Like that time he went to
the county fair last year, when all the other boys his age were
racing go-carts down Parson's Hill and he was stuck on the
kiddie rides. So what if he was small for his age. Did it always
mean having to watch the fun from the back of a pony?

Just then Gallund emerged from the house. His ever present
cane hung in the crook of one arm.

"I hope for your sake your mother doesn't get back early,"
he said as he approached. "Your room's a disaster. Here, this
is yours." He handed Ilien the house key. "And this." He
pushed a leather bound flask into Ilien's hands.

Ilien could feel its warmth. He hoped it wasn't what Thessien had been drinking last night. He didn't at all like hot ale
(not that he'd ever tried it)! He removed the cap and stuck his
nose in the rising steam. He could smell the earthy aroma.
Coffee! His mother never let him drink coffee! He looked
appreciatively at the wizard and took a careful sip.

"And let's not forget this," said Gallund, handing Ilien his
pencil. "You'll be a few days in Evernden. I wouldn't want you
getting bored."

Ilien eyed the mischievous pencil with disdain. It wasn't bad
enough that he was being left behind. Now he had to study to
boot. He jammed it into his back pocket.

"Let's get going," said the wizard, smiling. He leapt upon
his horse, and tipping his own flask of coffee, led them away
from the house and across the field, using his cane as a riding
crop.

Ilien gave one last look at his house, dark with shadows. It
appeared lonely now with no one in it, and for a moment he felt
relieved he would soon be returning. But only for a moment.

They traveled in silence, Gallund in the lead, choosing the

way in the gloom. Ilien brought up the rear, sipping his coffee while his horse jogged along to keep up with the longer strides of the others. They kept to the fields, avoiding the road and skirting the few houses they stole upon. They trudged forth blindly for fear of drawing attention by lighting a lantern, and Ilien couldn't help thinking about the amber-eyed men Thessien had seen. Could these amber-eyed men see in the dark—like wolves? If so, they could be watching from a distance even then. Ilien touched his bow beneath his cloak and looked around nervously. Gallund and Thessien rode on unfazed. Still, Ilien felt relieved to see that they drew near the forest. At least the trees would afford them protection from prying amber eyes. But then again, it surely opened up the possibility of ambush.

"Ilien!" cried Gallund. "Do try to keep up. We've only just started, for crying out loud!"

They rode for nearly an hour, winding their way between the trees. Ilien had long since lost his bearings, but Gallund led the way with marked assurance. Several times, as the old wizard looked to and fro, Ilien could have sworn he saw his eyes flash silver in the night.

Near sunrise they came to a stream that marked the boundary of the land Ilien knew. He had fished its deep pools often but had never ventured beyond it. Now he crossed with an unexpected feeling of excitement in his stomach. The splash of water in the darkness made his heart race for the want of mountains and unknown lands. But as they passed quietly through the slow current, he thought again of having to turn back at Evernden. With a kick he spurred his horse forward.

At noon they halted for lunch by a rocky brook where the water slowed into a large, sluggish pool. The sun shined down through the tangle of branches above and danced in the warm shallows, flashing brown and silver off the sandy bottom. The grey ghosts of fish spied on them from the cooler shadows of the pool's deep end. They had been riding up and down wooded hills all morning, and Ilien was glad to be off his horse, sitting on a mossy rock and eating a bit of bread and cheese. Gallund sat by his apprentice while he ate. Thessien had disappeared into the forest.

"Where did Thessien go?" asked Ilien.

"He's scouting ahead," said Gallund. He finished his bread and followed it with some water from a skin.

"Why? The trail is plain to see and these woods aren't dangerous." Ilien took the skin from the wizard. "Are they?"

A squirrel began to bicker at them from a nearby tree.

"No. True enough. But dangerous or not, Thessien is an Eastland soldier and it's his nature to be untrusting."

"A soldier?" said Ilien. "You mean he's in the army?"

"Of course he's in the army. What do you think I mean, a soldier in the air force? He rides a horse, Ilien, not a dragon."

Thessien called out from further down the trail, and Ilien followed Gallund, still thinking about what it would be like to ride a dragon. They found the soldier leaning against an oak tree on the crest of a small hill. On the ground before him were the ashes of an old campfire surrounded by stones.

Gallund approached and stooped low. He spread his hands over the ashes as if warming himself over an unseen fire. "Interesting," he said. "Very interesting."

The chattering squirrel had followed them. It swayed on a limb above, shaking the branches in warning. Gallund rose and searched the tiny knoll, prodding the ground with his cane. When he returned to the fire pit he looked troubled.

"What is it?" asked Ilien.

"Witches," said the wizard with a sideways glance.

"Here?" asked Thessien, his eyes hardening.

"Witches? How can you tell?" Ilien looked around, half-expecting to see a hag hiding behind a tree trying to cast a spell over them at that very moment.

"At first I couldn't," said Gallund, "but then I noticed these stones surrounding the fire pit and how they were arranged, five shaped like axe heads, set equally apart. It is the sign of witches."

He poked one with his cane. When he did it crackled with sparks. He pulled the cane away in surprise. "Very, very interesting," he said. He bent down and brushed away the leaves from around it. "A Runestone." He gave Thessien a sharp look.

Carved into the side of the stone was a strange symbol Ilien had never seen before. He couldn't help but notice that the forest had turned silent. "What are Runestones?" he asked, eyeing the trees and wondering where all the squirrels had suddenly gone.

"Not what," answered Gallund, "but who."

"You mean they're alive?"

Gallund looked up. "Not exactly, but they were. Runestones were once people, people foolish enough to bargain with witches."

Ilien stepped back from the fire pit. "The witches turned them into stones?"

"Yes," said Gallund, climbing to his feet. "But not ordinary stones. Ordinary stones are dead and unfeeling. Runestones are not. They contain imprisoned souls. There's a heavy price to pay for bargaining with a witch. Lying naked in the woods, frozen in stone, is just one of them. Remember that should you ever meet one."

"We won't, right?" asked Ilien. "Meet one, I mean. It looks like they haven't camped here in a while."

"It's not the way of witches to leave any sign at all," remarked Thessien, casting a watchful eye on the trees all about. "These witches must be young and inexperienced."

"From the look of things I can't say when they were here last," said Gallund. "But from the feel of it, I'd say they camped here just last night."

Ilien felt a chill climb his spine. A cold breeze moved across the knoll, rattling the branches above. The squirrel resumed its taunting.

"You may get some adventure after all," said Thessien with a grim smile.

"Can you release them?" asked Ilien, watching the stones as if they might jump at him at any moment.

"No," said Gallund. "They'll stay imprisoned forever until the stones are broken—and there's a heavy price to pay for breaking a Runestone."

"Your life," said Thessien suddenly, in answer to Ilien's gaze.

"We'd better march on," said the wizard. "We should put as many miles as we can between this place and our camp tonight."

They quickly returned to their horses, mounted up and rode on. But when they reached the witches' knoll the horses shied in fright and wouldn't pass by. They had to dismount and lead them by their reins until they were well past the campsite.

They traveled on even after the sun had set and the woods grew dark, moving silently through the thickening shadows. The bleat of bullfrogs from a nearby swamp rose up to drown out the whistles and chirps of the neighboring crickets and tree frogs. To Ilien their grunts and groans sounded like ominous warnings. "Goaway, goaway, goaway." The darkness deepened around them as the forest thickened, concealing even the most obvious of trails.

They finally set camp in a tiny clearing where the fallen trunk of an old oak gave them a place to sit before the fire they had built. Dinner was a hot meal of broth and cured venison. Afterwards, Gallund and Thessien withdrew to the outer edge of the fire and drank ale from a skin the wizard carried. They talked in hush tones while Ilien watched the moths fly reckless from the shadows and throw themselves into the dying flames.

The fire had burned itself down to a pile of glowing coals and a thin ribbon of smoke slithered away into the night. The steady thrum of the forest was lulling Ilien to sleep when the horses began to fidget. At first they only stamped their feet, but soon they were tugging at their tethers and snorting loudly.

Suddenly a shriek from the edge of the clearing sent the horses bolting into the forest, their broken tethers dancing madly behind them.

Gallund shot to his feet, his cane raised high. A bright flash lit the air. The fire, once but coals, leaped up blazing with rage. Ilien clutched his hunting bow, trying to blink away the spots before his eyes, forgetting to put an arrow to the string. Thessien stood in the firelight with his longsword drawn. Gallund stood beside him. Ilien blinked again. The wizard's cane had vanished. In its place he held a long silver wand. He pointed it across the clearing.

There, huddled together by a large oak tree, stood four of the ugliest witches Ilien had ever seen—in fact, they were the only witches Ilien had ever seen. Short and fat, they wore stained grey robes and pointy grey hats with their tips bent back as if they'd been caught in a wind storm. Eyes like black marbles peered past long, crooked noses. Their chins looked like knobby little knees and upon them grew thick, coarse hair.

Their leader stepped forward from behind them. Clothed in black, she was the fattest and ugliest of the hags. Her beard was the longest. Tufts of tangled hair poked out from under her pointed black hat. A yellow light gleamed in her eyes, like the light of a distant campfire seen through trees on an cold autumn night. She looked directly at Ilien.

"Who dares to camp in my hall?" she screeched, stooping so that the hat on her head slipped forward to just above her eyes.

She hid her hands in her long black robe, but when she spoke she raised one, pointing at Ilien in accusation. Upon her bony forefinger she wore a tarnished silver ring with the center stone missing.

"I am Gallund, Nomadin, and teacher of the True Language!" cried the wizard, pointing his silver wand at her in return. "Who are you to accuse me of daring?"

"Nomadin?" said the witch, changing her tone and pulling her gaze from Ilien to eye Gallund's silver wand. She stood up straight and pushed her hat back from her eyes. "Well then. Nomadin indeed." She cleared her throat, a strange gurgling sound like the trickle of muddy water over slime-slickened stones.

"As I was saying, my dear Nomadin, it seems that you've camped in our hall. Ordinarily we'd take quite an offense and have you for a nice bite to eat." She eyed her four companions uneasily. "But we are not an unreasonable people. Though, there is a toll to pay, for your trespassing, that is. I'm afraid you'll have to play a game with us. A witch's game. A game of luck! If you win, we shall forgive."

She made to bow, but the four witches behind her shuffled their bare feet and moaned their disapproval. "We shall!" she screamed, standing straight as a broomstick. Her sisters fell silent, but their toes still wriggled angrily. "But if we win," she continued, smoothing her robe with a smile, "we choose a prize for our toll." The glow in her eyes went out, and two black holes fixed firmly on Ilien. "We choose your wand and your lives."

The other witches shrieked in assent.

Ilien stood ready for another blinding flash as Gallund leveled his wand at the band of witches. There would be no bargaining, that he knew.

"I will play," said Gallund, signaling the others to put away their weapons.

Ilien's protest hung in his throat.

"But if I win I want more than just your pardon," said the wizard. "I also want a prize."

"As you wish," granted the black-robed witch, stepping closer to the fire. Ilien could swear that smoke poured from her hat like smoke from a chimney stack.

"If I win, my prize will be your hat," said Gallund, "and your promise of our safety tonight in this clearing."

Again the other witches lamented this new turn of events with moans and cries of "No! No!"

Their leader remained silent. Yet she clutched at her mangy head where her hat rested. From the look on her face, it was obvious to Ilien that the hat was precious to her—most likely magical. She clearly did not want to lose it. But a moment later, as if suddenly remembering something she'd forgotten, she smiled.

"Let's begin!" she hissed, showing her rotten teeth.

From a pocket in her robes she produced a tiny skull, probably that of a mouse or a shrew. She put it in her left palm and placed her hands behind her back. When she withdrew them from behind her robes she held them before Gallund.

"Which hand is it in?" she asked, her eyes flicking hungrily toward the wand.

Why, that's ridiculous, thought Ilien. *A game of luck? It's probably in neither hand, but in her back pocket!*

Gallund pretended to think hard on the answer. Then he chose her right hand, the one covered with warts.

"Wrong!" she shrieked in triumph, and the others shrieked with her. "Now give us the wand!" She reached out for it, her long, bony fingers grasping the air.

"Not fair! Show us the other hand!" came the muffled cry from Ilien's back pocket. Ilien grabbed his back end with both hands, nearly dropping his hunting bow in the process. He knew he should've left that idiot pencil behind. What good would it do to study if he was turned into stone, lying naked in the woods for all eternity?

"What did you say?" asked the witch, glaring at Ilien from under her pointy, black hat.

"I said show us your other hand!" repeated the pencil, mimicking Ilien's voice to a tee. "Cheater! Cheater!"

At that the black-robed witch cried out in anger—a gurgling, high-pitched peal of hatred that made Ilien cringe and squirm.

Thessien rested his hand upon the pommel of his longsword but remained silent.

"Come now, Ilien," said Gallund, a thin smile barely concealing his anger as he furtively plucked the pencil from Ilien's back pocket. "We must trust these fine ladies. We have lost, and now we must pay up."

To Ilien's astonishment, and to the surprise of the witches, Gallund held out his silver wand.

The black-robed witch snatched it away. The others gathered around her, murmuring to themselves and admiring the magical talisman.

"Now your lives!" she screeched, throwing the other witches back and raising the wand up high.

Ilien cringed and held his bow before his eyes. A rock! Eternity as a rock! He heard the rumble of a distant peal of thunder, then the sudden hiss of wind through tall grass. He looked and saw that the witch had vanished. A column of roiling smoke rose up like a sinuous, black snake where the witch had stood. It plumed upward and billowed out into a spreading hood, darker than the surrounding night. In its midst hovered a single yellow eye, reflecting the glow of the mounting fire, but in its center a burning red gleamed. Within the writhing smoke, Ilien caught the glint of Gallund's wand. The snake poised itself to strike.

"No, now your lives," he heard Gallund whisper. "*Mitra*

mitari mitara miru!" shouted the wizard. The power of his incantation resounded around the small clearing.

Up from his wand, within the black witch's shadow, leaped shooting stars of green and gold. The gleaming missiles sped to the tangle of branches above and burst into silver dust. The yellow eye peered upward, wide and bright. The other witches stared in awe as the glimmering dust hovered in the air. When it sprinkled down upon them they clung to each other in panic. The hood of the black witch flew out in warning, but it was too late. A loud crack split the air, a dazzling flash, and the witches, smoke and all, sprang into toads.

Ilien stood with his mouth wide open. He'd never seen such magic from Gallund before.

The fire died back down and Gallund walked over to the four grey toads, and one black one. His cane lay on the forest floor amidst the little throng. He scooped it up and the toads hopped away as fast as they could into the darkened woods. There also upon the ground was the witch's pointed black hat. Gallund picked it up and brought it over to the fire.

"You knew all along," said Ilien, still eyeing the woods where the toads had fled. "You knew she would win. But how did you know she wouldn't use the wand on you before you could use it on her?"

"Lucky, I guess," said the wizard, smiling. Ilien frowned. "If you really must know," said Gallund, "it had nothing to do with luck. After all, luck is for witches, not wizards. She couldn't use the wand even if she had all year to do so. My wand has no power, except perhaps to hold me up after chasing you all day." He leaned on his cane with a crooked smile. Ilien still frowned.

Gallund sighed. "Take your bow, for example. As you probably know, without an arrow it's worthless."

Ilien glanced red-faced at the bow in his hands.

"My wand is my bow," continued Gallund. "The arrows lie within me. I guess you could say I'm a quiver." He chuckled to himself, then cleared his throat. "The truth is that without my knowledge of Nomadin, my wand is no better than a riding crop, or a cane. But with the proper spell—well you get it. Now, this hat—" He turned it about in his hands. "It's different altogether. It's magical in itself and obeys the wearer."

Thessien threw more wood on the fire then sat down on the fallen trunk of the old oak to listen to the wizard. Ilien sat beside him.

Ilien looked in wonderment at the witch's hat in the firelight. He wrinkled his nose at its smoky odor. "What are those?" he asked, noticing strange letters embroidered inside the hat with yellow thread. "What do they say? Are they runes?"

Gallund peered into the hat's black hole as if a hand might reach out and grab him. "Hmm. No. Not runes. A spell, I think." He was silent for a moment, then said, "The writing is Nihilic, an evil and ancient tongue. When read, it summons a spirit. That is where the witch's true power lies. It's the dark spirit that fulfills her curse."

"A witch bright enough to learn Nihilic?" asked Thessien.

"Yes. Odd, isn't it?" said Gallund, squinting into the hat. "But I don't think so." With a snap of his wrists he turned the hat inside out. Ilien jumped to his feet as a large, hairy spider with spindly yellow legs fell to the ground.

"It seems that the hat is not the true talisman after all," said Gallund, eyeing Ilien strangely. He reached down and retrieved a frayed patch of cloth that had been hidden inside, a frayed patch of cloth embroidered with thick, yellow thread.

"It's only a scroll," said Ilien, wringing his hands in embarrassment and sitting back down. Though he'd never seen one, he'd learned about them in his spell book.

"Yes. A scroll," said Gallund. "A Nihilic scroll."

"Did the witch make it?"

"No," answered the wizard. "The making of scrolls is far

beyond a witch's skill. And this is an ancient scroll. Nihilic hasn't been spoken for many hundreds of years." He gazed at the small patch of cloth in his hands and closed his eyes. "Spoken by many. Written by one. Master of darkness. Reknamarken." It sounded to Ilien like a nursery rhyme, but when Gallund looked up, his eyes took on the fire's red hue. Ilien felt a strange sense of dread steal over him. "Most of the artifacts marked with the evil language were gathered up and destroyed," said Gallund, "after the second war with the Necromancer. This one must have escaped the purge."

"The Necromancer!" exclaimed Ilien. "The scroll was made by the Necromancer?"

"Most definitely," said Gallund. "No one else ever made such things."

"Then does it summon him?"

"Most definitely not!" cried Gallund, jumping to his feet. Again the fire flared high. The heat threw Ilien back and he toppled off the log to the ground. "The Necromancer can never be summoned!" said the wizard. "His weakened spirit lies imprisoned, trapped in a book, shut with a lock, and bound for the last five-hundred years. The first king of Kingsend placed his wax seal upon the lock and a powerful Binding spell was cast upon it. The Necromancer can never rise again unless the spell is undone and the wax seal broken."

"Like a Runestone?" squeaked Ilien, flat on his back, shielding his eyes from the blinding fire.

"Yes and no," said Gallund. He raised a hand and the flames receded. "A human soul imprisoned in a Runestone can never free itself. It is powerless to do so. But the Necromancer is not human. And neither is he powerless. He strains against his prison walls, always eager to be free. But the spell still holds, and if broken even then the key is needed to do the final unlocking." Gallund stood silent for a long moment, then sat down. The fire returned to normal once again, and Ilien scrambled back to his seat by the wizard. "But don't worry," said Gallund. "The Book is safely guarded by the Nomadin at Kingsend Castle, deep in the Southland."

The fire popped and Ilien jumped. "Why a book?" he asked. "Why not an iron chest or something stronger? A wax seal and some paper is little comfort against a Necromancer."

"It's not the object he's imprisoned in, Ilien, but the Binding spell I cast that holds him captive. He was tricked into the Book, thinking it to be a tome of great magic which would restore his strength."

"You cast the spell upon the Necromancer? But you said that was centuries ago."

"Do not be fooled by my youthful appearance, Ilien. You would be wise to remember that some appearances are not as they seem. Nomadin, though mortal, do not simply die of old age. And no, I did not cast a spell on the Necromancer. I simply cast a Binding spell on the king's wax seal."

"If the scroll doesn't summon the Necromancer, then who does it summon?" asked Ilien. "The NiDemons?"

"NiDemon, Ilien. NiDemon, as in geese not gooses. And no." The wizard poked the fire with his cane, sending a spray of sparks into the air. "The scroll summons a spirit. The world is full of such ghosts. They came here during the War of the Crossings nearly a thousand years ago. A few of the more powerful spirits served in the Nihilic Wars, the Necromancer's second rising. After his imprisonment, though, most simply wandered about causing mischief, or found rest in some dark nook of the earth. Many lie dormant in caves or at the bottom of the sea. Even now some still find strength enough to scare the unwary, but nothing more for their master is gone and their strength along with him. But talismans like this can cause some to rise at the sound of their forgotten tongue. I must keep this safe." He tucked it into a small leather pouch at his belt.

"Should you really keep it at all?" asked Ilien, jumping to

his feet. "Throw it in the fire! Let it burn! Destroy it!"

Gallund shook his head. "It wouldn't do any good. It's impervious to fire."

"Even a blacksmith's fire?"

"Even that, Ilien. It must be unmade, stitch by stitch. Only a Nomadin with the utmost patience could manage it."

"I guess that rules you out," said Thessien with a chuckle.

Ilien sat back down and shuffled closer to the campfire. "What of the Book, and the Binding spell? Can it ever be broken?"

"I think I've said enough for one night," said Gallund, finding little humor in Thessien's comment. "It's rumored that if you speak too long about the Necromancer, he can hear you from within his prison and will come after you some day if he ever escapes."

That was enough to quiet Ilien.

Thessien suddenly stood and put a finger to his lips. Gallund tensed and rose cautiously to his feet. Then Ilien heard it too—the cracking of branches, heavy footsteps. Someone or something was approaching their campsite. The slow trudge of feet stopped outside the firelight.

"Show yourself!" cried Gallund, raising his cane.

The soft nicker of a horse was followed by another. Into the clearing stepped their three mounts trailing broken tethers.

They all breathed a sigh of relief and hitched the horses to the fallen tree trunk within the firelight so they could be watched. Then each retired with his own thoughts to his own bedroll.

"Gallund?" asked Ilien when the wizard was nearly asleep.

"Yes," replied Gallund. Though he didn't look over, the tone in his voice conveyed his usual frown.

"Are all witches that ugly?"

Thessien chuckled, and Ilien sat up. "What's so funny?"

Gallund propped himself up and smiled. "Witches make you

32

see what they want," he said. Ilien fell silent.

"Witches appear differently to different people for different reasons," explained Gallund. "They can read a man's weakness, and always seek to use it against him. To you they appeared hideous because that's what would frighten you."

"Then what did they look like to you?" asked Ilien, and he picked up a stick and threw it at the fire.

"I am a wizard," said Gallund. "I saw them for what they were—smoke and shadows, nothing more."

Ilien turned to Thessien. The Eastland soldier merely smiled and peered up at the darkness above. "Let's just say they weren't that hideous," he answered.

Gallund shook his head. "Like I said, they know a man's weakness. Now get some rest. Morning comes early."

"And Ilien—" Gallund suddenly tossed Ilien his pencil. Ilien caught it deftly. "Please try to keep it quiet next time."

Gallund rolled over and said no more.

Ilien stuck the pencil in his back pocket and flopped back onto his bedroll. A moment later he cried out in panic. Gallund and Thessien shot to their feet, blankets flying in all directions.

"What? What is it?" cried Gallund.

"Nothing. It's okay. I'm alright," said Ilien, carefully removing his pet frog from under his blanket. It looked dry and wrinkled, and none-too-happy.

Chapter III

Whispers and Warnings

They had been riding all day in the rain and Ilien was beginning to think he didn't like adventures at all. If more of this was in store for them on the long trip to Great-tower he'd gladly stay behind in Evernden, if only to play dollies with some girl. Everything about him squished, his boots, his underwear—especially his underwear—and his thick cloak had sopped up so much water that it threatened to topple him off his horse if he didn't sit perfectly square in the saddle. He gathered that all the blankets were wet by now as well. Gallund and Thessien rode before him with their hoods up and their heads down.

Ilien's horse tugged at her reins and whickered. It seemed even she was sick of adventures by now.

"I bet old Winnie wouldn't mind," said Ilien, reaching up to knuckle the rain from his eyes.

His horse suddenly stopped and Ilien sailed forward with a cry. The weight of his water-logged cloak dragged him all the way up to her ears. He teetered on her head for a moment, looking to see what had spooked her. The rain's grey curtain blurred all but the closest trees.

"I'm sorry. I didn't mean it," said Ilien, shimmying back to his saddle. "I don't like this any better than you, but we're falling behind. Now come on."

He nudged her forward again. She stamped her feet and shook her head. He snapped the reins but she refused to move.

He kicked her. She moaned and blew out steam like an overheated engine.

Then Ilien felt it too—a sudden, unexplainable fear. His horse threw her head, her eyes wide with terror. He tried to call out but an invisible hand seized his throat, cinching it shut like a sack of marbles. He couldn't breath. Something held his arms. Fighting panic, he tried to remember the Lightning spell he had studied. Unable to speak the words, he recited them in his mind.

The mist roiled around him. The tree trunks hummed like plucked strings. The swollen air crackled and lightning crashed beneath the trees. He heard an angry shout, the bark of a mad dog, and his horse reared in fright. Another flash fingered the air, a skeletal hand clawing to reach him. The ground dropped away. Darkness closed over him as he fell, still on his horse, the wind howling in his ears as he plummeted into the void.

He stopped. The air smelled of earthworms and leaves, the sour smell of decay. His horse quivered beneath him, unable to move. He tried to move himself, but icy hands held him fast.

A voice broke the silence, a hiss in his ear.

Ilien Woodhill. I know you.

Ilien woke with a start and stifled a cry of panic. He held his breath, afraid to move. His heart pounded in his ears. It was only a dream, he told himself. Just a dream. Nothing more.

The cold night air washed over him and slowly he came to his senses. He suddenly felt foolish. Twelve, and still afraid of the dark. He blinked and sighed, feeling his muscles relax. Rain drizzled down through the darkness of their small clearing, pattering among the dead leaves around him. Surely the others were still asleep. He hoped they hadn't heard him, whimpering like a child. What time was it anyway, he wondered?

Without warning a shadow rose before him. He froze. The shadow stood motionless, watching him. He heard a whisper.

Ilien Woodhill.

Ilien lay paralyzed. Rain pooled in his eye sockets.

"Ilien Woodhill. Get up. It's time to go," said Thessien.

Ilien sat up and blinked the water from his eyes. Cold rain trickled down his back. "I'm awake," he said, but his heart still raced. His pet frog crouched on his pack, grinning at him in the rain. "What are you so happy about? Shoo! Go on! You're free to go if you like it here so much."

He bit his lip, watching the frog shift about. He really didn't want it to go. He had spoken out of anger. But it did look happier sitting in the rain instead of in his pack. He poked it gently and it hopped away into the forest.

Gallund and Thessien were already packed and ready to march. Ilien jumped up, wolfed down some soggy bread and grabbed some jerky for the ride. They mounted up just as the sky above the trees turned grey.

The forest canopy offered little relief from the rain. The cold water merely ran off the branches above and leaked onto their backs. But as they plodded further northward they found the going easier despite the steady downpour. The hills receded, the trees grew farther apart and soon their horses were prancing down the long, leaf-strewn lanes, their bodies steaming in the cool morning air.

Yet Ilien couldn't shake the nightmare. The smell of soil and worms still lingered in the mist. An aching cold had settled beneath his skin. He shivered. NiDemon. Witches and Rune-stones. Necromancers. He had learned more about evil in the past two days than he had in his first twelve years. He looked over at Gallund hunched in his saddle, cane in one hand, reins in the other. *Not quite the imposing figure of an all powerful wizard*, he thought.

Thessien steered his horse along side Ilien's. The big black trotted high-hoofed beneath the soldier, its back nearly level with Ilien's head.

"Something troubling you?" asked Thessien.

Ilien smiled up at him. "No. Nothing at all. Why?"

Thessien looked away, studying the surrounding forest like a surveyor. "I've spent twenty years judging the manner of people from the looks on their faces, Ilien. I'm a soldier. My life has often depended on discovering the lies hidden beneath cool smiles." He turned back and pinned Ilien with a solemn stare. "Men often tell me more with a single look than they've told anyone their entire lives."

Ilien slowed his horse, letting Gallund get further ahead. Satisfied that the wizard was out of earshot he asked, "What are these NiDemon that worry Gallund so much?"

Thessien too glanced up at the wizard, tightening his reins. When he looked back at Ilien his eyes admonished caution.

"They're hunters."

"Hunters?"

"Hunters of Nomadin," said Thessien.

Ilien's horse stumbled and Ilien grabbed its mane to steady himself. "What do you mean, hunters of Nomadin?"

"Could I have put it any clearer?" asked Thessien. "They are sworn to slay Nomadin, all Nomadin. They cross to our world for that purpose alone."

"Then Gallund is in danger?"

"Yes," replied the soldier.

Again his horse tripped, and Ilien asked, "But are they really powerful enough to kill a wizard?

"A wizard, yes," answered Thessien. "But Gallund is Nomadin, and Nomadin are not merely wizards."

Ilien steadied himself in his saddle. "But what's the difference?"

"A wizard is human, for one," said Thessien.

"If the Nomadin aren't human, then what are they?" Ilien glanced over at Gallund as if he might suddenly sprout wings and fly to Greattower.

"They are Nomadin, Ilien. And only a Nomadin can master the True Language of magic. A wizard merely speaks. A Nomadin understands."

"Well he sure looks human to me," observed Ilien, watching as Gallund scratched his back end with his cane.

Thessien laughed. "He does, does he?"

The wizard seemed to take no notice of them as they trudged along in the rear, but Thessien sat up in his saddle as if to end their conversation anyhow.

"One more thing," said Ilien. "You said the NiDemon had crossed to our world. Crossed from where?"

Thessien looked surprised. "From Loehs Sedah. From the realm of the dead. Has Gallund taught you nothing as an apprentice?"

"Nothing about NiDemon and crossings," said Ilien.

Thessien shook his head. "It's not my place to teach you the tales of old if Gallund thought it unwise to do so himself. Be content to know that Loehs Sedah is far away, but closer than you think, and the Crossings are gates from there to here, and here to there. The last one was shut a thousand years ago. Now a new one has been opened, or an old one rediscovered more likely, for not all the crossings could be found in the open spaces of the world, and the miners of Berkhelven have been known to delve deeper than is wise in search of gold and jewels."

At that Thessien turned away and fell silent, paying heed to the terrain before him.

"Last night Gallund spoke of the wars," said Ilien, not taking the soldier's hint. "He mentioned the second rising of the Necromancer. Just how many were there?"

Thessien spurred his horse forward. "Two. Three have been foretold, the third to be the last."

"The third to be the last?" said Ilien, bouncing about as his own horse followed at a trot. "That doesn't sound too comforting." He eyed the passing trees in the mist and suddenly realized how far from home he was. "And is the third yet upon us?" he asked.

"We shall see," said Thessien with a smile. "We shall see."

Throughout the day, Ilien noted a change in the forest. They'd been marching beneath old, fat oaks for nearly two days, but now young pine trees grew straight and lean in their place. Ilien noticed the crows also, big black brats that cawed at them from their front porches high above. At first he liked the familiar company of the crows, but after a while he thought their cries sounded like laughter. He felt miserable enough with all the rain. He didn't need to be made fun of as well.

At noon the rain stopped. The dark expanse of clouds parted and the sun speared down brightly through the hovering mist. They rode into a broad valley, a shallow basin surrounded by low, wooded hills. A grassy marsh, flooded by the day's downpour, stretched the length of the valley to the foot of a rocky slope forested with pines. They stopped and dismounted.

Thessien drummed a lean finger against his saddle as he studied the marsh. "It's too muddy. We'll have trouble with the horses."

Gallund raised a hand to shield his eyes from the sun. The marsh was nearly a mile wide, probably twice that in length. He poked the ground with his cane. Water pooled around its tip.

"I agree," he said. "We'll go around."

As they turned to mount up, Thessien called for silence. Ilien and Gallund both trusted Thessien's senses enough to freeze in their tracks. The breeze hurried over the tall marsh grass and a crow called somewhere over the hills, but no one moved. For a full minute they remained that way, Ilien and Gallund stone-still in silence, Thessien looking to and fro.

"Perhaps I'm wrong," muttered Thessien, "but for a moment it felt like we were to be ambushed."

39

"Yes. Perhaps you're wrong," said Ilien, eyeing a suspicious looking clump of grass anyhow.

"Perhaps. But I know the feeling well."

A bird flew up from the clump of grass in a rush of wings. The horses reared in fright. Ilien lost his balance and pitched face first into the mud. He pulled his head from the muck with a loud sucking sound and looked up at Gallund and Thessien. They were only grinning, but they might as well have been holding each other in fits of laughter.

"On second thought," said Thessien, scratching his chin, "perhaps I *am* wrong."

At that the two adults of the group burst out howling. Thessien stomped around in the rain soaked grass clutching his sides. Gallund buried his face in his saddle.

"It's not that fun—"

In all their hysterics they didn't notice that Ilien hadn't finished his sentence, until the grass grabbed them too.

Thessien reached for his sword, but the grass had woven itself around the pommel and he couldn't draw it forth. He fought to move but his boots were tied fast to the ground.

Gallund fared worse, even for a wizard. Quickly wrapped in grass to his waist, he called for Ilien. A crack opened in the ground beneath him and roots sprang up, gripping his legs and seizing his cane.

The sound of a sword ringing from its scabbard peeled like a bell over the marsh as Thessien tore free of his bonds. The tall grass cowered beneath his blade as he cut his way toward the wizard.

Gallund's cane burst into flames and in a searing flash it fell to ashes, revealing his silver wand beneath. He held the wand up high, but before he could utter a single word the roots pulled him beneath the ground and he vanished.

Ilien lay helpless, wrapped like a green ball of yarn, his pencil squirming in his back pocket. But as soon as the ground closed on Gallund the grass released him. He untangled himself and rushed to Thessien, who was already digging frantically in the spot where Gallund had disappeared. After several minutes they uncovered his silver wand in the soft earth—nothing more. Ilien buried his face in his muddy arms and began to cry.

Thessien rose and sheathed his sword. As if on cue, his horse approached and he swung himself up into the saddle.

"Get up."

Ilien wiped away his tears and began digging again.

"Get up," said Thessien. "We're leaving."

Ilien spun on him, his fists full of earth. "What good will it do to ride on now? Gallund is gone!"

"This is the work of the NiDemon, Ilien. We must ride north at once."

Ilien could feel his tears coming again. "For what? Your precious mission? In case you haven't noticed, it's over. You failed."

"You will turn back at Evernden," said Thessien evenly, "as Gallund had wanted. I will continue on toward Greattower. Now get up."

Ilien looked around the quiet marsh. He glanced down at the wizard's wand. He scooped it up and held it to his chest.

Thessien's horse took a step forward. "I grieve for him too," said the soldier. "I knew him twenty years. He was my friend and mentor. But my loss, and yours, pales now before what is at stake. We must ride on at once."

But Ilien was not a soldier on a mission, and though he held back his tears for the moment he couldn't bring himself to leave. He sat in the mire, staring at the scarred ground. Tears came again, stinging his eyes and streaking the mud on his face.

Thessien peered over the marsh at the lengthening shadows. He would be patient and let Ilien cry. It was a luxury he knew the boy would never have again. With Gallund gone, Ilien's chances of survival were slim. Oh, he would do his best to protect him. But even he, a soldier with a hundred kills to his name, would not be enough. He grimaced and glanced over at the grieving twelve-year-old. He hoped Gallund was right, that looks were deceiving, because if not, they were all doomed.

"At least let me lay a headstone for his grave," said Ilien, suddenly rising to his feet.

Thessien nodded as Ilien walked off to find a suitable stone. He watched as the boy returned and laid a small, flat rock on the ground where Gallund had disappeared. He also planted a tiny oak sapling nearby, as was custom.

Thessien stilled the thoughts running through his mind. A moment of silence for his fallen friend was only appropriate. Still, things were progressing quickly. The enemy paused for nothing, and they were surely under a dark watch now. They had to keep moving.

Ilien carefully arranged the soil around the base of the small sapling. He looked angrily at the marshland around him, then back at the tiny oak he had planted.

"Grow quick and strong," he said, gazing out over the scrub brush and tall grass of the marsh, envisioning a mighty oak forest in its place.

"Ilien. It's time to go," said Thessien.

Ilien climbed on his horse and they set off, leading Gallund's grey mount behind them. They skirted the marsh, staying a safe distance from its muddy edges, and soon were climbing the low rocky hill on its far side where the pines grew in small groves. Ilien looked back down on the ill-fated wetland.

"Farewell, Gallund," he said, then turned and gave heed to the terrain, crying silently as his horse picked its way between the boulders. All the while he held fast to Gallund's wand, wishing he could somehow cast a spell to turn back time, to make it all go away—to have Gallund back again. But he knew he couldn't. There was no going back. Not now. Not ever.

"The kingdom of Evernden," said Thessien.

Ilien looked up. They had reached the top of the hill. Below them, a vast forest of tall evergreens stretched to the horizon in a calm, green sea of needles. In the distance Ilien could see a tiny island of blue.

"There," said Thessien, shielding his eyes from the low western sun and pointing toward the blue land on the horizon. "Dry your tears and harden your heart, Ilien. We travel hard from here on out, but at least our aim is in sight."

As Ilien peered out over the still, green sea he saw a strange pool of darkness midway to the blue land of Evernden. But before he could ask about it, Thessien urged his mount down the hill and Ilien followed, leading Gallund's grey horse behind him.

Chapter IV

The Illwood Tree

Ilien lay awake in his bedroll, the heavy woolen blanket pulled all the way up to his chin. The pungent spice of pines laced the stinging cold that had settled over the forest since they had set camp.

They had stopped only once on their torturous journey to get where they were—to fill their skins and water the horses at a shallow stream. And when Thessien, hours after dark had fallen, had finally announced they could stop, Ilien had dropped his blankets where he'd stood and had quickly fallen asleep.

In the dead of night he'd woken cold and sad. He might have rekindled the fire, but he curled into a ball instead. Now, as he waited for his toes to warm, he could think of nothing but hot coffee, a blazing fire, and Gallund.

Ilien reached a hand through the blackness to the pack where he kept the wizard's wand. He still couldn't believe Gallund was gone. At any moment he expected to hear his heavy breathing and mumbled curses, the occasional "ah ha!" as he talked in his sleep. But all was quiet.

He rolled over to put his back to the memories. He needed sleep. At the rate Thessien was driving him he would need all the rest he could get.

Something suddenly jabbed Ilien in the rear and he jumped.

"Ouch! Stop it!" he cried, reaching for his back pocket.

"Well, why do you feel the need to lie on me all the time?"

came the muffled reply from his pencil.

"That's it! You're going in the pack!" said Ilien, but before he could pull his pencil from his pocket, a hand clamped over his mouth. Another held a cold blade at his throat. The pencil fell silent and Ilien was hauled to his feet, the weapon still under his chin. The hand at his mouth felt cold and sweaty.

Two shining, amber eyes appeared in the air before him, a long pointed nose dimly lit by their glow. The eyes disappeared as the face looked away. The luminescent nose seemed to float in the darkness as if hung on strings.

Ilien saw three more sets of eyes bobbing in the blackness near the horses. *These must be the amber-eyed men Thessien warned us about!* thought Ilien in a panic. Whatever they were, they were having a hard time controlling the frightened mounts for their eyes gleamed like wolves' eyes.

The face turned back. Its two burning eyes drew close. Without thinking, Ilien recited a spell in his mind. The back of his neck tingled. His hair crawled into the air.

A flash lit the night and he remembered no more.

Thessien pressed himself close to a small pine tree whose branches drooped to the ground like a giant umbrella. He had woken cold and damp earlier, setting off to find wood for the fire. Returning, he'd heard movement from ahead. At once he recognized the intruders for what they were.

Shape-changers. Lycanthropes. Wierwulvs! It was impossible to tell a wierwulf from a man in the daylight. Only at night did their amber-colored eyes give them away, glowing like dim lanterns.

At first the wierwulvs were only interested in what they had before them: fine horses, packs loaded with food and blankets, and a prisoner. But when the prisoner struck one of them dead with magic, they were shocked to their senses. As Thessien watched, they sent others to search the woods. To the wierwulvs, one prisoner and three horses meant two more men were hiding close by.

Thessien crouched low beneath the pines. His mind raced. A jagged spear of lightning had lit their campsite in a flash of white, striking one shape-changer dead. But he feared it had also struck Ilien. Under the cover of the drooping pine boughs he planned. He had to think quickly for the shape-changers were preparing to leave, taking Ilien with them.

As the amber-eyed pack led their booty into the forest, they failed to notice the shadow of a soldier following them in the darkness.

Thessien trailed them at a distance. Wierwulvs were extremely wary if not the most intelligent of creatures. They could sight the tail of a mouse on the darkest of nights. Their keen noses could scent the trail of a man after a heavy day's rain. Neither mouse nor man was ever safe from their rabid hunger.

Thessien followed the whisper of their passage with keen senses of his own. He masked his scent with the sap of pine trees as he tracked his way behind them. His sword was secreted at his side. Upon his back he carried Ilien's bow and quiver.

It wasn't long before he overtook two laggards loping lazily behind the pack, two men in all aspects except for their eyes.

"Run here, run there," growled the one who ran in the rear. He had an enormous nose and it shined brightly in the dark, illumined by the light of his eyes. "What does he think we are? Flippin' horses?"

"Shut up, Snout," said the other, his large eyes lighting the way before them like dying flashlights. "We run when Mutil says. He knows what he's doing."

"I don't think so," said Snout, frowning. "In case you haven't been counting, this is the third sacrifice we bring that wretched tree this week. Why does it get all the good eatins?"

"The Illwood doesn't eat 'em, you imbecile."

"Then who does?" Snout's empty stomach began to growl. "It's that cursed Groll, that's who, I tell ya. Why do we have to bring it food all the time? The bugger's got claws. Let it hunt its own lousy dinner." He pulled at the dirty cord around his waist that served as a belt.

"Don't be a dolt. Nobody eats the sacrifices. They're sacrifices! Besides, after we skewer 'em on those poisonous pickers they're not fit for eating anyhow."

Snout looked around at the darkened trees as he ran. "I still don't know why we had to come this far south. These woods aren't natural, I tell ya. Too dern peaceful. Not a sign of danger anywhere. At least back home we could count on an attacking do-gooder or two to eat."

"Will you please shut up!"

"Please?" said Snout. "Did you say please? You're not turning nice on me now, are ya? I'm famished, you know. I'd hate to have to kill you for a midnight snack. What time is it anyhow?"

He coughed and gagged—a wierwulf's attempt at laughter. In his hysterics he nearly choked up the lame rabbit he'd eaten earlier.

"Very funny. Quit your laughing or I'll show you the meaning of nice. Do-gooder to eat. We found one not ten minutes ago and you tucked tail and ran, climbed a tree like a stinkin' squirrel."

Again Snout looked around. He sucked at the air with his oversized nose. "That one's not right, I tell ya. He's magic. You saw it. He's a wizard or something."

"Wizard? Bah!" said the leader, looking back at his worried companion. "What do you know about wizards anyhow?"

Snout pointed to his unusually large nose.

"Oh yeah," mumbled the other, turning to light their path again. "I forgot about that."

Thessien almost felt bad for the two laggards as he silently bore down upon them.

When Ilien regained consciousness, he was being carried, slung over broad shoulders. The upside down shadows of passing trees jumped by him in the night. He thought it best to keep still and play dead even though his ribs hurt with every jarring stride. Besides, he could swear there were wolves following them, loping along in the dark.

As Ilien bounced about he tried counting the dancing eyes that swirled around him. Twenty-one? He abandoned his efforts when a single bloodshot eye shuffled too close.

All at once the company jogged into a brightly lit glade. A chorus of howls greeted them as they arrived. Torches burned on long, wooden poles in the ground and hundreds of amber eyed wierwulvs danced around a gathering of large bonfires. The flames cast an orange glow on the surrounding trees.

In the center of the glade stood the largest tree Ilien had ever seen. The massive, gnarled trunk stretched ten men wide. The tree towered so high above the clearing that its upper reaches disappeared into the darkness. As the wierwulvs carried him closer, Ilien guessed the tree was dead. A carpet of sharp, brown barbs covered its leafless limbs and rotted trunk. His captors dumped him beside one of the fires. He lay in a heap but kept one eye open.

The horses stood huddled together at the far end of the glade, their packs still fitted to their backs. *The wierwulvs must have used them to carry the gear*, thought Ilien. All at once Gallund's grey horse reared high, its hooves flailing in an attempt to escape. It surged forward, breaking free, and bolted into the darkened woods.

Ilien thought of running for it then, but he noticed the many wolves slinking about in the shadows between the fires. A few of the beasts pursued the fleeing horse, and Ilien gave up any ideas of escape. Perhaps Thessien would find him. But then what could the soldier do against so many enemies?

A commotion arose behind Ilien, but he didn't dare raise his head to look. Wierwulvs from all around raced past him, adding to the frenzy and confusion. It sounded as if a scuffle was breaking out—booted feet pounded the ground, shouts rose and fell. One wierwulf called for quiet above the din, and all fell silent.

"It's the boy!" cried the wierwulf. His throaty voice sounded like wolves eating flesh.

He must be the leader, thought Ilien, his mind racing.

"All the better to sacrifice," growled another. "The Illwood kills all, even—"

"To kill the One brings plague and ruin!" cried yet another.

"Says who?" demanded the leader.

"The Necromancer himself."

The group fell silent at that one.

"You whimpering jackals!" It was the leader again. "We don't toil for the Necromancer, do we. Besides, look at him. Does he look like a Nomadin to you?"

Ilien couldn't take it any longer. He had to escape before it was too late. He still had a chance. He jumped up and ran—

—straight into a tree!

"Nice one," piped his pencil from his pocket.

The wierwulvs howled with laughter.

"Mutil's right," said one. "He's no wizard!"

Ilien rubbed at the lump on his head, trying to think through all the pain. He had to do something. He looked up and saw the leader, a burly wierwulf whose eyes glowed more red than amber. The leader held Gallund's wand.

So that's what all the commotion is about, thought Ilien. *They've found Gallund's wand. But now what do I do?* He looked around in panic. *Think, Ilien! Think!*

Suddenly it came to him, or almost did.

"*Mitra mitara miru!*" he called aloud, still sprawled upon the ground.

The wierwulvs cringed and ducked, waiting for a spell to strike. Nothing happened. Ilien couldn't quite remember the spell Gallund had used on the witches.

"*Mitri mitaru mira!*" he cried again, edging away from his captors, who by now appeared confident that he knew no spells.

The wierwulvs looked up in surprise as two flaming arrows streaked from the darkened woods and buzzed over their heads. The burning arrows struck the Illwood tree high upon its gnarled trunk. At once the crumbling wood caught fire.

Ilien leapt to his feet. "*Mitra mitari mitara miru!*" he yelled triumphantly, recalling the proper words.

Up from Gallund's wand, even while in the grasp of the astonished leader, leaped blue and white stars that whizzed high above the clearing. They burst in flashes of silver light, and a haze of lustrous dust floated down toward the amber-eyed watchers below.

The frightened wierwulvs fled from the magical fireworks, all except the red-eyed leader. He simply smiled, revealing two gleaming fangs. He obviously wasn't afraid of a little silver dust.

Ilien watched the dust from the corner of his eye. It was caught in an updraft, swirling overhead in a small, shimmering cloud. The red-eyed wierwulf stepped forward, drawing a long, curved knife. His smile turned to an evil leer. Then something miraculous and frightening happened. All his features seemed to blur and melt like candle-wax in a hot fire. Where there once stood a tall, dark man, there now stood a large, bristling wolf.

The wolf crouched low, gathering itself to spring. Ilien fell back as the beast leapt forward. At that very moment a gust of wind from high above drove down the glittering dust. What fell upon Ilien was but a small, brown toad.

The pencil writhed in his pocket. "Run!" it cried.

Ilien swatted the toad into a tree and quickly snatched the wand from the ground. The light from the burning Illwood illuminated a ghoulish scene. Large, hairy men with eyes like embers jumped up and down to put out the mounting flames while howling wolves danced madly among them. In all the commotion no one noticed Ilien—until he ran headlong into one of his captors.

Cries of battle sounded across the clearing. Thessien attacked swiftly, driving toward Ilien, his sword flashing in the light of the fires, Ilien's bow strapped to his back. A knot of wierwulvs retreated before him, their swords glancing off the chain mail hidden beneath his cloak. The knot frayed, then broke. The wierwulvs fell over each other to escape his onslaught.

But one wierwulf stood his ground. The two warriors strove back and forth upon the battlefield in the glaring light of the burning Illwood tree. At first the shape-changer dodged neatly from Thessien's sword, unencumbered by heavy armor. But soon Thessien was driving him back, raining blows while the other parried with his sword in desperation. The wierwulf stumbled to the ground a dozen feet from the burning tree, his weapon flying from his grasp.

Thessien raised his sword but the sight before him stayed his hand. The wierwulf began to shimmer. A low moan escaped his lips. The moan turned to a growl as coarse, grey fur swarmed his body. His hands and feet sprang claws like stiletto knives. Thessien stepped back. The newly formed wolf rose, its head still human.

"Have you ever watched a wolf feast on its prey?" it asked. Its jaw snapped forward to form a snout. "We devour them alive." It smiled a mouthful of fangs.

Thessien braced for attack, but before the wolf could spring, a large, flaming bough from the tree's upper reaches came

51

crashing down between them. Fiery thorns sprayed in every direction, hissing and popping between the trees. Thessien dove for cover. The shape-changer was not so lucky. The poison of the many barbs worked quickly.

Thessien rolled to his feet, a sharp pain in his side. He saw Ilien by the horses, struggling with a guard. He rushed to his aid, making short work of the wierwulf guard, and in moments they were both astride their horses, tearing into the forest at a wild gallop.

Chapter V

The Bark and the Bite

Ilien squeezed the reins like he was strangling snakes as his horse raced through the shrouded forest. His pencil in his back pocket stabbed him mercilessly with every stride. He had lost Thessien in their flight from the glade, but he wasn't alone. The wolves flew after him like grey ghosts in the night.

A grunting figure surged forth from the shadows, closing the gap between them. His horse lunged forward, desperate to escape. The night jumped around him, a tilting landscape of darkness and phantoms. Ilien speared a hand into his saddle bag, hunting for something heavy. He plucked out a spare horseshoe. Casting a fleeting glance over his shoulder he let it fly. He heard a startled cry. The shadow fell back and disappeared, lost in the blur of receding trees.

Ilien's horse stumbled on, nearly spent, its strides growing shorter, its breath ragged. Sensing weakness, the shadow re-emerged, streaking forward. There was no time for another horseshoe. Ilien closed his eyes, waiting to be torn from his saddle in a flurry of slashing claws and snapping jaws.

It never came.

"Ilien! It's me!" shouted Thessien above the drum of beating hoofs. His fleeting form was a vague shadow in the rushing darkness. "Stop before you ride into a tree!"

A branch slapped Ilien across the face. The ghost of a limb sailed over his head. He hauled on the reins but his horse ran crazed, heedless of the rider on its back. It crashed through a thicket of laurels, maddened with fear, nearly ripping Ilien from his saddle. Ilien fought the panicked animal to a stop. It stood quivering beneath him, eyes wide, branches clinging to its mane. He quickly scanned the trees for signs of wolves. When he looked back at Thessien, he saw the soldier sitting bent in his saddle, clutching his side.

"Are you alright?" he asked.

"I don't think so." Thessien lifted his heavy cloak. His chain mail shimmered in the darkness, revealing a small rent in the linked vest. He plucked something from the gap and held it before Ilien.

Ilien squinted at it in the darkness. "What is it?"

"Poison," answered the soldier.

Ilien jumped as if pricked. He looked back toward the distant Illwood glade. The sky above the trees flickered orange. A cascade of glowing sparks rose in the night like a crown of fireflies. The Illwood was dying, and so was Thessien. He shuddered, fear choking his words away.

The yap of a wolf broke the silence.

"Follow me," said Thessien. He cast the thorn aside and spurred his horse forward.

They rode in silence, looking over their shoulders and urging their mounts on as fast as they dared. Every clop of hoof on stone or branch rattled their nerves like a rap on the door in the dead of night. *We're here! We're here!* But the shadows never altered. The night rushed by unbroken. Soon a pale light filtered down through the thick cloak of pine needles above, the trees taking shape in the gloom. The forest remained quiet and they slackened their pace.

Suddenly the horses perked up. They jogged their way forward unbidden, weaving eagerly through the trees. Then Ilien heard it too, the faint babble of water from farther ahead. A small stream tumbled over a thin line of rocks, and on seeing it, Ilien jumped from his horse. He scrambled to the mossy bank and plunged his face into the ice cold water. He looked up to see Thessien still slumped in his saddle.

"I'm dying."

Ilien stood up, blinking water from his eyes. The trees seemed to take a step toward him.

"What do we do?" he asked.

"You'll ride north," said Thessien, his voice tight with pain.

"But you said—"

"I said I'm dying, not dead!" Thessien's horse tossed its head. "Until then you'll do as I say! Now mount up."

Ilien leaped forward, his eyes wide with worry. "There has to be something we can do. This poison, there must be a cure."

Thessien rested his head against the neck of his horse. "The cure won't help now. And one of us has to reach Evernden to tell of Gallund's death." He looked at Ilien, eyes bleary, and slowly climbed down from his horse. "I pray you don't need this." He handed Ilien his bow, then leaned against a tree. "Ride due north. Evernden's not far. Now go."

Ilien felt a wave of heat flash across his face. "I won't."

The soldier shook his head. "Then you're a fool."

"I'm not going without you."

Thessien slumped to the ground.

Ilien rushed to his side and grabbed him by his collar. "Thessien!" he said, shaking him. "Thessien! Wake up!" When he got no answer, he changed tactics. "The cure! Tell me the cure! I can't make it to Evernden without you. Do you hear me? I'll die out here! Your mission will fail!"

Thessien stirred. An eye fluttered open. "Foolish boy."

Ilien winced, then slapped Thessien hard across the face. "Tell me!"

Thessien smiled, but his eyes remained closed. "Foolish boy. The bark. The bark of the tree. But it's too late." The soldier's breath grew shallow, and he said no more.

Ilien jumped up and leaped astride Thessien's horse. The big black reared high. Without hesitation it bolted in the direction of the Illwood tree.

The air grew thick with smoke, burning Ilien's eyes, blurring his vision. He rode on undeterred, yet as he did something tugged at the back of his mind. He was overlooking something, something important. Sure, he hadn't noticed bark on the tree earlier, and he didn't know what to do with the bark once he found it, but there was something else. He couldn't place it. Gallund's wand, tucked safely beneath his belt, gave him a measure of courage but didn't dull his underlying feelings of dread. He began wishing he'd been a better student; a Healing spell would have come in handy, but despite having a magical pencil there was still too much to remember, too many adverbial phrases, past participles, pronouns, adjectives, gerunds—

He shot out of his saddle and hauled back on the reins. Thessien's horse plowed to a stop. Before him stood the largest wolf he'd ever seen. It swayed on stiff legs, hair raised along its spine.

Ilien sat paralyzed—then blinked. It wasn't a wolf at all. It was a dog. A monstrous dog, the kind Farmer Parson kept to fend off the foxes, but bigger—much bigger. Nearly the size of a pony! He'd never seen anything like it. It too looked relieved. It took a hesitant step forward.

The wolves sprang from behind the trees, leaping on the dog's back. The dog reared high, meeting the sudden onslaught with a flurry of flailing claws and snapping jaws. The pack drove forward, forcing the dog back, trying to knock it off its feet. Their hooked fangs slashed at its sides from every direction. The dog fought back, battering the wolves with its massive paws, mauling any who came too close. But there were just too many. The dog was tiring. The wolves swarmed over it with renewed vigor, and it fell beneath the frenzied pack.

A shrill cry pierced the air and a wolf hopped straight into

56

the air. It fell to the ground dead, an arrow stuck through its neck. A second wolf died before the others knew what was happening. Fifty feet away, Ilien put another arrow to his bow string.

Instantly three wolves broke from the pack, bounding in wild leaps toward this new prey. The lead wolf never leapt twice. It fell in a tumbling heap.

Ilien stuck his next arrow to the string blindingly fast, faster than he could imagine as fear drove muscles that had done that single act a thousand times before.

Twang! The arrow flew. Another wolf dropped.

The last was nearly on him. He reached for an arrow. His fingers fumbled with the shaft and it fell from his grasp. He thrust his bow out before him and braced for the attack.

But it came too soon. He was knocked aside before the wolf could reach him. He struck the ground hard and looked up, gasping for air. The hulking form of the dog stood over him. A lifeless wolf hung in its jaws.

The dog dropped the body to the ground and fixed Ilien with a baleful stare. Cornrows of fur bristled along its back. It stalked forward, baring blood-stained fangs.

Ilien scrambled backward, his relief turning to worry. "Nice doggy. Sit boy."

To his surprise, it did.

Its enormous back end plunked to the ground, a thick tail squirming beneath it. A bright pink tongue lolled out and it began to pant. A paw the size of a hoof rose into the air. Ilien reached out with a trembling hand to shake it.

"Good boy," he said, lowering the thick front leg to the ground. He sat dumbfounded for a moment. "The bark!" He scrambled to his feet.

Grey bodies littered the deserted glade, twisted and broken remnants of the dog's battle with the wolves. Smoke billowed from the smoldering stump of the Illwood, snaking its way between the carcasses. Ilien turned and searched the ground, moving closer to the charred tree. All that remained of the Illwood now was soot and smoke. There was no bark to be found.

A dog's low growl stopped Ilien in his tracks. He scanned the forest for signs of danger. Clouds of smoke drifted between the trees, but there was no sign of wolves. He heard another growl, more urgent, and looked back at the dog. It held a branch in its mouth, a branch sheathed tip to tip in smooth, brown bark. It padded over and dropped it at Ilien's feet.

"Well I'll be. You're smarter than you look."

The dog sat quietly in front of him, but its dark eyes narrowed beneath its shaggy brows.

Ilien turned the branch over with his boot. Three large thorns crowned one end, but the other end looked smooth enough. He picked it up and held it out like a sword.

With Illwood sword in hand he ran back to Thessien's horse, mounted up, and fled back into the forest. The giant dog followed. It wasn't long before he arrived at the very spot he'd left Thessien. He looked around in dismay.

Thessien was gone.

Ilien jumped from the saddle and ran through the trees. "Thessien!" he called. Was he in the wrong spot? He could see his own previous tracks, and the impression left in the soft earth where Thessien had collapsed.

"Thessien!" he cried. But then he noticed other impressions too—two sets of hoof prints leading away into the forest. Someone had taken the Eastlander, and Ilien's horse. But who?

The giant dog snuffled the ground where Thessien had lain. Ilien watched as the dog circled through the trees, sweeping the forest floor with its nose. It stopped to look at him, then trotted off into the woods along the trail of hoof prints. The dog had Thessien's scent! Ilien climbed back on the soldier's black horse and followed the tracking dog into the woods.

They traveled for miles, the enormous dog with its nose in the wind, Ilien riding behind, clutching the Illwood sword. Whoever they trailed rode hard—they should have overtaken them by now. Occasionally the dog stopped to search a small clearing or patch of brambles, but little else broke their pursuit. They tracked the fleeing rider for hours, never stopping for rest. Dusk approached and Ilien began to lose hope of finding Thessien alive. A numbing sense of panic began to well up inside him.

Then without warning, the dog stopped stiff-legged before him, nose testing the air, hair rippling along its back. Ilien pulled Thessien's horse to a halt. The forest was quiet, too quiet. Even the crows had ceased their usual bickering. Then he saw it, a flash of grey between the trees. A twig snapped behind him. He turned in his saddle. Like curls of smoke the wolves emerged from the pines.

But they didn't attack. They watched from a distance, their lips pulled back in mocking smiles. As quickly as they appeared, they billowed back into the forest and were gone.

Ilien studied the trees in front of him. He had to keep going. Thessien's life depended on it.

"I wouldn't if I were you," said a deep voice behind him. Ilien spun around. There was no one there. He turned in circles. He looked at the dog.

"Don't be a fool," it said.

Ilien's mouth dropped open and he nearly fell from his saddle. Even Thessien's horse stepped back in surprise—it too had never heard a dog make human noises before.

The dog looked up at the sky and shook its head. "I was hoping this one had more sense."

Ilien sat blinking in his saddle.

"Make haste of your wits, boy!" said the dog. "What do you think will happen if you ride your beast of burden down that hill?"

Thessien's horse danced a mad step.

Ilien looked around in the gloom. A wolf drifted into view, eyes glowing like sparks in a plume of grey smoke. A moment later it faded back into the forest.

"Forget about riding on," the dog advised. "Collect as much wood as you can. It's our only hope. A fire might keep them at bay."

"You can talk!" cried Ilien. "But how is that possible?"

"You need wood, not answers. Now move!" The dog stepped forward, its great barrel-chest thrust out in anger.

Ilien retreated before it. "But Thessien—"

The dog's lips curled back, revealing razor sharp teeth. "You do as I say! If you don't you'll never find your friend, nor will he ever find you unless he looks in the bellies of a hundred wolves. Now gather wood and be quick about it! I'll guard you."

Ilien tried to think. He knew the dog was right. *Knew the dog was right? It was a dog!* A giant dog with very sharp teeth, he reminded himself. He climbed down off Thessien's horse and hunted the ground for wood, watching the dog out of the corner of his eye. Soon he had an armful.

"Pile it there—in that clear spot," barked the dog, running back and forth between the trees.

Ilien stacked all the branches and logs he could find in the center of the clearing. The pile of wood grew taller than him.

Thessien's black steed suddenly screamed. It threw its head and stomped about, the heavy scent of the wolves finally driving it mad. Ilien thought of unbridling it—freeing the big black of encumbrances in case of trouble, but the giant dog shouted out, "We need more wood than that! Follow me!" and Ilien left the horse to fend for itself. He had no doubt that it could.

"Move!" shouted the dog.

Ilien grabbed the Illwood sword where he'd left it, propped

against a tree. He eyed the three sharp thorns on its end. It would make a deadly weapon in a pinch. He shuddered at the thought, then moved down the hill after the dog.

They traveled only as far as they needed to fill Ilien's arms heaping with wood, then returned up the hill. The dog led the way, and thankfully so. Night had fallen quickly. But when they reached the woodpile, Ilien gasped and stumbled forward, dropping his armful of wood.

The pile was gone. So too was Thessien's steed.

The dog let out a low growl, and Ilien spun around. They stood surrounded by a jury of shining yellow eyes, peering at them from between the trees. The dog lifted its head to the deepening dusk. Its long howl shuddered the forest. The wolves stood unfazed, their grins only widening.

Ilien suddenly remembered Gallund's wand and the spell he had used on the wierwulvs. He reached to his side. His fingers fumbled at his belt. The wand was gone! He looked around in panic, holding the Illwood sword before him, turning in circles, anticipating attack from every direction. He wished he hadn't crept down the stairs that night not so long ago. If he hadn't been caught spying he might still be home, curled safely in his bed. If it wasn't for that pesky little light—

That was it! He could light the clearing with that pesky little light!

"*Kinil ubid illubid kinar!*" he cried aloud. The words tumbled over each other in his panic.

Nothing happened. He held out his hand, palm up, and recited the spell again. "*Kinil ubid, illubid kinar!*" Still no light. What was he doing wrong? It was a perfect magical sentence. No unnecessary adverbs. No double negatives. All the right tenses. It was perfect. It was a song, for crying out loud! He looked closely at the space above his hand. It was there. He saw it. The faintest of embers, like a hesitant firefly.

"*Kinil ubid illubid kinar!*" he shouted again.

The wolves attacked, their fury spent on the giant dog alone, as if Ilien didn't exist. A half dozen shaggy brutes piled in, snapping jaws seeking to hamstring their prey. More wolves raced past Ilien to join the fray. The valiant dog would be torn to pieces before his eyes.

The battle Ilien witnessed was a blur of fur and fangs. The pack swarmed over itself, a rushing wave of teeth and claws, swamping the dog, dragging it under. The clack of teeth and screams of wolves filled the air. Slowly the dog emerged, rising on a sea of twisting bodies. It shook itself free, snatching a wolf from off its back and tearing it to pieces. It waded through its enemies, ripping life from any it could reach. But there were just too many.

Ilien ran forward, the Illwood branch raised high. He shouted his battle cry above the din. Before he could strike, the darkness fled around him. The top of the hill grew bright. He looked up. A blazing ball of light hovered high above the clearing.

"Globe!" he cried.

But the wolves had tasted blood. They pressed their attack, undaunted by the magical light. Several turned on Ilien and he struck out at the air with the Illwood branch. The wolves circled, eager yet patient, fainting, darting out of reach. They soon found their mark. They leapt on Ilien from behind and he fell beneath a swarm of stinking, grey bodies.

As Ilien felt the first fangs strike, he heard the call of horns in the night. Moments later other horns called back. Still the wolves attacked, but their screams and howls faded away. A wolf chewed on his leg but he felt no pain. *Am I dreaming? Or is this what death is like?* he wondered. The horns called again. The din of the wolves disappeared. Darkness closed in around him. He looked to the sky, into Globe's brilliant light, and saw the face of a beautiful, young girl hovering over him.

Yes, he thought. *I am dying. I am. And this must be heaven.*

Chapter VI

Evernden

"Time to get up, Ilien. Rise and shine, sleepy-head. Come on now. It's getting late."

His mother's voice called to him from far away, muffled, as if heard through a thick fog. Her voice grew louder as it drew near.

"Good morning, Ilien. Or should I say afternoon? It's nearly one o'clock."

Ilien opened his eyes but all he could see was the inside of the blanket pulled over his head. Cheery light shined through and he felt warm and safe. The dream had felt so real. Thessien, the witches' clearing, the wierwulvs, the talking dog—it had all been a bad dream, nothing more. There hadn't been any adventure at all. He was safe and sound in his own bed, in his own house, on a bright, sunny Saturday. He shot the covers off and jumped out of bed.

"Where's Gallund?" he asked his mother, who was busy picking up his dirty clothes from off the floor.

"Downstairs reading, I think."

He bolted from the room and flew down the stairs. The midday sun streamed through the two kitchen windows and splashed all over in warm, shiny pools. Gallund sat in one such pool at the kitchen table, reading the morning paper. Ilien smiled. The paper, of course, was Ilien's spell book, disguised for the time being as the Southford Gazette. Gallund looked up, annoyed that he was being watched so intently.

63

NOMADIN

"Gallund!" Ilien threw his arms around the wizard. "I'm so glad you're not dead. You wouldn't believe the dream I had."

Gallund suddenly grabbed him and held him at arms length. His cheeks flushed bright red. "Ilien, listen to me. Go back at once."

Ilien pulled away, but the wizard tightened his grip, drawing him close, his brows raised in alarm. "Go to the front door and leave. Don't look back, no matter what happens. Remember what I say, some appearances are not what they seem."

He released Ilien just as his mother came into the room.

"Would you like some breakfast, dear?" she asked.

Ilien rubbed his arms. He was about to answer when Gallund shot him a warning look, then continued reading his paper.

"How about some scrambled eggs, your favorite?"

Ilien froze. His mother knew he hated scrambled eggs. He turned and eyed her uneasily, but as soon as he saw her casual wink he realized it was just a joke. His mother was always joking like that. Of course she knew he hated scrambled eggs. He looked back at Gallund, relieved.

The wizard was mumbling under his breath. Ilien stood just close enough to hear what he was saying.

"*Illustus bregun, illustus bregar.*"

As soon as the last word was spoken Ilien's mother flickered. She actually flickered, disappearing for an instant. If Ilien had blinked he would have missed it completely.

"Is something wrong?" she asked, moving into the sunlight and suddenly holding a frying pan.

Ilien gasped. Her eyes shimmered in the light, glowing like two hot coins.

"Run!" cried the wizard. "To the front door and don't look back!"

Gallund shot to his feet. Hot, blue flames poured from his fingers, igniting the kitchen into a raging fire. Ilien heard a

64

loud clang as the frying pan his mother held crashed to the floor. He raced for the door. His mother screamed in pain.

My god! he thought. *He's burning her alive!* He froze short of the door. Then Gallund's words came back to him. *Some appearances are not what they seem.* He reached for the knob.

"Ilien, help me!" His mother's scream tore through him.

The wizard's voice rang out. "Run, Ilien! Run!"

Ilien opened his eyes, unsure if he was awake. The grim face of Thessien hovered over him. He tried to talk, but couldn't. Thessien turned and spoke to someone beside him.

"He's coming to."

Ilien flinched in pain. There was movement in the room and a young girl dressed much like a man came into view.

"Don't move," said the girl. "Lie still. You were bitten many times."

Ilien tried to speak again and managed a croak. The girl moved close and brought a polished, silver cup to his lips. He drank a cool, sweet liquid and closed his eyes. The strange liquid warmed him, clearing his wits. He opened his eyes with a start. The face of the girl before him was the same face he had seen in the forest. He tried to speak again, this time managing a few words.

"You saved me."

"Rest," said the girl.

Ilien suddenly remembered the giant dog who had fought to save him.

"Dog?" she said in response to his mumbled question. "I didn't see a dog. Only wolves. Now rest, Ilien. You have no worries here. You are safe in the king's castle at Evernden, and your courage has saved your friend's life. Lie still and rest."

Ilien closed his eyes and fell into a deep, dreamless sleep.

He stayed in bed for three more days, Thessien by his side. His room was small and drab, with walls of rough hewn stone.

The bed, and a chest at its foot, were the room's only furnishings, except for a single chair in the corner. In that chair Thessien kept vigil. Every morning the girl came and offered Ilien the polished, silver cup with its strange, cool drink. And each day his strength grew quicker than he thought it possibly could. All the while he wondered about the mysterious dog who had befriended him, the monstrous canine who could somehow speak. He feared the worse, that it had been mistaken for a wolf and shot with arrows, only to slink off into the forest and die.

On the third day, Ilien looked at his wounds. They were completely healed! Only a razor thin scar remained, the trophy of the deepest of his wounds on his left leg. That afternoon the girl came to see him again as he was getting dressed. His clothes had been washed and mended. He found his house key and pencil, miraculously quiet, still in his pocket.

"I'm glad to see you're feeling better," she said.

He was about to ask her what had been in the silver cup, but he fell speechless again. Where before she had worn the clothes of a woodsman, she now wore a dress of green and gold that lightly brushed the floor as she walked. Her hair, rather than tied short, fell in loose curls down past her shoulders. And her face—emerald green eyes, skin pale and smooth like egg shells, one small dimple beside her mouth. She was looking at Ilien curiously.

Before Ilien could come to his senses, a tall, broad man with a windburnt face and rusty-brown hair piled high upon his shoulders stepped into the room and stood behind her. Hard lines creased his red face, and a pale scar curled the left side of his mouth into a permanent snarl. The scar flushed crimson as he regarded Ilien with distaste. He put a hand on the girl's shoulder. The hand was missing a finger.

"Kysus, I trust all is ready," she said.

The man nodded, withdrawing his hand to place it in the

pocket of his tunic. "All is ready, My Lady." His voice was deep and gruff. When he smiled, his upper lip pulled back like an angry dog's.

The girl turned back to Ilien. "I've been asked to bring you before my father," she said. "He is eager to hear your tale, and curious to learn why you're here."

"Why we're here?" said Ilien. "Hasn't Thessien told you what's happened?" He looked at Thessien, puzzled.

"My father wants to hear it from you yourself. After all, you are Gallund's apprentice, and Thessien, well, he is only an Eastland soldier."

Kysus chuckled. Thessien remained silent.

"And who is your father?" asked Ilien.

"Why the king, of course," she said, slightly bemused.

Ilien suddenly felt foolish. "I meant no disrespect," he said. "It's just—I mean—I've never met a princess before."

"I've never met a wizard's apprentice before. We have much in common. Later we will talk. But now we must see the king."

The princess led the way, with Ilien and Thessien following. Kysus trailed behind.

Ilien was astounded at the magnificence of the castle. Where his room had been bare, dim and stuffy, the hall outside was decorated handsomely with portraits and colorful tapestries. On one side, large-paned windows overlooked the forest, letting in the bright afternoon sunlight to warm the gleaming stone floor beneath their feet. On the other side, scores of doors, intricately carved with battle scenes, winged dragons and unicorns, opened into other well-lit rooms. Ilien couldn't help slowing to peer in at the men who went about their business. The rumors back home were all wrong. Evernden did have a castle—a true king's castle!

They stopped before wide, splendidly carved double doors. "I'll tell my father you're here." With that the princess pushed through the doors. They closed behind her with nary a sound.

Kysus regarded Ilien with a wan smile, then set about sharpening a knife he had tucked into his belt. Neither Ilien nor Thessien felt much like talking anyhow. Thessien stood as if at attention. The look on his face spoke of his apathy toward the castle's beauty. Ilien, on the other hand, couldn't take his eyes off the double doors in front of him. The scene carved into them was enormous, covering every inch from top to bottom. It showed two armies at battle. Hundreds of intricately cut horsemen and foot-soldiers waged war in the very center where the two doors met. Farther back near each door's hinge camped the opposing armies. Hundreds more men lay wounded in between under the banner flags of their kings.

Ilien moved forward to get a better view of a particular scene near the center of the battle. A lone figure stood on a small crest of earth with his hands outstretched toward the advancing enemy. A halo encircled his head. A wounded man lay sprawled at his feet. A sheet of flames fanned out from the lone figure's fingertips, shielding the wounded man from his enemies. Ilien peered closer and saw that the man on the ground wore a crown. He looked at the standing figure again, leaning nearer the door. The figure looked familiar.

The door swung open.

"My father will see you," announced the princess.

Ilien was still rubbing the lump on his head when he came before the king.

The king of Evernden was not a large, imposing man as Ilien had imagined. He was rather small and plain for a king, looking much like Ted the grocer back home. The room past the double doors was also not impressive, lacking the extravagant trappings of the rest of the castle. In its center stretched a long, rectangular table. Around it sat ten men in high-backed chairs wearing grim, ill-tempered looks. The king sat at its far end.

When Ilien entered the room, everyone, including the king, rose from their seats.

"I'm glad you are well, young Ilien," said the king.

Ilien felt surprised and flattered that a king, any king, knew his name, let alone called him by it.

"Please. Sit," bade the king.

There were four empty chairs at their end of the table. The princess sat opposite Ilien, with the ever-present Kysus beside her. Thessien, though, remained standing by the door. Ilien thought he acted a bit rude, and was worried about what might happen to someone who acted a bit rude to a king. But the king ignored him.

"My daughter has informed me as to how you came here," he said, raising an eyebrow in her direction. "But I do not know why you are here. So tell me, why has Gallund sent his apprentice through my backyard to see me? And why hasn't he come himself? I dare say, he could have saved you a lot of trouble sending you by road."

Ilien shifted in his chair, all eyes upon him. He looked at Thessien. The soldier only nodded.

"I bear bad news," said Ilien, nearly choking on his words. "I'm afraid Gallund is dead."

Shouts rose around the table and some of the king's men jumped to their feet, knocking their high-backed chairs to the floor. The king remained unruffled, sitting quietly amidst the uproar.

"Gallund dead? What of the spell?" asked one of the men.

"Who is responsible?" asked another.

"The Necromancer—that's who!" shouted someone else.

Ilien tried to listen to what everyone was saying, but soon the room grew too loud for him to hear anything at all. Thessien watched quietly from the doorway. The entire room hushed, and Ilien saw then that the king had risen from his seat.

"Even though I feared it was true, how am I to believe this?"

he asked. "Who could kill a Nomadin? These are not dark times. Tell me. Who?"

It was then that Thessien stepped forward. "I will answer that question." Whispers and coughs moved about the room as the Eastland soldier addressed the king uninvited. Ilien could see the distaste for Thessien in the men's eyes as they exchanged sour looks.

Kysus rose to his feet, pounding his four-fingered fist on the table. "You are in the king's court, Eastlander, and should I remind you, far from home. You might chance such dishonor at your father's table, but here, oh brat of Ashevery, you would be wise to hold your tongue until spoken to."

"I am glad you so cherish wisdom," said Thessien, turning cool eyes on the red-haired warrior. "You will soon need it tenfold to what you have."

The room hushed at his words, each of the king's advisors trying to decipher if Kysus had been handed an insult.

"Yes, Gallund is dead," continued Thessien in a loud voice. "You think you know what that means, but you do not. The dark years were well before your time. Your kingdom has been a safe haven for as long as your grandparents' grandparents can remember. But my father's kingdom knows not this squalid splendor you call peace. There is a darkness that touches the land still, but like the evening shadows, it touches the West last. Yes, Gallund is dead, and so too is the Binding spell that holds the night from falling."

No one spoke. Even the king sat back down in silence. Thessien seemed to grow taller as he formally addressed the king.

"King Allen, I mean no disrespect, and though it is true that I hold no love for rule or regency, I speak only the truth. We must put our nations' dark history behind us. I ask you to listen and heed my advice, for all our futures hang in the balance. Evil dwells in your backyard. Wierwulvs and servants of the

Necromancer have grown powerful. A NiDemon has crossed."

Thessien stood silent for a moment, his eyes scanning the men before him. They fell last on the king. "Yes. A crossing exists," he continued. "The power of Nihilic remains. I have seen it with my own eyes, in a scroll Gallund found nearly on your doorstep. The Third Rise is upon us. The NiDemon's hand is in this, and if it is then already the Book may be open."

"But what of the key?" asked one of the king's men. "Is it not true that the Book cannot be opened without it?"

"Yes," said the king. "Though the Binding spell dies with the caster, we are still safe, so long as the key is safe."

"True," said Thessien, "but Gallund was the keeper of the key. We must assume the enemy now has it."

"But wouldn't he have hidden it?" asked one of the king's advisors. "Surely he wouldn't have kept it on him."

"True again," replied Thessien, "but NiDemon have ways of discerning the secrets of dying men, dying Nomadin as well."

Kysus slapped the table. "You worry too much!" he said. "Let's not get ahead of ourselves. The sky is not falling as our Eastland friend suggests. Don't forget, the Book is safely guarded by the Nomadin at Kingsend Castle."

"Is it?" said Thessien, silencing the room with his question.

"What would you have us do?" asked Kysus. "Are we to raise an army and march on an unseen enemy? Or raze the forests with flames and rout out the wolves and the rabbits?"

Thessien leaned forward, placing both his hands on the table. "No army you could raise would suffice to do either." He turned to the others. "Do not let yourselves be fooled by wolves—or rabbits. Some appearances are not what they seem. Evil takes many forms. King Allen, I implore your reason. No one outside this room knows of Gallund's death. Yours is the only kingdom able to send riders to Kingsend Castle to warn the Nomadin. They must be told that the spell is broken. The Book must be protected, if it's not already too late."

71

Again the room fell quiet as everyone waited to hear the king. Ilien's head was spinning. He was trying to understand all that was being said. On top of that, he had never heard Thessien speak so much at one time.

"Gallund was not only a buckler against evil, but he was also my friend and teacher," said the king. "Not unlike you, young Ilien, and yes you also, Thessien, Gallund sought to be my mentor in a great many things. Ours is a history that dates back to my grandfather's grandfather, you might say. In fact, if it wasn't for Gallund I wouldn't be here at all. He saved my great, great grandfather, King Braul, from the army of the very man who stands before me now. His death is a great blow to my heart."

The king steepled his hands, bowing his head in silence. When at last he looked up, his eyes held a flame of hope, but a flame like an oft burned candle, pale and wavering.

"Yet I wonder," he said. "Is not the Necromancer's prophesy of some importance? Is it not true that only the Prophesied One can release the Necromancer from his prison? Has there been no diligence on the part of the Nomadin? Are we to fear and call to arms if the Nomadin have kept to their oath?"

"Prophesies are but well-trodden paths for sheep," said Thessien, "and oaths are broken always, if given enough time. We should not be sheep led to the slaughter by the Dark Shepherd. And the Nomadin mark their days in our years a thousand to one. There may yet be a grandchild of the First Line, hidden, unknown to any but a few. We can be certain of nothing, save that all I've said is true."

The king's advisors fell silent and Kysus shook his head. King Allen, though, rose from his seat, the flame in his eyes suddenly bright. "I have been aware of the dangers brewing in my own backyard for some time now. I fear my delay in dealing with them has been a grave mistake. But no longer will I delay good judgment. You are right. The Nomadin must be warned. I will send riders to Kingsend Castle come daybreak."

"My Lord," said Kysus, "to send troops south, what would our people think if they knew our reasons? NiDemon? Dark magic? Old tales retold, that's what. They have outgrown such Eastern mythology. Would you have them think we pin our medals on the jackets of the East?"

"Perhaps Thessien is right," said King Allen. "Perhaps our people have lived too long in the squalid splendor of peace. But we all know that peace is only an illusion. Gallund's death should be proof enough of that." The king looked at the carved double doors and shook his head with a sigh. "But you are also correct, Kysus," he said, turning to the red-haired warrior. "I will send only three men to Kingsend Castle. Their departure will not be noticed, and three will travel faster than thirty." The king then turned to Thessien. "You serve your father with honor. Will you serve our cause as well? Will you ride south with my men?"

"I still serve the cause that was set before me from the start," said Thessien, straightening, "though I may already be too late. My mission travels a different road from yours. I must ride north in the morning."

"So be it," said the king. His eyes fixed on Ilien. "And what of you, young apprentice?"

Ilien was stunned silent. The king had actually asked him for an opinion. He cleared the frog from his throat.

"The apprentice stays here with you," said Thessien. "It was Gallund's wish before we left."

Ilien bit his lip. So much for his moment of glory.

"Very well," said the king, nodding. "My daughter will enjoy the company." The princess smiled at Ilien. "Thessien, we part ways in the morning. I pray our next meeting brings better news between us. When you return home, tell your father that we prize the squalid splendor of peace above all else, and will not hand it over so easily. The West will make a ready ally in the battle against the Necromancer. Now go, and fare well."

The men around the table rose and left with many mumbles and silent curses, but Ilien remained sitting, eyeing Thessien curiously. Brat of Ashevery? If he'd heard right, Thessien was a prince, a prince who wished he wasn't. Why hadn't Gallund told him that he'd be traveling with a prince? He might have been better behaved. And what of this prophesy the Necromancer had made? Gallund never told him about any prophesy either.

As Ilien watched the room clear, he remembered Thessien's words and shuddered. *There is a darkness that touches the land still, but like the evening shadows it touches the West last.* Ilien would soon be returning home, but with all that he now knew, and with all that had happened, he wondered if he'd ever truly feel safe again.

Chapter VII

The Groll

The evening was fast approaching when the princess brought Ilien and Thessien out to the west gardens of the castle, under the shadow of the surrounding forest. Kysus, as usual, followed close behind. When Ilien asked the princess about the red-haired warrior, she answered him in low tones.

"He's supposed to be my bodyguard, something my father so graciously supplied against my wishes. He's not a very good one either, which is fine with me. I don't dare tell my father that he's hardly ever around, that he's always mysteriously disappearing, sometimes for days. If he knew, he might find me a better one and then I'd never get any privacy."

She looked back to make sure Kysus wasn't within hearing range. "He goes off into the forest, you know. I saw him once, at dusk, when I went gathering teaberries. I don't think he saw me, but I saw him."

Ilien glanced back at Kysus, but Thessien ignored the princess' remarks, caught up in his own thoughts. Tomorrow Thessien would continue north to Greattower, and Ilien could sense the restlessness in the Eastland prince, as if the late afternoon sun chastised him for not riding onward even then. But they both knew there was no sense leaving till morning, so for now they let the princess indulge them in a leisurely tour of the castle and its grounds.

"These gardens might be of interest to you, Ilien," said the princess. They walked through a large, brown tract of land spotted with small beds of green plantings. A row of wooden trellises stood empty to their left, while to their right a low wall of stone separated the garden from the castle grounds. "It's here that we grow the wolfsbane that kept Thessien alive until your timely arrival with the Illwood bark. As you know, wolfsbane is thought by most to have magical healing properties."

Ilien, of course, did not know this.

The princess stooped to pull a few weeds from beside a prickly looking bush growing in one of the beds. "We grow many healing herbs here in the west garden. The plants fare well in the shade. When the last frosts have gone we'll plant the annuals. They're the most potent healers."

The garden was immense, even compared to the large garden kept by Farmer Parson, Ilien's closest neighbor back home. Arranged in neat rows from the foot of the forest to the low stone wall, it stretched left and right as far as Ilien could see. Most of it lay unplanted—a tangle of dry, brown refuse with here and there a square, green patch thrown in.

"My father permits these gardens because plants are things he can see and feel. But like you, Ilien, I have a different understanding. I also know the power of magic."

"Are you an apprentice to a wizard too?" asked Ilien.

She laughed. "No. I'm afraid I'm not that gifted. I looked at your spell book but it made no sense at all."

Ilien straightened in surprise. "My spell book? You have my spell book?"

"Don't be angry. I was going to return it to you. It was in the saddle bag of Gallund's horse."

"You have Gallund's horse, too?" Ilien looked at Thessien, who merely raised an eyebrow in surprise.

The princess motioned toward a nearby bench. "I'm sorry. I should've told you. Sit down and I'll explain everything."

They sat on a long stone bench beside a small bed of deep

green holly. Kysus remained standing some distance away. The shadow of the forest lay dark and cool around them, the tall trees casting their long, spiky images up the castle walls.

"Six days ago," began the princess, "while in the forest at night, I came across a magnificent grey horse. To tell the truth, it came across me while I was gathering teaberries for a potion. As you probably know, teaberries only come out at night."

Ilien didn't know that either. "A potion?" he asked.

"Yes. You do know what a potion is?"

Ilien nodded. "Of course. I was just—"

"Well, I was gathering teaberries for one," continued the princess, "when I heard a soft nicker. A beautiful, grey horse stepped out from behind a tree into my lantern light. It let me approach. That's when I saw that it had been attacked by wolves. The wounds weren't severe, but I took it straight back to the castle anyway, to Kemp, my stable master. He recognized it right away as the grey mount of Gallund the wizard. I sent him to tell the king immediately. Meanwhile, I unsaddled the poor wounded creature. It was then that a book spilled out from the saddle bag. It was obviously a spell book. After all, what other book would a wizard carry with him, a history book?"

More than likely, if you knew Gallund, thought Ilien.

The princess smoothed her long dress on her lap. "Being interested in magic as I am, and being a mage, I looked inside."

"A mage?" asked Ilien.

"Yes. A mage." The princess stressed the word to give it special meaning. "You know, a user of magic." She ruffled her dress before continuing. "As I said, I couldn't understand a single word. Most of what I read was jibberish, even though I am quite skilled in the use of magical items."

"Magical items?"

"Ilien, you're beginning to sound like a parakeet," said the princess, trying not to lose her patience. "Magical items?

Talismans? Enchanted things? You know, magical items." She tilted her head and smiled. "How do you think I managed to save you from those wolves single-handedly?"

"Single-handedly?" Ilien's eyes narrowed. "But I heard the horns of a small army."

"If you'll just let me finish I'll explain everything!"

Thessien was his usual guarded self, but from the amused look on his face even he was interested in the story's ending, or the princess' complete loss of patience, whichever came first.

She took a deep breath. "Now I've lost my train of thought." She looked around the garden as if she might actually find it again. "Oh yes—I was saying I couldn't understand a word in the spell book. And that's when my father received the news that Gallund's horse had been found, without Gallund on it. He was concerned, of course. He began to talk about Gallund lying wounded in the forest, or worse yet, dead. He called his advisors together." She stopped and looked over to see if Kysus was listening. "My father can't seem to make a decision without consulting his advisors."

Thessien chuckled.

"Precious time was passing," continued the princess, throwing Thessien a dark look, "and if Gallund was lying wounded in the forest then I couldn't see how calling a council of men together was going to solve anything. So I rode back into the forest, to the spot where I found his horse. It wasn't hard to pick up its tracks and follow them back along the route it had come. And that's when I found what I thought was a wizard. I didn't know it then, but it was only an Eastlander."

She glanced at Thessien. "I mean no disrespect, you know."

"None taken," said Thessien.

She pushed him a smile, then said to Ilien, "I managed to coax him back onto his horse."

"You mean *my* horse," corrected Ilien.

"Your horse, his horse—what's the difference?" argued the princess. She stopped and smirked openly. "Though, now that you mention it, it was a bit small."

Ilien ignored her and turned to Thessien. "Your horse—the wolves—they—" He frowned and hung his head.

"I'm sure old Talamar is fine," said Thessien, placing a comforting hand on Ilien's shoulder.

"Sure he is," said the princess. "He's in my stable."

Ilien looked accusingly at Thessien. The Eastlander's smile widened to a grin.

"He's fine," Thessien assured him. "A few nips here and there, but no worse for the wear. He showed up two days ago."

"As I was saying," continued the princess, smoothing her dress upon her lap again. She evidently wanted to tell her tale without further interruption, for she looked hard at both Ilien and Thessien and cleared her throat. "After I found him, I managed to coax him back onto your horse."

"Coax isn't the word," said Thessien, rubbing his cheek with a wry smile.

"I did what I had to," countered the princess, her hands at her hips. "Now if the two of you don't mind, I'll finish my story now, thank you very much."

"Please do," said Ilien.

Thessien turned mock-serious and nodded.

"Anyhow," said the princess, turning back to Ilien with a sigh, "after I found him, I brought him straight to the king. My father didn't know who he was at first, but he did know that he wasn't Gallund. I think he was a little upset that I had gone back into the forest alone because he began ranting about councils and procedures." She shook her head in annoyance. "He said he had met with his council and they had decided to wait and search the forest the next morning. He forbade me to go looking for anyone else in the forest that night. I promised I wouldn't."

She smiled. "But I did go hunting for teaberries again. That's when I found you, and might I add, not faring so well for a wizard's apprentice."

"And how did you know I wasn't the wizard himself?" asked Ilien.

"Come now, young Ilien," said the princess, rolling her eyes. "Even I am not that blind."

Thessien chuckled again. Ilien quieted him with a bewildered look.

"But I was also not so blind as to overlook your courage and resourcefulness. Left alone in the forest amongst wolves and wierwulvs, you still managed to find the bark of the Illwood and nearly make it back to the castle. How you accomplished all that is still a mystery to me."

"What's a mystery is how you drove off those wolves single-handedly," said Ilien. He thought it best not to mention the talking dog. Not only would it sound unbelievable, but it might make him seem less courageous and resourceful, and he liked being thought of as courageous and resourceful, especially by a princess.

"I'm a mage," replied the princess. "My powers lie in my talismans. I used the Horn of Plenty to drive off the wolves."

"Horn of Plenty?"

"My, you're full of questions, aren't you?" She sighed and glanced over at Kysus, who all but ignored her and kept looking out at the surrounding forest. "Yes, Horn of Plenty. A single call sounds like the calls of a hundred horns coming from every direction. It was more than enough to trick the wolves into thinking I was a small army. I have a collection of magical items. Would you like to see them?" Without waiting for an answer she called out to Kysus. "We're going now."

The princess led them back into the castle through a small hidden door between two large rosebushes. The door had been carved to look like the side of the castle, faced with thin slabs of stone. Ilien would have missed it completely unless he knew it was there all along. The princess touched a series of stones beside the door and it swung open with a groan. The afternoon sunlight fell into a large room beyond. They all filed in and the door shut behind them, sealing them in utter darkness.

"This is one of the castle's storerooms," called the princess through the inky blackness. "Now where is that lightstone? Blast! I thought I had put it in my pocket."

The air around them brightened as Ilien incanted his Light spell. Globe rested in the palm of his hand, growing larger at his bidding. Its pale light threw wavering shadows on the floor. Satisfied with its size, he tossed it in the air toward the princess. It bobbed up and down above her head, the shadows bobbing with it.

The princess stared at the tiny light above her. "Thanks," she muttered. "I must have left my lightstone in my room."

Without another word she led them toward a door at the far end of the store room. Globe hovered along above her like a balloon on a string.

"Where do those go?" asked Ilien, noticing stairs leading downward into darkness.

"To the castle's cellars," answered the princess with a wave of her hand. "They're mostly wine cellars, but we also have food stores below. It's not very nice down there though, too damp and smelly if you ask me, but we do have a fine collection of wines. My father is quite fond of the whites, but I like the reds—much sweeter."

"He lets you drink wine?" asked Ilien, still looking back at the darkened stairway. "How old are you, anyhow?"

"I am the princess, Ilien. I drink what I like."

Daylight streamed in to end the conversation as the princess pulled open the door leading out of the storeroom. They entered a cramped, circular room with a long, spiral staircase leading upwards in its center. Small windows had been cut into the walls, casting a patchwork of sunlight on the rising steps. Ilien extinguished Globe with a nod.

"This is the back way to my room. It's near the top of the tower."

Soon they were plodding up the tall, spiral staircase. Ilien looked to see if he could spot its top, but it continued up so high that the turning curves became a blur in the distance.

"I like my privacy," said the princess. "I just wished it didn't take me twenty minutes to make it down to breakfast."

She laughed, and so did Ilien. Thessien and Kysus, though, were not amused. Ilien counted two hundred and fifty-eight steps, and that was just from the spot where he began counting, when they finally came to a small door. The twisting stairs continued upward into shadow.

"Isn't there an easier way to get to your room?" asked Ilien, still puffing from the climb.

"Of course there is. I usually go through the castle."

"What's up there?" questioned Thessien, pointing up the darkened stairs.

"Nothing yet, but soon there'll be an observatory. My father hasn't finished it, though. He keeps promising that someday I'll get to use my telescope." She rolled her eyes and produced a small, silver key. She quickly unlocked the door and placed the key back in her pocket.

The room of the princess of Evernden surprised Ilien. He had expected it to be frilly and girlish, decorated with bright tapestries, furnished with a plump feather bed sprinkled with lacy pillows. But it was almost like his own room back home, which meant there was nothing special about it at all. From the small, hard bed to the bare walls to the cold, dusty floor, it made him feel right at home.

The princess closed the door behind them and it disappeared, blending perfectly with the stone pattern of the wall. Another, more obvious door, stood closed on the opposite wall.

"This is your room?" asked Ilien, checking out a corner where a number of books lay piled in a heap.

"Yes. Why? You think it's unbefitting a princess?"

"Of course it is," said Ilien. "I mean, it does seem a bit common," he stammered.

The princess turned away in satisfaction. "Good."

Thessien raised an eyebrow. Kysus shook his head.

"Well here it is," said the princess as she struggled to pull something from under her bed. Ilien joined her in tugging until a large, flat trunk sprang free, sending both of them falling back on their bottoms.

"This is it!" beamed the princess. "My collection!" The trunk was shut tight with a polished silver lock. "Now where is that key?" she muttered, fishing in her pockets. "I just had it."

"Ouch!" Ilien jumped up as something jabbed him painfully where he sat. Beneath him was the silver key, standing, oddly enough, on end.

"Sorry about that. It's a bit unruly, as magical keys go."

"You should meet my pencil," mumbled Ilien, rubbing his sore bottom. The moment he said it a tumble of muffled yells erupted from his back pocket. The princess raised an eyebrow.

"What is that?"

"It's nothing, I promise you."

"Nothing!" shouted the pencil. "Well I never! All this time you keep me stuffed away in this suffocating little hole with god knows what else. What is this anyway? A leftover sandwich? How disgusting. It stinks in here!"

Ilien snatched the pencil from his pocket. "There is no leftover sandwich in there and you know it." He glanced at the princess, red faced. "So quit your loud-mouth antics and be nice," he said, holding it before the princess like it was an unruly child. "Now say you're sorry."

The pencil fell silent.

"Come on now," said Ilien. "You're being rude. Say you're

sorry, or I swear, I'll give you to Peaty when we get home. You know how he likes to stick pencils up his nose for attention."

"Sorry," muttered the pencil.

The princess stepped back. "Oh my!" she exclaimed. "Apology accepted." She looked at Ilien. "It's amazing."

"At least *she* appreciates me," replied the pencil. "You—"

Ilien jammed it back into his pocket. "I don't know why I keep you," he mumbled.

"Because you don't know a right angle from a hypotenuse," came the answer, and muffled laughter.

The princess unlocked the chest, and with help from Ilien, swung open the heavy lid. She smiled, and with a flourish of her arms cried, "Ta dah!", revealing a number of quite ordinary looking items. A horseshoe, a brown feather, some small rocks and a bit of string, to name a few. Most of it looked like useless junk to Ilien.

"My talismans," said the princess.

Beneath an old leather boot lay Ilien's spell book. "Ah ha!" he cried as he pulled it out. Someone had stuck a bookmark in it. He looked at the princess accusingly.

"What?" she asked.

He fingered the strange bookmark.

"Don't look at me. It was there all along. I even left it right where I found it. I didn't want to lose your place."

He opened the spell book to the marked page. He had flipped this far ahead only once before, and was surprised to see writing this time. Pages this far ahead were usually blank, the consequence of a spell Gallund had cooked up after Ilien had nearly flooded the house with a Rain spell last summer. *The Concealing spell must be broken,* he thought. He looked at the writing on the page and an ache of sadness crept over him. He read the spell anyhow. "Truth Sear Em. When invoked, this spell will burn the hands of a liar until the truth is told."

"*Istru benot, isnot behot,*" he mumbled before he knew it.

84

"Ouch!" cried the princess.

Ilien looked up, wide eyed, apologetic.

"Darn needle," she said. She stuck her finger in her mouth. In her other hand she held a small sewing needle trailing green thread.

"What does that do?" asked Ilien, assuming it was part of her collection.

"Sews. What else?" She pinned it to her dress. "A lady always carries a needle and thread with her, just in case her dress tears in an embarrassing spot."

Ilien closed the spell book, but removed the bookmark. On it were the words, *Princess with a capital P.* He tossed it to her without looking up.

"Hey, I recognize this!" he said, pulling out a polished, silver cup.

The princess snatched it out of his hands. "Be careful with that. It's a very valuable talisman." She polished it on her sleeve. "It turns water into a potent healing potion. It worked wonders on you." She turned it over in her hands, her enthusiasm suddenly waning. "Though I have to say, it didn't seem to help Thessien all that much." She tossed it back into the chest.

Suddenly her eyes lit up. "Here it is!" she gushed, lifting out a small, round stone that immediately began to glow as she held it. "My lightstone! You see, it works just as well as your spell."

She quickly slipped it in her pocket.

"Ah ha!" she squealed, lunging back into the chest to pluck out the large, brown feather. "This is one of my most magical of talismans. I bought it from a lady in—get this—Anderbar. She's famous for her collection of talismans."

Ilien raised an eyebrow, as if Anderbar meant anything to him.

"It looks like an ordinary chicken feather," said Thessien.

"Yes, but it's not ordinary at all. With it you can fly."

"That is extra ordinary," said Ilien. "Let's see it work." He half-expected the princess to begin hovering around the room.

"Not right now," she said. "There's really not enough room in here. I'd just end up bumping into the ceiling."

She slipped the feather into her pocket along with the lightstone.

"And this—" She reached in and pulled out what looked like a toy bugle. "This is what saved you." She turned it over in her hands. She put it to her lips and Ilien covered his ears. She laughed and tossed it onto her bed.

"What about that horseshoe?" asked Ilien, looking back into the chest with renewed interest.

"This?" She pulled it out from under the tangled mess. "This gives the horse who wears it unearthly speed and stamina."

"But you only have one," said Thessien, hovering over Ilien to get a better look. "Don't you need four?"

"Sadly, yes." She threw it back on top of the old boot.

Ilien couldn't help but dig through the odd-ball assortment. "What's this?" he asked as he lifted up a painted wooden doll and baby bottle.

"Oh. Those aren't magical." She grabbed the doll and baby bottle and quickly tucked them under her bed. Her face flushed crimson.

"Where did you get all these things?" asked Ilien.

"Some of them were gifts from other mages," she answered. "Some were given to me by my father, even though he doesn't believe they're magical at all. But most I bought abroad. Sadly, that's the only good things about being a princess. You get to travel quite a bit."

Ilien looked skeptically at a few of the more doubtful items in the chest: a length of frayed rope, a worn slipper, a rusted knife, a bent candlestick.

"But how do you know they're really magical?" he asked. "Have you tried them all?"

SHAWN P. CORMIER

"Of course I've tried them all. I'll admit not all of them contain practical magic. But now and then I find a really useful and powerful talisman, like the Horn or lightstone, or better yet my flying feather. I only wish—"

Thessien sprang to the front door, raising his hand in warning. The princess left the sentence unfinished. There was a long moment of quiet before distant shouts could be heard outside. Kysus stepped forward, but before he reached the door it flew open and a man clad in chain mail rushed in. He held a sword in one hand. A small shield was strapped to his forearm.

"Your Highness, I've been sent by the king himself. There is a battle at the gates. Wolves and wierwulvs are assaulting the castle. You're to come with me at once."

"Wolves and wierwulvs my arse!" raged Kysus, stepping out and looking up and down the hall. "Where is the king's guard? Where is the night watch?" He turned back and stood in the doorway. "Surely they can handle this disturbance."

The armor-clad man held his sword at his side, his face hard and grim. "Sir, the night watch is dead. The king's guard have been repelled. We fear the castle has been breached. The princess is to come with me by order of the king."

Ilien scooped up his spell book. The princess began grabbing talismans from the chest. The man in armor stopped her.

"There is no time."

Thessien pushed past Kysus and the rest followed. Kysus brought up the rear, his eyes darting nervously to and fro. Once in the hallway the mail-clad man turned to the two men present.

"Be prepared," he said. "There may be a Groll in the castle."

Ilien didn't know what a Groll was, but Thessien's eyes hardened at its mention, and the Eastlander drew a long dagger from beneath his cloak.

Kysus followed suit. "A Groll? What makes you say that?" he asked.

87

The man answered without so much as a glance. "A wier-wulf told me, thinking it would save his life."

Ilien noticed then the red tinge to the man's blade.

The man led them quickly through the bustling castle. They flashed past open doors where men hastened to don leather armor and longswords. They pushed their way through the crowded hall, shouldering past men headed the other way. *The way toward battle,* thought Ilien. Toward a sea of wolves and wierwulvs, of men with amber eyes and freshly sharpened swords. He shivered and quickened his pace to keep up.

They continued on, making their way down a wide staircase of cut stone, along another hallway and through a set of double-doors. There they entered into a darkened ballroom, empty except for a few long tables pressed against the nearest wall. Long cloth curtains covered the windows, cloaking the room in shadows. The double-doors swung shut behind them and the room grew hushed, the only sound that of their padding feet echoing faintly around them. The heavy silence seemed ominous after the clamor of the hall. The armor-clad man continued on into the gloom, beckoning them to follow.

The princess pulled the lightstone from her pocket. It shined fiercely in her hand, casting its light ahead of them into the darkness. Ilien was about to strike up Globe, but thought better of it when he saw the look on the princess' face.

"Wait!" Her voice hurried around the ballroom, seeming to come from all directions at once. "Where are you taking us? This way leads no where. There is no exit from the Grand Ballroom."

Silence fell as everyone stopped. The shadows seemed to press in close, dimming the magic of the lightstone. Ilien looked around the room, trying in vain to see through the darkness. The silence was broken by a quiet snap—the sound of Thessien unfastening his sword from its scabbard. It was a simple message sent.

SHAWN P. CORMIER

The man's eyes narrowed as he turned his gaze on the Eastland prince, his hand white-knuckled around the pummel of his own sword. "You would be a fool to meddle in the king's affairs, Easterner. He has bound me to protect his daughter with my life, but yours would do just fine."

"You have not answered my question!" shouted the princess. "Where are you taking us?"

"My Lady," said the king's soldier, taking a kinder tone, "not all the king's passages are known, even to you. I have my orders. Now come." The man strode forward.

"Which are?"

"Do you question the king?" he asked, turning to face her.

"I question my father when I may," replied the princess smoothly. "I'll go no further until you answer my question."

The man fell silent. His eyes darted past her to Kysus.

Ilien's heart jumped. The man's eyes flashed amber in the glow of the lightstone! Ilien looked around at the others. No one else seemed to notice. Was it a trick of the light?

"What is your name?" asked the princess.

The man turned back, distracted. "I'm sorry, My Lady. I mean no disrespect. If you will just follow me, you'll soon understand everything. Now come."

"Tell me your name," she repeated. "I don't recall your face, and I know most of my father's coolies by sight, if not by smell. So have out with it. Your name!" The princess had her hands at her hips, and from the look of it, wasn't going anywhere until her question was answered.

Ilien tried to catch Thessien's attention. Surely *he* had noticed the strange glow of the man's eyes. But the Eastlander's gaze was fixed on the princess. Kysus too seemed oblivious.

Ilien looked back at the armor-clad man, then back at Thessien. Suddenly words came to him, as if from out of a dream. *Some appearances are not what they seem.*

89

"*Illustus bregun, illustus bregar!*" he cried, squeezing his spell book tight.

The suddenness of his spell jolted everyone as it reverberated painfully around the darkened ballroom.

Nothing happened.

"Ilien! What do you think you're doing?" demanded the princess, her hands clenched into fists at her side. "You scared me half to death. If I—"

Her eyes flew wide in terror. "Behind you!" she screamed.

Thessien's sword rang free from its scabbard. He rushed forward and knocked Ilien aside. Ilien sprawled to the floor, his spell book flying from his grasp. He looked up in terror at the monster crouching where Kysus had stood.

Hooked teeth leered from a long, pointed snout. Taller than a man, and twice as broad, the beast stood upright on its wolfish hind quarters, hairy human arms hanging down where front legs would have been. It fell to all fours, warg-like and stiff-legged, lowering its head warily. Up from its back curved a thick, prickly tail covered with mottled, black fur. Like a scorpion's, a sharp black barb dripped steaming liquid from its splayed end.

The Groll roared and charged forward.

The armor-clad man grabbed the princess by the arm. The lightstone fell from her hand, bouncing along the cold stone floor and thrusting them all into darkness.

Globe flashed to life above Ilien's head, lighting the ballroom with its dazzling light. The Groll froze, stunned by its sudden appearance.

"Run, Ilien!" shouted the princess as the king's soldier hurried her toward the door.

Ilien hesitated. He couldn't leave Thessien to fight alone. On instinct he reached for his hunting bow. It wasn't there.

"Get out of here, boy!" shouted Thessien, dodging a strike of the Groll's tail and lashing out with his sword.

Ilien felt a hand on his shoulder.

"Come on!" The princess pulled him away.

Ilien turned to the king's soldier. "We can't leave Thessien!"

"My duty is to protect the princess, nothing more," said the mail-clad man grimly.

Ilien stole one last look at Thessien. The prince's sword flashed in the gloom as Globe danced madly above his head.

They fled back the way they came, through the double doors, down the hall and back up the stairs. The halls were eerily empty now. Every last man battled the wierwulvs outside the castle. As they neared the princess' room, Ilien looked over his shoulder, hoping to spot Thessien bounding toward them.

"Your friend was a brave man, even for an Eastlander," said the princess. With that she raced into her room, dragging Ilien with her and latching the door behind them. They dashed to the hidden back door. There was no handle, only a small key hole.

"Now where is that blasted key?" cried the princess, eyeing the empty silver lock on the chest.

Ilien expected another jabbing, but unfortunately the key didn't appear.

Suddenly they heard a piecing howl from out in the hall, and the distinct rattle of the Groll's tail growing louder as it moved up the corridor toward them.

The princess and Ilien hunted frantically for the key, throwing open drawers, knocking over lamps. The king's soldier stepped forward. Cursing, he knocked them both out of the way.

"Why anyone values magic is beyond me!" He kicked the secret door open with the heel of his boot.

The screech of claws on stone followed from out in the hall as the Groll rushed forward. The front door buckled under its assault but held. Another blow sent nails flying from the hinges. There was a moment of breathless silence, then the knob began to turn. The soldier drew his sword and stood before the princess.

Out of the corner of his eye Ilien saw a flash of silver. The magical key shot from under the bed and raced for the door. Ilien ducked as it buzzed past his head. It reached the lock in the nick of time and the bolt fell into place with a loud click. The key breathed an audible sigh of relief.

The knob turned again. The door shook but wouldn't open. The Groll howled in rage and the key raced to the princess' pocket, squealing like a stuck pig.

"Go!" bade the soldier. "The lock won't hold for long."

At that the door burst apart, splinters of wood flying inward. The Groll lowered its head and stepped into the room. Its scorpion's tail hovered in the air above it, black barb quivering. A deep gash dripped blood onto the floor, a mute reminder of the power of the steel tooth its last victim had wielded. It approached its new prey cautiously.

The armor-clad man advanced a step and stopped, his sword held steady before him. "Get out of here!" he cried.

The princess grabbed Ilien's hand and they fled through the secret door, leaving the king's soldier to face the Groll alone.

When they reached the spiral staircase they looked down in terror. Several turns away three pairs of shining red eyes raced upwards toward them.

The princess pulled Ilien up the stairs. The wolves ran close behind. Three turns up and the stairs abruptly ended at a small door. The princess stopped.

"Don't tell me!" cried Ilien. "You can't find the key!"

"No!" said the princess, falling back against the wall. "I'm afraid of heights."

"What does that have to do with anything?"

She flung the door open. A violent gust of wind knocked her back into Ilien's arms. Ilien looked past her in awe. The door opened onto nothing. The night sky stretched out before them

92

like an endless void. A small ledge snaked away on either side into darkness.

"Like I said, the observatory's not finished yet!" exclaimed the princess.

The wolves drummed up the wooden stairs. Ilien turned in a dizzying circle. There was no where to go.

The princess suddenly drew him close, wrapping her arms around his waist. "Hold tight," she whispered. She pulled her magical feather from her pocket and gave him a quick kiss. "We jump on three."

"What!?" cried Ilien.

A blast of wind slammed them backward, threatening to knock them from the tower.

"Don't let go, no matter what!" she shouted. "One, two—"

Ilien flung his arms around her in disbelief.

The wolves rushed at them from the top of the stairs.

"—three!"

They leapt as one.

As they rushed headlong toward the ground, Ilien could hear the princess scream above the roaring wind.

"She told me it was magical, I swear!"

Chapter VIII

The Drowsy Wood

The rushing wind swept their screams away. They clung to each other in panic, neither noticing the other, mindless terror overwhelming them as they fell.

Ilien's thoughts flashed to his warm house back home, his mother's reassuring voice, the smell of paper in his father's study. His final seconds were spent in shocked, serene silence. The piercing cries of the princess washed past him like a distant, peaceful wave.

Laughter suddenly crashed over him, bringing him back to his senses. The screams of the princess had turned to exuberant shouts.

"It works! It really works! We're flying!" she cried.

They swooped down over the battle below, the heat from the bonfires sweeping over them, the smoke stinging their eyes, their toes inches from swinging swords and snapping jaws. The clang of metal and cries of battle rushed around them in a dizzying accord. Ilien's boots blind-sided a wierwulf and it fell to the ground before its astonished opponent.

They sailed back into the sky, climbing above the din, Ilien clinging tightly to the princess. The waging battle receded beneath them, men and wierwulvs growing small as toothpicks. The clamor faded. The bonfires shrank to burning match sticks.

"We made it!" shouted Ilien. "We really made it!"

They laughed and wept, howled and whooped, hugging each other tighter as they soared above the melee.

"We're safe! We're safe!" they cried.

They rose on the stiff night wind, flew higher above the castle until the bonfires below appeared as tiny sparks. The stars above glimmered like ice crystals. A cold breeze blew them upward again until the battle beneath them was all but lost to darkness. Their laughter trailed away to silence.

"How do we get down?" asked Ilien, hugging the princess tight and beginning to shiver.

"I don't know," said the princess, an edge of panic in her voice.

"What do you mean, you don't know?"

"I'm not a bird. It's only one feather! Can't you cast a spell or something?"

Together they screamed as a frigid gust blew them higher. Ilien's fingers grew numb. His arms ached. Shivers tore through him, and his grip loosened on the princess.

"Don't let go!" she shouted above the wind.

"I can't hold on much longer. I can't feel my hands. We have to get down!"

Again the night winds drove under them, lifting them toward the crystalline sky. Ilien held on with the last of his strength.

"I d-don't even know your n-name," he said, his teeth beginning to chatter.

The princess held tightly to Ilien, but her arms were tiring. "Ilien. Hold on."

"I don't even kn-know your n-name," he repeated. "What's your n-name?"

"Windy. My name's Windy," she replied, starting to cry.

"W-windy?" Ilien laughed. His grip faltered.

"No, Ilien! Hold on!"

Ilien caught himself, wrapping his arms around her legs. She reached down to grab him. "Don't let go!"

A dark shadow passed overhead, blotting out the starlight.

Windy looked up in fear. A roiling, black cloud descended from out of nowhere, screeching as it came, falling like a net of flapping black wings from the sky. A flock of giant birds flew down upon them, clawing at their eyes and clinging to their hair. One had Ilien by the ear. Another hammered its long beak into his back.

Ilien hugged Windy's legs, his arms weakening. He slipped and cried out, catching himself around her ankles. The birds beat their wings against him, ripping at his clothes. Others flew beneath him, stabbing him with their beaks. But the pain in his arms had eased. The birds were holding him up!

At the same time they were also descending. He heard Windy scream above him. Down they sailed, faster with every second, back down to earth, down toward solid ground and safety. They were going to make it! They were going to make it after all!

Ilien's arms gave out, and he fell with a cry.

He quickly struck the ground in a daze.

"Hey!" cried his pencil from his back pocket. "That hurt!"

Ilien had fallen only a few feet but it was enough to knock his wits away for a moment. Above him, the princess came in for a gentle landing, a score of flapping black wings easing her gently to the ground. The birds set Windy down beside him and flew off in a thick, inky cloud. The clatter of their wings receded into the night.

Ilien sat in stunned silence as the night wind played around him, hissing through the tall grass. The stars hung distant and cold above.

"What just happened?" asked Windy.

"I don't know," answered Ilien, nursing his throbbing arms and trying to gather his wits again.

They sat in the middle of a large field, its edges indiscernible in the pale starlight. The horizon behind them glowed orange, the pulsing orange of fire.

"What do we do now?" asked Windy. She looked a bit like a rabbit searching for a hole.

Ilien climbed to his feet. Overwhelmed with dizziness, he sat back down.

"Hey! Watch it!" shouted the pencil again.

"We can't go back, that's for sure," said Ilien, ignoring the pencil's outburst. "The castle is under siege. We'd just be killed with the others."

Windy hugged herself and turned away.

Ilien started. "I didn't mean—I only meant—" He put a hand on her shoulder. "I'm sure your parents are safe," he said quietly.

"You mean my father," said Windy. "The king of Evernden has no queen." She said this last part bitterly. Tears made her eyes glow dimly in the dark, but she quickly wiped them away. "I'm sorry about Thessien," she said, turning back. "He was your friend. And Gallund—now you're alone too, I suppose."

Ilien looked away, back toward the bright ribbon of light on the horizon. His pencil wriggled in his pocket but remained silent. The wind hurried over the tall grass around him and through the shrouded brambles, sighing in the shadows.

"Why is this happening?" whispered Windy. "Why was that creature after us?"

The answer came before Ilien could speak. "It was after Ilien." The giant dog emerged from the shadows, its imposing bulk rising over them. Its eyes glowed like two pale moons.

The princess fainted. Ilien caught her, lowering her gently to the grass. He looked up at the dog. "How—"

"It's no coincidence that I've found you," said the dog. "In fact, nothing that has happened has happened by chance. The birds of the Lady have spared you, but I am your only hope now."

"What do you mean?"

"Not now. Wake your friend. We must go at once."

97

"Go where?" asked Ilien.

The monstrous dog crept closer. Its fangs hung down like gleaming icicles. "You're still being hunted. There's a Groll in the wood."

Windy stirred. She sighed as if lost in a pleasant dream.

"Hunted?" said Ilien. "Me? But why?"

"Do you think we have time for a tale?"

Windy slowly woke. When she saw the massive dog, she bolted upright, scrambling to get behind Ilien.

"It's okay," said Ilien. "He's a friend."

"But, it, I heard—"

"Yes. He speaks. Listen to me Windy. We have to go with him, right now. That thing is still after us."

Her eyes went wide, her face pale. "Why? Why is this happening?"

"I don't know. But we have to go. Come on."

The giant dog lifted it head, testing the night air with its nose. The tall grass bowed beneath a chill wind, a wind that minutes earlier had danced past the prowling form of the Groll.

"You'll have to ride me," said the dog.

"Ride you?" said Ilien.

The dog growled fiercely, baring its teeth. "I like it no better than you! Now quick! Get on my back! It's near!"

The wailing howl of the Groll sounded in the distance. They scrambled on top of the dog. Windy sat in the front, grabbing the scruff of its neck.

"Not so tight!" growled the dog. "Hold on with your legs."

They bounced about awkwardly at first as the dog trotted off, Ilien holding fast around Windy's waist. Soon the dog cantered along and they found the going easier. They traveled across the open field, the only sound to break the silence that of the dog's heavy strides as it ran through the swaying grass. The shadow of the forest rose up before them, climbing above the calm field like a towering black wave. They dove into the woods, the dog's keen eyes guiding them through the inky gloom. Ilien looked back at the receding landscape. The trees seemed to close in behind them, stepping together to block their retreat. There was no sign of the Groll.

"I think we lost it," he said.

"Don't be so sure," panted the dog, looking back over its shoulder. "Now keep quiet. We've a ways to go."

They rode beneath the dark forest canopy for nearly an hour, the dog keeping a steady pace, eating up the miles in silent monotony. Ilien thought about what it had said. He was being hunted. But why? He was only a wizard's apprentice, and not a very good one at that. He had nothing anyone could possibly want. He didn't know anything that anyone else didn't already know. It made no sense. Yet somehow it was true. A Groll hunted him, a creature with razors for claws, a venomous dagger for a tail, a monster that could kill with a single touch.

He shivered, pressing himself closer to Windy's comforting warmth. Now, because of him, she was in danger too. And without his spell book or Gallund's wand they were helpless. He held tightly around her waist. She squeezed his hand in return.

They emerged from the trees and entered a wide field. The forest's dark shroud dropped away to reveal an endless star-speckled sky. They galloped on, climbing steadily up the rising grassland. At the top of the hill they stopped. The field sloped away before them, stretching out into a sea of grey fog. The pale orb of the moon balanced on the tree tops behind them.

"Just a little farther. Hold tight." The dog trotted quickly down the hill.

"Where are we going?" whispered Windy.

"I'm not sure," answered Ilien. The field rolled out before them, unbroken except for the square outline of a small grove of pine trees in the distance. "Maybe there's a town past those trees. We'd be safe in a town, I think." He looked back as they drew near the grove. Behind them the moon had crested the hilltop.

Framed in its light rose the loping shadow of the Groll, its tail raised like a sickle behind it.

"It's found us!" cried Ilien.

The Groll's silhouette vanished as it tore down the hill after them. The dog lunged forward, throwing the princess back into Ilien's arms, nearly toppling both of them to the ground. They held on in desperation as the night jumped around them.

"Listen up!" barked the dog as they approached the small pine grove. "Enter the grove five trees from the left. Any other way and you're dead. Go three trees in, left two and right three more. Don't stop until dawn. Now go!"

"I don't understand." Ilien had never been good with numbers.

"Fifth from the left, in three, left two, right three more!"

The Groll poured down the hill, its tail swaying wildly in the air.

"Go or I'll rip you to shreds myself!" shouted the dog.

They jumped off the dog and ran to the edge of the grove. The tall pines grew in straight, even rows. The grove was so small they could see straight through to the other side. They looked back, unsure what fleeing into the trees would accomplish. The dog pelted up the hill to meet the Groll's onslaught.

"Five trees from what side?" asked Ilien.

"Don't men ever listen?" berated Windy. "Come on!"

Ilien tagged close behind as Windy entered the forest between the fifth and sixth tree.

"One. Two. Three," she counted as she strode forward. "Now left."

A shrill howl split the night and Ilien spun around. The dog and Groll fought on the hillside just outside the trees, a frightening frenzy of fangs and claws, limbs and jaws.

"Ilien! Come on!" yelled Windy, pulling him backwards.

Ilien backpedaled as he watched the battle unfold. The princess ran ahead, counting off trees. "One. Two. Now right!"

Ilien stopped. His jaw dropped open. He rubbed his eyes in disbelief. The world outside the grove had suddenly disappeared, dog, Groll, battle and all. In its place grew more straight pines as far as his eye could see. He blinked and rubbed his eyes again. The forest around him stretched neat and even into the distance. Everything outside the once small grove had completely vanished.

So too had the princess.

"Windy!" shouted Ilien, turning in circles. Endless green halls ran off in every direction, bathed in pale moonlight. "Windy! Where are you?"

He glanced up at the thick lace of pine boughs overhead. A small patch of sky peered down, flat and starless. It hovered close above the treetops like a vast grey sheet of paper.

"Windy!" he called, crying her name down each long lane. But there was no answer, and he soon realized that he'd lost his sense of direction. Every row of trees looked exactly the same. He was stranded alone in an endless forest of identical pines.

He closed his eyes against the confusing monotony and tried to think. "Now what did the dog say? Don't stop until dawn? But which way do I go?"

Since everywhere he turned looked the same, he figured any direction would do. He forced his legs into motion, peering left and right down the straight forest paths to either side. The air grew colder as he walked. His breath plumed around him. He crept down the trunk-lined halls for what seemed like forever, keeping one eye on the broken sky above.

"The sun should be rising soon," he said aloud. The hovering pine trees muffled his voice, as if he was locked in a vast green closet full of identical green overcoats. The ground beneath his feet felt soft and pillowy. It seemed an effort just to walk. Finally he stopped, overcome by exhaustion and despair.

It was all he could do not to lie down on the needled carpet beneath him and sleep. He looked up at the sky through the pine branches again. The low grey ceiling remained unchanged.

"Don't stop until dawn," he mumbled sleepily, the springy ground grabbing at his feet as he tried to walk forward.

Then something out of the ordinary caught his eye. Farther ahead a single tree arched over the straight, plush lane. It was as out of place amidst the evenly spaced tree trunks as he was. He approached the bent tree cautiously.

"What's this all about?" He took a step closer.

The tree jerked straight. His legs kicked out beneath him as a well-hidden snare yanked him off the ground. Now thoroughly awake, he dangled ten feet up, a thick rope wrapped around his ankles.

"Heel, Bleak! Heel!"

The booming calls of a man were followed by the sounds of crashing trees. Ilien twirled in circles at the end of his rope. With each revolution he struggled to look in the direction of the voice. Soon he was so dizzy that all he could do was close his eyes and hope not to get sick. Slowly the rotations stopped. His head pounded. His stomach churned. He opened his eyes.

Below him sat the giant dog. Or at least it looked like the giant dog upside down. He screwed his eyes to focus. It was a massive dog alright, but not the same one. This one was black, a bit smaller, and definitely not as friendly. It sprang up at him, jaws snapping inches from his dangling head. It gathered itself to lunge again.

"Bleak!"

The thundering bellow sent the dog cowering behind a tree, and Ilien grabbing for his ears. From his unusual vantage point, Ilien saw a pair of behemoth legs clothed in numerous animal skins lumber closer. He craned his neck to see the rest of the towering body.

Even upside down the Giant was terrifying.

"What do we have here, Bleak?" The Giant spoke as if there were stones in his throat. His head was nearly level with the treetops, and he peered evenly at Ilien, regarding him suspiciously, either unsure whether his catch was safe to approach, or safe to eat. To Ilien, both thoughts were equally frightening.

"Well I'll be." The Giant spat tobacco onto the ground in a black, oily clump. He ran a massive hand across his weather-beaten face, wiping tobacco juice off his chin. "I can't believe it." He let out a laugh like the howl of a gale force wind. "A man-boy. Now how did a man-boy get into my trap?" He tapped Ilien with his finger, sending him spinning again.

"Look, Bleak," he said. "We've got ourselves a man-boy. I don't think I've ever seen one in these woods before. I wonder if they're good to eat." The Giant suddenly grabbed hold of the rope.

Ilien twirled to a stop. He felt suddenly sick, and not just because he was thoroughly dizzy. The Giant was looking at him grimly, his stone wall forehead furrowed in worry.

"Yeah. I don't think I've ever seen one of *these* in here before," said the Giant. "In fact, I know I haven't."

He brought his face, big as a boulder, close to Ilien's. His nostrils, large enough to fit fists into, flared even wider. Ilien's hair blew back as the Giant smelled him with a loud, wet snort. Bleak sat patiently below, as if waiting for a tasty biscuit.

"No. I don't think we'll eat this one," said the Giant. "Too bony. Besides, it ain't no man-boy. It's Nomadin."

Chapter IX

Kink and Crank

"S ir?" chirped Ilien when he finally found his voice again. "I'm awfully sorry I fell into your trap." He could think of nothing else to say, having never fallen into a Giant's trap before.

The Giant ignored him, carrying him by the rope like a freshly caught fish. Bleak trotted behind them, eyeing him hungrily.

"I meant no harm, sir," he said louder, noticing the thick hair that grew out of the Giant's ears. "I'm really pretty harmless. If you'd let me go I promise I'll—"

"Harmless you're not," said the Giant. "Nomadin are never harmless."

"I think you've made a mistake, sir."

The Giant stopped, lifting Ilien so his face was level with his own. He drew him closer until their noses nearly touched.

"I, I didn't mean it like it sounded, sir. I—"

"Be quiet. And stop calling me sir." Again the Giant's cavernous nostrils flared open. He sniffed Ilien up and down as if he was smelling a ham. "Nope. Definitely Nomadin."

The giant lowered Ilien and continued on, swinging him back and forth like a school boy carrying his lunch bag. He whistled as he walked. "You see, my nose is never wrong. Just last night the missus sat telling me the goat's milk was still good. But I knew better. Should've seen her face when she drank hers. Now that was a good one."

Ilien jiggled up and down as the Giant broke into a fit of laughter. He noticed that Bleak had crept closer, sniffing the air as if he trailed fragrant steam.

"And you say you're harmless. Bah! You're a Nomadin-child! That makes you as dangerous as Reknamarken himself."

"Who?" asked Ilien. Where had he heard that name before?

"You think you're smart, don't you?" continued the Giant, turning his head to target a nearby pine tree with tobacco. "You know who I mean."

He spat hard, splattering the tree with black goo. "You're just lucky I found you before Reknamarken did. You'll be safe here, in my collection."

"But I really don't know what you're talking about," said Ilien, grimacing at the foul odor of tobacco that hung in the air. "Collection? What collection?"

The Giant jerked the rope sharply. "Be quiet, boy. You're as bad as that nagging wife of mine. I'll have none of it from you."

Ilien did as he was told. What else could he do? His head throbbed. His feet ached. And everything in the middle felt queasy. The Giant carried him casually down the lane, stopping now and then to look around. It appeared to Ilien, even upside down, that he was lost.

"Blast it!" bellowed the Giant, the fifth time he stopped. "Where is that tree?"

By this time Ilien's feet were numb where the ropes had cut into his ankles.

"Bleak!"

The black dog eyed the Giant with disapproval. It opened its mouth to speak.

"Don't give me any lip, dog. Just find the tree. And be quick about it!"

It glowered at him and skulked off, mumbling what Ilien thought was something about a paper bag. The Giant followed.

Soon the dog placed a paw on a tree where an X had been chopped into the trunk.

"That's a good boy," said the Giant.

"And you think you're the master race," it muttered.

A hard cuff behind the ears sent the dog tumbling down the lane.

"Quit your talking! I won't have it, not from dogs. I swear, I'll add your kind to the list!" He turned his attention back to the tree in front of him. "In three. Right two. No. No. That's to the swamps. In three. Left two." He paused to think, tapping his broad skull with a thick finger. "No. No. I think that's to the meadow." He looked sheepishly back at the dog. "In two, left three?"

The dog barked once.

"Now come on!" pleaded the Giant. "You know I can never remember if one bark is yes or no. Just tell me, or I swear—the list!"

The dog padded slowly over, its tail tucked between its legs. The glow in its eye told another tale, though. "In two. Left three," it growled.

"In two left three," the Giant repeated, carrying Ilien forward.

Two trees passed Ilien upside down. He turned and passed three more.

Even hung from his feet Ilien was astonished. One moment he was staring at the straight trunk of a tree, the next, the timbered wall of an enormous cabin. The dog materialized beside him, still wearing a sour look.

"Home sweet home," sighed the Giant, setting Ilien down.

Ilien rolled to his side, the cabin at his back. He lay on a hill littered with stones and branches. Below, a vast, mirrored lake spread out before him, reflecting the glow of morning that painted the far horizon in shades of pink and gold.

"Now don't you go anywhere, boy. Bleak, watch him." The

Giant lumbered over to the cabin. He turned back at the door. "Now how am I gonna explain this one to the missus?"

The door slammed behind him and he was gone.

Ilien sat up and rubbed his wounded legs. Bleak bared his fangs, then yawned. Ilien glanced back at the cabin. A row of shabby, wooden dog houses had been built along one side, their open entries filled with gloom.

"He sure treats you like dirt," he commented as he worked to untie his ankles.

"Shut up! And leave those knots alone," said Bleak. "I have a list of my own you know, and little boys are already on it, Nomadin or not."

Ilien quit fiddling with the knots, but he knew he'd hit a nerve. He looked back at the row of dilapidated dog houses. "Is that where you live?"

"What's it to you?"

"It's just, well they don't look too comfortable, that's all. A little cramped, don't you think."

"I said shut up!" snapped the dog.

A pair of yellow eyes sprang up inside one of the dog houses. A moment later a second set appeared inside another.

"Now you've done it. You woke Kink and Crank."

Two monstrous dogs emerged simultaneously from the darkened openings. One was a yellow hound, its back end bent painfully sideways. Its rump seemed to take the lead as it shuffled forward. A long tongue hung out the side of its mouth, bobbing up and down like a pink cigar as it spoke.

"Hey, Bleak. What's going on?"

Bleak shook his head. "Hey, Kink."

"Knock off that racket!" barked the second dog, a shaggy grey brute. "Can't a dog take a cat nap without some lousy cur chatting away like a flipping squirrel?"

"Sorry, Crank," said Bleak.

"Yeah, sorry, Crank," repeated Kink.

The hair along Crank's back rippled. "It wasn't your fault, you idiot!"

Kink looked confused as he scratched his crooked behind. "Oh yeah. You're right."

"Who's that?" Crank pinned Ilien with a glare. "Don't tell me those Giants finally bred. That's all we need around here, another Giant."

"It's not Giant," said Bleak. "It's Nomadin."

Crank's jaw dropped open. He took a step backward, falling on his haunches.

Kink grinned stupidly, chewing on his tongue.

"Anselm found him in one of his traps," said Bleak.

Crank looked back at the cabin. "Does that fool know what he's caught?"

"Excuse me," interrupted Ilien. "But—"

"Shut up!" Bleak and Crank barked in unison. Kink sat smirking.

"What's he gonna do?" asked Crank.

"What do you think he's gonna do?" said Bleak. "What did he do with us? He can't eat him. I don't think Nomadin are on the list. He's gonna keep him."

"He can't keep a Nomadin boy here."

The heavy silence between the two dogs was broken by Kink.

"Uh. Why?"

"Don't you remember what the Swan told us?" said Crank.

Kink's tongue switched sides. "Um. No."

"She said a Nomadin-child is as dangerous as the Necromancer himself. If he's allowed to stay here it'll be the end of the Drowsy Wood for sure."

"Shush!" warned Bleak. "He's coming out."

The door opened and the Giant emerged, a stream of sharp rebukes spilling out behind him. He quickly shut the door. "If ever a Giant could be a witch, it's that woman. I swear." He walked over to Ilien, shaking his head. "Get back to your kennels you mutts! Get!"

Crank growled menacingly but slunk back to his dog house. A quick smack finally wiped the imbecilic grin off Kink's face, sending him yelping back to his. Bleak stood by Ilien, wagging his tail coyly.

"Good boy, Bleak." The Giant turned a bewildered look on Ilien. "Well, she won't let you in the house. Says she'll have none of it. You'll have to stay out here with the dogs. I'll bring you food when I can, and there's plenty of dog houses to choose from. Just don't go near the last one over there, unless you're wanting to be torn to bits." He untied Ilien's legs. "No point keeping you tied. There ain't no escaping anyhow. Isn't that right, Bleak?"

The Giant laughed all the way back to the front door.

"Remember, any one but the last one," he warned, pointing a finger at the row of run-down houses. He listened at the door before opening it. "I swear that woman never stops." He yanked the door open and waded through the continuing shouts of his wife, slamming it closed behind him.

Bleak padded over to his dog house and disappeared inside, leaving Ilien alone with three sets of yellow eyes peering out at him. The Giant's cabin leaned against the very edge of the forest, the even lanes shrouded in shadows. The glassy lake stretched out in front of it. The tall trees stood over the still water like silent sentinels. The horizon remained unchanged, morning's fingers frozen at the lake's far end. Ilien glanced over at the last dog house. No eyes peered out from the round, black hole. He wobbled to his feet, all pins and needles.

"Um, Bleak?" he said.

Bleak's shining eyes wavered within his house then disappeared. Crank was already asleep. Only Kink's eyes continued to blink back at him from the darkness.

"Is that you, Kink?" asked Ilien.

A long snout poked out the entry, still wearing its ever-present grin. "Yeah. Whatchya want?" asked Kink, his tongue dancing in the darkness.

"Can I ask you a question?"

"Sure. Okay." He emerged, his back end so crooked he walked like a horseshoe.

"How did you get that way, anyhow?" asked Ilien.

"What way?"

"All crooked like that."

Kink looked at himself as if for the very first time. He nodded toward the cabin.

"The Giant did that to you?" asked Ilien.

Kink's smile slipped away. "Yeah."

"Why? What did you do to deserve that?"

"Tried to get in the house, that's what. Slammed the door on me. But it ain't that bad."

Ilien looked back at the imposing bulk of the cabin. "I don't get it," he said.

"Get what?"

"Why you stay with him?"

"Because there's no escaping, that's why," answered Bleak as he crawled out from the cramp confines of his house. "This side of the forest is enchanted. There's no way out. You can go in, but you can't get back to anywhere but here, or the swamp, or the meadow. I've been to them all. It's all the same. There's no getting home."

"What about the lake?" asked Ilien.

Bleak looked out over its serene surface. "Let's just say there was never an empty dog house until we tried escaping across the lake." He fixed Ilien with a grim look. "Hungry fish."

"Well, then how did you get here?"

"The same way you did. Caught in a lousy trap," said Bleak.

"I still don't get it," said Ilien.

110

"What's there to get?" asked Bleak. He shook his head and turned away.

"Well, for one," said Ilien, stepping forward, "where exactly are we? I know I'm in some sort of enchanted forest, but where? And why? And where do all you dogs come from? And why are there so many of you here to begin with? You can't all be that dumb to get caught in the Giant's traps."

Bleak spun on Ilien.

"Well, I don't see any other animals here!" cried Ilien, gesturing at the forest all around.

Bleak was about to speak but turned away and only grunted.

Kink stepped forward, a grin across his face. "You're in the Drowsy Wood, the only enchanted forest left in all the world," he said. "I don't know why *you're* here, or where *you're* from, but *we're* from the other side of the lake where the sun always sets. And yes, other animals do get caught in the Giant's traps, but they're on the list."

Ilien stared at Kink, perplexed.

"He eats them," said Kink.

"Now do you get it?" asked Bleak, looking over the lake again at the frozen dawn. The giant dog fell silent. He sat back on his haunches and peered longingly at the sun.

Ilien drew a deep breath and let it out slowly. It was obvious that the dogs, talking or not, couldn't help him. He was lost, stranded, marooned on a thin slice of mystical forest, literally in the middle of nowhere. And he still had to find Windy.

"Is it always like that?" he asked, following Bleak's gaze across the lake.

"You mean never quite morning?" said Kink behind him. "Yeah. I haven't seen the sun in years. How I miss lying in it."

Ilien scanned the shoreline. Straight, even pines wrapped around the mirrored lake, a brown picket fence topped with green.

"There's got to be a way out of here," he said.

111

"Well there isn't," snapped Bleak. "You just forget about getting out of here, or you'll bring trouble to us all. Bad enough you're here at all. You'll be the ruin of the Wood for sure."

"But I don't understand," said Ilien, turning to face Bleak. "Why does everybody keep saying that?"

"Because you're a Nomadin-child. Don't you get it?"

"But I'm not. And no, I don't get it."

"Shut up out there!" howled Crank. "Can't you see I'm trying to sleep!"

"Sorry, Crank," said Kink.

"I wasn't talking to you, you idiot!" Crank stuck his head out the door. "I was talking to those other two idiots!"

"Oh yeah. You're right," answered Kink.

Crank extricated himself from his dog house with considerable effort. "For howling out loud, there's no getting any rest around here, is there! You're dangerous because you're still alive, boy. The Nomadin were never to have children, not while the Necromancer still lives."

"But I'm telling you my parents aren't Nomadin," said Ilien. "They're not magical at all." He stopped and turned away. "At least my mother isn't."

"What do you mean, at least your mother isn't?" asked Crank with a sideways glance.

"Well, I never knew my father. He left when I was very young."

"Well then, there you go," said Crank. "Your father was Nomadin."

Ilien considered his comment in silence.

"And Nomadin children are forbidden!"

"It can't be," said Ilien, thinking of his father. "It just can't be."

"Well it is!" said Crank. "Your parents understood the dangers. At least your father did. He knew Reknamarken would hunt you down when the time came."

"It's impossible."

"What's the matter with you? Haven't you heard a word I've said? You're about as thick as that girl the Giant brought back today. You're a danger to us all, boy!"

Ilien spun on Crank. "What did you say?"

"I said you're a danger to us all!" Crank took a step forward. "What's it to ya?"

"Not that! The girl. What girl?"

"The pretty one the Giant caught right before he caught you," said Kink. "She was real nice. She even petted me." Kink looked over at the cabin. "There she is now!" he gushed, jumping up and down.

Ilien turned to see Windy watching him through the cabin window high above, her breath steaming the cold glass.

Chapter X

Into the Dog House

W indy!"
Ilien ran to the window, trailed by an excited Kink. The cabin was built for a Giant, not a boy. The window was well out of reach. Windy peered down at him from ten feet up, pressing a finger to her lips.

"Windy! Are you alright?"

She looked behind her, then motioned for quiet again. She attempted to open the window but it was just too heavy. Twice the size of a normal window, it wouldn't budge.

"We've got to get her out of there," Ilien whispered to Kink.

"We can't. She's locked in," said Kink. His twisted rump sat next to him on the ground and he eyed it as if it might begin to itch on its own accord. "She's part of his collection now," he said, beginning to sniff his fur for fleas.

"What do you mean? Collection?"

Kink looked up from his flea hunt. "Oh, he has such a nice collection. Candlecranks, boondogglers, parakites."

"Don't you mean parakeets?" asked Ilien.

"No. I don't think so," said Kink, and he scratched behind his ear with a thick paw.

"How in the name of all that's canine do you know what he has in his collection?" It was Crank, of course.

"Well—" Kink began to itch his bent behind, and soon fell into a fit of scratching and gnawing.

"Well what, you contorted cur!"

"Well—ooh that feels good—oh yeah—that hits the spot."

Crank leapt on top of Kink in a fit of rage, knocking him to the ground. "I swear I'll straighten you out right quick if you don't answer my question!"

"Well I've been inside and seen it," whined Kink. "Now get off me!"

"Yeah, get off him!" said Ilien, stepping forward. "No one likes a bully."

Crank turned an angry glare on Ilien. He stepped off Kink and advanced stiff-legged toward him. "I've about had it with you, boy, Nomadin or not. Maybe your parents didn't have the fortitude to end you like they should have, but I do."

Bleak stepped forward in front of Crank. "And I've just about had it with you. Come closer and I'll end your complaining once and for all."

The two dogs faced off in heavy silence.

"Stop it," pleaded Kink, still sprawled out on the ground where Crank had left him.

"Cool off, both of you," said Ilien. "The important thing is that Kink's been inside. If he's been inside then we can get her out."

"And he never saw fit to mention that before?" growled Crank. He held Bleak's challenging glare for a moment, then fixed Kink with a deadly stare. Kink cowered in fear. "What good will it do, anyhow?" said Crank, regarding Kink in disgust. "We all know that there ain't no way out of here."

Crank's right, thought Ilien. Even if he could free Windy from the Giant's cabin, then what?

"We could go see the Swan," offered Kink. "Maybe she could tell us how to get out of here."

All heads turned toward Kink.

"What did you say?" asked Bleak.

"I said we could go see the Swan. Maybe—"

"Jumping cat crap!" yelled Crank. "If we could go see the

Swan then we'd be out of here already, you tearing idiot!"

Kink cowered before Crank's anger. "Oh yeah. You're right," he whimpered.

"Hold on," said Bleak. He padded over and put a paw on Kink's head. "Kink. Have you been to see the Swan?"

"Yes?" answered Kink uncertainly.

Everyone was stunned to silence, except Ilien. "Who's the Swan?" he asked.

"I can't believe it," said Bleak. "I can't believe you've been to see the Swan."

"Don't be angry," said Kink, slinking to his feet. He glanced over at Crank, looking like he was ready to bolt into the forest at any moment.

"We're not angry," answered Bleak, taking a kinder tone. "You didn't do anything wrong. We're just surprised, that's all. But I am a little curious, Kink. How exactly did you go see the Swan?"

Again Kink looked ready to run, but instead he fell cowering to the ground. "I knew it was wrong! I knew I shouldn't have done it! He told me not to! I'm sorry! Please don't tell him!"

"What are you talking about?" yelled Crank. "Don't tell who?"

"He'll skin me alive! Please don't let him get me. He told me not to go near it. Now he'll rip me to shreds!"

All eyes turned toward the last dog house. It stood ominously empty.

"You've been inside the last dog house?" asked Crank.

"Don't be mad," pleaded Kink. "I didn't mean to get in trouble. I didn't mean it. It's just that the Swan is so nice to me. She's so kind. And it's so terrible here."

He curled into a shaking, quivering ball and began to cry. "I'm just so lonely."

"Oh for crying out loud," said Crank in disgust.

Ilien moved to Kink and stroked his head. "It's alright boy," he soothed, looking back at Crank in disapproval.

"Look! He's treating him like a pet!" Crank stalked over. "Get up! You're disgracing us all!"

"I'd be proud to have a dog like Kink for a pet," declared Ilien, scratching him behind the ear.

Kink looked up. "You would?"

"Of course I would."

"Now I've seen everything," said Crank.

"Will you shut up!" shouted Bleak. "Look Kink, just tell us—"

He stopped as Kink cowered in fear again. He drew a deep breath and continued more cautiously. "Look Kink, are you telling us that we can go see the Swan through the last dog house?"

Kink still looked worried.

"It's alright," assured Ilien, patting him gently. "You can tell him."

Kink swallowed and looked up. "It takes you right to her."

It was as if the air had been kicked out of everyone present. The silence was finally broken by the faint sound of someone tapping on a window.

"Windy!" cried Ilien. "We've got to get her out of there. You've got to help me."

"Count me out," said Crank. "I'm not staying here any longer than I have to." He trotted over to the dilapidated dog house at the end of the row. Without looking back he squeezed through the front door and was gone.

Bleak looked at Ilien, then back at the dog house. "All these years," he whispered. "It was always right under my nose, all these years." His eyes opened wide and he turned to Kink. "And Kink—you never left us. You always came back. But why?"

Kink began to shiver. "He told us not to go near it. He said

117

he'd rip us to shreds. If he ever found out . . ." Kink's eyes glistened. "I was afraid he'd hurt you."

Bleak looked sadly at Kink. "Oh Kink," he said. "Come on." He headed for the dog house. Ilien watched in dismay as Kink followed suit, his tail between his legs. But Bleak suddenly stopped. He stood silent for a moment, shaking his head. "I know I'm going to regret this," he muttered.

Kink's tail shot up and began to wave. Ilien smiled broadly.

"Alright! I'll help you!" cried Bleak, spinning around. "But I have a life to get back to, you know, so let's make this quick!"

Ilien jumped into action. "Kink, you said you've been inside the Giant's cabin. How did you get in?"

Kink padded over and sat by Ilien, his ever-present tongue hanging out. "Through the front door," he replied.

"You mean you just walked through the front door?"

Kink nodded. "The Giant leaves it unlocked. How else do you think I got in? Down the chimney?"

Bleak approached, chuckling.

"Okay," said Ilien. "Once we get inside, then what?"

"This is how it is," said Kink, jumping to his feet and taking the tone of a Commander in Chief explaining his plan of attack. "We'll have to wait until the Giant and his wife are sleeping. Then we have to move in real quiet-like, you see. Down the hall, careful not to wake them. That's real important. Then we pass five doors on the left, or is it five on the right? Anyhow, then left, or is it right again? Well, it's past the kitchen and past the dining room, the living room, den, spare bedroom, trophy room, wash room, a closet—at least I think it's a closet—knitting room and the kitchen again." He stopped his narrative, looking a bit confused.

Ilien looked at the cabin in astonishment. "All that fits in there?"

"Yeah. Can you believe he has two kitchens?"

"I think I'll stay out here and keep watch," said Bleak, suddenly eyeing his escape route.

"Okay. Let's go," Kink said to Ilien.

"Shouldn't we wait until they're asleep?" asked Ilien.

Kink sat down. "Oh yeah. You're right."

Ilien looked back up at Windy, who by now appeared annoyed for having been ignored for so long. "We'll get you out of there soon," he mouthed up at her. He gestured with his hands as he spoke, as if translating a foreign language. "We—have to wait—until the Giant—is asleep. Then we —will come in—and free you."

Windy shook her head and threw up her hands. She couldn't understand a word he was saying. Ilien started again.

"We—have to—" He suddenly stopped and pulled out his pencil. "Does anyone have any paper?" he asked.

Silence fell as the dogs looked at each other in disbelief. "We're dogs," said Breach. "Does it look like we have any paper?"

Ilien smiled. "Oh yeah. You're right," he said, red-faced. He placed the pencil back in his pocket before it could comment. Then he repeated his mime routine to Windy. She seemed to understand this time.

Ilien turned back to Bleak and Kink but was stopped by more tapping behind him. Windy was trying to ask him something. He watched her through the glass as she mouthed something to him, signing with her hands as well.

He shook his head. "I don't get it. What did you say?"

She glared down at him, going through the motions again.

"Sorry. Still don't understand."

Again she tried to ask him, this time more animated.

"*But then?*" said Ilien. He looked back at Kink. "But then? What does that mean?"

"How should I know?" said Kink, looking more confused than ever.

119

By now Windy was jumping up and down as she tried to tell him yet again.

"Oh! What then! What then!" cried Ilien, finally understanding.

"I still don't get it," said Kink.

"Kink here," Ilien pointed to Kink, "knows a way out of here. We're gonna—" Windy suddenly disappeared from the window. "Now where did she go? Boy, she's touchy."

The crash of the shattering window was followed by a whirlwind of objects flying through it—books, potted plants, candlesticks, pictures, forks, knives, dinner plates. As each one hit the ground Ilien could swear they all cried, "Ouch!"

The steady stream of items suddenly stopped and out popped Windy's head.

"Look at all this stuff!" she cried. "It's the most wonderful collection of magical items I've ever seen!"

"Are you crazy?" asked Ilien. "What are you doing? Get out of there right now! The Giant will catch us all!"

"There's just one more thing. I've got to have it!" She disappeared again.

Bleak watched in horror, then sprinted over to the last dog house. "Half the legs, half the brains," he said. "She's lost her mind!" He leapt through the entryway and vanished.

Kink sat calmly on his crooked haunches, his tail waving in the air next to him. "I bet I know what she's getting," he said matter-of-factly.

Windy appeared at the window again, struggling to pull something behind her. She crawled through the broken window and dropped lightly to the ground holding one end of a string. Whatever was on the other end was still inside and, from the sound of it, wanted to stay that way.

"Let go of me at once!" came an angry shout from inside the room. "Ouch! That hurts!"

"I've just got to have it!" cried Windy, pulling on the string as if she was trying to land a prized fish. "It's just amazing!"

"Stop it!" came another shout from the other end of the string.

"Windy! Let go," said Ilien. "We don't have time for this."

Windy yanked hard on the string and fell backward as out from the window sailed a very belligerent—kite?

"I said let me go!" it screamed as it tried to pull away.

"A parakite!" cried Kink with delight.

The door to the cabin burst open and the hulking form of the Giant emerged, knuckling sleep from his eyes. The shrieks of his wife blasted out the open door.

"You tell those dogs of yours to keep it down or I swear you'll be sleeping with them on a permanent basis!"

The Giant looked in surprise at the scene before him. "What the—Hey! Let go of my parakite!"

"Run!" yelled Kink.

Kink and Ilien were halfway to the last dog house when they heard Windy scream. Ilien looked back. The princess still stood below the window, surrounded by the litter of magical plates, pictures and candlesticks. The parakite was dive-bombing her in an attempt to break free of her clutches.

"Let it go!" cried Ilien. "The Giant is right behind you!"

Windy released the magical kite just as the Giant's two massive hands closed around her waist.

"Gotchya!"

But the Giant's relief soon turned to disappointment as the parakite floated up and out of his reach.

"I'm free!" it shouted. "Free! Free at last!" It flew higher, twirling and circling in the air. "You'll never catch me now! Never!"

The Giant watched in disbelief as the kite disappeared into the flat, grey sky. "Come back," he pleaded. He wiped away a tear. His face tightened in rage. "Now look what you've done! You've lost my kite!" He lifted Windy into the air, his brow knitting in anger. "You're gonna pay for this." He turned to Ilien and Kink. "You're all gonna pay for this!"

The front door to the cabin flew open with a bang and out strode the Giant's wife. "Look at this mess!" she screeched, her fists clenched in fury like two hairy war hammers. She shook them at her husband. "I've had it with you, mister! I've simply had it! That's it, out it goes, all of it!" She stormed about, picking up the magical items strewn around the yard. "And look at that window! First it was that stupid kite, then the dogs, now that, that Nomadin boy! Well no more! It's all going in the trash. All of it!"

The Giant watched his angry wife with a panicked look on his face.

"Now get over here and clean up this mess. Right now!" she screamed. "You just wait until I get my hands on you. You've had it!"

Kink crept over to the Giant, his tail tucked between his legs. When the Giant glanced down at him, the massive dog curled into a pitiful, shivering ball.

"Move it, mister!" yelled his wife, standing with her muscular arms crossed upon her bulging belly. A hairy, bare foot tapped the ground in staccato. "Well, what are you waiting for? You're in enough trouble as it is, so stop your lollygagging and come pick the rest of this junk up at once!"

The Giant cast a distressed look at the empty sky and gave out a loud sigh.

"If you don't come this instant you can sleep out here with the dogs!" cried his wife. Her feet picked up their tempo. "In a dog house!" she screamed.

A smile suddenly lit up the Giant's stony face as something in him seemed to snap into place. He set Windy down. He placed a hand on Kink's head, scratching him tenderly behind the ear.

"Come on boy," he said. "It's alright. Come on." Kink

looked up, his tongue quivering in fear. "That's a good boy. Don't be afraid. Come on. Let's go."

"And where do you think you're going?" his wife screeched. She watched him walk toward the row of rundown dog houses. "Fine! Go then. Sleep with them forever, for all I care!"

The Giant turned to Windy and Ilien. "Well, aren't you coming?"

Ilien looked at Windy and shrugged. They followed the Giant to the last dog house.

"Goodbye dear," the Giant called back.

"Goodbye? Get back here! Who's gonna clean up this mess?"

The Giant knelt down and reached a thick arm into the dog house. It almost didn't fit.

"Frankly my darling, I don't give a—" His image froze. His hulking form blinked once, then disappeared.

"No!" cried his wife. "Anselm, come back! Don't leave! I'm sorry!"

Next, Kink threaded his way into the dog house and vanished.

Ilien looked back at the Giant's wife as she began to sob. When she saw him staring at her, she renewed her screeching.

"Get out of here, Nomadin! You're to blame for all this. I knew you'd be trouble. Go and good riddance!" She stooped down and picked up a magical item to throw at him.

Windy tried to wait and see what it was, but Ilien quickly pulled her back and into the dog house.

Chapter XI

A Shadow in the Dark

Ilien ran around inside the spacious dog house (after all it was made for a giant dog) half-expecting bells and whistles to sound off. But to his surprise nothing happened. He scratched his head. For some reason he was still surrounded by plank boards and the unpleasant smell of wet dog.

"I don't think it's working," he said, pressing himself against the back wall and staring at the entrance. At any moment he expected to see the craggy face of the Giant's wife peeking through the doorway.

"You don't think what's working?" asked Windy, a bit too loudly.

"Sshh!" whispered Ilien. "This! Look around. We're still in the dog house."

Windy lowered her voice. "Considering that's what we're actually in, I'd say things are working just fine."

"No. You don't understand. This is a magical dog house. It's supposed to take us to the Swan, wherever that is."

"A magical dog house?" said Windy. She looked around as if she'd suddenly found herself in a grand cathedral. "You don't say." She glanced back at the open entrance way. "You don't suppose she's still out there?" she asked, seemingly oblivious of their predicament. "Boy, was she mad. I just wish you hadn't pulled me back so soon. I might have caught whatever it was she was throwing at us."

Ilien shook his head and stared out the door, wondering

what to do next. He glanced about. Maybe there was a lever he had to pull, a button he had to push, anything.

"Maybe I should peek and see if she's still out there," offered Windy. "I bet I could grab that magical talisman she threw. It must be right outside the door."

"No!" said Ilien. "No peeking, and no grabbing."

"I'll peek if I want to," replied Windy. "You can't tell me what to do."

"Fine. Go ahead and stick your head where it doesn't belong. But don't come crying to me if the Giant's wife is right outside, waiting to snatch you the way a hungry bird plucks a worm from its hole."

Windy looked back at the gloomy entryway, her face suddenly drawn with concern. "You think so?" she whispered.

"Peek out and see."

That was enough to quiet Windy for the time being.

"Why are we still here?" asked Ilien. "Why are we still in this god-awful dog house?"

"Maybe you have to tell it where you want to go," said Windy, still peering out the door. She looked back at Ilien. "You know, like a carriage driver or something."

Ilien shot her a sharp look.

"Well I don't hear *you* coming up with any bright ideas," she said.

Ilien shook his head, but despite his misgivings he tried it anyhow, just to quiet her again. "Take us to the Swan," he announced. Nothing happened. He cast another bothered expression in Windy's direction.

"I wouldn't take you either," said Windy. "Rather rude, I'd say. Try it again. And try to be more courteous, why don't you."

Ilien moaned.

"Well how would you like it if—"

"Okay," he said, holding his head in his hands. "Jeez, you're something else." He cleared his throat to address the dog house once more. "Will you please take us to the Swan, please?"

"Pretty please," Windy coached.

"Pretty please," said Ilien through clenched teeth.

Nothing happened.

"Oh well, it was worth a try. Courtesy never hurts, my Aunt Olive used to say."

"Oh for crying out loud," said Ilien. But before he could continue berating the princess, she cried out in delight.

"Look! Look at the doorway. It's changing!"

The same flat grey that hung like paper above the forest now filled the entryway. Yet somehow a pale light still lit the inside of the dog house. As they watched, the grey gave way to black, littered with a glittering of tiny stars. Soon a myriad of bright, multicolored lights speckled the entrance. Tiny orbs of red and yellow glowed here. Pinpoints of blue and white shined there. Though it looked exactly like the night sky above Ilien's house, it was oddly disturbing.

"What do we do now?" asked Windy, hovering closer to Ilien.

Ilien shrugged and pulled away. "Maybe you should peek and see what's out there."

"Will you please stop?" she cried. "I think this dog house has made you a bit cranky."

Ilien had no response. He was too busy studying the starry entrance with a strange fascination. There were two red suns in the center of the doorway that seemed to be looking in at him, like two ruby eyes. Now and then they twinkled as if they were blinking. Their presence began to make him feel uneasy. The air inside the dog house grew uncomfortably warm. He pulled at his collar and swallowed.

Something wasn't right. The ruby eyes appeared larger than they had been a moment before. The feeling of uneasiness grew into fear, but Ilien couldn't seem to take his eyes away. Caught in their spell, he was only vaguely aware of Windy talking to him.

"Ilien. What are you doing?"

The ruby eyes began to pulsate, swelling in size, drawing him deeper into a trance. A numbing fear swept over him like a cold wave, but still he was helpless to turn away.

"Ilien?"

He closed his eyes and cried out weakly. Windy grabbed his arm and spun him around.

"Ilien. What's wrong? You're trembling."

"There's something out there," he whispered, opening his eyes.

The princess backed away in fear. "Ilien! My god, your eyes!"

"What? What's wrong with my eyes?"

"They're red. They're blood red!"

Ilien clutched at his eyes in panic, spinning to face the entrance again. The ruby eyes were gone. Staring back at him were his own brown eyes. He reached out a trembling hand. The eyes widened as they watched it approach. Then they swiveled back and fixed him with an angry glare. Ilien tried to pull his hand away, but couldn't.

"Ilien!"

Windy's shout sounded as if it came from somewhere outside the dog house.

"*Ilien,*" came an echo from the eyes. Ilien sat frozen in fear as the eyes drew closer, growing larger. "*Ilien,*" they whispered.

"Ilien!"

He heard Windy's voice again, hushed, receding, as if calling to him from somewhere above the surface of a still lake as he drifted slowly to its murky bottom. The eyes followed him downward into the shadowy depths. Deeper he descended, darkened silence closing in around him. But the eyes, always the eyes were there, sailing down with him, their soft, brown glow just visible above him.

Windy's voice called to him once more, almost imperceptible now. "Ilien! Can you hear me?"

"Can you hear me?" whispered the eyes. The darkness deepened around them. *"There is no reason to be afraid. Come closer."* The eyes drifted nearer, swelling like flooded pools as they approached. *"Closer,"* they urged.

Soon they hovered so close above him that Ilien could see an image of a man reflected in their glassy surface. A man with glowing eyes, streaming hair as black as cinder, skin grey as ash. Long, black robes hung loosely around his lean frame. It was an image not wholly unfamiliar. It wasn't until Ilien reached his own hand to his face that he realized the reflection was somehow his own. He pulled his hand back in fear.

"*Do not be afraid,*" said the eyes. "*Look deeper.*"

The eyes pressed closer, pupils dilating into two black pits. A distant light, like the flicker at the far end of a tunnel, shone in their depths. Ilien felt himself walking, packed earth beneath his feet.

"*Deeper.*" The sound of the eyes reverberated down the length of the tunnel. *"Go to the light. I have something to show you."* Ilien's footsteps echoed in the darkness. The light grew brighter as he drew near its source. *"Come closer. Do not be afraid. Behold!"*

Ilien exited from the shadows into the bright light of day. He stood at the base of a low, wooded hill. Behind him a tunnel stretched away into blackness, bored into the green earth. He knew where he was immediately.

"This is Southford."

He jumped back in surprise. He heard the words come out of his mouth, but the voice was not his own. "This is the hill behind Parson's farm," he heard himself speak again, his voice deep and commanding.

"Do not be afraid," echoed his real voice from the cave. *"There is something you must see."*

Ilien spun around but the tunnel remained empty. He caught a glimpse of his hands, held in fists before him. They were the hands of a man, lean and hard. He looked at himself in awe. Black robes hung loose around his shoulders. He was tall, his long, lean legs clothed in tight, black pants, his feet in black leather boots.

"Who am I?" he asked, still afraid of his own voice.

"I will show you," his real voice said from within the cave.

Ilien peered hesitantly into the shadows. He still could see no one. "Who are you?"

"I will show you that too. Trust me. I will show you every-thing. But first you must go to your house."

"My house?"

"Yes. I will show you everything."

As Ilien walked along the stony trail leading from the cave he became aware of the unearthly silence surrounding him. The air hung heavy and still. The raucous calls of the crows that normally roosted in the tall pines around Parson's farm were absent. Even his footsteps on the thick carpet of dead leaves beneath his feet were silent.

He moved out from beneath the forest canopy and into a freshly tilled field. He breathed deep the sweet smell of earth mixed with decay. Everything looked different from the unusual vantage point of a tall man. As a boy he would have walked with his head bent to the ground, searching for stones to throw, or sticks to use as makeshift swords. Now the earth below his feet seemed so distant, less important. He glided forward with long, easy strides, head up, eager to arrive at his destination. What before would have taken thirty minutes was shortly completed. He stood before his house, outside the fence surrounding the front yard.

For a moment he thought it odd that he hadn't seen a single

soul as he had walked along. The hired field hands Farmer Parson would have had toiling in his fields, the ever-present town folk traveling the road, even the cows normally grazing by Parson's pond, all were missing. He was completely alone, as if he was the only person left in the entire town.

"Do not be afraid," soothed the voice of a child in his ear, his real voice. *"This is your home. Go inside. There is nothing to fear. Go inside. You will see."*

But Ilien could not move. He stood with his man's hands gripping the fence, staring at his house. A sense of dread stole over him, like the feeling he had one summer after he had broken Farmer Parson's window with a stone. He had stood outside the fence until supper time then, afraid to enter his house and tell his mother what he'd done. Now as he looked at its familiar facade that same fear returned.

"There is nothing to fear," the house seemed to whisper, the second story windows staring at him blankly. Ilien found himself trembling, his knuckles turning white as he gripped the fence. *"All your questions will be answered. Open the gate. Come inside. To the study. There is something you must see."*

"What is it?" asked Ilien, startled again by the sound of the man's voice he spoke with.

"You are confused. You have questions," his real voice answered. *"You want to know who you are, who I am. Inside you will find the answers."*

The gate swung silently open beside him.

"No!" Ilien jumped at the fierce shout from his back pocket. "Don't listen to him. Go back!" yelled his pencil.

The front door flew open. Framed in a pale light stood the unimposing figure of Gallund.

"Stop!" cried the wizard, raising a hand in Ilien's direction. "Go back, Reknamarken. You have no power here. Your strength has grown but you are still imprisoned. You are only a shadow. Nothing more!"

Ilien stood dumbfounded. Gallund was looking directly at him. Sudden movement from the second story window caught his eye. He looked up to see his mother peering down, her eyes aglow with a strange, red light.

"*You are wrong, Nomadin*," came Ilien's real voice from the air around him. "*I am free. I have always been free.*"

As quick as a cat his mother moved back from the window.

"Flee, my boy!" cried Gallund, looking past Ilien. "You mustn't let them catch you!"

Ilien's mother appeared behind the wizard. Gallund spun to face her, stepping forward to block her way. The door slammed shut behind him, leaving Ilien all alone, still gripping the fence around the front yard in clenched hands.

"*Do not be afraid.*" His real voice spoke again, but this time not in his ear. It came from somewhere behind him. He spun around.

A boy with soft, brown eyes stood staring at him, arms crossed, smiling—an image of himself so perfect that Ilien stepped back in alarm.

"Who are you?" he asked.

"You heard the wizard," said the boy. "The question is, who are you?"

The front door to Ilien's house opened and the sound of his mother's voice spilled into the yard.

"Ilien! Ilien!"

His mother was hurt! Without thinking Ilien jumped the gate and ran for the house. Halfway there his mother appeared in the doorway, eyes ablaze, hands on her hips. Her hair stood out like a frightened cat's. Her lips stretched thin and angry across her face. When she saw Ilien she softened her expression. She forced a smile, and tried to pet down her disheveled hair.

"Ilien," she said. "Why not come inside, dear?"

Ilien tried to peer past her for signs of Gallund, but she stepped forward, blocking his view.

131

"You are not my mother," he said evenly in his deep, mannish voice. "And don't call me dear."

"Of course I'm your mother," she replied, still trying to tame her wild hair. "Don't be silly."

Ilien glanced back at the boy, who by now had moved closer.

"Who are you? Who are you?" taunted the boy.

"Come inside, dear. It's getting late."

"Who are you? Who are you?" chanted the boy again.

"I said come inside," demanded the woman with the untamed hair, the woman who looked like his mother. "Come in this minute!"

Ilien ran. The boy moved to intercept him but Ilien dodged his outstretched arms, jumped the fence and streaked away, his long man-legs propelling him faster than he had ever run before. The shrieks and wails of his mother receded as he sprinted up the road, and disappeared as he raced past the pond toward Parson's Hill. He had to get back to the dog house.

When he reached the tilled field he looked back the way he had come. The boy was nowhere in sight. With a burst of fear-driven energy he ran through the forest and back to the cave. To his relief, it was still there.

He rushed into the darkness, running along the stony corridor, stumbling forward with amazing speed. Soon the entrance shrank to a pale moon behind him and the lack of light forced him to slow. But fear kept him moving, one hand on the rough hewn wall to guide his way. The tunnel entrance soon dwindled to a faint star and vanished.

He continued on. Now and then his fingers closed on empty air as a side tunnel forked away in a different direction. He didn't recall making any turns on his way out of the cave so he figured he shouldn't make any on his way back in. His footsteps echoed around him, sounding like followers in the dark. Unsure of where he was, not knowing what to do, he finally stopped. The muffled clap of his last step bounced along the unseen walls and faded to silence. He was alone in the void, afraid to call out for fear of hearing his strange, deep voice in the blackness, or worse yet, his own familiar voice answering back.

But in his mind he wondered, *who am I?*

That there came no answer was a relief. He might have been lost, but at least he was alone. He had escaped to a dark, silent prison, but darkness was better than seeing his mother's burning red eyes, and silence better than hearing her screams.

He took a deep breath to steady himself. He had to find his way back to the dog house. He had to keep moving.

A single footfall sounded in the blackness behind him.

He froze. The cold tunnel wall felt slick beneath his hand as he strained to detect the sound again. Had he imagined it? Or was someone following him?

He raised his foot to move again. Two more footfalls echoed behind him, louder, closer.

He wasn't alone.

A whisper drifted to him, a chill movement of air. "I know who you are."

Ilien started forward in the dark, slowly at first, feeling the walls, stepping carefully so as not to trip. The footfalls resumed behind him.

"I know who you are," came the whisper again, closer this time.

Ilien moved faster, looking over his shoulder as he ran. Forward or backward, the void was impenetrable. Behind him, the sound of feet on the tunnel floor drew nearer. He sprinted ahead, his hands held before him, his head down.

"I know you! I know you!" cried the voice behind him.

Then up ahead, like a glorious beacon, Ilien saw a star, blue and bright. The exit! Freedom! He sped toward it, not caring if it was a trick, only that it was there.

"I know who you are! I know who you are!" shouted the voice.

The blue light ahead widened into a sky-filled hole in the void. Ilien shot forward, desperate to elude his pursuer. But the voice sped past him, screaming in fury.

"You will never get out!"

The light disappeared as something stepped in front of it. Ilien rushed ahead, heedless, furious, maddened. He dropped his shoulder and hit something hard, a barrier between him and the light, a raging wind that sought to cast him aside.

"Get back, Reknamarken!" he cried.

The cave jumped and shook like the throat of a laughing man. The floor spilled out beneath him and he fell to his knees. Rising, he fought his way forward, head down, arms raised. One step, then another, he marched toward the hidden light. A blast of cold wind battered him backwards. He had to get through! He had to get through!

Suddenly he did . . . and he fell into sunlight.

"I'm free! I'm free!" he heard himself shout.

But he hadn't said a word.

Chapter XII

The Swan

W here am I?" asked Ilien. He lay on his back, on something soft yet prickly. The blurred outline of a face hovered over him.

"You're safe," soothed a woman's voice.

But Ilien sensed something was wrong. As his vision began to return, so did his fear. The face that slowly took shape before him was something from out of a nightmare. White as a ghost, horribly stretched and emaciated with one yellow eye that seemed to quiver and writhe about, the face peered at him from atop a long white neck, swaying back and forth like a giant, albino snake.

Ilien tried to move, but couldn't. He was completely paralyzed—except for his mouth.

"Stay away from me! I'm a wizard!" he cried, giving the still blurry face as fierce a look as he could. "Come any closer and I'll—I'll turn you into a toad!" It was a lie of course, but one he counted on the monster leaning over him not knowing.

"You're safe here, Ilien." The monster's yellow eye blinked as it spoke, as if it were speaking through it. "There's nothing to fear. You'll see. Your vision will return shortly."

And so it did, rather abruptly. And when it did, Ilien found himself face to face with—a duck? No, not a duck. A swan! A massive, snow white swan with a shiny, yellow beak.

"You're the Swan." Ilien smiled up in relief. "Then I really am safe."

135

"Yes. You are safe," said the Swan, peering down at him. The great bird's eyes seemed like deep, black pools. She lifted her head and stretched out her wings, ten feet in each direction. The massive wings folded silently back into place and the swan lowered her head once more, her eyes opening wide.

"Safe for now," she said.

"For now?" asked Ilien. He struggled to move. "Why do you say it like that? And why can't I move? What have you done to me?" He peered at the Swan's yellow beak for signs of teeth. "You're not going to eat me or anything, are you?" He realized the Swan was large enough to do just that.

"Of course not," laughed the magnificent bird. "You're a bit too scrawny for me. And besides, I hear Nomadin tastes horrible."

There came a hearty chuckle from somewhere close by and the Swan shot off a disapproving look to its maker. Ilien strained to see who it was. He could see lush green grass all around and a deep blue sky above, but little else in his state of immobility.

"Your body has been drained," said the Swan, still pinning someone beyond Ilien's field of vision with an icy glare. She looked back at Ilien with a soft smile on her beak, if that was possible. "You've passed through Reknamarken's shadow. But don't worry, your motion will return in time, very soon really, if I'm not mistaken."

"A bit scrawny," chuckled the someone again, this time ignoring the Swan's warning glance and falling into a fit of laughter filled with snorts and shouts and quite a bit of knee slapping.

"Anselm! I said you could stay if you kept quiet!" scolded the Swan.

"Anselm?" asked Ilien. "That sounds like—like that—"

"That Giant?" said the Swan. She shook her head. "Yes. I'm afraid so."

She glanced at Anselm and ruffled her feathers. "But have no fear, Ilien. This is actually a rather kind Giant, as Giants go. He won't harm you, no matter what he says."

"Windy!" cried Ilien with a start. "Where's Windy?"

There was silence, even from the bemused Giant.

"I could only save you, Ilien," said the Swan.

"What do you mean? Then she's in trouble. I have to help her!" He struggled to move.

The Swan bent her long, graceful neck downward, bringing her feathered face close to Ilien's. Again her dark eyes spread out like black pools of water.

"I could only open one door," she said. "And even then it nearly drained me."

Ilien stared at her blankly.

"The NiDemon has her," she said.

Ilien shivered as an icy chill swept through him.

"But your strength is growing fast," she continued. "Already your motion is returning. Soon you will be well enough."

Though the Swan's face remained impassive, Ilien sensed something else beneath her words, something left unsaid, or unfinished. "Well enough for what?" he asked.

The Swan flapped her massive wings once, then folded them back at her sides. The breeze sent grasshoppers springing from the grass in all directions.

"Why, well enough to rescue her," she said.

Ilien felt like running, but he couldn't. "Me? Rescue her?"

"Yes, you."

"But what can I possibly do against a NiDemon?"

The Swan's great head darted forward and she snatched a grasshopper from out of the air. She swallowed it whole. "You forget you are Nomadin," she said. Another grasshopper buzzed by and she caught it with a snap of her beak.

Ilien stared at her in wide-eyed disbelief.

"Oh, sorry," she said, looking sheepish. "Instinct."

"But I'm just a boy," said Ilien. "I'm not even a wizard. I'm just an apprentice."

The Swan's eyes narrowed into shiny, black marbles. She leaned in closer, until her beak was only inches from Ilien's face.

"You are right. You are not a wizard. A wizard's power pales to yours."

A jolt of pain jumped through him and Ilien cried out. For a full minute he lay on the ground, stiff and breathless, while the Swan fanned cool air on him.

"It will pass," she soothed. "Be thankful. For most, the agony left by Reknamarken's shadow is the last thing they ever feel."

Slowly the pain receded and Ilien moved his hand to wipe the tears from his eyes, surprised he could do so.

The Swan stood straight and beamed down at him. "Even the most powerful of wizards could not have passed through Reknamarken's shadow and have recovered so quickly, Ilien. But you are no ordinary wizard, that much is evident. You may even be no ordinary Nomadin, if ever there was such a thing. I knew when you were first brought to me that you were different. Your parents knew as well, I suppose."

"My parents?" asked Ilien, propping himself up. "My parents brought me here?"

"Yes, when you were a baby. But not the parents you know, Ilien. Your real parents."

Another spasm of pain coursed through him and Ilien fell back, clutching his chest.

"Yes, I'm afraid there is much you don't know that will hurt," said the Swan. "Your parents back in Southford are not your birth-parents."

Ilien lay still, bearing the pain in silence until it subsided again. His head hurt, and he felt like he was suddenly going to be sick.

"Then who are my parents?" he managed to ask. "And who am I?"

The Swan nodded to Anselm, who had been so quiet that Ilien had forgotten he was there at all. "I will tell you every- thing I know," she said. "But first you must rest. The shadow still hangs over you. You need to recover your strength."

Anselm came into view, his massive, stony features set in a sympathetic frown. A large, hairy face suddenly eclipsed the Giant's, a thick, pink tongue licking Ilien's face.

"Kink," said Ilien, reaching up to scratch the ever-grinning dog behind the ear. "Kink, my boy."

Kink was so excited he rolled around in the grass beside Ilien like a crazed wind-up toy. The Swan looked on, amused. "Anselm will take you to a place where you can rest out of the elements." She looked at the Giant. "Gently, Anselm."

Anselm bent down and scooped Ilien up. His trunk-like arms were as hard as wood, and Ilien winced. Anselm shot the Swan a worried look.

"To Hemlock," she instructed, "and watch over him."

"But I have so many questions," said Ilien.

The Swan waved them off with a wing. "Go now. Rest. We will talk more soon." The Swan turned and waddled away.

As Anselm carried him off, Ilien looked around from his perch high up in the Giant's arms. They were leaving the grassy field, heading for a dense evergreen forest not unlike the one around Anselm's house. Behind him, the sun sat poised above the outstretched lake, unmoving on the horizon, its long rays warming the back of Ilien's neck. Kink tore past them, running back and forth across the lawn in a fit of glee.

"Where are we?" asked Ilien as he bounced along in the Giant's arms.

Anselm stopped and looked back toward the water. "We're clear across the lake. My house is on the other side." His face bent in sorrow as he gazed out toward the bright horizon.

"You miss your wife, don't you?" guessed Ilien.

The Giant locked eyes with him. "No. I was thinking of my parakite." With that he resumed his march toward the forest.

As they traveled, the field gave way to patches of wild flowers Ilien had never seen before. Low clusters of purple and white blossoms blanketed the grass before them. Among them, tall green stems shot upward, bursting with tiny, multi-colored blooms. Beyond these, and to either side, thick hedges tangled with crimson-colored roses spilled to the ground, pooling like wine on a lush green carpet. A sweet smell hung in the air, and a myriad of tiny hummingbirds zipped here and there, dancing to get out of their way as they walked. Kink chased after them, pawing and nipping at the air.

And the forest! As they drew closer, Ilien saw that it wasn't like the one behind the Giant's house at all. The trees grew so tall and wide around that the green forest canopy seemed suspended on gigantic, brown marble columns.

"It's paradise," he said.

Anselm looked around with a smile. "It's the way the world once was. Now only the Drowsy Wood remains, hidden from all but the animals." He noticed Ilien looking at him. "And a special few," he added proudly.

"But why is it so different across the lake where you live?" asked Ilien, waving away a hummingbird trying to feed in his ear.

"That side is the entrance to the Wood—the mud room, so to speak. It's where I keep guard against all the unwanteds who accidentally find a way in. It's my job."

"You're the doorman?"

"You could say that."

"But what about the dogs? Kink, Crank, Bleak. How come they were there? Why wouldn't you let them go?"

Anselm turned a shade of red, his ears burning brightly. He watched as Kink sprinted joyfully by. "I have issues," he said.

"What?"

"I have issues. That's why they put me over there on the other side of the lake." A yellow hummingbird landed on the Giant's forehead. His hands full, he tried to blow it off. It hopped to his nose and took hold with its claws, refusing to let go. Cross-eyed, Anselm continued. "Those dogs fell into my traps and tore them all to pieces. They shouldn't have been there in the first place." The hummingbird began to peck him. Anselm's ears turned from red to purple, and a thin trickle of sweat ran down the side of his face as he tried to ignore the little beast.

"So I got angry," he continued, breathing heavy now. "I hid the way back under a dog house and told them they were never gonna leave again." He stared across the field. The hummingbird stared with him. "They weren't that bad off. They could hunt for themselves. But no way was I gonna let them free after what they did to my traps!" His face turned hard, his stone wall forehead deeply furrowed. "I lost my temper, that's all." He looked abashed. "It's a problem, I know."

The hummingbird began grooming itself. Anselm shook his head in crazed derangement. "Will you get off my dern face, you stinking feathered freak!"

The bird flew off like a shot.

Anselm looked stone-eyed at the approaching forest. "I'm working on it."

They passed from the field and entered the trees, making their way down a wide forest lane. The air grew dark and heavy, and Ilien looked up in amazement. The forest here certainly was quite different from the one across the lake. More ancient and less tended, the boughs of the trees were woven into a thick, needled web above, spreading out like a tangled stone ceiling to block out the sun. Ilien peered forward into the shadows. Columns of trees marched into the gloomy distance, sooty pillars in an underground hall.

141

They walked in silence through the shrouded forest. Kink trotted behind, sniffing loudly in the dark. Now and then Anselm stopped, looking left and right as if lost. But always he continued on down the lane they were in. Before long they stopped in the shadows beside an ancient tree, its moss-grown trunk so massive that an entire house could have been carved within it. Through the darkness, Ilien saw that was precisely what someone had done. A door, concealed by the overhanging moss, and so well hidden that it seemed only etched into the tree's rough bark, was vaguely visible in the center of the trunk. Two windows, one on each side of the door, were covered by tight-fit shutters cut from the tree's very surface.

Anselm stepped up on the front stoop, a low root that grew out of the ground just in front of the door. He looked at Ilien.

"Do you think you can stand?" he asked.

Ilien nodded, staring in wonder at the secreted tree-house before him.

Anselm set him down. "Good. I'll get the door."

It wasn't until Ilien watched Anselm grab and turn a raised knot, sending the front door swinging silently in on invisible hinges, that he realized he was actually standing.

Anselm rushed to catch him. "Whoa there! You'd better lie down." He scooped Ilien up and, ducking to get through the door, carried him inside.

Kink knew better than to try and slink past the Giant a second time, and curled up on the stoop.

The door swung shut behind them, sealing them in utter darkness. Ilien breathed in the heavy scent of sap and spice that filled the warm air, and tried to peer through the inky black-ness. Anselm crashed into something in the dark and cursed. He changed directions, knocking over something else, sending it clattering to the floor. After a few more curses, he set Ilien down upon something large and soft. Ilien heard him move back toward the door. A moment later the shadows fled as the

Giant lit a lamp. He lit another, then another, and soon the tree-house filled with warm, cheery light.

"It's amazing," said Ilien.

Carved from the very heart of the ancient tree, the circular room shined like hand-rubbed amber. The vaulted ceiling stretched high overhead in a gleaming, honey-colored arch. It was so high up that Anselm could stand with room to spare. Except for the bed on which Ilien sat, the only other furnishings were a table and chair, currently knocked on their sides. Both were fashioned from the tree's golden marrow.

The Giant bent down and righted the chair and table. "This," he said, "is Hemlock."

Ilien's eyes danced about the room. Though the furniture was sparse, Hemlock was anything but bare. A wood-burning stove, the color of the walls, sat opposite the door. Beside it, a small pile of golden logs lay stacked. Cabinets of wondrous make lined the walls, built cunningly into the tree's interior. Not a single seem was visible. It was as if everything had been milled from the singular block of the tree. Ilien felt suspended in a magnificent, wooden bubble.

"It's incredible!" he marveled.

"Yeah. I think so too," said Anselm, following Ilien's gaze about the room. "Much nicer than that cabin with that Missus of mine in it." He suddenly began pounding his hand to his head. "If I could just learn to control my temper!"

"Why is it that the dog house didn't send Windy and me straight to the Swan?" asked Ilien, hoping the question would take the Giant's mind off of bludgeoning himself.

Anselm looked over, a meaty fist poised in mid-strike. "You were captured, seized by the Necromancer. That can happen when you portle."

"Portle?"

"You know, travel magically?" Anselm lowered his fist. "When you portle, you're no longer where you started, nor where you're going, neither here nor there. It's precisely when you're in-between that Reknamarken can reach you."

The cheery brightness of the room dimmed when Anselm spoke the Necromancer's name. Ilien eyed the corners, where he could swear a few, bent shadows crept back up the wall. "But what does Rektum—"

"Reknamarken," corrected Anselm.

"Yeah. Him. What does he want with me?"

"Well let's see," replied Anselm, putting on his best thinking-face. "Have you got anything on you that he might want? Any magical items or such?"

"No," said Ilien. "I lost my spell book and Gallund's wand both." His pencil jabbed him in the rear. "Ouch!" He shot to his feet. "Oh yeah. I do have this," he said, rolling his eyes as he pulled the pencil out and held it before the Giant.

Anselm squinted at the pencil in Ilien's hand. "I doubt Reknamarken would want that."

"What do you mean?" railed the pencil. "You doubt he'd want me? I'm not good enough, is that it? Too small to be of value? Well I'll have you know that I'm—"

"You want I should give you to him?" said Anselm, his temper beginning to rise.

The pencil fell silent.

Ilien put it back in his pocket.

"Now, where were we?" said the Giant. "Why else would Reknamarken be after you? Well, do you know anything important? Trade secrets? Powerful Unbinding spells?"

"No. But I can do this." Ilien incanted his Light spell and Globe sizzled to life above the Giant's head. Anselm looked up at the mischievous light in obvious annoyance. Ilien had flashbacks of the hummingbird incident and quickly sent Globe chasing the shadows in the corners of the room.

"How about dirt?" asked Anselm, as he watched Globe dance about the room.

"Dirt?"

Anselm turned back, looking more annoyed than ever. "Yes. Dirt," he said. "Do you have any dirt on Reknamarken? Do you know anything that could lead to his untimely demise?"

"Definitely not," said Ilien.

"Too bad."

Ilien sat back down on the edge of the bed. "This is serious! How would you feel if the Necromancer wanted you for reasons unknown?"

Anselm pinned Ilien with a chilling glare. "I'd feel angry."

"Try scared and confused," said Ilien, meeting his gaze.

"Never been scared before. Confused?" Anselm scratched his head. "I'd have to think about that one. Hmm. Let me see."

"And now he has Windy," continued Ilien. "What could he possibly want from her?"

Anselm snapped out of his thinking pose. "Why that's easy. You. He wants you. And he knows you'll come to get her."

Ilien flopped backward onto the bed. "But what could he possibly want from me? I'm just a boy. It makes no sense." He stared at the high, golden ceiling in silence.

Anselm's usually ruddy complexion turned white as a bed sheet. The oil lamps flickered as if a chill breeze blew through the room. He stooped low, bringing his chiseled face close to Ilien's, looking like a weathered, limestone statue come to life. He grabbed Ilien's shirt collar between two thick fingers and pulled him to his feet.

"You heard the Swan," said the Giant. "You're no ordinary Nomadin. There's something different about you—something special. There's divine blood coursing through you. There's powers untold, and maybe that's what Reknamarken wants. But the real question is what are you going to do about it? Sure you're scared and confused, but make haste of those feelings, Ilien. They will be your undoing."

Anselm released his grip on Ilien's collar, discovering that he'd nearly lifted him off the floor in his excitement. "You have a lot to think about," he said. "But first I think you need some food. You look a little pale." He turned and lumbered over to the cupboard.

As Anselm rummaged through the cupboard's contents, knocking things over and cursing, Ilien realized that the Giant was right. He was famished. He felt like he hadn't eaten in days, which was probably true.

He walked none-too-steadily to the golden table and sat down. As he watched Anselm prepare his food, he pondered for a moment all that the Giant had told him. He was wanted by the Necromancer. That much he knew. But why? Because he had powers untold? *Divine blood*? What did he mean by *that*? To top it all off, the Giant talked as if *he* could actually do something about it. But what? What could he do to stop the Necromancer? He was just a boy. Even the weakest of spells eluded him. It was all too unreal. It made no sense, yet . . .

He suddenly felt dizzy. Not for the last time, he wished Gallund was there with him.

Anselm returned with a large tray laden with food. Large for Ilien, small for a Giant. Anselm tried his best to place it on the table without tipping it, but his massive fingers seemed to overrun everything and soon he was wiping up spilled milk.

In no time at all Ilien managed to wolf down everything the Giant could put in front of him. Sweet bread with honey, a hunk of soft cheese, a bunch of grapes, a bowl of blueberries, several ears of corn and some bread and butter. The grapes and blueberries took the brunt of Anselm's best efforts and resembled jam more than fruit, but the meal was the best Ilien had ever tasted. He followed it all with a tall glass of warm milk. When he was through he felt both impossibly full, and incredibly sleepy. He watched as Anselm cleared away the dishes.

"The Swan said I passed through the Necromancer's shadow," remarked Ilien. "What did she mean by that? Isn't the

Necromancer imprisoned in a book?" He grimaced as he watched the Giant simply stack the dirty plates back in the cupboard. He found himself wondering when they were last properly washed, and felt queasy.

"Yes," answered Anselm, closing the cupboard and turning to wipe the table. "But just as you can cast a shadow out the door, so too can Reknamarken. And his shadow falls the farthest. His shadow is darkest of all. There's danger in darkness, evil magic—death itself! Reknamarken's shadow is all that and more."

Anselm finished cleaning up and turned down the lamps. Even in the gloom the room glistened like a vein of solid gold. "I know there are questions without answers tumbling around in that head of yours," he said as he helped Ilien up and led him over to the bed. "But now you need to sleep. You still look a bit sickly. Soon you will know more than you do now, and you'll need your strength if you're to rescue Windy."

"Anselm?" said Ilien as he lay back on the bed.

Anselm pulled off Ilien's shoes and placed them on the floor. "Yes," he answered.

"I'm sorry about your parakite."

Ilien was vaguely aware of the covers being laid over him, and the soft rumble of Anselm's voice singing him a sorrowful song as he drifted off to a deep, dreamless slumber.

Chapter XIII

The Test

Ilien awoke suddenly, his face drenched—not from a cold sweat, but from a sickening mixture of dog slobber and bad breath. Kink sat by his side, painting his face with long strokes of his enormous tongue. Ilien shot straight up in bed, waving him off with a yell.

"I'm awake! I'm awake!"

Kink laid his monstrous head on Ilien's chest, pinning him back down on the bed.

"Hey!" cried Ilien. "Watch it with that thing. It's heavy!"

Ilien tried to push Kink off but the giant dog wouldn't relent. Kink's head weighed as much as a small boulder. His tail thumped the floor like a hammer.

"Kink," he croaked. "It's a bit hard to breathe." He reached up and scratched the giant dog behind the ear. "Please, Kink."

After a few moments lost in ecstasy, Kink lifted his head and looked down at Ilien. "Are you alright?"

Kink had acted so much like a regular dog that Ilien was almost surprised to hear him talk.

"I'm fine. I'm both rested and bathed now, thank you very much."

He wiped his face with his sleeve and knuckled the sleep from his eyes. The lamps had been relit, casting their golden light about the room. A warm breeze blew in through the windows, bringing with it the faint scent of flowers.

"The Swan told me to come and wake you," said Kink. "She

148

says to meet her down by the lake right away. Says it's urgent." He fell into a scratching fit, oohing and aahing as he attacked his crooked back end. "Buh uf ur tard," he continued, his mouth full of his own hide, "I cud teller yuh neeg mur resk."

Ilien climbed out of bed. His legs felt solid once more, his head clear. To his amazement the clothes he wore looked and smelled as if they had been freshly washed and pressed. He felt his pockets. His house key and pencil were still there. He shrugged. He hadn't felt this good since the last time he'd slept in his own bed. "I feel fine," he said. "Besides Kink, you just told me it was urgent. Let's go."

Kink stopped his chewing and looked at Ilien in embarrassment. "Oh yeah, you're right."

Even though he felt fine, Ilien left Hemlock with a knot in the pit of his stomach. He glanced back at the magnificent tree-house, with its front door magically hidden and its windows thrown wide, lit like enchanted eyes, and he felt somehow homesick. The pervading gloom only added to his sense of foreboding. He looked long and hard at the secreted sanctuary, wanting to commit to memory everything about it. He had a sinking feeling it would be the last time he would ever see it again.

He made his way slowly through the forest, Kink leading the way through the shadows. Ahead, he could see the bright outline of the forest's end, where the trees fell away and the sun shined slanting upon the field far away. Behind him, the bright glow of Hemlock's open windows dwindled, then died away, lost among the intersecting rows of trees. He quickened his pace. He longed for the comfort of the sun, even if it did always teeter on the moment of sunset.

Soon he reached the field, and broke out into the sunlight. He slowed, stopping to admire the strange and beautiful flowers again, telling himself that it would be his last chance to smell them. But he knew he was only lingering to put off the inevitable. Sooner or later he had to face his fears—his fear for Windy, his fear of finding out the truth, his fear of facing Reknamarken.

Anselm's words came back to him. *Make haste of your feelings.* But he couldn't. With Kink dragging his tail beside him, the stroll to the lake felt like a march to judgement.

Ilien found the Swan exactly where he thought he might, swimming in the shallows of the lake, just off the sandy shore. She moved effortlessly through the water, wielding slowly about to face him. Ilien quickened his pace to meet her. Kink trotted at his side.

"You look well," she said, her eyes glinting in the sunlight. "I trust you are."

"I am," was all Ilien could say. He walked to the water's edge. Kink followed behind him.

"You have many questions."

Ilien nodded.

"I will try to answer all that I can. But first there is something you must know."

"Like who my parents are?" asked Ilien.

The Swan hovered backward in the water, her long neck bowing gracefully in a gesture of acquiescence. "Yes, for one."

Ilien looked out over the water. Ripples from the Swan's passage pressed silently on the shore. "If I am Nomadin," he said, his gaze coming to rest on the Swan, "then my parents must be Nomadin."

The Swan nodded.

"Then is Gallund my father?"

At that the magnificent bird paddled forward and climbed ashore, shaking her back feathers dry. "I don't know who your father is."

Ilien looked at Kink, then back at the Swan. "How can that be? You said yourself that my parents brought me here. You saw them."

"You were brought before me by three Nomadin," said the Swan as she walked past Ilien. "One was Gilindilin, the wizardess. The other two were wizards. Yes, one was Gallund, that's true. But the other was the wizard Genten. It was clear from the start that Gilindilin was your mother, but neither wizard claimed to be your father, though I suspected one was."

"And you didn't ask?"

The Swan slowed and stopped, but she remained peering forward along the sandy shore. "Having a child is forbidden by the Nomadin, Ilien," she said, watching a gull as it played near the water's edge. "It took great courage for them to come to me, and even greater courage for Gilindilin to proclaim herself your mother. It was not my place to ask."

"Courage to proclaim herself my mother? You say it as if I'm a shame to her."

The Swan was quiet for a moment. The gull she watched lifted suddenly from the beach and sailed out over the water. "Not a shame," she replied, turning to face him. "A tragedy."

Ilien was stunned silent.

"You may want to sit. There is something you should understand."

"I'll stand, thank you."

The giant bird sat down, and though Ilien remained standing, her head still towered above his.

"Nomadin are forbidden to love so deeply as to have children," she said. "They must live without the love so many others take for granted. It is a lonely existence, to be bound so, but to permit themselves the greatest joy in life is not only to doom the greatest treasure they could ever have, but to doom all creation as well."

"What do you mean?" asked Ilien.

"Having a Nomadin-child is to release the Necromancer himself," said Kink. "It is prophesied so."

Ilien looked at the Swan in disbelief.

151

"It's true," she replied. "Reknamarken foretold that a Nomadin-child would free him, and thus would begin the third and final war, as it must. For it was prophesied from old that the Dark Shepherd would rise three times, the third to be the last, and that three generations of Nomadin would meet him in battle. But the final words of Reknamarken would prove a bane indeed, for the Nomadin forbade themselves from ever bearing children, and now the Sons of the First Line are old and weary, and no heir exists to carry on their work. Until now."

"But why would they believe him?" asked Ilien.

"If you knew the Necromancer, you'd believe him too," said the Swan. "The Nomadin understood what Reknamarken was up to, that his prophesy would doom them to extinction, but as first-hand witnesses to the destruction he had caused in the past, they decided not to take any chances."

"Well someone sure did," said Ilien.

"Yes, they did," said the Swan, eyeing Ilien with a half-smile.

"But Reknamarken's prophesy has to be wrong. I have no intentions of freeing him."

"His prophesy makes no mention of your intentions, Ilien."

Ilien sat down beside the Swan, digging his heels into the sandy shore. Kink plopped down next to him, doing the same with his front paws.

"If I was such a tragedy, then why did she bother to bring me here in the first place? If I was destined to doom creation itself, then why didn't she just—"

"Gilindilin could never have slain her own son!" exclaimed the Swan, rising to her feet. "But don't be naive, there were others who would have. She brought you here to hide you from the Necromancer, for even though he is imprisoned in the Void, he yet sees, and though his body has long been destroyed, he has many hands abroad. It is only here, the Drowsy Wood, that remains unreachable to Reknamarken still."

152

"And my parents back in Southford? They just found me one night on their doorstep, I suppose."

"Of course not," replied the Swan. "You needed to be hidden better than that! No matter how hard Gilindilin tried, she could not hide your birth from Reknamarken. From the start you were sought by the Necromancer's servants, the NiDemon. Oh, she cast what spells she could to mask her pregnancy, but word would soon get out, that she knew. A Nomadin was to have a child, the prophesied child. She fled, finally coming here, where Reknamarken could not see, to seek an answer, to hide you."

"No, she could not simply leave you anywhere, Ilien. Whoever she chose to leave you with would need to believe that you were their son, through and through. There could be no doubt to anyone that you were nothing more than a common child from a common woman, that your mother in Southford was truly your birth-mother."

"But that would be impossible," said Ilien, "unless she actually gave birth to me."

The Swan ruffled her feathers, then carefully groomed them back into place with her beak. Kink laid his shaggy head in the sand and looked up at Ilien.

"But that's impossible," said Ilien.

"It's not impossible," said Kink, jumping to his feet. "It's incredible!"

"Twice born you are, Ilien," said the Swan. "Much is possible when your parents are Nomadin."

Ilien looked at her doubtfully. "If what you say is true, then that means my mother back in Southford really is my birth-mother."

Kink looked at the Swan.

"Yes. In a way," she answered. "But no."

"But you just said—"

"You are Nomadin, Ilien," said the Swan, "and not just any

153

Nomadin. You possess powers beyond compare. It is foretold that you will free the Necromancer. Reknamarken must find you. He needs your powers. Gilindilin could take no chances. She hid you well, better than you may ever know. Yes, your mother in Southford gave birth to you, but only to what you see in the mirror, not to who you really are, not to what you really are. You would be wise to remember that not all appearances are what they seem."

Ilien started. "Gallund used to say that."

"Yes, I know." The Swan sat down again, lowering herself gently, as if she roosted on eggs. "He was a worthy guardian. He watched over you from the beginning. He was wise to enter your life as a teacher, though I dare say he should never have taught you magic. That was forbidden. But he never was one to put faith in prophesies."

"And the Nomadin named Genten?" asked Ilien. "Was he also my guardian?"

"No," replied the Swan. She rose and hastened to the water's edge. "Gallund, I'm afraid, was your only guardian." She stopped short of the water and fell silent. She regarded the frozen sun on the horizon as if it held an answer she couldn't see. "There was another, though, who would protect you should something befall him."

"Thessien," surmised Ilien.

"No," said the Swan, turning to face him. "Thessien Atenmien followed a different path, though one that unfortunately crossed yours. No, Gallund knew well enough that there was still a chance, even though you were hidden, that Reknamarken would find you. If anything were to befall him—"

"Then my brother Breach was to protect you," said Kink, solemnly.

"The giant dog that saved me from the wierwulvs?" asked Ilien.

"Yes," said the Swan, and she took to the water again,

paddling slowly away from shore. When she swung about, her eyes fell briefly on Kink. "When Gallund fell in the marsh, Breach embarked to find you. Unfortunately, he was not the only one searching for you."

"The Groll," whispered Ilien.

"Yes. A Groll was already hunting you."

Ilien looked out across the lake at the sun, frozen in time at the water's edge, a glowing red ball poised between dusk and dawn.

"Are they all dead?" he asked.

No one answered.

"Then it is all my fault," he said, casting his eyes downward. "And now Windy too."

"There is no one to blame except Reknamarken himself," said the Swan as she paddled closer to shore. "His way has always caused suffering. He is responsible for Gallund's demise. He is the one who sent the Groll. And it is he who has Windy now. Blame not yourself, Ilien."

Kink prodded him with a nose like a cold, wet sponge, looking at him sorrowfully. "It's not your fault you were destined to doom all creation."

Ilien stroked the massive dog's head more for Kink's sake than his own, but when he spoke next he couldn't still the quivering in his voice. "What do I do now? How am I to save Windy when I can't be trusted to save myself?" He looked up at the Swan circling slowly in the water. "So many have tried to protect me while I've stood by and let them die."

Kink propped his head on Ilien's lap.

"You evidently don't understand what a Nomadin can do," said the Swan with a splash. She surged through the water in excitement. Her wake roiled behind her. "Nomadin possess divine power. They've been created to touch the very Source. And if I'm not mistaken, you are the most powerful Nomadin of all. You just don't know it."

NOMADIN

"You've got that right," said Ilien, inspecting Kink's head gloomily. "I can't even master the simplest of spells."

"Anything worth doing is worth doing poorly," said Kink.

"Until you can do it well," finished the Swan as she glided to a stop. "Very well put, Kink. And Ilien here can do it better than any. He only needs to be shown."

"Are you saying that you can teach me how to defeat the Necromancer in the next two days?" asked Ilien.

"Two days?" exclaimed the Swan. "There isn't that much time! And I'm afraid I am no teacher of magic as Gallund was."

Ilien looked away at the mention of the fallen wizard.

"But don't worry, Ilien. You need only learn one thing, and that, I'm happy to say, is something I can teach you. Anselm!" The Swan's shrill cry caught Ilien by surprise. Kink jumped to his feet. "Anselm!" she called again. "Now where is that Giant?" The feathers of her brow crisscrossed with annoyance. "I gave him one simple task and—oh—there he is now. Good."

The Swan paddled forward, smiling, and climbed onto shore. She shook the water from her tail feathers, soaking both Ilien and Kink in the process.

Ilien looked out across the field. Anselm came running toward them. "I'm coming!" bellowed the Giant.

The ground shook as Anselm approached. Ilien saw then that he cradled a small, curved tree in his arms. On closer inspection, and to his surprise, Ilien realized the tree was actually a wooden bow, giant-sized to be sure. Anselm stopped breathless before the Swan.

"You see, Ilien," continued the Swan, inspecting the bow with obvious satisfaction, "you have more magic in you than you realize. In fact, you've been using it all along."

Ilien didn't hear a word. His attention lay on the enormous bow in the Giant's arms, and the inch-thick arrows held in a quiver upon his back.

156

The Swan circled behind Anselm, pleased with Ilien's reaction. "Though Gallund made you study your spell book night and day, it did you no good," she said. "It couldn't."

"I learned my first spell studying that book," said Ilien, wresting his eyes from the enormous bow to defend his beloved tome.

"No you didn't," said the Swan, her feathery brow lifting in anticipation of what she was going to say next. "Magic for you is not something you learn. You already know everything there is to know, and perhaps more, if I'm not mistaken."

"What do you mean, if you're not mistaken?"

"Haven't you cast spells you've never studied?"

Ilien sat quietly.

"Mitra mitari mitara miru?" prodded the Swan.

Ilien eyes sprang wide and he cringed in fear, expecting at any moment to see green and white stars shoot forth from her wingtips.

"Ilien!" scolded the Swan. "Gather your wits! Do I look like a wizard?"

Ilien glanced at her skeptically.

"You know as well as I that spells are simply words," she said. "Some people can learn their use for magical purposes. But not you. You've no need to learn. Now answer my question. Why is it that you were able to cast that spell without ever having studied it?"

"I had Gallund's wand," answered Ilien, his eyes revealing his lingering doubt. "And how do you know about that?"

"The same way I know about Gallund's ambush in the marsh, and the Groll that was sent to kill you. I can see more than most. Do you really think that flock of birds had nothing better to do than save you from floating to the moon? And as far as Gallund's wand is concerned, you know as well as I that it holds no power. A wand merely focuses a wizard's magic. It works only for the wizard for whom it was made. It is useless to all others. Yet look what you were able to accomplish with Gallund's. Imagine what you could do if you had your own!"

The Swan suddenly advanced, the feathers on her neck standing stiff as needles.

"Why is it that your wounds healed so quickly in Evernden?" she asked.

Ilien looked at her blankly.

"Think, Ilien!"

"I drank from a magical cup," he answered.

"Did you? If it was a healing cup then why didn't it work on Thessien's wounds?"

"Windy said the wolfsbane worked better."

"Yes. It did. And do you know why?" She didn't wait for his answer. "Because that silver cup held no more power than her magical feather."

Ilien shot to his feet. "That feather saved our lives! We soared through the air!"

"Yes," said the Swan, her eyes growing wide. "You did." She nodded to Anselm behind her.

Into the span of stunned silence from Ilien came the loud creak of the giant bow being drawn back. Ilien froze. He looked at the Swan in disbelief.

"Don't worry," she said. "If I'm not mistaken, this won't hurt a bit."

The buzz of an arrow cutting the air dropped Ilien to his knees. He tightened like a knotted rope, jerking forward, crying out in anticipation of the missile's deadly assault.

It never came. He knelt trembling in the sand, staring blindly ahead. The Swan stood before him. Her face beamed with delight.

"Well I'll be," she marveled. "I'm not mistaken after all. Look! See for yourself the power you possess!"

Ilien turned slowly around. The razor-tipped arrow hovered before him, as still as the frozen sun. He reached out a trembling hand and it dropped to the ground and broke in two.

"Yes, Ilien. You stopped the arrow that was meant to kill you, just as you healed your own mortal wounds, just as you flew from the towers of Evernden. You have passed the test, the test Gallund could never bring himself to give you. Do not be afraid of what you are, for only when you accept your fate is it possible to do something about it. Then and only then will you control your own destiny."

Ilien stared at the broken arrow in bewilderment. "And it's this power I've known nothing about till now, this power I can scarcely control, that will allow me to face Reknamarken?"

"No, Ilien," answered the Swan. "It is courage that will allow that."

Ilien rose, looking as though he had just been handed a scolding. He glanced at Anselm, and the Giant looked away. He regarded the broken arrow once more as Kink sniffed at it warily.

"If I'm destined to release the Necromancer, then why have me face him at all?" he asked.

"Like Gallund, I too put little faith in prophesies," replied the Swan. "I see little power in them. But this I see crystal clear. Windy is in grave danger. You must go to Greattower and face the NiDemon, or she will die."

A bitter taste rose at the back of Ilien's throat. "How can I when I have no control over this magic within me?"

The Swan's eyes lit up. "Ah, but you carry the answer with you, Ilien."

Ilien felt something wriggle in his back pocket. He pulled his pencil forth.

"Yes," said the Swan. "Your very own wand! Gallund knew that the Necromancer would search for you. That's why he found you first, watched over you, taught you magic. He was afraid you'd be discovered before you were ready. And that's why he made you the wand."

Ilien inspected his pencil as if for the very first time.

"This is my wand?" he asked.

"Something wrong with that?" remarked the pencil in a tone that begged for an argument.

"There's one more matter," said the Swan. "The matter that prompted me to wake you in the first place, a matter that makes your mission that much more important. Kingsend Castle has been sacked."

"The Book!" cried Anselm.

"Yes. The Book," said the Swan. "It's been captured. It's on its way to Greattower as we speak."

"Then all is lost," said Ilien. "The Binding spell has been broken. The Necromancer will soon be free."

"All is not lost," said the Swan. "They don't have the key, and the key is needed to do the final unlocking. But that's another reason why I fear for the princess. My vision is not clear, but I fear she has yet a part to play in Reknamarken's plans larger than simply luring you to Greattower."

Ilien felt a cold wave of fear run through him. "My god! She has the key. I've seen it. A magical key that flew into her pocket. She has it with her."

"I feared it was so," said the Swan. "If she does have the key, you should ride at once. Take the fastest horse in the Wood. You must make it to Greattower in front of the Book. You must retrieve the key."

Ilien narrowed his gaze. "Don't you mean rescue Windy?" he asked.

"Yes. Of course."

There was a moment of tense silence before the Swan spoke again.

"There is one more thing, Ilien. The Groll hunts you still. It waits for you outside the forest."

Kink stepped forward. "Then I'm going with him."

"Kink," said Ilien. "No. You don't have to."

"I want to," said Kink.

The Swan looked at Anselm.

"What?" said the Giant, looking from face to face as if he'd missed an important point.

"They could use a mighty warrior. Someone with Giant-like strength, and courage to match. Unless, that is—" She motioned across the lake.

"Okay, okay," said Anselm. "It's been a long time since I've been on an adventure anyhow." His ears turned pink. "Unless you count living with that missus of mine. And I'm not going on that one again! Count me in too."

"A company of three!" said the Swan. "Excellent! Come. You should leave at once."

She took a step forward then stopped. She turned to face Ilien, her smile gone. "Always remember what's at stake, Ilien. Never forget what's most important."

"I won't," said Ilien. But as the Swan turned and led them away, Ilien wondered just what she had meant.

The three traveling companions trod in silence as they followed the Swan across the field toward the forest. Anselm walked in the lead. Kink sniffed the ground as he followed behind. Ilien brought up the rear, his apprehension growing into fear as the enormity of the quest ahead settled over him. He thought of Windy, who at that moment sat huddled in the darkness under the cold stone of Greattower Mountain. He clenched his fists. He needed courage! It seemed he had everything else.

"Will you stop?" he said, suddenly grabbing his back pocket.

"I think I deserve a little better treatment, now that I'm your wand," snapped the pencil, poking him again. "Starting with where you keep me. You think I like being sat on all the time?"

"What do you mean, now that you're my wand? You've always been my wand. I just didn't know it."

"Well it was news to me too."

"Oh great," said Ilien. "That's just great. Not only is my wand a talking pencil, it doesn't even know it *is* a wand!" He put the pencil in his front pocket anyhow, and quickened his pace to catch up with the others.

A moment later Ilien stopped. "Anselm?" he asked.

"Yes?" answered the Giant without looking back.

"Did you know I would stop that arrow?"

Anselm slowed and studied the ground in front of him. "No. But I'm sure glad you did," he replied.

"Make haste!" called the Swan from up ahead. "The NiDemon won't wait forever!"

Anselm turned with a smile. "At least I think I am."

Chapter XIV

Runner

As far as Ilien was concerned, the Swan was leading them on a wild goose chase. The giant bird had said they were to leave at once, but an hour later they were still walking through the outskirts of the forest, weaving their way in and out of the even rows of tall, straight trees that grew beside the field. The way Anselm described it, there was only one way to the grove where the horses roamed, and though it was actually very close by, you needed to walk a long way to get there.

"Distance here in the Drowsy Wood is sort of like time back where you come from," he said to Ilien as they trudged past yet another massive tree in an endless sea of massive trees. "Some days, when you're busy having fun, the whole afternoon flies by like it was hardly there at all. Other days, when it seems like the chores will never get done, a few minutes lasts an eternity."

Ilien still wasn't sure if he understood, but to him it didn't matter. At the rate things were progressing, they would never get to Greattower.

Nearly another hour elapsed and Ilien looked back the way they had come. The lake was still clearly visible from where they stood. They had walked miles to get nowhere! He was about to complain when the Swan stopped and looked back with what Ilien decided was an annoying smile on her face.

"Well, we're nearly there," she said, flexing her webbed feet in excitement. "A few more zigzags past that tree behind you, and a loop or two around that one beside you, and you won't believe your eyes."

"I already don't believe my eyes," moaned Ilien, looking back at the very spot near the lake they had left nearly two hours and five miles earlier. "This doesn't make any sense. None of this makes any sense. A few more zigzags, a loop or two around that tree—doesn't anything here work in a straight line?"

"We can't be too careful here in the Drowsy Wood," said the Swan. "If it all seems a mystery then that's as it should be. It is the one and only place in all Nadae that remains a secret to Reknamarken."

"Nadae? What's Nadae?" asked Ilien.

"Nadae," answered the Swan, gesturing with her wing at the land all about. "It is the world you live in. From Greattower to Evernden, from across the Clearwater River to your very own town of Southford and beyond, to places you'll never see, places as far as you can be from home, where one step further brings you closer to the way you came. It is our world, and the Drowsy Wood is but a part."

The Swan looked at the forest around her like she would never see it again. After a few moments of silence she laid soft eyes on Ilien.

"The Drowsy Wood is like a fantastic dream. While in it you should never question its logic, or else you might wake and discover that it's only a memory. Remember this, and remember it well. If all the world falls, this will be its last hope. Reknamarken must never discover its secrets. Never." With that she turned and walked away.

Sure enough, after a few more zigzags and a loop or two, Ilien couldn't believe his eyes. He found himself facing the lake again, the wind fingering the tall grass of the field before it. Nothing had changed. Nothing at all.

"Well, here we are," said the Swan. Anselm stood beside

SHAWN P. CORMIER

her, smiling in satisfaction. Kink's tail waved back and forth like a victory flag. Ilien frowned.

"Wait," said Anselm. "They're coming."

Ilien waited. The tall grass churned in the breeze that came off the lake, dancing and swirling before the playful gusts of wind. One quick gust blew in their direction, parting the grass as it approached. Ilien felt a warm breeze blow past him. He breathed in the sweet scent of flowers.

"Runner must like you," commented the Swan. "She's being a bit obvious, if you ask me."

Ilien did as he always did when he figured he'd missed something. He kept quiet, hoping to catch it the second time around.

"So what do you think?" asked Anselm, grinning.

"Yeah, what do you think?" echoed Kink.

Ilien shuffled back a bit, stuck his hands in his pocket, and tinkered nervously with his house key and pencil. He had no idea what they were talking about! He was about to say so when something suddenly breathed down the back of his neck. He spun around, but it was only the breeze.

"Isn't she beautiful?" said Anselm.

"Magnificent," said Kink.

"Absolutely!" agreed the Swan.

Ilien waved his hand in the air before him, feeling foolish. "Okay. What are you talking about?"

"Why Runner, of course," said the Swan. "I must admit, I haven't seen her myself in quite some time, but she's still the most inspiring horse in the Wood. Surely you agree?"

Ilien stood dumbfounded.

Kink fell back on his haunches. "He can't see her," he said. "He can't see her at all."

"See what?" shouted Ilien.

Anselm's hands flew to his mouth. "Surely this can't be good."

165

"What can't be good?" asked Ilien.

"Look. She's nuzzling him even now and he doesn't even know it!" cried Kink.

Ilien did feel a tickle run down his side, but as far as he could see it was only nerves at being cast a fool. "Will you stop?" he said. "There is nothing nuzzling me."

Even the Swan looked surprised. "But there is."

"Tell me you can see her," begged Kink, jumping to his feet.

Ilien's silence was followed by a low whistle from Anselm. "What does it mean?" asked the Giant.

"It means he walks," said Kink, his crooked back end plunking back to the ground.

"It means nothing of the sort," replied the Swan, walking over to stand beside Ilien. In a low voice she said, "You really can't see her?"

Ilien shook his head, looking from disappointed face to disappointed face.

"Not at all?" she asked.

"No. Not at all." He screwed his eyes to focus at a fixed point in mid-air before him. "Is that bad?"

The Swan thought for a moment. "Not necessarily."

"That doesn't sound comforting," said Ilien.

"What I mean to say is I'm not sure what it means. The horses of the Drowsy Wood are visible to all but mortal men."

"And Reknamarken," added Kink.

"Yes. And Reknamarken," said the Swan. "But you are Nomadin, Ilien. You should have no trouble at all seeing Runner."

The Swan cocked her head in the direction of the field. "Uh huh. Yes. Of course, Runner." She looked back at Ilien and smiled. "No matter. Runner has agreed to take you anyhow."

"You can't be serious," said Ilien. "I can't even see her. How can I ride her?"

"What was that?" asked the Swan.

"I said I can't—"

"No, no. Not you. I was talking to Runner. What was that dear?"

The Swan listened intently. Anselm and Kink paid rapt attention to the silence as well. A moment later she turned to Ilien. "Runner says to have faith."

"Faith?" said Ilien. He searched the empty air before him, and threw his hands up in defeat.

"Yes. Faith," said the Swan. "You do know what that is?"

"Of course I know what faith is!"

"Good," replied the Swan. "Now climb aboard. You really must leave at once."

Ilien looked hard at the space in front of him, the space that everyone thought was rideable. "You can't be serious," he repeated.

"Do I look serious?" said the Swan, smiling. "You have ridden a horse before. Haven't you?"

"Of course."

"Then let's go. There should be nothing to it."

Ilien shook his head, but reached out to grab the invisible reins anyhow.

"Um. Ilien?" Kink nodded in the other direction. "She's behind you."

Ilien turned around with a grimace. He stuck out his hand, grabbing empty air again. He reached further, feeling more foolish than before.

"Just lift your leg in the air and Runner will do the rest," assured the Swan.

Ilien did as she asked. He stood like a dog taking a—

"Oh my!" he cried, rising into the air as if levered off the ground by an invisible teeter-totter. He fell forward, clutching at thin air. "Whoa!"

His hands hit something almost solid, and somehow warm. He felt a strange tingle run up his fingers and into his arms.

167

Soon he was able to steady himself. He sat six feet up, eyeing the ground suspiciously.

"Don't worry," said Kink. "You'll get the hang of it."

Ilien doubted that, but patted what he thought was Runner's neck in a friendly sort of way. *Can't be too careful*, he thought.

"Now, when you exit the Wood," said the Swan, "you'll find yourself in a small, nondescript grove of pines in the middle of the Near Plains, fairly close to Greattower Mountain."

Anselm cleared his throat. "That grove was cut down some time ago."

"Cut down?"

"Yes," said the Giant, "by some men who wanted to build a river-boat casino."

"A river-boat what?"

"Well you see, the Far Hills River runs right through there, and—"

"Never mind," said the Swan. "I guess you'll have to exit by way of the small grove near Bamber Lake."

Anselm shook his head.

"Cut down as well?" asked the Swan.

"Yes. To help build the town of Bamber."

The Swan snapped her beak shut with a loud snap. "Well, are there any exit groves left?"

Ilien waved his hand in the air. "Hello. Can anyone tell me what in the world you're talking about? What is an exit grove?"

The Swan stared blankly at him for a moment. "Oh. Yes. I quite forgot. You're new at all this." She shook her head at her foolishness. "As you have already so eloquently pointed out," she said, "nothing here works in a straight line. The Wood, after all, is enchanted."

She glanced at Anselm and Kink and winked.

"I think I get that much," said Ilien, frowning.

"Ah. Yes," continued the Swan, growing serious. "Well, to put it plainly, there are only six ways into the Drowsy Wood, or more accurately put, were six ways in." Her eyes narrowed on Anselm as she said this. "And so it goes that there are, or were, six ways out. Each way led a traveler out or in through a small grove of pine trees, which as you know, had to be navigated just so in order for their enchantments to work." Her brow bunched in thought. She raised a wing and began ticking off feathers, counting silently to herself. She shook her head again. "Was it actually six, or more like eight? Hmm." She looked up, remembering where she was. "Anyhow, back to the question at hand." She turned to Anselm. "Are there any exit groves left?"

"Well—" began Anselm.

The Swan shook her tail. It thrummed in the air like a five-foot feather duster. "Just forget it," she snapped. "We do have a map here, don't we?"

Ilien, being fond of maps, looked on with interest. The Swan saw him peering intently at the empty air in front of her.

"I didn't exactly mean here," she said. "Really Ilien, not everything in the Drowsy Wood is invisible."

"I have the map," announced Anselm, pulling it from his pocket. It was in very poor shape, folded many times, with edges frayed and torn. Ilien absently nudged his invisible mount forward to get a better look, and to his surprise he floated through the air and hovered near Anselm. The Giant began gingerly unfolding the map, as if afraid the aged parchment might suddenly crumble to dust before his eyes. Ilien soon learned the real reason for his caution, though, when the Giant accidentally tore a corner.

"And there goes the fabled city of Worcester!" cried the map. "How many times have you folded and unfolded me? And each time I get the same treatment. Another precious piece of me lost forever. You'd think you'd have learned by now! Pretty soon they'll be nothing left of me but the very spot you stand on. Giants! Really!"

"Calm down you wretched piece of paper!" said Anselm. He turned the map over in his hands, trying to decipher how it had been folded to begin with.

"I swear!" he said, shaking his head. "You're as bad as my wife! Nag. Nag. Nag. You'd think you'd treat me better after all I've gone through for you. Every time we're out she tells me, "just ask for directions." But no. No matter how much trouble it brings me, I always use you, don't I? And what thanks do I get? You know, if she'd had her way you'd have been used to paper the parakite cage years ago!"

That silenced the map.

"Now open up and show us what we need," said the Giant.

At that, the map unfolded in the Giant's hands. Ilien craned his neck to get a better look. Though the map looked tattered and worn, he saw that its surface was exquisitely detailed. Too much so, in fact.

"How can anyone read that?" he asked.

Anselm rolled his eyes and moaned.

"I beg your pardon," answered the map, "But you don't read me. I am not a book, I'll have you know. I am a map."

"I beg your pardon back," said Ilien. "What I meant to say was how can anyone possibly find where they are, not to mention where they're going, with all those unintelligible scribbles all over you?"

"Well, I never!" And the map rolled into a tight, little tube.

"I think you hurt its feelings," said Kink.

"All you have to do when you have an enchanted map is ask," explained Anselm with a wink. "Unfortunately, we have a temperamental map at best."

"Really, I'm sorry," said Ilien to the sulking map as he wobbled atop his invisible horse.

"Don't worry," said Anselm. "This always seems to do the

trick." He placed the map on the ground at his feet and pulled a flint and tinder from his pocket. No sooner were the flint and tinder revealed when the map unrolled and lay seamless and silent before him. "That's better," said Anselm.

"What can I show you, oh mighty one?" intoned the map.

"Knock off the dramatics and just show us the exit grove nearest Greattower Mountain."

The map was quiet for a moment, as if thinking. "Why, the nearest exit grove is the only exit grove. It can be found outside of the Kingdom of Evernden."

Anselm gasped. Kink growled. The fur on his back bristled. The Swan, though, merely closed her eyes and was silent.

Ilien looked hard at the map. A red X suddenly appeared, marking the grove's exact location. "If I'm not mistaken," he said, trying to sort through the tangle of markings, "that's where I came in."

"Precisely," answered the map.

"Why that's not close to Greattower at all," said Ilien. "It'll take us a week to get there."

"And it won't put us that far ahead of the Book either," said Anselm. "There has to be another way."

"Well there isn't," said the map.

The Swan sighed and opened her eyes. "If this map is correct," she said, "and I'm sure it is," she added with a wan smile at the magical parchment, "then this is bad news indeed." She turned to Ilien. "The Groll will be waiting for you."

Kink's ears pricked up at the mention of the Groll. He bared his fangs and sniffed at the map warily. "So be it," he growled.

The Swan placed a wing on Ilien's shoulder. "Don't fret," she said, in answer to his worried look. "I have a plan."

Chapter XV

The Best Laid Plans

The plan is a simple one," said the Swan as they gathered in one of the even forest lanes.

They had traveled back across the lake, this time by boat, to the entrance side of the forest—the mud-room as Anselm had called it. The Swan had been tight beaked on the long boat ride over, refusing to tell anyone her plan until they had arrived in the very lane where Anselm had caught Ilien in his trap. At Anselm's behest, they had been careful to avoid his cabin.

"You'll leave the Drowsy Wood exactly as you entered," said the Swan, "except in reverse of course, which is exactly no different than the former."

Ilien squinted at her.

"To put it plainly," she said, "simply pass between those two narrow trees over there, walk three trees forward, turn left, walk two more, turn right, walk three more again. It's the only way out of the Drowsy Wood, and you'll find yourself in the very spot you entered. And it's there that the Groll will be waiting for you."

"Isn't there another plan we could follow? Perhaps a more complex one?" asked Ilien, standing between Anselm and Kink. His invisible horse was tethered nearby, at least that was what they'd told him.

The Swan looked cross. "No, Ilien. Just listen. You haven't even heard my plan yet."

"I heard the part about the Groll. That was enough for me."

"Yes, the Groll will be waiting for you. But if you'll just listen I'll tell you exactly what to do." The Swan rattled her tail feathers and sat down on the needle-covered ground. "Good. Now where was I—oh yes—when you exit the Wood you'll come face to face with the Groll."

She stood back up, spreading her wings in excitement. "When the Groll sees you it will charge, bearing down on you like a lion upon an unsuspecting foal, expecting to catch you easily, which of course it can, and rip you limb from limb in a frenzy of bloodlust and rage. Oh, only after impaling you several times with its venomous tail."

Ilien stuck a fist in his mouth to keep from screaming.

"But," she continued, growing even more animated, "you will not be an unsuspecting foal because you will have listened to my plan and will know exactly what to do!" The Swan stood triumphantly before the company of three, beaming proudly.

"Which is?" they asked in unison.

"Why run, of course," answered the Swan, bouncing excitedly up and down.

"Run!" cried Ilien. "That's your plan? I may not be an unsuspecting foal, but I'll still be a dead one!"

"Always jumping to conclusions, aren't we, Ilien. No, no. You will not be a dead foal. You will not be a foal at all. You will be bait."

"Bait?" Ilien hung his head. "I'm dead for sure."

"You will retreat back into the forest," said the Swan, as if she hadn't heard a word he'd said, "back the way you came, in three trees, left two, right three more and the Groll will follow you."

Anselm raised a hand.

"Yes," snapped the Swan. "What is it?"

"But that will lead the Groll back here," said the Giant.

The Swan smirked openly. "Don't worry, Anselm. You'll play a part in this too before all is through. Actually, come to

173

think of it, you've played your part already." She shrugged and turned back to Ilien. "Now, when you arrive here, in this lane of the forest, you must move quickly. The Groll will be hot on your heels, after all. Run as fast as you can, count ten trees and jump."

"Jump? What good will that do?" asked Ilien.

"Why, it'll save your life!" said the Swan.

"I say we go back to before I was a foal and start over," said Ilien, looking at the others for help.

"Listen," said the Swan as she walked down the lane away from them. "When you re-enter the Drowsy Wood you'll find yourself right here."

She stopped, then walked back toward them, counting the trees as she went. She passed Ilien at number six. "Seven, eight, nine, ten." She turned and smiled. "This is where you should jump. Come. Look for yourself."

"What in the world is she talking about?" muttered Ilien.

Anselm shrugged. Kink trotted over to stand by the Swan. He looked down at her feet, then back at Ilien.

"She's right," he said. "You'd better jump, and hard."

Ilien walked up to Kink, shaking his head. "Knowing this place, she'll probably have me jumping into tomorrow," he muttered.

At the Swan's feet was the carefully hidden coil of a rope snare, an enormous rope snare to say the least.

"That's right. My snare!" said Anselm. "Now I remember."

"How could you possibly forget?" asked Ilien, remembering how it had yanked him painfully off his feet.

"That's precisely what I asked him the last time he stepped in it," said Kink.

Anselm's ears flushed red. "Just keep quiet, will ya?"

Ilien looked up at the Swan. "But will it hold a Groll?"

"It held a Giant," chuckled Kink.

"Why you cantankerous, crooked canine," said Anselm, his

ears burning red as he advanced on Kink. "If you don't keep your mouth shut—"

"It will hold the Groll," said the Swan, raising a wing between Anselm and Kink, "at least long enough for the three of you to get very far away."

Ilien looked down the lane, counting the trees with his eyes. "Ten trees is a long way to run."

"Run fast," offered Kink.

"Very fast," added the Swan.

Anselm stewed silently.

"Now off you go," urged the Swan, shooing Ilien forward with a wing. "Remember, in three, left two, right three more and run like the wind. Oh. And jump! Don't forget to jump!"

Ilien stopped short. "I'm going alone?" he asked.

The Swan looked at the others as if to ask what she had missed. "Yes. Of course. There's no point in *all* of us being bait."

"You mean foals," said Ilien.

"Now Ilien," said the Swan, placing a wing on his shoulder and pulling him close. "You know I mean bait."

Ilien pushed her away. "That makes me feel so much better."

But there was nothing else to do. The Swan was right. He just hoped she was right about everything else. So Ilien walked forward, weaving in and out of the trees in the correct, and he thought, ridiculous procedure that would transport him back to the world outside the Drowsy Wood where the Groll lay waiting for him. Just before the last turn he pulled his pencil from his pocket.

"You've got to be joking," it said. "What is it you think I can do, give the Groll a geometry lesson?"

"Don't worry, I know a spell or two," said Ilien. "Just be ready. I have a plan of my own."

"I don't like the sound of that."

"You heard what the Swan said. Wands focus magic. If I can turn a wierwulf into a toad using Gallund's, imagine what I can do to a Groll with you."

"I think I'll wait here with the others," replied the pencil.

Ilien smiled. "Consider this payback for all the times you've gotten me in trouble with Peaty."

"But—"

Ilien squeezed the pencil silent and waved goodbye to the others. With a few steps he disappeared from their sight. But to Ilien those three steps seemed no different than the last twenty. There was no flash, no shaking of the earth, nothing to signify that he had been magically transported out of the last mystical realm in all Nadae. He simply placed one foot in front of the other and soon found himself standing in the moonlit field outside the small grove of pines.

And face to face with the Groll!

Ilien froze, hoping his pencil was smart enough to keep quiet for once. Curled in a ball, like an overgrown puppy with a black, barbed dagger for a tail, the Groll slept soundly in the grass not ten feet away. Ilien quickly aimed the pencil at his unsuspecting target.

For a terrifying moment he wasn't sure if he remembered the spell correctly. But then it all came back to him in a rush. "*Mitra*—"

"Wait!" whispered the pencil in a panic. "I think you're holding me backwards!"

"What do you mean, you think I'm holding you backwards?" Ilien whispered back, one eye fixed on the sleeping Groll. "Isn't that something you should know by now?"

"This is my first time as a wand. I've never cast a spell before. What if it backfires?"

The Groll began to stir. Its tail shifted about. It arched its back and stretched its legs. Its claws spread out like garden rakes. Ilien spun the pencil around.

"*Mitari*—"

"No! Wait!" said the pencil. "I was wrong! Turn me back! Turn me back!"

"What? Are you sure?"

The Groll's slobbering lips drew back in a yawn, revealing long, curved fangs. One eye opened, blinking away its weariness.

"Yes. Do it now!" cried the pencil.

Ilien re-aimed. *"Matara miru!"* he shouted, finishing the incantation.

The Groll opened both eyes just as the burst of bright red stars shot forth—from the wrong end of Ilien's pencil! The magical fireworks shot backwards past Ilien, missing him by inches. They smoked and sizzled, bouncing among the trees behind him. The Groll stiffened in surprise, as did its four hairy legs, sending it leaping into the air. It landed before Ilien, its tail rattling like a box of broken plates.

Ilien looked deep into the Groll's yellow eyes—then ran.

The Groll stood mesmerized, stunned for the moment by the multicolored lights dancing wildly between the trees. Ilien stopped and looked back. He had to be sure that the Groll followed his trail exactly as he laid it. If he ran too far ahead, the Groll would make a bee line to cut him off. It too had to follow the invisible maze—in three trees, left two, right three more—or the Swan's plan would fail from the start.

He held his station near the third tree, sweating and trembling as the Groll came to its senses. Slowly it looked his way. Their eyes met. Ilien leapt forward again as the Groll streaked after him. He turned left, then right, the Groll closing fast. Three steps later, Ilien began counting trees. *One. Two. Three.* The Groll's clawed feet tore up the forest floor behind him. *Four. Five. Six.* The Groll surged forward, closing the gap between them. Ilien cried out in panic. *Seven. Eight—*

Ilien tripped, falling flat on his face. Like a spike he stuck fast in the soft earth. Surprised, the Groll ran past, leaping over him in a single bound, landing square in the center of Anselm's snare.

The rope sprang tight, yanking the beast off its feet. It flew screaming into the air, thrashing wildly in an attempt to escape. The tree from which it dangled swayed precariously under its weight.

The others sprang out from behind the trees. Anselm stared in wide-eyed awe. Kink, on seeing the Groll hanging helpless from its hind legs, stalked forward, fangs bared. The Swan stepped before him with both wings spread wide.

"Don't be a fool. Run as fast as you can. The snare won't hold forever." She turned to Ilien. "Ride at once!"

Ilien searched frantically for his invisible mount. "Runner! Where are you?" he shouted. He groped about in desperation, felt something warm, and leapt into the air. He landed on his back on the soft forest floor. Anselm rushed over, picked him clear into the air and set him on Runner's back.

"Ride!" cried the Swan.

Ilien turned to call for Kink, but the words hung in his throat. Behind the Swan rose a black, barbed tail. The Groll crouched low in the center of the straight forest lane. The broken end of the snare dangled in the air above it.

Before Ilien could shout a warning the tail drove downward, striking the Swan in the back with a sickening crunch. It lanced straight through her and out the other side, venom spraying in all directions. The Swan's wings spread wide in crucifixion. Her beak opened mutely, her eyes filling with anguish. She looked at Ilien, stepped haltingly forward and toppled to the ground, impaled upon the Groll's deadly tail.

"No!"

Ilien's scream erupted from a place he never knew existed, from so deep down it crippled him upon Runner's back. Unknowingly, he thrust out his pencil to smite the Groll down.

A jet of blue flames leapt from the pencil's end, rushing forward and striking the Groll's tail. Ilien's wild magic engulfed both Swan and Groll in a torrent of blue fire. The trees blew back like reeds. Ilien's scream continued, pouring out of him like water from a drowned man's lungs. Still the flames streaked forth, intensifying into a blinding shaft of white hot magic, kindling the treetops into flames.

The Groll pulled its dagger from the Swan's back. It reared in the air on its wolfish hind legs, roaring in pain. The Swan lay motionless, frozen in the blue aura of Ilien's magic. The gaping hole in the center of her back began to glow, filling with flames. Slowly the hole closed as fire seared the wound away. The flames faded. The wound disappeared. The bloodstained feathers bleached to white.

As quickly as the magic began, it ended.

The Groll fell backwards to the ground. The Swan jumped up and stared wide-eyed at Ilien, reeling from a wound that was no longer there. Without a moment's hesitation she sprang into action.

"Flee!" she cried, rushing forward, flapping her wings in warning. Anselm and Kink leaped to her aid, but she snapped at the air with her beak. "This is a battle you cannot win! Now go!"

She whirled about to face the fallen Groll, her strength renewed, her long neck outstretched in anger. The Groll slowly rose, wobbling to its feet, its tail extended to ward off attack. A low growl rippled in the back of its throat. The Swan stepped back in fear and the Groll advanced, grinning a mouthful of fangs.

That was all Ilien saw before Runner raced away, weaving through the trees to safety. Try as he might, Ilien couldn't stop his invisible mount. In moments they exited the forest and emerged from the pine grove. Once in the moonlit field it was only through sheer luck that Ilien caught hold of the unseen

179

reins and pulled Runner to a stop. He watched as first Anselm then Kink came running from the trees.

The Giant sprinted past him in leaps and bounds. "Come on!" he called.

But Kink stopped short. He wagged his head from side to side and sniffed at the air.

"Kink! Let's go!" shouted Ilien.

Kink glanced over. His teeth flashed white in the gloom. He whirled about and sped off parallel to the trees. Ilien turned to call for Anselm but the Giant was already running past him again, following Kink. Ilien spurred Runner on.

A hundred yards away, they found Kink sitting in the grass beside the body of his brother.

Breach lay on his side, the earth scarred and torn from the battle that had taken his life. He might have seemed sleeping, if it wasn't for the hind leg twisted horribly beneath him.

Kink lowered his head and breathed deep the scent of his brother. He sniffed his ears, and touched his face. A low whine escaped him as he read the story of how Breach had died. He laid his head across his brother's neck where the Groll's fatal sting had left it swollen with poison, and sank to the grass, his crooked back end curling around his fallen brother in a tender embrace.

Anselm knelt beside him. "Kink. I'm sorry."

Kink shivered in the warm night air. He nuzzled his brother's neck and licked the blood from off his face. "I will avenge you," he whispered. He looked up at Ilien. "I will, you know."

"We all will," said Anselm. "But not here." He looked back at the silent grove. "Not here, Kink."

Ilien stared at the painful scene that played out before him. Pain. Fear. Vengeance. He knew the first two by heart. He would learn the last, he promised himself. He would learn the last.

Kink rose to his feet. Tears cast dark shadows beneath his shining eyes. His shoulders drooped and a low moan escaped his lips, but nothing more.

"I'm sorry, Kink, but we have to leave," said Anselm.

With a quick glance back at the trees they moved on, leaving Breach lying in the field beneath the waxing moon.

Chapter XVI

The Giant's Tale

The sun rose like a tired old man, casting a weary light upon the land. That was how Ilien saw the sunrise as he struggled to stay atop Runner for the fifth hour in a row. In that time, and to his dismay, he found that riding an invisible horse didn't save one from getting very visible blisters.

The land had blown by in the night, the featureless landscape a march of dark clouds and phantoms. The moon had kept silent pace above, sailing tirelessly over their shoulders as they made their way northward. Anselm had led them from the exit grove with haste, his long legs putting miles between them and possible pursuit. Now as Ilien clung to Runner, fear quickening his heart, his thoughts turned to the Swan.

Was she dead too, another innocent victim to perish in his defense? The memory of her silent scream as she fell before the Groll flashed over and over in his mind. Yes, he had saved her. Wild magic from some hidden place within him had healed her deadly wound. But then he had fled, had left her to face the Groll alone. There would be no one there to help her if she fell again.

He looked over his shoulder at the receding landscape. Kink loped along, silent and brooding. Ilien searched the horizon behind him. To his relief, they ran alone.

At length, he pulled his invisible horse level with Anselm. "There's no sign of pursuit," he said. "Shouldn't we rest for a bit?"

"Just because you can't see it doesn't mean it's not back there," replied Anselm, his eyes fixed ahead, sweat running down his face as he ran. "If you're hungry there's food in your saddlebag. Otherwise, we keep going."

Ilien grit his teeth. He was hungry but that wasn't the point. He was exhausted. He didn't know how much longer he could keep riding before he simply fell off. Besides, what saddlebag?

"It's on the other side," said Kink, next to him. "It's there, behind you, behind your right leg."

"Here we go again," muttered Ilien, spearing an arm behind him and to the right. "I suppose the food is invisible too."

"For your sake I hope it is," said Kink. "No. No. Lower."

Ilien leaned to the side, groping lower. His hand disappeared. He drew it back, startled.

"No. No. Don't worry," said Kink. "It's just the saddle bag. It's invisible."

Ilien reached down again. His hand vanished once more.

"That's it," said Kink, growing excited, his tongue flopping up and down as he ran. "You've got it. Now dig to the bottom. No. Deeper. That's it. You feel something hard? Good. Now pull it out. Careful. Don't drop it. It's heavy."

As Ilien withdrew the item from the unseen bag, he marveled as his hand grew visible again. Along with his hand there appeared a five pound, two foot—bone? Kink's eyes lit up. He drifted closer as he ran beside Ilien's invisible horse.

"Now hand it down here," he said, beginning to drool. "Slowly now. Slowly. Don't drop it." Kink snatched it and wheeled away, dropping back to chew on it as he resumed his steady, crooked march in the rear.

A few minutes later, after he grew tired of watching his hand vanish and reappear over and over again, Ilien fished out what appeared to be bread—flat, stale, off-smelling bread. He placed it back in the bag with a grimace, hoping to find something else, anything else. His search proved fruitless. He plucked out the bread again, glancing back at Kink chewing happily on his bone and wondering who had the better deal. But there was nothing to do but eat it. He tore off a hunk with his teeth. It had the texture of raw meat. It tasted like a sour mushroom. At least it took his mind off the endless riding.

They finally stopped as darkness descended. A few sooty clouds hung low in the sky, puffs of black smoke above the vast expanse before them. The tall grass of the plain stretched as far as the eye could see in every direction, a grey sea in the dying light, and though there was none to be seen, Ilien decided to look for firewood. He made sure he handed Runner's reins to Anselm first. There was no sense in his trying to unsaddle an invisible horse when the Giant could unsaddle a visible one.

"I still don't like it that you can't see her," said Anselm. To Ilien it looked as if the Giant moved in pantomime as he tended the invisible mount. "I don't know what it means, but it can't be good."

"It's good for him," said Kink, curling up in the grass. "It means he doesn't have to unsaddle her."

Ilien wandered around the campsite searching in vain for something to burn. The thought of a damp and chilly night without a fire was almost more than he could bear. "There wouldn't happen to be any wood around here that I can't see, would there?"

"Don't bother," said Anselm. "We've entered the Far Plains. You won't find wood in any direction for a hundred miles or more. But don't worry. I brought some fireflies."

"Fireflies? You've got to be joking," said Ilien, flexing his fingers. "I can do better than fireflies."

"They're not what you think," said Anselm, reaching into his pocket. But before the Giant could show him, Ilien pulled out his pencil.

"Are you sure you're holding me the right way?" asked the pencil, outlined in the gloom. "I wouldn't want to—"

"Keep quiet," said Ilien, and he circled it above his hand. "*Kinil ubid, illubid kinar*," he whispered. The tiny light took shape in his palm.

"Unfortunately, this seems to be the only spell I can control," he said as the light grew brighter. "Throw me from the highest tower, shoot me with an arrow, chase me with a hungry Groll and I'll somehow save the day. But let me try a simple Lightning spell and it's *run for the hills*!" Globe grew to a bright moon, pulsing softly. Ilien stroked it gently, as he might a cat. Soon there was enough light to see twenty yards in all directions. He laughed. "Globe and I, we go way back. Don't we boy?" He looked at Anselm and smiled.

Just then Globe shot from his hand in a spray of hot sparks and hissed up into the sky. Ilien watched in dismay as Globe arched over the grassland. It disappeared in the distance with a tiny flash.

"You don't say," chuckled Anselm in the darkness. "Me, I just got these fireflies yesterday." He drew forth a glass vial, holding it up for Ilien to see. Three bright pinpoints of light milled about at the bottom of the small container. "Guaranteed not to fly away."

"You don't say," said Ilien, staring off into space where Globe had disappeared.

"Yeah," said Kink. "He tore their wings off."

"Just keep quiet!" said Anselm. "These flies will start and keep a fire all night, with or without wings."

Ilien moved to take a closer look at the three glowing lights. Sure enough, they were bugs alright, fireflies actually, sans wings of course. "They're just plain old fireflies," he said. "I used to catch those back home."

Anselm pulled the stopper off the glass vial. "They're not plain or old when caught in the Drowsy Wood." He fished out the more sluggish of the three, holding it in a cupped hand. He replaced the cover and dropped the bottle back in his pocket.

"No wood needed. Behold." With a flourish he placed the bug on the grass. Immediately a small fire jumped up as if consuming the very air itself. Anselm held his hands to its warmth.

"But what about the firefly?" asked Ilien, peering into the dancing flames. "The poor thing's cooked for sure."

Anselm looked to Kink and back again. "For crying out loud, Ilien. You can't reuse it. It's a bug!"

They ate a hot meal of steaming, flat, off-smelling bread. It seemed, to Ilien's horror, that they carried little else. Kink wolfed his down and promptly curled into a massive fur ball in the grass. Anselm ate his share gingerly, as if it were some sort of delicacy.

"What is this stuff, anyhow?" asked Ilien, trying to chew without gagging. He poked his piece suspiciously.

"Dragon dung," said Anselm as he licked a hunk off his finger. He tore out laughing as Ilien choked and coughed. "It's just Awefull," said the Giant with tears in his eyes.

"You can say that again," said Ilien, spitting his dinner to the ground. "Tell me I haven't really eaten dragon dung."

"No," said Anselm, holding his sides. "It's not dung. It's Awefull. It's just Awefull, bread made from the rye grass of the Drowsy Wood. Awefull. It's good for you."

"Awefull?" Ilien turned it over in his hands, unconvinced. "I think I've lost my appetite."

"No matter," said Anselm wiping his hands on his animal skin pants. "You've eaten enough to last all day and then some. Awefull goes a long way." He finished his and reached for Ilien's. "If you're not going to finish that—"

Ilien handed it over gladly and reclined in the grass. The night was still, the only sounds that of Kink's snoring and Anselm's chewing. The plains allowed for an unobstructed view of the night sky. The moon chased a swarm of bright, white stars across a black velvet canvas.

"Do you think the Swan is still alive?" asked Ilien. He

closed his eyes, fearing Anselm's answer. The chewing stopped. There was quiet for a moment. Even Kink's snores fell silent.

"I think the Groll still lives," was Anselm's answer.

Ilien contemplated the blackness behind his eyelids. So many had fallen into the void. So many had perished because of him. Somehow he knew he should feel grateful for their sacrifices, but he only felt lonely, lonelier than ever.

"I'm sorry," he whispered, opening his eyes to take in the stars again.

Anselm swallowed loudly. "Don't apologize, Ilien. I know it seems you're to blame for everything that's happened, but you're not. We've all chosen the course laid before us for our own gain. Despite the prophesy, you're perhaps our only hope against Reknamarken's rising. The fact that you alone have the power to save us is not of your choosing. Our path is."

"I have choices too, you know," said Ilien sitting up, his face flushing red and hot in the darkness. "You talk as if my entire fate is foretold."

"But it isn't," said Anselm, putting down his Awefull. "Remember what the Swan told you, Ilien. Only when you accept your fate is it possible to do something about it. Then and only then will you be able to control your own destiny."

"That makes no sense whatsoever."

"It makes perfect sense," laughed Anselm.

Ilien hunched into a stubborn knot.

"Look at me, Ilien." Ilien ignored him. "Look at me." Anselm grabbed Ilien's shoulder between thumb and forefinger. "Look!" Ilien had no choice but to look as the Giant swiveled him around. "What do you see?" asked Anselm.

"I see you," answered Ilien, rolling his eyes.

Anselm shook his head. "But what am I?"

"A Giant. What else?"

"Exactly," said Anselm. "I am a Giant. My fate was foretold

187

the moment I was conceived. I never had a choice. I was destined to be a Giant whether I liked it or not."

"So," said Ilien, turning away.

Anselm turned him back again. "Have you ever wondered why you haven't seen anyone else like me in the Drowsy Wood?"

"There's your wife."

"Besides her," said Anselm. Ilien was silent. "She and I are the only Giants in the Wood precisely because we are Giants."

"Are you telling me the Swan doesn't like your kind?" said Ilien, pulling away. "Because that doesn't sound like her at all."

"No. I'm telling you that Giants don't like *her* kind, or your kind, or any kind. Giants, Ilien, are evil. They have always been allied with Reknamarken."

"But that's impossible. You're not."

"Exactly."

Ilien shook his head and gazed back up at the stars. "You make no sense at all."

Anselm sighed and shuffled closer. He studied Ilien in silence for a moment. "When I was young," he said, but then he stopped and looked away, and Ilien waited for him to speak again.

When Anselm turned back, his face was grim. He continued in a low voice. "When I was young, I was trained in the ways of my people. Taught to fear others who were different, to hate those who didn't follow Reknamarken. To kill without feeling." He clenched his hands into fists and examined them in the firelight. "I excelled in my training. I had a great teacher. The greatest among Giants. I was taught by my very own father."

He regarded the flames of the firefly fire before him, and let out a long sigh. "But my heart was never in it, really. Even the simple things, like besting my fellow Giants in feats of strength, always made me feel bad. And the more difficult things . . . well, I cringe now at my own cruelty."

The lines of his face filled with shadows. The hiss of the fire filled the empty silence. "I was a hunter," Anselm said at last, "trained to track and kill unbelievers. To be a hunter was a great honor." He dropped his hands at his sides, and Ilien could see that he struggled with what he was going to say next.

Anselm stared into the flames, and though Ilien couldn't tell for certain, he thought he saw tears in his eyes. "I was called on one night for a hunt," said Anselm. "An important hunt. An unbeliever had fled into the hills. But this was no ordinary unbeliever. My prey had once been a leader among our people, the one who had taught me all I knew. That night, I was to hunt my very own father."

He pulled a handful of grass from the ground and threw it into the fire. A shower of sparks rose into the night.

"Hunting my father was a great show of faith," he said. "The kind of show that would prove my absolute allegiance to Reknamarken. After all, if my father could stumble from the truth, then surely I could too."

Kink whined and padded over to Anselm, curling up next to him. The Giant stroked the great dog's head in silence for a while.

"I trailed him hard," he continued. "With me were four other Giants, to make sure I did the job right, to make sure I didn't lose my nerve."

He looked at Ilien with eyes of stone. "My father died that night."

Ilien moved closer to the fire's warmth, suddenly aware how small he was sitting next to the Giant.

Anselm cleared his throat, and his expression turned bitter. "When we finally caught up to him, he was sitting alone with his back to a tree. I told the others to stay, that I'd take care of it myself so my faith could never be questioned again. I drew my knife and started forward, but halfway there I stopped.

189

Before me, my father rested unaware. Behind me, the others urged me on, their eyes gleaming with murder from the shadows. I hesitated." Anselm lowered his eyes.

"I couldn't do it. I knew then, that like my father, I too was an unbeliever." The fire popped and let out a loud hiss. The muscles of Anselm's jaw tightened, knotting in the half-light of the flickering flames. He leveled his gaze upon Ilien. "When the others saw my lack of faith, they attacked."

"What happened?" asked Ilien, feeling himself shrink even smaller before the Giant.

"I killed them. I killed them all."

A chill ran through Ilien. "And your father?"

"He was dead, dead before we even got there. He knew they had sent his son to murder him. He had killed himself so I wouldn't have to."

Anselm rose and walked to the other side of the fire. Kink followed. Ilien watched him sit back down, not knowing what to say.

"Listen and listen good," said Anselm, peering through the dancing flames at Ilien. "I'll say this once and we'll never speak of this again. I finally accepted my fate that night, but it was too late for me to do anything about it. I was born a Giant, raised a Giant, trained in the Giants' ways. It was always within my power to change all that, to control my own destiny, like you. But I chose too late."

Anselm leaned forward. The fire lit his craggy face in bright shades of orange. "We're not so different, you and I. Your fate is to be the child of Nomadin wizards, to be the one who will loose Reknamarken upon the world, to doom us all. But I've seen the powers you have. You can change all that. Just don't wait until it's too late." He lay back in the grass and was silent. "Get some rest," he said suddenly. "We rise early."

Ilien rolled over, putting his back to the Giant and his story. He thought of all the pain in the world, all the pain that seemed to come from him, all the pain he'd caused. Gallund, Thessien, Breach. He thought of Windy too. A sudden sadness overwhelmed him and he turned back to Anselm. He wanted to say something, something kind and comforting, if only to hear the words himself, but he couldn't. He watched the magical firelight in silence, the orange flames licking the air like hungry little dragon tongues. Fighting back his tears, he closed his eyes and went to sleep.

Chapter XVII

Kink's Revenge

The marble stairs beneath Ilien felt as slick as ice. His breath steamed the air as he struggled to climb them without falling. Where was he? He wanted to look but he couldn't. He was transfixed by the sight of his feet on the stairs. They were shod in huge black boots. He managed to lift one, placing it on the next stair up. Ice crystals scattered around it, tumbling past him down the stairs. His hand came into view, a man's hand, lean and hard. He looked up with a start. A row of mirrors hanging on the wall beside the stairs revealed what he already knew. Tall, with streaming black hair, he stood wrapped in a long black cloak that hung loose to his knees. He marveled for a moment at the image before him. He watched his hand in the mirror as it touched his mannish face.

"He's here!"

The shout came from farther up the stairs. It was followed by the echo of booted feet on the cold stone floor. Ilien looked up. A wizened old man clothed in emerald green robes stood above. He looked down at Ilien with eyes hewn from the frosty marble beneath him, a long, golden wand clutched in one hand. The ringing of boots on stone stopped as a dozen men clad in armor appeared behind him.

"You are a fool to come here, Reknamarken," said the old man, pointing his golden wand in Ilien's direction. "Do you really plan to defeat us all?"

His own boots were silent as Ilien began climbing the icy

stairs again. "Yes," he heard himself say in a deep, commanding voice. "Yes, I do."

The guards behind the old man shuffled their feet. Their armor filled the hall with clamor. The old man frowned and fingered the tip of his wand as if to test its sharpness. "You always were arrogant," he said. "Now you will pay for that arrogance."

Ilien expected the soldiers to step forward, but they held their positions like so many empty suits of armor. As if a bystander, Ilien watched his broken image in the mirrors beside him as he moved up the stairs. His enemies waited above, making no move to stop him.

Something's wrong, he thought suddenly. The cold in the air seemed to deepen. The light in the room dimmed, adding fear to the foreboding silence. But the man whose body he possessed was oblivious to the sense of dread he felt. His boots kept their steady march up the icy stairs. His smile remained unflinching. Yet something was very wrong. The further he moved up the stairs, the closer Ilien knew for certain he came to danger.

"You misunderstand me," he heard himself say in a voice that echoed off the rising stairs. "There is no need for fear. Your defeat will not be painful. I have no intention of causing you harm."

Still the old man waited with his clutch of soldiers. Still they made no move. But when Ilien ascended the next step they flinched as a sharp click sounded at his feet. He froze where he stood.

"Your intentions mean nothing to us," said the old man as he backed away. "And ours, well, let's just say they're not yours."

At that the old man left. The soldiers followed. The clanging of their armor faded to silence. Ilien remained as still as stone. The click at his feet could only have been one thing. His eyes searched the walls and ceiling for traps, holes designed for poisonous darts, slits for blades, anything out of the ordinary. He saw nothing. His mind reached outward, combing the smooth stone for signs of danger. The magical search was dizzying, and he nearly fell. Everything seemed normal. Cold, seamless marble surrounded him in every direction. He looked back up the stairs, but before he could proceed he heard another sharp click. This one from behind him. This one distinctly familiar. This one claws on stone.

The Groll crouched at the bottom of the stairs. A grin of curving fangs split its face from ear to ear. Smoke rose where its dripping poison pooled on the floor.

Something flashed in the mirror to Ilien's left and he gasped. The reflection he saw was no longer a man's. It was his own. Ilien spun back to face the Groll as a twelve year old boy draped in baggy man's clothes. A shrill howl pierced the cold silence and the mirrors along the wall shattered, shards of glass flying around him like stinging bees. The Groll lunged forward.

Ilien jumped in the darkness, trying to recall where he was, fighting off the urge to scream. His heart thrummed in his chest. His breath steamed the air. The cool night breeze chilled his damp skin and slowly he came to his senses. It was just a dream. He breathed deep and lay back down, pulling his discarded blanket all the way up to his chin. *Just a dream*, he thought. He curled into a tight little ball and stared out at the inky darkness. He wondered how long it would be until morning and began to shiver.

He sighed and rolled onto his back. The sky above looked thick and perilous. Low hanging clouds covered the stars. He listened to the soft hiss of the wind through the grass. Anselm mumbled in his sleep. Kink softly snored. He closed his eyes and tried to fall asleep, but he couldn't shake the fear that began to settle over him. The dream had felt so real. The confrontation with the old wizard played out in the air before him. He closed his eyes and his middle aged reflection stared back at him with that unflinching smile. The Groll's howl echoed in his ears. *You are a fool to come here, Reknamarken,* the old man had said. But where was here? Who was the old man? Was it a scene from the past? And if so, why was he witness to it?

He let his mind wander to more comforting thoughts of fishing in the small stream behind his house. He drew his pencil from his pocket, clutching it to his chest. He was glad it remained silent, and he felt a measure of comfort holding it close. He wondered if it ever slept.

Kink's snores fell silent. Anselm sat up in the darkness.

"What was that?" asked the Giant.

Ilien squeezed the pencil tight, shutting his eyes against his fear. As if from out of his dream, the Groll's howl rose like a distant siren in the night.

The darkness exploded as Anselm shot to his feet.

"Kink?" he said. "How far?"

Kink was already up, his nose tilted to the wind, his ears on end, searching. Anselm didn't wait for an answer. He rushed around the campsite, hastily packing the gear. He saddled Runner. He turned to Ilien, but Ilien had already gathered his blankets and was shoving them into his hands even then.

Another howl sounded over the plains, louder, more urgent.

"I knew we shouldn't have had a fire!" said Anselm. "Kink! How far?"

The giant dog's nose continued to test the air.

"Kink!"

Kink's shining eyes grew wide. "Less than a mile."

Anselm pulled the map from his pants pocket. "Open up, you filthy piece of paper!"

Slowly the map unfolded. "Keep your pants on!" it shouted. "Even maps need their shut eye, you know."

NOMADIN

"Wake up!" commanded Anselm. "I need to know how close we are to the Quinnebog River bridge."

"What's your rush?" asked the map, crinkling in obvious annoyance.

Anselm snapped it tight. "Just tell me!"

"The Quinnebog bridge is exactly 2.3 miles away, 3.7 kilometers if you want it in metric, that's precisely 1.75—"

"Show me!" said Anselm.

The words *you are here* appeared in red on the map, followed by an X in blue a little to the north.

"Let's go," said Anselm. He stuffed the map back into his pocket and lifted Ilien onto Runner's back. "Follow me. And stay close."

They fled their camp like ghosts in the gloom. Runner followed behind Anselm, the invisible horse a silent gust of wind, propelling Ilien forward. Kink brought up the rear, casting furtive glances over his shoulder. Ilien too looked back at the receding darkness, wondering how fast a Groll could cover a mile. At any moment he expected to see its sprinting form emerge from the shadows.

"Runner!" shouted Anselm. "Take Ilien ahead!"

Before Ilien could argue, the invisible horse surged forward. Ilien fell back, his hands grasping for the invisible reins. He flew through the air and the night whistled around him. Anselm and Kink disappeared. He soared alone through the darkness, away from danger, but he had the presence of mind to keep hold of his pencil.

"Wake up!" he shouted. "I'm gonna need you!"

The wind drowned out the pencil's complaints. Ilien peered back at the condensing gloom. He couldn't leave his friends to deal with the Groll alone. He had to help them.

"Runner! Stop! We have to go back!" He might as well have been shouting to the wind. He hauled back on what he hoped were the reins. Runner only sped faster, till the ground became a blur beneath him. The wind threatened to rip Ilien from the saddle. Soon all he could do was hunch forward, hoping not to fall off a horse he couldn't see.

A moment later the wind subsided. The ground slowed to passing grass once more. The whistling in Ilien's ears stopped as Runner checked her speed. A low rumble shook the air and Runner pulled to a sudden stop. Ilien looked up in surprise. The river thundered past them in the darkness, a boiling black scar across the plain.

Ilien tried turning the invisible horse around. "Runner!" he cried. "We have to go back!" He wasn't sure if the horse could hear him over the coursing river, let alone understand him. And no matter how he kicked and screamed, Runner wouldn't move. All he could do was turn and wait for Anselm and Kink, his pencil held ready.

"The bridge!" he cried suddenly, spinning in his saddle. "Where's the bridge?" He beat at Runner's neck. "We're trapped! We have to find the bridge!"

Suddenly Giant and dog emerged through the gloom. To anyone else they would have seemed straight from out of a nightmare, two behemoth monsters rushing forward in the night, but to Ilien they were—

Ilien's blood ran cold.

The Groll ran fast behind them.

Runner leapt forward.

"No!" screamed Ilien, but she sped toward the river, picking up speed. The water's rumble grew deafening. He shut his eyes. He couldn't watch. She was going to jump. He held on to the air in front of him as tight as he could. But at the last moment Runner veered away. She galloped along the shore and up a steep rise. Ilien looked back. Anselm and Kink still followed.

Ten yards back, so did the Groll.

Runner leaped to the side and Ilien nearly flew from the

saddle. The clop of hooves on wood sounded above the water's roar. Ilien looked down in surprise. Worm-eaten planks raced by beneath him, now and then empty air as well. Runner sped on, navigating the broken boards without missing a stride. Ilien looked up. A narrow rope bridge slithered out ahead of them, thrashing up and down in the darkness. He wondered for a moment just how much an invisible horse weighed, but before he knew it they had reached the other side. Runner stopped and spun around.

Halfway across the bridge, Anselm moved forward, gripping the side ropes, pulling himself along. His massive weight threatened to tear the bridge apart. Kink straddled the missing planks behind him. The Groll picked its way forward, closing the gap between them.

"Hurry!" shouted Ilien. But Kink and Anselm could only move so fast. As it was, Anselm had broken through the boards several times. Only the side ropes held him from the rushing torrent below. Kink fared better, but could move only as fast as Anselm. The Groll gained ground.

The boards beneath Anselm buckled again. He hugged the ropes, pulling himself upward. Kink was forced to stop. The Groll struck out eagerly with its tail, and clawed its way closer. Kink spied Ilien on shore. Their eyes locked briefly.

"Kink! No!" cried Ilien.

Kink turned to face the Groll.

"Kink!" cried Anselm. The Giant was helpless to stop him.

"There has to be something I can do," said Ilien. "I can't just sit here and watch them die."

His mind raced over the few spells he knew. Lightning? No good. He'd shock them all. Transformation? As frogs they'd fall off the bridge for sure.

"Think! Think!" he screamed.

"I am! I am!" shouted his pencil.

The remaining boards around Anselm shattered and fell into

the rushing current below. Trapped on the ropes, Anselm watched as Kink and the Groll navigated the swaying bridge toward each other.

"I've got it!" cried the pencil. "I remember!"

Words tumbled over each other in Ilien's mind, nouns and verbs, a magical sentence from out of the very ether, summoned without his knowing. He rose into the air.

"What's going on?" he cried, struggling to keep his balance. "Runner, stop!"

"It's not Runner!" shouted the pencil. "It's you. You're flying!"

"How in the—"

"Shut up and fly! You once carried Windy, now carry a Giant!"

Ilien looked in horror at the behemoth Giant clinging precariously to the swaying bridge below.

"Carry Anselm?" he said. "I can't carry Anselm. He's too heavy!"

"And you can fly?" retorted the pencil. "Now go! You can do it! I know you can!"

With a cry of desperation, Ilien leaned forward and kicked his legs.

"Stop swimming!" shouted the pencil. "Just aim me where you want to go!"

Teeth clenched, eyes wide, Ilien pointed the pencil at Anselm and shot forward, out of control.

"Watch out!" bellowed Anselm, swatting him away.

Ilien wheeled in a circle above him. "Grab hold of me!" he shouted as he swooped down toward him again. "Grab my legs!"

Anselm reached up. His massive hand closed around Ilien's ankle. Ilien pointed the pencil skyward.

"Hold on!"

A dog's shrill cry pierced the roar of the river. Ilien looked down in horror. The Groll held Kink by the neck with its human-like hands, its scorpion's tail poised to strike.

Anselm fought free of the ropes. "Kink! No!" He took a step forward and fell.

A blinding pain tore through Ilien's leg as Anselm's crushing weight dragged him toward the river. A surge of magic rushed through him, crackling and buzzing in his ears. He stopped in mid air, held aloft by an uncontrollable power. The pain in his leg vanished as anger and frustration swept through him. He dangled from the end of his pencil, and Anselm dangled from him.

"Fly! Fly!" screamed the pencil.

Ilien's body tensed rigid as a plank. Over and over he shouted his magic spell. Over and over the words rang clear above the thundering water. But he couldn't lift the Giant. By inches he sank toward the river below.

Another shrill cry sounded over the tumult. The Groll cast Kink to the planks. Its tail drove downward. The bridge shifted and the razor sharp barb arched past its target, severing a side rope. Kink twisted free, raking the Groll's face with his claws. The Groll reared in pain, clutching at its eyes, exposing his neck. Kink lunged forward.

The Groll's tail lanced out unbidden. Kink's eyes flew wide. He stood tall on his hind legs, and straight as an arrow, his chest thrust outward. The tail drove deep, pushing him back against the ropes. It quivered as it poured forth its venom.

"No!" A blinding flash accompanied Ilien's cry as he struggled to rise above the bridge. Anselm still hung from his ankle. Lightning stabbed the darkness, illuminating the scene before him. Kink crumpled to the planks. The Groll pulled its pulsing tail from Kink's body and turned toward Ilien. Deep scratches furrowed its face, exposing rich red flesh beneath its fur. Another stroke of lightning fingered the blackness above. The Groll advanced, eager to end its hunt.

Anselm loosened his grip on Ilien's ankle.

"Hold on!" cried Ilien.

"Don't look back!" shouted Anselm. "When you get to shore, ride and don't look back!" He let go of Ilien and dropped into the water below.

Ilien sailed into the air, lightning splintering the sky around him as he catapulted above the bridge. The Groll howled in rage as its target shot up and out of reach. Ilien turned and stopped twenty feet up, hovering like a storm cloud. Hot magic boiled in his veins as he looked down upon the wounded bridge. He struck out with his pencil. A bolt of lightning knifed the churning waters below, revealing the Groll as it clawed its way toward shore. He struck out again and the bridge buckled under the assault, flames pouring forth from the singed wood. The fire spread quickly, igniting the ropes. The Groll continued on undeterred.

In the light of the fire an arm rose from the river, the churning water boiling around. A hand reached up and gripped the edge of the bridge. Anselm pulled himself from the rushing current. He clung to the ropes in exhaustion, unable to defend himself as the Groll scrambled to reach him. He looked up in time to see its spiked tail hovering over him. But before the Groll could strike, the bridge shifted violently, tossing the beast off its feet. The Groll looked up in surprise.

Kink stood a dozen paces away, his powerful jaws set to sever the last remaining rope holding the bridge aloft. The Groll turned in panic. The bridge shuttered and split in two, dropping into the river below.

Ilien landed and staggered to the water's edge. He fell to his knees, his eyes searching the thundering darkness for signs of life. The river swept by him, unaffected by the sacrifices it had claimed. It tugged at the tattered remains of the rope bridge still attached to shore, its roar drowning out his cries as he held his head and wept.

201

How many more must die? he thought. *Who will be next?* He dropped his pencil and clenched his hands into useless fists. *Who will be next?*

Let it be me, he thought. *Let it be me.*

Suddenly a hand gripped his shoulder and he turned with a cry. Anselm stood behind him like a rain soaked tree. Ilien threw his arms around the Giant's leg. "Kink," he sobbed. "Kink's dead."

Anselm lifted him off the ground and cradled him in his arms. Together they stared across the tumbling water as to the east the black of night began its slow turn to grey.

Chapter XVIII

Herman the Heretic

Neither had the stomach for food but they ate a meager meal of Awefull under a flat, grey sky anyhow. They had traveled without rest all morning, making their way north toward Greattower with all the haste they could muster. They reminded themselves that their mission still lay ahead of them, but all they could think about was what lay behind.

"How much farther to Greattower?" asked Ilien. He speared his portion of the damp, spongy bread with a finger, then pulled it back in disgust.

"Not far," answered Anselm, his mouth full and slowly chewing. "A hard day's ride perhaps."

Ilien had convinced the Giant to stop and eat. Not only were they safe from pursuit, but Ilien was sure he'd get sick if he was forced to eat something as nauseating as Awefull on horse back. So they sat amidst the tall, swaying grass, their conversation a mask against the sadness they felt for Kink's loss.

"I think when this is all over I'm gonna go back home and make amends with my wife," said Anselm, chewing thoughtfully. "She may have her faults, but . . ." He trailed off into silence.

Ilien couldn't think that far ahead. Too much lay ahead of him. Windy still huddled alone under Greattower Mountain. The NiDemon still awaited him. And if he ever did get back home, how could things ever be the same again? His life was changed forever now.

"I suppose we should go," was all he said. They mounted up and rode on.

They traveled hard across the plains, keeping a watchful eye on the distant horizon. Anselm ran like a Giant possessed, flying over the earth in long, powerful strides. Runner matched the reckless pace with ease. Ilien wasn't sure if the Giant was running to reach their destination, or fleeing from where they'd been. *Probably a little bit of both*, he thought.

The sun arched slowly across the sky and dusk approached. Ilien kept looking over his shoulder as they traveled, expecting to see Kink running crookedly behind them. Each time he glanced back it felt like waking from a bad dream into a nightmare. Each time his heart grew heavier with the realization that Kink was gone forever.

"Look!" said Anselm, slowing from his reckless pace to catch his breath. The afternoon sun laid a golden blanket across the flat expanse of grassland that stretched out before them. But far in the distance a pile of pale purple rose from the land, casting a jagged smear of shadows beside it. "Greattower!"

Ilien rose up and down in the air as Runner cantered along beside the Giant. "How far?" he asked, squinting into the light.

Anselm lifted a hand to shield his eyes from the angled sun. "Tomorrow midday."

Tomorrow midday, thought Ilien. *Then there'll be no turning back.*

"Come on," said Anselm. He picked up the pace again.

They traveled a few miles more but the mountain never moved. It seemed stuck on the horizon, refusing to be approached. Anselm ran on faster, but Ilien held Runner back a moment. He eyed Greattower's purple peak, his stomach tied in knots. Purple, the color of childhood, once his favorite color. He took a deep breath. Somewhere under that innocent hue lurked a demon.

"Ilien!"

Anselm's cry spurred Ilien forward. The Giant had stopped up ahead. When Ilien drew near he saw what had halted him.

The ground before them had been beaten to a muddy pulp. A path twenty men wide had been trampled into the plains. It came from the east and swung northward in front of them, stretching out into a straight, brown line toward Greattower. Anselm put out his hand to stop Ilien from riding on it. He walked along its edge, studying the grass as he went.

Ilien looked close. At the Giant's feet were footprints that matched his own.

"Those are Giant's prints," said Ilien.

Anselm placed his foot over a muddy impression. It was as if he had made it himself.

"Aren't they?" asked Ilien, taken aback by Anselm's sudden silence. The Giant nodded.

"A hunt?"

"No. Not a hunt," said Anselm, his eyes brighter than usual. "An army."

Ilien watched the hair on Anselm's arms stand straight on end. "An army of Giants, headed for Greattower? What do we do now?" he asked.

"What do you mean, what do we do? If they lie between us and Greattower then we'll have to go around."

"But we don't have time," said Ilien. "There's an army of wierwulvs carrying the soul of the Necromancer behind us. If we go around we'll never make it to Greattower before the Book."

"Have you ever seen an army of Giants?" asked Anselm. He stepped toward Ilien, rising above him, blocking out the light of the sun. "I'm considered small among my people."

"But we can't go around," argued Ilien. "There isn't time."

Anselm stood over him a moment longer, as if to take measure of the small boy who stood in his shadow, then he stepped back.

"The Giants must be waiting for the wierwulvs to arrive with the Book," he said, turning his attention to the muddy track again. "We'll have to move fast. We'll head east, and follow the trail they came along until nightfall. Come morning we'll head north again. That should keep us a safe distance from any Killer Scouts trailing the main army."

"Killer Scouts?" Ilien's glare faded away and he was just a boy once more, frightened and bewildered.

"I know you're worried about Windy," said Anselm. "Too much has been placed upon your shoulders already. This is my decision to make. Trust me. We don't want to meet with an army of Giants. We have to avoid them at all costs. It's the only way." The Giant tousled Ilien's hair. "You remind me of my own boy, you know. He was proud and brave too."

Ilien started, but before he could say anything further Anselm took off running.

"Come on!" cried the Giant.

As they sped along the trampled ground, Ilien felt relieved that Anselm had decided on their current course. Some of the tracks they passed were enormous. He could only imagine the size of the Giants who had made them. And imagine he did, until he had Runner flying so fast over the plains that Anselm had to struggle to keep up.

Soon the overcast grey of day began its descent into darkness and they were forced to stop. Their campsite was little more than a few blankets laid on the grass in the dark, a few for Anselm, one for Ilien. Anselm insisted they not light a fire, so Ilien reclined in the gloom, peering into the small vial of fireflies. The two remaining bugs wandered aimlessly about its bottom, their rumps lit like tiny glowing cigars. Every time they reached the side they turned and wandered back the other way.

"What makes everything in the Drowsy Wood so different from the rest of the world?" he asked, tipping the jar upside down to watch the bugs fall from top to bottom like miniature shooting stars.

"The question you should ask," said Anselm from somewhere in the grass to his left, "is what makes the rest of the world so different from the Drowsy Wood. The Drowsy Wood came first, after all."

"What's the difference?" asked Ilien as he leveled the jar again, secretly desiring to open the lid and free its captives. "Either way it's the same."

"It's not the same at all," said Anselm.

"It is if it doesn't change the facts."

"Why the fox eats the rabbit is a completely different question from why the rabbit gets eaten by the fox," said Anselm. "But as you know the facts are the same. The rabbit gets eaten. Point of view makes all the difference."

"Okay, okay," conceded Ilien, rolling onto his back and placing the vial of fireflies up to one eye. "Then why is the rest of the world so different from the Drowsy Wood?"

"Because of the wizards."

Ilien looked over at the darkness surrounding Anselm. "Did the wizards create the Drowsy Wood?"

"No," replied Anselm. "They destroyed it, all except what's left today."

"They destroyed it?" said Ilien, sitting back up. "Why would they do that?"

"To keep Reknamarken from winning the war, why else?"

Anselm sat up in the dark. To Ilien he looked like the shadow of some gigantic boulder tossed onto the plains from the mountain far away.

"You know," said Anselm, "for a Nomadin, you don't know much."

"Just tell me," said Ilien

"Alright. Here we go, then. History of the Drowsy Wood, lesson one," laughed the Giant.

"Will you knock if off?" said Ilien. "I'm serious."

Anselm chuckled to himself, then cleared his throat. He sat in silence for a moment, as if collecting his thoughts. When he turned back to Ilien, his eyes held a measure of caution. Ilien had the feeling that what he was about to say was a close-held secret.

"When Reknamarken came to Nadae," Anselm began, "the Drowsy Wood stretched the world over. Nadae was a paradise, more beautiful than you could ever imagine." The Giant leaned forward suddenly, his face losing all merriment. "And Reknamarken desired it all for himself."

Anselm frowned and sat back up. "His lust for power was insatiable, uncontrollable, even by the combined armies of the four kings. Soon Reknamarken and his minions crushed any who stood in their way, and it looked like he would win the war for no one knew how to stop him. Even the Nomadin were no match against him. Only through sheer luck did the Nomadin discover the source of his power and turn the tides of battle."

"How's that?" asked Ilien. He was so wrapped up in the beginning of Anselm's tale, he didn't notice that the vial of fireflies had fallen from his hands.

"As the war progressed," continued Anselm, "there were patches of enchanted forest that were literally obliterated by the forces of battle, scraped clean to the dirt below, to the very bones of the earth. The Nomadin noticed that Reknamarken avoided these areas whenever he could. Every battle fought in one of these blasted fields or decimated glens went decisively to the Four Armies. And where the Drowsy Wood remained, the bones of brave soldiers littered the ground. There, without exception, Reknamarken prevailed. It was obvious then."

"What was obvious?"

"It was obvious that the magic of the Drowsy Wood filled the Necromancer and his armies with power," answered

208

Anselm. "And once the wizards realized this they at once set about cutting the Wood to ribbons, burning it to the bare ground. Soon nearly all the enchanted forest had vanished, and soon too had Reknamarken's army. After the Necromancer's defeat, what little that remained of the Drowsy Wood was hidden from the rest of the world forever."

"So that's why the Swan said Reknamarken must never discover its secrets," said Ilien as he picked up the vial of fireflies once more.

"Yes," answered Anselm through the gloom.

"But why leave any at all? Why didn't the wizard's just finish the job so Reknamarken and his armies could never rise again?"

"Would you want to be the one to completely destroy paradise?" asked Anselm.

Ilien watched the fireflies crawl up the side of their jar. "I guess not," he said.

But deep inside he knew that if the prophesy proved correct, he might just do worse than that.

The next morning found them staring once more down the length of the trampled mud highway that led back to the east. The newly risen sun was beginning to bake it brown and hard, releasing an odor of tilled soil and cut grass. The smell reminded Ilien of Farmer Parson's neatly rowed fields back home.

Anselm peered out toward Greattower, now a little ways off to their left. "I think we can head north now without fear of stumbling on any Killer Scouts," he said.

"Are you sure?" asked Ilien. He had conjured up images of Giant Killer Scouts all night long and didn't at all like what he had seen.

"Well no," said Anselm. "But we can't circle all the way around to the other side of Greattower. The wierwulvs weren't that far behind us. We'll have to take our chances if we're to beat them to the mountain. So mount up."

Ilien put two fingers to his lips and whistled. Over the last few days he'd finally gotten use to having an invisible horse; or maybe Runner was getting use to things, he wasn't sure. Either way, he knew that once he whistled Runner would be standing to his left, ready to ride. He turned to mount up and saw four Giants racing toward him with drawn swords.

"Killer Scouts!" he cried, clawing at his pockets for his pencil, his mind fumbling for a spell. But before one could come to him, Anselm stepped forward, and with a swipe of his forearm sent the attackers sprawling into the grass. Peering from between Anselm's legs, Ilien saw that they weren't Giants at all. They were men, men with razor sharp swords. They quickly assembled into a tiny regiment and prepared to attack.

"Wait!" came a shout behind Ilien. The men stopped but held their swords at the ready.

Ilien turned and froze. He couldn't believe his eyes. "Thessien?"

"Ilien?" The Eastland prince held his sword in one hand. The other he ran across the stubble of his face. "Well I'll be," he said. "It *is* you."

"Thessien!" cried Ilien, and he ran to meet him.

Thessien sheathed his sword and grasped Ilien by the shoulders. "I can't believe it! It really is you!" he said, pulling him into a bear hug. He looked around suddenly. "The princess, Ilien. Where is she?" He looked at Anselm and reached for his sword. "What's going on here?"

"Anselm's a friend," said Ilien, quickly. Thessien pushed his way forward. "A friend," repeated Ilien, grabbing the prince of Ashevery by the arm. "Windy's been captured. We're out to save her."

"Captured?" said Thessien, keeping his hand where it was, but finally looking down at Ilien. "By the Giants?"

"No. By the NiDemon."

Ilien related to Thessien all that had happened since they'd last parted—their flight from the Groll, the Drowsy Wood, Windy's capture, Anselm, the Swan, the stealing of the Book by the wierwulvs, and finally the battle at the bridge. He purposefully left out his own part in all of it, and wondered if Anselm would let him keep it secret. He didn't feel like telling Thessien that he was destined to doom the world. At least, not just yet. The Giant kept silent after he finished, but Thessien looked oddly at Ilien nonetheless.

"Yes, I know the Book's been captured," said Thessien. He looked at Anselm. "But not by the wierwulvs. By the Giants."

"The Giants?" said Ilien, looking to Anselm.

"Yes. The Giants," answered Thessien. "They sacked Kingsend Castle and took the Book with them. We've trailed them for the last four days." Thessien's men stepped forward with a silent signal from the Eastland prince. "Tell me," said Thessien. "Why is it that you travel with a Giant?" He drew his sword halfway from its sheath.

Anselm remained as still as stone, but Ilien could plainly see that his ears were beginning to turn red.

"And what does a NiDemon want with the princess?" asked Thessien. "Tell me Ilien, what has this Giant told you?"

"Wait," said Ilien as Thessien's men advanced a step on Anselm. "Anselm's my friend. He's my protector. There's more to my story than I've told you."

Thessien raised a hand to halt his men, but his eyes never left Anselm. "Then let me hear it from him," he said, fingering the pommel of his sword. "So, Giant, tell me what he's not telling us? Why is it that we find you bringing this boy to Greattower when a NiDemon hides beneath the mountain and an army of your own kind holds the Book that imprisons the Necromancer?"

Anselm stared unblinking at the man half his size before

him. "As you well know, Thessien Atenmien, oh Brat of Ashevery, this boy is the prophesied child."

Thessien's sword rang free of its scabbard, but he made no move to attack. "I know too that you would like nothing better than to unite this boy with the Book to release your Master!" he cried. "Speak quickly your case for our sparing you, for all I see is a Giant stealing candy from a child!"

"And all I see is a prince who meddles where he shouldn't," replied Anselm, his hands clenching into fists. "Though your fame will never equal that of your brother, you are far more notorious. They don't call you brat for nothing, oh prince who forsook his title."

Thessien strode forward, undaunted by the Giant's size.

"Stop!" shouted Ilien, grabbing Thessien's sword arm and pulling him up short. "It was my decision to come here, not Anselm's. I chose to rescue Windy. She's been captured to lure me before the NiDemon. I have to face it or she'll be killed. There is no trickery, Thessien. Anselm saved my life."

"Am I to believe that a Giant is out to help you defeat the Necromancer and rescue the princess of Evernden?" said Thessien, leveling his sword at Anselm, the look on his face one of disbelief.

"Yes," said Ilien, refusing to let go of Thessien's arm.

"And why?"

"Because Anselm isn't evil. He doesn't follow the Necromancer. He's wanted for treason by his own people."

Thessien's eyes opened wide. "A heretic?" The other four men exchanged knowing glances. "Tell me, Giant," said Thessien, his brow raised questioningly, "what is your name?"

"I've already told you his name," said Ilien.

Thessien raised a finger at Ilien to silence him. "Tell me, Giant. Your name. What is it? And be truthful. It may save your life."

A crimson wave of fury passed across Anselm's stony

features. His ears burned like hot coals. His neck turned purple. Ilien squeezed his pencil tight. There was about to be trouble—big trouble.

"Herman Hedrick Humphrey the Third," replied Anselm between clenched teeth.

A snicker from one of the men sent Anselm into a tirade.

"You think it's funny?" he said. "Well I'll have you know that there's more to a person than just his name. What do you think your precious king of Kingsend's real name is? Ruppert! That's what! Ruppert Ruppert Ruppert the Fourth! That's right, three Rupperts in a row!"

The men backed away, trying not to laugh. Even Thessien cracked a smile as he sheathed his sword.

Ilien looked on in confusion. "So you believe him because his name is not Anselm?"

"No," said Thessien. "His name is definitely not Anselm, but that's not why we believe him. You don't know who this is? He's none other than Herman the Heretic. He's legendary—or almost legendary. I never much believed he existed until now. Herman Hedrick Humphrey the Heretic. Once and future king of the Giants."

"King of the Giants?" said Ilien, looking at Anselm as if for the very first time.

"Why of course," said Thessien, "until he was driven into hiding by his own people."

Anselm was still ranting under his breath about the evils of name calling and the harm it can do to a person's fragile self-esteem, especially children, when Thessien approached him and held out his hand.

"My apologies, Lord Herman," said Thessien.

Anselm froze. He regarded Thessien's hand with a frown. "It's Anselm to you," he said.

Thessien grabbed Anselm's hand, or tried to. He could barely fit his fingers around the Giant's thumb. "Welcome

213

aboard, Anselm. I'm sorry for the rude treatment but I had to be sure you weren't, well, you know . . . a Giant."

The red in Anselm's body began to drain away. At that the other men gathered around.

"I'll be. I don't believe it," said one, dropping his sword to the ground to shake Anselm's hand with both his own. "To think I got a black eye from Herman the Heretic!" He rubbed at the spot where Anselm's forearm had struck him.

The tips of Anselm's ears flushed red. "Call me Herman again and you won't believe what else I'll give you."

The man smiled weakly and retrieved his fallen sword.

"Well," said Thessien, clapping Ilien on the back. "I do believe our stumbling on you is a stroke of luck twice over. Not only is it a blessing to find you still alive, but now we have what we've been looking for all along."

"What's that?" asked Ilien, finally breathing a sigh of relief.

Thessien smiled. "A way to steal back the Book!"

Chapter XIX

The Giant's Encampment

N o way," said Anselm when Thessien laid out his plan to steal the Book from under the very noses of five-thousand Giants. "It's suicide."

Ilien shook his head. He too couldn't believe what Thessien was proposing. It couldn't possibly be done.

"Let's go over it again," said Thessien. He spoke like a college professor talking to grade-schoolers. "It's really quite simple. Anselm will enter the Giant's encampment at nightfall. He'll locate the Book, wait for our diversion, then steal it back." The four men behind him were all nodding their heads. "It doesn't get any simpler than that."

"Except you left out one minor complication," said Anselm.

Thessien put his head in his hands. "Now what could that possibly be?"

"I'll be caught and hung on the spot!" cried Anselm.

"No you won't," said Thessien, throwing up his hands, his face turning red. "Listen. Our diversion will be such that the whole camp will have no choice but to leave their posts. Then you'll only be left with a guard or two protecting the Book."

"How do you know there'll only be a guard or two protecting the Book?" asked Anselm. "There could easily be a dozen."

"Trust me. There won't be after the diversion we'll create."

"And what would that be?" asked Anselm. "Will the sky fall down around them? Will you conjure up the armies of King-send from thin air?" He turned to Ilien and rolled his eyes.

"Yes," said Thessien, and he reached into the pocket of his cloak and produced an ordinary looking horn.

"The Horn of Plenty," said Ilien, stepping forward.

"Yes, the Horn of Plenty," said Thessien as he admired the magical talisman, turning it over in his hands. "The princess was thoughtful enough to leave it behind. After the Groll stung me and left me for dead, I raced back to her room and found it on her bed."

"You were stung by the Groll?" asked Ilien. "But how—"

Thessien parted his cloak to reveal his armor beneath. "The blow left me stunned, nothing more. Funny, really, the spike of a Groll's tail fails where a small thorn succeeds. Once I recovered my wits I raced after you, but you were already gone, and so was the Groll."

"And the king's soldier?" asked Ilien. "The one who helped us escape? What happened to him?"

"Bad chain mail," said Thessien, shaking his head.

"I hate to interrupt," said Anselm, "but can we possibly go over how a little boy's bugle is going to help us steal the Necromancer's imprisoned soul from an army of Giants."

"It's a magical horn," explained Ilien. "A single call sounds like the blast of a hundred horns from every direction." He looked at it, his enthusiasm suddenly waning. "At least that's what Windy told me."

"Like I said," said Thessien, "it's really very simple. You'll enter the camp and locate the Book. We'll blow the horn which will fool the Giants into thinking they're under attack. They'll undoubtedly send every available Giant out to meet what they think is an large opposing army. You'll overpower whatever guards remain and simply walk out of the camp the other way, Book in hand. Once a safe distance away, make your way to Berkhelven. We'll meet up with you there."

"But how will you know when Anselm's located the Book?" asked Ilien.

Thessien's eyes lit up. "That's where you come in," he said. "You'll shoot that pesky little light of yours into the air. That'll be our signal."

Ilien looked doubtful. "But how will *I* know when Anselm's located the Book?"

"This will never work!" came a muffled cry from under Anselm's animal skin shirt. The moving bulge beneath made the Giant appear pregnant—fifteen months pregnant. He chuckled each time it shifted positions. Ilien popped his head out from Anselm's collar. "This is just ridiculous!"

"No it's not," said Thessien, a bit too seriously in Ilien's opinion. "It serves two purposes. It will get you inside the camp so you can send us the signal, and you'll create a perfect disguise for Anselm. Between the growth of several days' beard and the appearance that he's a hundred pounds over-weight, no one could possibly recognize him as Herman the Heretic."

"Hey!" shouted Anselm. "What did I tell you about calling me that name?"

"It will never work," said Ilien, ignoring Anselm's outburst. "How do you know that horn is really magical? Most of Windy's talismans turned out to be . . . well . . . me."

"Trust me. It works," said Thessien. "Just keep your head down and everything will go as planned."

Anselm pushed Ilien's head below his collar.

It popped back out.

"It smells in there!" cried Ilien. "I don't think this is such a good idea." He started to climb out of Anselm's shirt. "Besides, I can't waste my time on this suicide mission when there's already a NiDemon waiting for me elsewhere. I've got my own suicide mission, you know. I have to get to Greattower."

"Why is that?" asked Thessien, stepping forward and suddenly turning serious. "To beat the Book there? It's already

217

there, Ilien. The Giants are camped on Greattower's doorstep and if we don't get the Book back now you won't ever be able to help the princess. This is her only chance."

Ilien froze halfway out of Anselm's shirt. "What makes you think that they're not taking the Book to the NiDemon even as we speak?" he asked. He looked like some strange two-headed monster with his head and shoulders still poking out from Anselm's collar.

"We don't have time for this," he said.

"Yes we do," said Thessien. "Giants are extremely superstitious. They believe that Book holds the very embodiment of God. They won't bring it before the NiDemon until later tonight, possibly morning, after their dark ceremonies."

Anselm nodded and craned his neck to look at Ilien. "He's right. You can bet the Book hasn't been delivered yet. Giant ceremonies are long, drawn out affairs with lots of incense burning, seances and sacrifices."

"Sacrifices!" Ilien would have shrunk back under Anselm's shirt but the smell was prohibitive.

"It's not what you think," said Anselm. "It's mostly goats and pigs. The smell of roasting bacon is actually quite nice."

"We only get one chance at this," said Thessien. "It's now or never."

Ilien writhed about under Anselm's animal skins. "But what about the Killer Scouts. There's sure to be Killer Scouts trailing the main army."

Thessien broke into laughter. "Killer Scouts? Trailing the main army? Where did you ever get that idea?"

Anselm looked sheepish. Ilien gave a kick to his ribs.

"Hey! Watch it!" cried the Giant. "I had to say something to keep you from following the Giant army like a fool."

Thessien turned to go. "Now climb down from there, Ilien. We're leaving."

Ilien crawled out from under Anselm's collar. "Killer

Scouts," he mumbled. He scaled his way down Anselm's torso none-too-gently.

Thessien blew a sharp whistle and five horses rose up from the grass where they had been lying low. Ilien and Anselm jumped in alarm at the sudden sound of bits and bridles and flailing hooves. Thessien smiled.

"There's nothing like a well-trained horse," said one of Thessien's men, patting the neck of his mount.

Ilien too gave a sharp whistle. A snicker went up from the now mounted men. A gust of wind ruffled their hair.

"Horse run off on ya?" laughed one.

Ilien climbed aboard Runner.

The man fell out of his saddle.

"No. Why?" asked Ilien, holding the invisible reins with both hands. Anselm laughed and shook his head.

According to Thessien, they would reach the Giant's encampment by nightfall. Ilien couldn't see how that was possible. Compared to Runner, the other horses only limped along. Ilien had to keep a tight rein just so they could keep up. And by the looks the men gave him, one would have thought they had never seen anyone ride an invisible horse before.

Ilien sighed. He eyed the looming mountain on the horizon. The late afternoon sun painted its smooth sides purple and grey. There was nothing else to do but make the best of it. Besides, there was no point in rushing toward his death just to stop short of the gallows and wait for his executioners to catch up. *Steal back the Book*, he thought. He shook his head at his own foolishness.

"So, you're a king?" asked Ilien as Anselm jogged beside him. "Should I call you Your Majesty?"

"Call me whatever you want," said Anselm with a sideways glance. "Just don't call me Herman."

Ilien nudged Runner closer. "And you have a son?"

Anselm nodded and wiped the sweat from his forehead.

219

Though the pace they set was anything but vigorous, the angled sun fell warmly on them as they traveled.

"How old is he?" asked Ilien.

"Eighty-two," replied the Giant.

Ilien lurched in his invisible saddle. "Eighty-two?"

Anselm jogged along without missing a step. "Yup. Eighty-two. And currently king of the Giants."

"But how's that possible?" asked Ilien.

"I know," said Anselm. "Eighty-two is a bit young for a king. But he was next in line when I fled."

"No. Not that. I mean eighty-two, that would make you at least . . ." Ilien calculated in his head for a moment. "At least a hundred!"

"A hundred!" said Anselm. "I've always been told I look good for my age, but a hundred? I'm flattered." Anselm watched Ilien out of the corner of his eye. Finally he broke into laughter. "Giant's don't age the same as humans, Ilien. We move a little slower. Mature a bit more carefully."

Ilien frowned. "I suppose you're going to say, like fine wine."

Anselm smiled and puffed out his chest as he ran.

"So just how old are you?" asked Ilien.

"Two hundred and fifteen."

"That's some old wine," replied Ilien.

Anselm's look turned sour.

"And your son?" asked Ilien. "Does he still follow Reknamarken?"

The Giant stared off at Greattower and wiped the sweat from his forehead again. "For now," he said. "For now."

Anselm remained silent in contemplation, and Ilien knew that the conversation was ended. He had plenty to contemplate himself, but every time he thought of what they were doing, his mind froze in terror. He busied himself with a small piece of Awefull instead. The putrid taste kept his thoughts in the present, and deep down he knew that it might be his last meal for a while.

They traveled without break for nearly an hour more. The setting sun cast their shadows long and thin behind them. They struggled on through the dying light until darkness pushed the glowing sun beneath the horizon. Ilien led the way on Runner. The others filed out behind him. They stopped at the crest of a small rise, and the land curved and fell away before them—a gigantic bowl with Greattower rising up from its center, cold and glistening in the starlight. Lights twinkled around it, the distant fires of the Giant's army.

"Not far now," said Thessien, and they made their way wearily into the valley.

It wasn't long before they stopped and dismounted, only a few hundred yards from the first of the Giant's many bonfires. Thessien and his men laid their horses down in the grass again. Ilien simply whispered, "Stay close, Runner. I have a bad feeling about all this."

Thessien motioned for his men to set up watches in four different directions. He turned to Ilien. "Okay. It's time." He looked suddenly around. "Anselm? Where's Anselm?"

Anselm appeared through the gloom, fiddling with the buttons on his pants. "Sorry," he said sheepishly. "Like my mum used to say, go now or forever hold your pee."

Thessien shook his head. "Just get over there by Ilien!" He cast a cold glance at Giant and boy standing side by side. "Good. Now up you go, Ilien."

Anselm held out his hand. Ilien looked at it disdainfully.

"What?" asked Anselm.

Ilien raised an eyebrow and began climbing up the Giant's body without assistance.

Anselm looked at his hand, then back at Ilien again. "What? What's the matter?"

Thessien gave a quiet whistle, and four quiet whistles from

221

his men called back through the gloom. "Good. All is set," he said. He turned to Anselm. "Now, you *do* know what to do?" Anselm nodded. "Just remember to stay calm, and follow the plan," said Thessien. "Don't panic if things go wrong. Act natural." He studied the Giant for a moment as Ilien writhed about beneath Anselm's animal skin shirt. "Oh, and Anselm?"

"I know," said the Giant, turning to go. "We'll meet you back at Berkhelven."

"No. Not that," said Thessien as Ilien still struggled to get settled. "Try to keep to the shadows."

Ilien coaxed Globe to life beneath Anselm's animal skins with a whisper. The magical light flared brightly then settled to a dim burn. The faint illumination turned the interior of the Giant's shirt into a small, dingy cave. "You know what to do," said Ilien to Globe. "Don't screw this up. Wait for my command." Globe's pale light revealed a small hole in Anselm's shirt and Ilien poked his finger into it. "Isn't this a stroke of luck," he said, removing his finger and peeking through the hole. Though Anselm would scarcely have noticed it, the small rent in his shirt was just big enough for Ilien to see through.

As Anselm padded off toward the Giants' encampment, he looked like a goose fattened for the feast. He avoided the first bonfire he came to where a few lonely Giants reclined in the grass cooking some sort of meat on sticks. The smell of real food made Ilien's stomach rumble beneath Anselm's shirt. He wasn't really hungry with all the Awefull he had eaten, but Awefull was anything but appetizing, and the thick, sweet smell of roasting meat was almost more than he could bear.

They passed through the shadows unnoticed, heading for the center of the camp. At first they found it easy to make their way all but ignored, just another solitary soldier wandering about. But the further they went the more bonfires they passed. Soon there was hardly a shadow to cling to. It wasn't long before those around the fires began looking up to see who was so eager to make his way past. Ilien realized then that Anselm wasn't so much walking as running. He poked him in the stomach and the Giant slowed, continuing on at a more leisurely pace.

Beneath the shirt things were beginning to get hairy as well. Anselm's nervousness was taking its toll on Ilien. The Giant was sweating profusely.

"Hey! Hey you there!" called a rather short Giant, as Giants go, from around one of the bonfires they passed. "Yes, you. Come over here."

Through his peephole, Ilien could vaguely discern two other Giants sitting on the sawn off stumps of trees. A third emerged from the shadows rolling another log toward the fire.

The short Giant pointed a blunt finger at Anselm. "You, soldier! I said get over here right now!"

Anselm hesitated and Ilien wondered what he was doing.

"Don't stop now," he whispered. "Keep going! Keep going!" He was about to give Anselm an elbow to the ribs when he heard a shout.

"That's an order!"

Anselm jumped forward. Ilien lost his balance and fell back against the Giant's hairy chest. He scrambled to regain his footing, attempting to maneuver his way back to the peephole while trying to keep as still as possible at the same time.

"What's your name, soldier?" asked the Giant as Anselm approached.

Ilien reached the hole and looked out. The Giant stood before them, and his short, bandy legs nearly formed an O, he was so bowlegged.

"I said what is your name?"

"An—Andrew," replied Anselm, an octave higher than usual, stopping a few paces away.

"Andrew sir!" shouted the Giant, thrusting out his barrel chest. "Don't you know how to address an officer?" Upon his

223

dirty tunic he wore a tarnished pin, a lump of lead that Ilien assumed was some sort of medal of honor.

Anselm kept his head down. "I'm sorry sir," he said in his falsetto voice.

"Sorry?" screamed the officer. "Why I ought to court-martial you right here and now! Get over here. I said come closer and let me get a look at you!" Anselm moved forward. Ilien held his breath. The officer studied Anselm closely, and Ilien was so certain he would be seen peering out the hole in Anselm's shirt that he closed his eyes tight.

"Boy, you sure are a big fellow," remarked the officer. "I guess you'll do. We need a fifth for cards. Now sit down."

Ilien let out a breath and looked back through his peephole. One of the other Giants had broken out a deck of cards. His fingernails glistened black and oily, and he smelled to Ilien like a ham gone bad, even beneath Anselm's shirt.

"I don't know how those stupid humans play with these god-awful things," said the Giant. "They're so darn small. Whose idea was it to steal 'em, anyway?"

"Shut your trap, Willy, and get this soldier a stump," commanded the officer.

A stump was rolled out and Anselm took his place around the fire, careful not to sit too near Willy.

"We're playing War," declared the officer. " Deal 'em, Will."

As Will attempted to shuffle the cards, cursing under his breath, the Giant sitting opposite Anselm said, "Are you as excited as I am? I still can't believe it." His left eye protruded as he spoke, bulging forth with every word, and snot leaked from his nose, running down across his lips. Anselm looked away in disgust. Ilien winced but didn't dare move.

"I mean, how much easier could it be?" said the Giant, spraying snot all around. "First we sack Kingsend Castle like there was nobody home. And the Book, being unguarded and all. It was like stealing mutton from a twenty year old." The Giant sniffed the air and sucked a drooling green puddle back up his nose. "Speaking of mutton, when are the ceremonies gonna start? I'm starving."

Will threw cards at everyone until the deck was spent. Anselm's cards collected in a loose pile on his lap.

"You don't look so good," said Will, nodding at Anselm's distended stomach where Ilien's knees pushed out his shirt. "What'd you do? Eat a goat, hooves and all?"

The others roared with laugher.

"Shut up!" barked the Giant in command. "This ain't no sorority. Play cards!"

In the moment that everyone gave heed to their cards, Anselm pushed Ilien's knees back down—a bit too hard. Ilien grunted in pain.

"Bad goat," said Anselm in response to everyone's stares, and he put a hand on his stomach to hide Ilien's movements.

They soon settled down and played war, the object of the game being to throw out a card and hope it was the highest in the pile. The problem was, no one could read the writing on the tiny cards.

"Hey!" yelled Will. "Kings beat queens! Give up the pile!"

"That's not a king, you idiot," replied the other, rising to his feet in a surge of anger. "That's a three! The pile's mine!"

As Ilien saw it, Anselm's ace beat them all. He hoped Anselm knew better than to point this out. It was best to keep quiet before war really did break out. As it was, the two opposing Giants had thrown their cards at each other's faces and were reaching for their logs.

"Knock it off! That's an order!" shouted the officer.

The two warring Giants returned their stumps to the ground and their rumps to the stumps.

"Pick up your cards. Save it for the real thing," said the officer. "There'll be plenty of skull bashing when those men bring their army down here. And believe me, they will. So save your strength. Let's play."

The Giant sitting near Willy grinned a mouthful of crooked teeth. "I can't wait to see their faces when Reknamarken rises again. I bet you he's free already." A shiver of joy coursed through his massive body.

"For the love of Evil! Another idiot!" shouted the officer. "Reknamarken won't be free until we bring the Book before the NiDemon! Now shut yer mouth and play!"

The other Giant shivered again, this time without the smile. "NiDemons give me the willies."

"Me too," said Willy, suddenly pulling a roasted ham leg from his pocket. He waved away a swarm of flies that came out with it.

"I don't like 'em any better than you," said the officer, straightening the medal upon his shirt. "But the NiDemon does have the Nomadin-child, and she does has the key. As unpleasant as a NiDemon can be, it can't be helped." He patted the medal twice before looking up with a leer. "Reknamarken will be free soon enough."

Beneath Anselm's shirt Ilien couldn't believe his ears, and it wasn't because of the loudest growls he'd ever heard a stomach make. The Giants believed Windy was the prophesied child! Ilien was so surprised that without thinking he popped his head out from Anselm's collar.

A moment of silence fell around the campfire. Ilien's eyes were as wide as Anselm's. The eyes staring back at him were double-sized.

The blast of horns split the night, and Ilien dove back beneath Anselm's shirt. What was going on? He hadn't given the signal. Globe was still there with him. The horns sounded again and a cry went up. "The ceremonies are starting! The ceremonies are starting!"

The Giants around the fire jumped to their feet, caught between the confusion of the moment and the excitement of the entire camp. When they looked back at Anselm, he was gone.

Anselm melted into the throbbing crowd, losing himself in the rush of massive bodies. He flowed along the river of Giants, careful to keep his head down. When he looked back, his pursuers were nowhere in sight.

"Nice going," he grunted to his shirt. He veered off into a shadowed area where no one would notice him, and poked his belly hard. "You could've gotten us killed!"

"Sorry," came the muffled answer. Ilien's head slowly crept out. "It just happened. But didn't you hear them? They think Windy is me."

"I know. I know," said Anselm. "I never said my kind were very bright." A pig-nosed Giant ran past, squealing with joy. "Or good looking." He pushed Ilien's head back beneath his shirt. "Now get back down. We have to locate the Book."

Ilien's head sprang out again. "We're surrounded by a stampeding herd of Giants," he said. "How do you suppose we do that now?"

"We follow the herd to the ceremonies," said Anselm. "After all, the Book is the guest of honor."

Ilien cried out his protest but Anselm stuffed him back down to the smelly dungeons below his collar.

"Just keep your head down this time, and wait for my signal," said the Giant, and he took off running. Ilien tucked himself into a ball and tried to ignore the growing pool of sweat beneath him.

Anselm stayed alert as he jogged along amidst the throng of

other Giants. His card-playing buddies could show up at any moment and finger him as a traitor—again! It wasn't that he minded being a traitor, but he had a sinking feeling he wouldn't escape so easily this time around. Fortunately, no one took notice of him in all the excitement.

Within moments the crowd thickened to a land-locked sea of sweaty, jostling Giants. Anselm shouldered his way forward as gently as anyone can shoulder their way forward, keeping an eye out for any sign of those who might recognize him. A cry arose up ahead and surged among the bystanders. Anselm ducked down, but his fears were soon allayed. In the light of the many fires, an unusually large Giant, even as Giants go, stood above the crowd on a tall, sawn off stump. The other Giants danced around and cheered as the monstrous Giant held up a hand to calm the crowd. The other hand he held behind his back.

"I'm going in to get a closer look!" cried Anselm.

Beneath the thick animal skins of Anselm's shirt, Ilien had no idea what was happening outside. The roar of the crowd was deafening, even from under an inch of cow hide. And as he listened and waited anxiously for a sign from Anselm, he swore he heard the Giant yell, "Ilien! It's the Book!"

Chapter XX

Alone In The Night

Caught! Ilien still couldn't believe it, though a quick check of reality left no doubt. His hands were bound behind his back with thick rope. His legs were tied tight as fence posts, and a dirty rag plugged his mouth. The musty smell of Giant permeated the air of his prison—a large tent with a damp, sandy floor.

The Giants had left nothing to chance, or almost nothing. They had found his pencil while searching him, but having no idea of its true nature had simply tossed it into the corner of the tent. The firelight from outside filtered through the thin cloth walls, illuminating its outline ten feet away. If only he could reach it. He wriggled three feet forward and stopped. His ropes were tied fast to a stake in the ground.

He cursed himself. How could he have been so stupid? The plan had been so simple. Everyone had followed it perfectly. Even Globe had dutifully done its job. Ilien moaned as he played it all back in his mind. He was the only one to make a mistake—and such an awful mistake. He could have sworn he heard Anselm give the signal.

Now all was lost. The Giants were interrogating Anselm at that very moment in the tent next to his. He could hear their shouts through the darkness, and the low moans of pain from Anselm that followed. Ilien shuttered with each blow the Giant received. How much more could Anselm take? Tears sprang to his eyes. It was all his fault.

He suddenly wondered if Thessien and his men had been captured too. He'd heard the blast from the Horn of Plenty seconds after he'd sent Globe shooting into the air to the astonishment of everyone around him. When the Giants saw Globe fly out from Anselm's collar they seized him at once. They must have guessed the horn call was a trick because they simply gathered around and waited. When an attacking army failed to show up, they quickly sent a dozen of their kind to search the surrounding fields. As far as Ilien knew, no one had come back with a catch. It was possible that Thessien and his men were safe. A glimmer of hope remained at least.

And to think that the Book had been nowhere in sight.

"Psst. Over here," whispered his pencil from the corner of the tent. "I'm over here."

Ilien mumbled heatedly under his gag and tugged at his tether. *What did that idiotic pencil want him to do? Dematerialize?*

"You don't know how to dematerialize," whispered the pencil.

Ilien mumbled something unintelligible.

"Yes. I can read your thoughts," said the pencil. "I've always been able to read your thoughts, though not all of them have been a pleasure to read. So quit your grumbling and get over here. I've about had enough of your insults."

Ilien mumbled again.

"You don't have to talk," said the pencil. "Just think. I know you're not in practice but—"

I can't move! thought Ilien, loudly, if that was possible. *I'm tied tight.*

"If only I could roll toward you," said the pencil. It rocked back and forth, caught in a divot in the sandy floor. "Oh, for the want of legs! If only you could reach me I might be able to get us out of this mess."

But I can't! I can't move! screamed Ilien in his head.

"Alright. Alright," said the pencil. "You don't have to get snippy about it."

How's that? thought Ilien.

"You're yelling at me, that's how," answered the pencil.

No, thought Ilien. *How would you get us out of this mess? You're only a wand. You can't cast spells.*

"I'm a little more than a wand, Ilien. I may not be able to cast spells directly, but I can help you remember them."

Remember them? Ilien looked around the tent.

"Ilien, do try to concentrate!" scolded the pencil. "You're letting your mind wander, and it's getting more than a bit confusing trying to sort through all those nonsensical thoughts of yours!" It rolled back and forth in the divot again, then gave up. "Don't you remember what the Swan said? You have no need to learn magic. You already know everything there is to know. I just need to help you remember."

Then jog my memory and make it quick, thought Ilien. *Idiotic pencil.*

"I heard that!" cried the pencil. "And it doesn't work like that. You have to be holding me. That's the rule. Something to do with the time-space continuum."

The what?

"Never mind," said the pencil.

The tent flap flew open and in stooped a rather short Giant—the officer Anselm had played cards with. He held a burning brand in one hand, and he looked to and fro around the tent. He studied Ilien for a moment while he fingered the medal on his tunic.

"That's odd," he muttered. "I thought I heard . . ." He shined his light about, shrugged, and left.

When the torchlight had faded away the pencil whispered, "That was close. I can't keep talking like this."

Then don't, thought Ilien. *I could do with the quiet. Do you know how to read minds?*

231

Ilien struggled to sit up straight. *I don't think so.*

You just did! the pencil thought back at him. *You do have powers unlimited!*

Tell that to Anselm, thought Ilien, staring at the tent flap. *If it wasn't for me he might be eating Awefull by a warm fire right now, instead of—*

The sounds of Anselm's interrogation from the nearby tent silenced his thoughts.

Then it's up to you to get him out of this mess, isn't it? retorted the pencil.

But how? thought Ilien.

There has to be something you know that will help get you out of those ropes.

Fat chance. Even if I did know an Unbinding spell I'd probably turn myself inside out trying to cast it. As for the last two spells I cast without actually saying the words, one nearly set my father's study ablaze and the other one electrocuted me.

That's it! thought the pencil.

You really don't like me, do you? thought Ilien.

No. Not the Lightning spell, thought the pencil. *The Kindle Candle spell.*

Ilien's eyes opened wide. *You're right. I can burn the ropes with the Kindle Candle spell.*

Do it. Do it now! urged the pencil.

Ilien looked down at his ankles. He recited the spell in his mind. A thin wisp of smoke rose from the ropes. He furrowed his brow in concentration, squinting at the darkening spot before him. A small flame jumped up, feeble, on the verge of going out. He cocked his head and recited the spell again. The flame held steady for only a moment. Then it sank to a wavering yellow ghost, and vanished with a puff of white smoke.

No! thought Ilien, his anger rising. *This can't be happening. It's supposed to be a simple spell!*

At that, the ropes around his ankles burst into flames. The

fire devoured them in seconds. He shook his legs free of the hot ashes.

Quick! thought the pencil. *Your hands.*

The orange light of an approaching torch lit the side of the tent. Ilien kicked at the smoldering remains of the rope as two Giants stopped outside the entrance.

"He won't tell us anything, sir," he heard a hoarse voice say.

"Let him be for a while," came another voice. Ilien didn't need to see him to recognize who it was, but the short shadow the Giant cast didn't hurt. "Let him sit with his thoughts, and his wounds," continued the officer. "He knows he's dead in the morning if he doesn't tell us who his friends are and what they're planning. That kind of knowledge tends to loosen tongues."

"Isn't he dead in the morning anyhow?"

"Of course," replied the officer. Ilien heard him spit on the ground.

The light outside grew brighter as the first Giant pointed toward Ilien's tent with his torch. "What about this one?"

"He's harmless," said the officer. The Giant's shadow turned, and Ilien could see the outline of his hand adjusting the medal on his chest. "Let him be. We'll be rid of them both come morning," said the officer. "Any word on the search parties?"

"They haven't all reported in, but those that have didn't find anyone."

"Keep searching. Herman the Heretic was not alone."

There was a moment of silence. "He did have the boy with him, sir."

The Giants' laughter faded away along with their torchlight.

Good, thought the pencil. *Excellent, in fact.*

Ilien glared openly. *Good that they're going to execute us in the morning, or good that they think I'm a joke?*

No. Didn't you hear them? They're going to leave you and

233

Anselm alone for a while. Now's our chance. Burn those ropes around your wrists and let's get out of here.

Ilien twisted about, trying to bring the knots within sight. *But I can't see them,* he thought.

It isn't like you've never seen your hands before. Just think. Visualize the ropes.

Ilien closed his eyes. He pictured his hands behind his back. He wriggled his fingers to get a feel of where they were, how the ropes wrapped around his wrists. As he recited the Kindle Candle spell he hoped his aim was better than his memory. He anticipated the pain and smell of burning skin, but to his relief and amazement got neither. In fact, in moments he heard the distinct sizzle of singeing ropes, and a puff of dark smoke rose over his shoulder. He shook free of the ropes and pulled off his gag.

"Now what?" he asked aloud.

Sshh. Keep it down! thought the pencil. *It's best if you think instead of talk from now on.*

Now what? thought Ilien.

Come get me, that's what.

Ilien tiptoed across the sandy floor and picked up his pencil.

Now, the pencil began, its thoughts whispering in Ilien's mind, *what do you think we should do?*

Ilien locked his fingers around the pencil and brought it close to his face. *What do you mean, what do I think we should do?* he thought through clenched teeth. *You said you could get us out of this mess!*

I can only help you remember, Ilien. I can't tell you what to do. I'm not the wizard. You are. Remember?

Remember what?

Remember what it is that'll get us out of this mess!

You're unbelievable, you know that? thought Ilien. *Look at this!* He gestured around the tent, pencil in hand. *Stuck here, surrounded by an army of murdering Giants and all you can*

234

think is, *"So Ilien, what do you think we should do?" Truly
unbelievable.*

He threw his hands up in disgust. *Some help you turned out
to be. Why Gallund ever made you I'll never know. Sometimes
I wish you'd just disappear from my life completely.*

"That's it!" shouted the pencil out loud.

"Quiet down!" cried Ilien, looking quickly to the tent flap.
"I thought you said it was best to think, not talk."

"Sshh! Quiet!" said the pencil.

"My god!" said Ilien. "You're incredible!"

"No. Sshh! Someone's coming."

Two large shadows appeared, framed in the light against the
wall of the tent. The shadows looked left then right as if afraid
to be seen.

*I thought you said they were going to leave us alone for a
while,* thought Ilien. *What do we do now? We'll be caught for
sure.*

*No we won't. Remember what you just said, about disap-
pearing? Well, you can do it. You know how. You must know
how. You just have to remember.*

Remember how to disappear?

The shadows outside lumbered closer, gesturing with their
hands. The outline of an arm pointed toward the tent entrance.

Hurry! whispered the pencil. *Remember! You have to
remember!*

I can't. I don't know how to disappear!

*Yes, you do. It's just like in geometry class. I never told you
the answers but you got the questions right every time.
Remember?*

"I just thought I was smart," whispered Ilien.

Really, Ilien.

But the pencil was right. It had always been like that.
Whenever he took a test using his pencil the answers seemed
to magically pop into his head. The pencil never actually came

out and told him the correct answer, but he scored A's nonetheless. Now as Ilien watched the approaching shadows grow larger on the tent wall, a feeling stole over him like the sinking feeling he had in class when the time was running out and the page of geometry problems still lay blank on his desk. The teacher was coming to collect his test. There wasn't much time left. His face flushed hot and itchy.

"I just don't know!"

Did he really just scream that aloud?

The shadows began moving. Quickly. Purposeful. Words whispered in Ilien's mind, words of a half-remembered song. He tried to listen but fear shouted through his mind, drowning out his thoughts. The words came again, louder. He could almost make them out. He willed himself to understand but he couldn't keep his concentration. Something strange was happening. He could see it out of the corner of his eye. The shadows—they were growing smaller. Were the Giants leaving? The sound of approaching footsteps told him otherwise, but still the shadows shrank. The tent flap rustled.

"*Inhibi inhabi hababi viru.*" The words tumbled from Ilien's mouth before he knew it.

The entrance to the tent parted, and in stepped two of the smallest Giants Ilien had ever seen. Three feet tall from head to toe, bald as fish and thin as eels, they looked more like hairless cats than Giants. And they looked directly at Ilien.

"I told you it was empty," said one in a voice two octaves too high even for a hairless cat. "See, no one here. My intuition is still as good as ever."

Ilien realized they weren't Giants at all, and they weren't looking at him. They were looking through him.

"Yeah. Yeah. Right. Right," said the other strange creature in annoyance, which added an octave more to its voice. "But now what?"

The first looked around, still obviously pleased with its

intuitive abilities. "We wait here and give my intuition a rest," it said. "It's gotten us this far and it's a bit tired. Give it some time to figure out where the Book is being kept."

A pale light flickered in the eyes of the other, eyes large and lidless. "You and your intuition have nearly gotten us killed several times over already. Let's squelch and keep looking."

"Why squelch now?" said the first. "There's no need to squelch when simple stealth will keep us concealed. Why waste precious energy becoming invisible. I need all the energy I can get to keep my intuition sharp."

"And I say blast your intuition!"

The two tiny creatures advance on each other as if to come to blows, circling and hissing. But instead of fighting they suddenly embraced.

"I'm sorry," squeaked one.

"Me too. Me too," squeaked the other. "All this pressure is making me crazy."

"Yeah. But think of our reward when we finally get the Book back for our new employers."

The cry of baby pigs followed as they squealed with laughter, then a sudden hush.

"We must keep quiet," said one, looking around like a squirrel off its tree.

"Yes. Yes," piped the other almost inaudibly. "Quiet will do your intuition good."

During their silence Ilien wondered what the two strange creatures could be. On closer inspection he saw that not only were they bald, but they had no ears either, only shallow impressions where ears should have been. Their mouths were little more than slits, their noses merely buttons on a child's sweater. And as for clothing, they wore none at all. Their skin resembled soft, supple leather, smooth and brown all over. Though they had no tails, Ilien would have thought them to be some strange woodland creatures he had never seen before, if they hadn't spoken, and if it wasn't for their eyes. Larger than any human's, they looked very human-like. Almond-shaped, they held a gentleness within them, a hint of perpetual worry too. And when the strange creatures spoke, their eyes filled with a light of their own, changing colors with their mood, sometimes deep blue, other times green or silver.

Whatever their appearance they couldn't be all bad. They did want to steal the Book from the Giants. Perhaps they were sent by the wizards.

"I think I've got it!" said the intuitive one. "I think I know where it is."

"Where? Where?"

"Not far. Come."

The first one dashed to the entrance and looked out.

"I hope you know what you're doing," said the other. "If we don't get that Book back we'll be as dead as that Groll they sent to kill the boy."

His companion looked back from the tent flap. "The Groll's demise is our blessing. Being the last hope to stop that child will only raise our reward when we succeed. Then maybe they'll realize we really are the best thieves in all Nadae."

They slipped out the entrance and were gone.

It worked! said the pencil in Ilien's mind. *They couldn't see you at all. You're invisible. You did it!*

Did you hear that? thought Ilien, staring in disbelief at the tent flap where the two creatures had fled.

"Hear what?"

Ilien watched the entrance as if it were a trap door, ready to spring open at any moment. "Whoever hired those things sent the Groll to kill me."

"Then let's go before anyone else who wants you dead arrives."

Ilien couldn't argue with such sound logic. He stole to the entrance and peeked out. The strange creatures were gone.

Anselm's tent stood twenty feet away. Ilien looked left then right as if he were about to cross a busy street.

You don't have to be so paranoid, thought the pencil. *You are invisible, you know.*

Ilien stopped to inspect himself. He waved his hand before his face. He felt it breeze by his nose but saw only the tent flap in front of him. Now here was something he wished he knew how to do earlier. How he could have wreaked vengeance on Stan and Peaty!

Ilien crept the distance to Anselm's tent anyhow. When he reached the flap he stopped and looked around. Oversized tents rose in the night around him, run-down tenements in some grey, desolate city. He wondered which one held the Book. A lone Giant stood a hundred feet away, picking his nose in the shadows, glancing to and fro to make sure no one saw him. Ilien parted the flap to Anselm's tent and peered in.

A small fire smoldered in the center of the tent, its thick ribbon of smoke rising to exit a large hole in the roof. Several lanterns had been lit and hung from long poles in each corner. Anselm sat slumped over beneath one of the sputtering lamps. He was bound with rope to a heavy stake in the ground. Even from where he stood Ilien could see the bruises on the side of the Giant's face. He entered like a soft breeze to stand near his wounded friend.

Anselm looked up then, and even though he couldn't see Ilien, his eyes burned with the fierce fire of wariness.

Ilien pulled off Anselm's gag.

"Who's there?" asked Anselm, startled, looking to and fro.

It's me, replied Ilien.

When Anselm didn't respond, Ilien realized he was still thinking instead of talking.

"It's me, Ilien," he repeated, this time aloud.

Anselm's gaze crisscrossed the tent. "Ilien? But how? Where are you?"

"I'm here. Right in front of you. I'm invisible."

Ilien began untying Anselm's feet. The Giant looked on in fascination as the knots unraveled, seemingly on their own.

"Don't," said Anselm, and he pulled his feet away. "Leave them be."

"What do you mean?" whispered Ilien. "We've got to get you out of here before the guards return."

"No, Ilien. Don't."

Ilien shuffled forward and continued working on the knots. "I'll have to burn through them. Shield your eyes."

"No!" said Anselm, fiercely. Ilien looked up. Even though he was still invisible, Anselm looked directly at him. "If you free me, all will be lost," said the Giant.

Ilien hunkered down to work on the knots again. "All will be lost if I don't."

"Listen to me," said Anselm. Ilien had moved from his gaze and Anselm spoke to the air beside him. "When they discover I've escaped, how far do you think we'll get before we're found? You may be invisible. But I'm not."

Ilien stopped and looked up at Anselm. "But I can't leave you here. You're to be killed at dawn."

Anselm's eyes moved to Ilien's again. "It doesn't matter."

"What do you mean, it doesn't matter?"

Anselm's hand speared forward. He grabbed Ilien by the collar. "We all have choices to make," he said, his eyes peering into Ilien's as if Ilien stood plainly visible in the clear light of day. "This one is mine. Yours should be to leave, right now. You can still beat the Book to Greattower. They have no idea how important you are. They won't worry about the small boy who fled in the night, but they'll tear the plains apart to find me. They'll never let Herman the Heretic escape them again."

Ilien pulled away. With trembling hands, he resumed his work on the knots. "No. I'm not leaving here without you."

Anselm kicked his legs. "If you love all that you know to be true, then you will leave me now to save it!" he shouted, sending Ilien flying across the floor.

The tent flap flew open. Four Giants marched in. "What's going on here?" said the officer, stepping from behind his soldiers. "I thought I told you this Giant was to be gagged."

"He was gagged, sir," answered one of the soldiers.

The officer's eyes flicked about the tent. "He was, was he?"

Ilien held perfectly still, even as several times the officer's gaze washed by him. "Stand at the entrance!" commanded the officer. "Don't let a breeze pass by you." His eyes continued to dance around Ilien. "You are well aware, Heretic, that you will die come morning, as are your friends, whoever they may be." The Giants guarding the entrance followed the officer's eyes around the tent. "If only you would tell us what we want to know. Surely you don't take us for fools. We know much already, perhaps everything. So come, confirm our suspicions. It might just save your life."

Ilien looked from the officer to Anselm. Just then his heel slipped forward in the sand.

"Guards!" cried the officer. Though he hadn't seen the sand move, he sensed something was amiss. The guards leapt to attention, unaware of what was happening. "Link arms and spread out!" They did so at once, stretching across the tent.

"This heretic came here to steal our Lord, but he did not come alone. No. He no doubt has accomplices more powerful than little boys. In fact, he is being helped even now, even here."

The officer reached to his side and yanked forth his sword, a nicked and bent blade too short for a Giant. "There is a wizard among us, boys."

The guards exchanged nervous glances as the officer took his place to block the exit. At his signal they walked forward, arms linked, legs forming a moving picket fence.

"What makes you think you could ever catch a wizard,

Molnius, when you could never catch me?" said Anselm, trying to distract the officer's attention.

Molnius lunged at Anselm, leaving the door unguarded. He seized him by the throat. "But I have you now!" he spat.

Ilien crawled backwards, bumping into the small pile of Anselm's belongings that had been cast to the side. There at his fingertips lay the map. He snatched it up and tucked it beneath his shirt. It disappeared without a trace. The pencil's thoughts cut through his mind.

It's now or never. Let's get out of here!

Ilien's neck felt hot and prickly. The hair on his head stood on end as he fought back his growing anger, an anger he'd felt only once before, a rage from which he knew there would be no turning back. *I'm not leaving Anselm*, he thought wildly. Sparks flew at the edge of his sight, unseen to anyone but himself.

No Ilien! Anselm's right. If you love all that is true then you must leave him to save it! There's no other way!

Ilien watched as Molnius raised his hand. He felt the singe of wild magic burn at the back of his throat. The hand came down, striking Anselm across the face.

Anselm merely smiled. "One day soon, my people will rise above this evil," he said. "One day soon, the shadow of the Necromancer will lift from the heart of my son, and you will be the first to follow your Master into the darkness."

Molnius struck again, this time with the flat of his sword. Anselm fell back, covering his face. "Leave me!" he cried, struggling back up. "Leave me!" His eyes searched the tent, and Ilien knew for certain that they searched for him.

Molnius hit Anselm again.

Ilien! cried the pencil in his mind. *The guards!*

The guards had stopped to watch Molnius, but now they resumed their march across the tent, arms linked.

We have to get out of here! thought the pencil.

There was no way past the net of guards. *But how?* thought Ilien as they drew nearer.

The hole in the roof! Fly out the hole in the roof! thought the pencil in a rush.

As Ilien looked up, his hand struck something small and hard. The vial of Fireflies popped out from the pile of Anselm's belongings and rolled across the sand toward Molnius. The officer spun around. He looked directly at Ilien. Anselm looked up too, his eyes beseeching his invisible friend to flee.

Fly! cried the pencil in his mind. *Fly now!*

The guards jumped forward, arms linked, eyes dancing. They reached the far end of the tent and looked back at their angry leader. Ilien floated silently toward the hole in the roof, his feet gliding inches above them. He closed his eyes against the haze of stinging smoke rising from the fire, but tears streamed down his cheeks anyhow. He sailed up and out, and into the cool night air, leaving Anselm behind.

Up he drifted over the Giants' encampment, like a balloon lost by a heartbroken boy. Anselm's tent shrank below him in the gloom, and his tears fell upon its roof, the first lonely raindrops of a storm to come. He rose higher into the night until the camp resembled a gathering of fireflies on the grass below. A cold wind pitched him forward, propelling him toward the imposing shadow of Greattower.

Chapter XXI

Greattower

I'*m so tired,* thought Ilien as he sailed through the air under a skyful of stars. *Why am I so tired?*

"It's the magic," answered his pencil, aloud now.

"Magic?" muttered Ilien, like a child being carried to bed well after bedtime.

"You're flying invisibly, Ilien. That takes a lot out of you."

The shadow of Greattower filled the northern sky, a black hole in the night, growing larger as he drifted closer, spreading out to devour the stars. Below him the fires of the Giants' camp stretched into a glittering spiral of lights.

"You have to land," said the pencil. The sound of its voice in the void startled Ilien. "It's not safe even for birds to fly this high for this long, let alone little boys not dressed for the occasion."

"I'm not a little boy," muttered Ilien.

"Set down over there, at the foot of the mountain, before you fall to the ground frozen."

Ilien slapped his cheek and shook his head. "Yes. Down," he mumbled.

The impenetrable shadow of the mountain loomed higher as Ilien glided down through pools of warmer air layered between sheets of heavy cold. The stars began to fade, their icy crispness melting pale and watery. The glowing canvas of the Giant encampment tilted and shifted as Ilien descended. Soon it pitched out of sight, lost to distance.

Ilien felt solid ground beneath his feet and sank to his knees, curling up on the cold rock that had risen up out of the blackness to meet him.

He never remembered closing his eyes.

He woke slowly, driven from dreamless slumber by a dull headache. He stirred and opened one eye, reaching beneath his head to remove the jagged stick he'd been using as a pillow. He rolled onto his back and moaned.

The gloom of early morning exploded into brilliant light. The spiked top of Greattower shined above him. He propped himself up on his elbows, hanging his swimming head to focus on the soothing dimness of the rock beneath him. The plains below still slept in nighttime shadow. His bedroom, a small shelf of rock, the first tall step of a giant staircase leading up the mountainside, hung in twilight limbo.

Ilien trained his eyes upward, squinting against the painful light of the glowing peak. The sheer side of the mountain loomed over him. He dropped his gaze to the comfort of the dull rock beneath him once more. His head throbbed, and he felt like throwing up. He spied his wooden pillow, snatched it up, and threw it from his mountain perch in disgust.

"Good morning, sleepy-head," chimed his pencil.

The pencil's high-pitched greeting pierced Ilien's aching head like a needle. "Things made of wood are not high on my list this morning," he said, eyeing the pencil where it lay a few feet away.

"You've got a hangover," it said, cheerfully. Ilien lunged an arm out to grab it. "But don't worry it'll pass," said the pencil, rolling out of reach.

"A hangover? If this is what a hangover feels like, may I never drink ale for as long as I live."

"Yours is a magic hangover. Overdid yourself, I'd say, but thank heavens you did."

245

"No one ever told me I could feel like this," said Ilien, clutching his head.

"Yes. I know," said the pencil. "All magic users tend to think they're invincible. But even the best of them have their limitations."

"Mine seem a bit low," said Ilien, closing his eyes and rubbing his temples. The pain in his head began to work its way south and he grabbed his stomach. "Why do you think that is?" he asked suddenly.

"Invisibility is not a spell to be taken lightly. To tell you the truth, I didn't think you could pull it off. It may seem like a simple enough concept, but believe me, it isn't. On top of that you were flying. Fairly impressive, I'd say."

"I'm not so sure," said Ilien. "What if I'm not as powerful as everyone thinks? What if they're wrong about me?"

The pencil rolled toward him. "Doubt me. Doubt Anselm. Even doubt the Swan," it said. "But always believe in yourself." It rolled right into Ilien's hand. "The fact that the NiDemon believes Windy is you is misbelief for a good cause. It gives us an edge. But believe me, most misbelief isn't."

Ilien closed his eyes. "Whatever you just said, I hope you're right."

"Now let's get going," said the pencil. "We may be ahead of the Book, but we won't be for long if we stay here and mope."

"I'm not moping," said Ilien as he tried to get his bearings. "I'm wallowing. Besides, there's no way off this rock unless I fly, and I'm not sure I can."

"Quit your driveling and act like a man," scolded the pencil. "There's more at stake here than just your sore head."

Ilien stewed in silent shame. The pencil was right. He knew it, but his body didn't. Another wave of nausea swept through him. He fought back his sickness, then remembered Anselm, and retched on the cold stone.

"It's too late to save him," said the pencil, reading his thoughts. "Don't let it be too late for Windy."

Ilien winced and wiped his mouth. "I know," he said. "I know."

The mission was still before him. The importance of what was at stake did nothing to ease his sickness, but the thought of Windy in danger speared through him, snapping him to his senses. He wretched again and rose to his feet.

When the pain in his stomach had finally quieted to a dull ache, and his vision began to clear, he consulted Anselm's map. He discovered that if he flew upward only fifty feet or so, he could land on a narrow ledge. The ledge led to a sheer wall of rock, but if he could manage to fly a hundred feet higher he'd reach a small landing. There he could rest before undertaking the final, and longest, flight up to a small opening in the rocks. The opening ran into the mountain and led to tunnels which branched out like veins into the very depths of Greattower. The map assured him that it could guide him safely through the maze of tunnels, to the very heart of the mountain where Windy was being held.

Ilien steadied himself against the side of the cliff. "I don't have to fly invisibly again, do I?"

"Don't be silly," said the pencil. "Of course not. No one can possibly see you up here."

Ilien looked around anyhow, if only to delay the inevitable. He didn't relish the idea of making himself feel even more ill than he already was, and grammar was the last thing he wanted to think about just then. But there was no getting around it.

"*Lever belie, belever beflie,*" he muttered. With a groan he rose into the air. He repeated the spell again and sailed slowly up to the next ledge, keeping his eyes closed against the dizzying ascent. By the time he lit on the narrow landing, the pounding in his head had faded to a dull ache.

"That felt pretty good," he said.

"Wait till tomorrow," said the pencil.

"What?"

"Never mind."

In fact, the more Ilien flew the better he felt. By the time he reached the final landing his headache had vanished, his nausea had fled, and the sun no longer burned holes in his eyes. Compared to how awful he felt when he woke up that morning, he now felt as if he could take on the world.

"Don't get ahead of yourself," said the pencil, reading his thoughts again. "That time may soon come."

"Why do I feel so good all of a sudden?" he asked.

"There's nothing quite like magic to ease a magic hangover. But remember—"

"I know," said Ilien. "Just wait until tomorrow."

The entrance to the tunnel lay open before him, a dark mouth with rocky teeth all around. He peered into the impenetrable darkness. Without a thought he conjured up Globe to light the way, and strolled into the mountainside.

The tunnel ran straight, sloping downward for nearly a hundred feet before it branched left and right. Two other tunnels veered away in a yawning Y while the main way continued onward. Ilien looked back at the bright eye of the entrance and his newfound courage began to fade.

He thought about flying along the tunnel—he longed for the exhilaration of magic to make everything seem alright. But something told him that it wouldn't be right. He needed to stay put in reality, keep his feet on the ground. He was headed into the heart of Greattower where a demon lay waiting for him. He turned from the bright light of the entrance to face Globe's soft glow, pulling out Anselm's map. It unfolded without a word.

"Which way now?" he asked.

In the hazy illumination of the magical light, Ilien could discern the outline of a complex rendering of tunnels and chambers drawn upon the map, graphed out in a series of rectangles, squares and, most disturbing of all, blank spots. A red X appeared. Beside it the words, "You Are Here" could be faintly seen. What followed was a dotted line tracing the proper path through the tunnel maze. It ended abruptly at one of the blank spots.

"Go straight," said the map. "Veer left two tunnels down, then right, then straight again until the next four way crossroad, then—"

"I can read a map," said Ilien. "But what's with all the blank spots?"

"Interference. Something's blocking me," said the map. "It's as if some powerful force wants to hide those parts of the tunnel from prying eyes."

Ilien counted five blank spots in all. "That can't be good," he said, looking back the way he had come.

"At least we only have to pass through one," said the map.

Ilien turned from the beckoning light of the entrance. "Let's go," he said before he could change his mind. He started down the tunnel with Globe hanging above his head like a halo.

As Ilien made his way forward, he became aware of troubling changes around him. The cold hung silent in the blackness. The compression of air made breathing difficult. The utter darkness dulled his thoughts until thinking became nearly impossible. He had to stop several times to gather his wits. He had never felt the weight of the earth press so heavily upon him before. The snug caves beneath Tipton Rock hardly qualified as subterraneous caverns a mile below the earth.

What he noticed most of all were the smells. As he crept along the sooty halls, nearly each new step brought a different and disturbing odor, some swampy and pungent, some sharp and flinty, and others—the others were the worse. Once, long since he'd seen the prick of light from the tunnel entrance vanish, the dull plodding of his footsteps suddenly sounded like fat, wet kisses in the dark. He would have imagined he was walking over melted chocolate, if it wasn't for the smell. At least he hadn't encountered the putrid odor of Spanstone yet.

Time ceased to exist for Ilien in the dark, far beneath the floor of the earth. What seemed to him to have taken scant minutes had eaten up hours. He finally stopped at a curve in the tunnel that, according to the map, was the last curve before they ventured into the mysterious blank spot. Globe flickered then dimmed to a dirty brown. Ilien peered fearfully at the map.

"What's the matter?" asked the map. "Let's go."

In the soiled orb of light Globe cast around him, Ilien's mind began to conjure up images of what might qualify to be hidden from prying eyes when it was already buried a mile beneath a mountain. The best his imagination of twelve years could come up with was a magical stretch of tunnel where snakes as white as maggots hung from the ceiling, their fangs like bloodthirsty needles in search of wandering prey to drink the liquid from their upturned eyeballs. Beyond that he felt he had nothing better to offer.

"Are you sure there's no other way around?" he asked in a shaky voice, as if he'd just witnessed albino snakes drinking heartily from a pair of white-eyed explorers. "Are you sure there's no other way to get to Windy?"

"No," replied the map. "I'm not."

"Well then take another look!" cried Ilien, his voice echoing around him. "If you're not so sure then search some more! If we don't have to pass through a tunnel that someone, oh, let's say the Necromancer, doesn't want us to pass through, then let's not!"

"Keep it down," said the pencil. "Ilien's right, you dried out piece of scratch paper. Look again!"

"It won't do any good," said the map.

"Why?" cried Ilien and the pencil at once.

"Because I don't know how to get to Windy."

The map's final words echoed down the tunnel, then silence.

"You don't know how to get to Windy?" whispered Ilien.

"No."

"But you said, you assured me you knew." Ilien looked into Globe's pale light for comfort.

"I said I could lead you to the very heart of the mountain where Windy was being held," replied the map. "I never said I could lead you to Windy."

Again silence.

"For crying out loud, haven't you ever used a map before!" yelled the map. "I'm geographic, not demographic!"

Ilien put his head in his hands. "What can possibly go wrong next?"

Suddenly Globe streaked away, flying down the corridor like a bat chasing moths. It bounced off the walls, dwindling in the distance until it finally rounded a corner and disappeared from sight.

Ilien stood trapped in utter darkness.

"Globe!" cried Ilien. "Come back!" He recited the Light spell again, and again, and yet again. But Globe was gone, and Ilien was left with the unmistakable knowledge that he was utterly, and hopelessly, lost. He dropped to his knees in the darkness. There was no going forward. There was no going back. He huddled in a knot, fighting off the blackness that pressed in around him, that seeped into his mind to snuff out his very thoughts.

The darkness played tricks on Ilien then, for it was not the simple gloom of night that he was used to in his room. It was complete and utter darkness, like the dark in his closet at midnight, or the dark behind his eyes while squeezing them tight against a still fading nightmare. Darkness so thick that a light shined through it in his mind because that's what he wanted to see—that's what he needed to see. A light shining through mist which he knew was not there, but which brought him comfort when comfort couldn't be found with his eyes. As

251

Ilien crouched on the tunnel floor, he fancied he saw his feet, snug beneath him, his legs lit in a soft blue glow as if Globe still hovered nearby. But try as he might to keep the vision from fading, in the farthest corner of his mind he knew it was just an illusion, and the darkness closed in once more.

Except that when he blinked the light was still there. And when he wiggled his toes he actually saw the tips of his boots move up and down. He threw his gaze upward and there, hovering before him, speckled in lights like a withered Christmas tree, stood the glowing image of Gallund, bent and crooked without his cane. Ilien looked back at his toes and wiggled them again. He closed his eyes and opened them. He sprang to his feet. He pointed his pencil at the image before him. It was a trick! A ghost sent to lure him down the tunnel and into the blank spot to his doom!

"Get back, Reknamarken!" he shouted, but it came out as a squeak and he sank back to his knees. "Get back," he pleaded, his pencil held at his side.

Gallund's image shimmered bright, then dimmed. It flickered, playing with the shadows on the tunnel walls. Ilien expected it to disappear and prove his assumption correct, but the darkness suddenly sprang away and Gallund's image blazed forth so brightly that Ilien shielded his eyes.

"How you ever made it this far I'll never know," said the image before him. "Get up! Get up at once and turn back! I didn't raise you to be a fool, Ilien Woodhill."

"Gallund?" Ilien peered sideways into the wizard's shining aura. "Is it really you?"

"Who else would bother to look for you in a rat-infested place like this?" said the wizard, looking ever so cross as usual.

Ilien glanced around nervously. "Rat-infested?"

Gallund's luminescent image flushed red in anger. "That's the least of your problems! Now turn back at once. Get to Berkhelven as fast as you can."

"Gallund!" cried Ilien, jumping to his feet. He ran to hug the wizard but passed straight through him instead, stumbling into the far wall. He spun around with a gasp. "You're—you're a ghost?"

"I'm as much a ghost as you are a wizard!" said Gallund, his hands at his hips. "Now do as I say and turn back at once!"

"But I can't," said Ilien. "The NiDemon has captured the princess. She holds the key that unlocks the Book. I have to rescue her before the Book arrives."

Gallund's image flared bright. "No, you don't," he said. "The princess doesn't have the key. You do."

Ilien stared in silence at Gallund, but his hand strayed to his pocket where he kept his house key.

"That's right," said the wizard, his image growing larger, more imposing. "You've had it all along. Now turn back before it's too late. There is no gain in rescuing Windy. You're not ready to face a NiDemon. He will take the key from you, and all will be lost."

Ilien shrank back against the wall, feeling the hard outline of the key in his pocket. "But what about everything the Swan said?"

"The Swan was wrong," said Gallund. "You will free Reknamarken if you face the NiDemon. The Swan was fooled by her visions, as most people are by their eyes."

"Or by their ears," said Ilien, studying Gallund's glowing image. "The Gallund I know would never let an innocent girl die."

"Things are not as simple as you make them," said Gallund. "Yes, if you turn back now Windy may die. But if you don't many more surely will. You are prophesied to release the Necromancer. Don't rush to fulfill your destiny. Everything appears hopeless now, but remember—"

"Some appearances are not what they seem," finished Ilien, suddenly standing tall. "You are not the Gallund I know!" he

253

cried. *"Illustus bregun, illustus bregar!"* His incantation echoed down the tunnel.

He half-expected Gallund to flicker, but the wizard put a finger to his lips and shook his head instead. He seemed about to say something, then he looked over his shoulder as if he heard someone approaching. He turned back to Ilien, but when he spoke he made no sound at all. Ilien pressed himself against the tunnel wall in fear. A cross expression flashed across the wizard's face. He glanced over his shoulder again. When he turned back, Ilien saw something he'd never seen in the wizard before—the brittle look of fear. Gallund's lips moved again. This time Ilien could hear the words in his mind.

She's coming for me. Turn back now, before it's too late. Then his image turned grey as ash and froze in the air.

"Gallund!" cried Ilien. "Where are you?" He ran forward, careful not to pass through the wizard again for fear that he might disappear completely.

But the frozen image faded anyhow, until all that remained was a neon ghost before Ilien's eyes, a floating red phantom in the blackness of his mind.

"I knew it was you. I knew it," whispered Ilien, dropping to his knees and sagging to the cold, wet floor. He closed his eyes, his mind a void, filled with the pressing darkness and the faint chatter of rats somewhere down the tunnel.

"What should we do now?" whispered the pencil.

Ilien clutched the hard outline of the key through his pants. His mind turned in circles, first to images of Windy huddled somewhere nearby, awaiting her death if he didn't press onward, then to thoughts of the NiDemon prying his hands from the key, releasing the Necromancer, proving the prophesy true. The only safe course seemed to be kneeling for eternity in the cold slime beneath him.

"Staying here and turning back are one and the same," said the pencil. "Your choosing not to choose is a choice nonetheless. You probably don't want to hear what I think, but Gallund told you to turn back, and I agree. If you're careful you can make it out safely. I know you can."

Ilien closed his eyes, though he could have left them open. In the absolute darkness, with his mind frozen in fear, it was all the same. "I won't let Windy die," he said suddenly. He shoved to his feet. "We're not going back. If the map can lead me out in the dark, then it can lead me in."

"But Ilien, you don't know where the princess is," protested the pencil.

"Then we'll try every tunnel, pass down every passage, every snake of an entryway until we find her."

"But you have the key. The NiDemon will take it from you. All will be lost. You have to go back. You heard Gallund. He said there was no gain in rescuing Windy."

"He was wrong," said Ilien. "And as for they key . . ." He shuffled forward, digging his hands along the slimy floor until they fell into a deep crack. "No one will have it." He dropped the key into the crack. He expected to hear its small clink as it hit bottom, but no sound ever came.

"Now let's go," he said. He rose, stroking the wall to get his bearings in the dark. He dug out the map. "You'll have to tell me where to go, not show me."

"No. I won't," said the map.

"You're right," said Ilien. "I could try a Kindle Candle spell." He rolled the map into the shape of a candle.

"No! No!" cried the pencil. "What he means is Globe is coming back!"

Ilien's heart jumped and he peered around in the darkness, but the void remained unbroken. Then suddenly he saw it, the light of a single star in the distance. It grew to bright moonlight and the shadows fled before it. It was Globe! A blazing sun spinning toward them up the tunnel!

"Globe! You've come back!" cried Ilien.

"Boy, you sure are an easy sell," said the pencil. "Now if I had pulled a stunt like that you'd have stuffed me back in with the left-over sandwiches."

Globe careened toward Ilien like a love-sick puppy. Ilien had to shield his eyes from its blinding light.

"Down, Globe. Down. Not so bright!" he laughed as the magical light frolicked around him.

"She's excited!" said the pencil.

"She?" asked Ilien.

"She says she's found Windy!" said the pencil. Globe spun in circles and the shadows danced a jig on the wall. "She's not far!" said the pencil. "Back one turn and straight on, with no blank spots to pass through."

Ilien peered down the tunnel. The shadows squirmed beneath Globe's pressing light. *Back one turn and straight on to Windy? With no blank spots to pass through?* "It's too easy," he said. "It's just too easy."

Globe dimmed and came to rest on Ilien's shoulder.

"It's about time something came easy," mumbled the pencil.

Chapter XXII

NiDemon

Not far now, whispered the pencil in Ilien's mind. *The tunnel runs straight, then loops left. After that—*

"I know. I know," said Ilien, pinching his nose. The putrid smell of spanstone filled the air. The NiDemon was close. But that meant Windy was close too. As an afterthought, Ilien waved his pencil through the air as Gallund had back home. "Is the smell gone?" he asked.

"Ilien. We don't have noses," replied his pencil.

"Oh yeah." Ilien removed his hand. The smell was gone. He couldn't believe it. He nearly smiled, until he remembered what had caused the smell in the first place.

The NiDemon. The most feared of Reknamarken's servants. A creature of the netherworld. Even Gallund had paled at its mention. And here he was, a boy who weeks earlier had nothing better to do than lay stretched out by the stream behind his house, hoping not to catch a fish that would disturb his slumber. A NiDemon. A creature that chilled the hearts of the Nomadin themselves. And at that very moment it held Windy prisoner. The thought of the princess in danger suddenly filled Ilien with a fierce desire to run forward, like a king's knight with his shining sword held forth to save her. But he held his place in the gloom, a small boy with nothing more than an obnoxious number two by his side.

"I heard that," said the pencil. "Would you really feel better if I was a sword? Do you think a sword is going to help you

257

face the NiDemon? Think again. No sword, magical or not, can harm a NiDemon. Even I, an obnoxious number two, am powerless. It's you, Ilien. Only you have the power necessary to stand before it."

"I know that! Don't you think I know that? Isn't that what everyone keeps telling me?" Globe dimmed at Ilien's outburst. Ilien himself cringed to hear his voice echo loudly down the tunnel and around the looping left.

"But you have to believe it," whispered the pencil. "If you don't, there's no point going any farther. If you don't then the next steps you take may be your last. And Windy will die too."

Ilien looked around at his friends, everyone of them an inanimate object, not one of them a real person. Globe shed barely enough light to see by, and in the dusky silent moments that followed Ilien could almost believe he had finally lost his mind. He crouched in a smelly puddle of muck a mile from daylight talking to his homework.

"But we are real, and so is the NiDemon," said the pencil through his thoughts. "And so is the danger Windy faces, we all face, including you. Especially you, if you refuse to believe in yourself."

But how could he believe in himself? How could he believe everything the Swan had told him when she'd been so wrong about so much? Maybe Gallund was right. What if he wasn't ready to face the NiDemon? What then? He was just a boy after all, a boy who desperately wished he were back home and had never heard of Giants and magic and adventures. A boy. A boy dammit! Why wouldn't anyone believe him?

"I'm just a boy," he whispered, hanging his head.

Globe floated down to hover over his shoulder, brightening until Ilien could see his own wavering reflection in the puddle of slime beneath him. The frightened face of a twelve-year-old stared back at him through the darkness.

"I'm no more a powerful Nomadin than Globe here is a

person," said Ilien, turning from his reflection.

"Don't be so sure about that," came a whisper.

Ilien jumped and fell back. He peered up at Globe in surprise.

"Yes," said Globe, pulsing with each word it spoke. "Looks are deceiving, aren't they?"

"What are you?" asked Ilien, lifting his hands from the slime and wiping them on his pants. "Why is it you've never spoken before?"

"I could always speak," replied Globe. "You were just never ready to listen. The question is, Ilien, what are you?"

Globe hovered closer and Ilien searched deep within its light for a sign of what it was. "Make up your mind who you want to be," said Globe, "or life will choose for you."

Ilien's face was lit with wonder as he gazed into Globe's soft aura. "But what if I'm not who I choose to be?" he asked. "What if I'm only fooling myself?"

"Will choosing otherwise help?" replied Globe. "Be, then do, then have, Ilien."

Ilien turned away, suddenly preferring the darkness to Globe's piercing questions. "Stop talking in riddles! Now is not the time for riddles!"

"It's no riddle," said Globe, floating closer. "First you must be. Be the person you want to be. Then you must do. Do the things that he would do. Then, and only, then will you have it."

"Have what?" Ilien turned toward Globe once more, her gentle glow softening the hard outlines of his face.

"Have what you wanted all along, the name you chose for yourself at the start." Globe floated all the way down to the tunnel floor and Ilien couldn't help catching his refection again. The sulking boy was gone. An awe struck young man stared back. "Be, then do, then have," said Globe.

Ilien looked hard at himself. What he saw didn't fit. His hair was long, no doubt from spending the summer as far away as possible from his mother's shears. But there was more. His face had lost the boyish curves he remembered seeing reflected in the lazy ponds around Southford while fishing. Now it stared back sharp and angular. His eyes fixed himself with an icy glare, hard and unforgiving. When had he come by those eyes? How had all these changes occurred without his knowing? He glanced down at his hands, strong, almost man's hands.

He scooped up Globe from off the floor. He rose from the puddle of drool and cast the magical light into the air before him. "If the NiDemon wants the child of Nomadin wizards, it'll be sorely disappointed," he said as bravely as he could. "It'll get a Nomadin instead."

"That's the spirit!" cried the pencil.

Ilien turned on the pencil in anger. "Keep it down!" he cried.

"No respect," said the pencil. "I'm telling you, no respect."

Globe cast just enough light to show the way as Ilien continued on. His footsteps echoed forward, and around the looping left of the tunnel. Almost immediately, a thin light from further ahead painted the tunnel walls a soft orange, and a faint thump, like a distant drum, rose to drown out Ilien's footfalls.

The light grew brighter and the drumming louder as they rounded the bend, only now a sharp click followed each drum beat. Thump-click. Thump-click. Thump-click. Ilien looked at Globe, who only dimmed in reply. The tunnel curved sharply to the right and they came to a door, a small wooden door that leaked bright light from its edges. The thump-click, thump-click behind it beat on.

Now what? thought Ilien.

"Open it," whispered the pencil. Globe seemed to agree for she moved over to light the wooden surface.

"But how?" asked Ilien. The door was a smooth, polished slab of wood with no visible handle, no hinges for that matter, only a small circular hole in its center at eye level. *A peep hole,* thought Ilien.

Or an eye, thought the pencil.

Ilien hung back for a moment. When it didn't blink, he tried looking through it.

"I can't see a thing," he said, leaning on the door.

The door swung suddenly open, and Ilien tumbled into bright yellow light, falling flat on his face onto a thick, wooly rug. The thump-click of the beating drum stopped and Ilien scrambled to his feet. Globe all but disappeared. She hovered in the air like a dust mote.

Bright lights hung from the ceiling—strange, flameless torches. The room was small, no bigger than his father's study back home. Pictures hung on the white, painted walls, portraits of brooding men, some standing, some sitting behind ornate desks. The pictures were everywhere. A desk and chair dominated the center of the room, more pictures sprinkled upon it. Beside the desk, poised over a small box was—Gallund?

No. Not Gallund, but a man with such a resemblance that it could have been the wizard's brother, except for his strange clothes. The man wore a striped blue and grey coat, tight fitting, like an officer's uniform, with matching grey pants and shoes as bright as polished onyx. As he bent over the box, he held a small rod in one hand, one end of it attached to the box, and beneath it a black, circular disk revolved on a spinning, round platform.

He looked up in surprise, and stopped the disc from turning with his hand. "May I help you?" he asked.

Ilien stared at the man without speaking, then glanced at the black disc.

"Oh. This? It's nothing," said the man. "Really. None of your concern." He picked up the box and placed it under his desk, muttering, "Why do they always seem to see it on magical worlds?"

He turned back to Ilien. "That's that." He pulled a handker-chief from a breast pocket and wiped his hands. "Now. How may I help you? Yes. Right. You must be lost." He moved from behind the desk. "Well, back out the door, that's a good child, now run along. If you hurry you can make it home for dinner." He guided a dumbfounded Ilien toward the door.

Ilien stopped and turned to face him. "Wait," he said. "Who are you?"

The man rolled his eyes and moaned. "Listen, kid. I'm being awfully patient here. No questions, okay? Just run along home, before it's too late."

Ilien looked around the brightly lit room. The faces of the men in the pictures glared at him. He glanced back where the strange box with its spinning disc had been. There, on the other end of the desk, lay a feather, a small smooth stone and a key—a silver key.

Ilien pulled away from the man's grasp. "Where is she? Where's Windy?"

The man threw up his hands. "That's it. Now you've done it," he said. He pulled something from his pocket, aimed it at the door and walked back to his chair behind the desk. "Time's up. Too late. You've had your chance."

The door behind Ilien vanished.

"Unbelievable," said the man. "Truly unbelievable." He began opening drawers. "What those Nomadin won't stoop to. Incredible. Sending a boy to do a man's work."

"Where is she?" asked Ilien again. His mind raced. This was not how he pictured things happening. A room beneath a mountain, a room with a desk and pictures on the wall, and that strange box. And now him, this oddly dressed man with the shiny black shoes, this—this—

"NiDemon?" said the man, looking up from the drawer he was rifling through. "That is what they call me, isn't it?" He looked back in the drawer and smiled. He reached a hand inside. He fumbled for a moment with the item he'd been searching for. "It's too bad you didn't leave when you had the chance," he said. "Now, I'm afraid, it's too late. Now you must pay for your ignorance."

Ilien looked to the drawer, then back at the leering man before him. He shrank back in fear.

The NiDemon pulled out a small, black book and laid it on the table. "Name?" he said, throwing the book open.

Ilien's mind raced. There had to be a spell he could remember, a spell to defend himself against the NiDemon's dark magic. Something! Anything! He throttled his pencil.

"What was that?" he asked suddenly. He looked at the NiDemon in confusion. "What did you say?"

"Your name," said the man, drumming his fingers on the desk. "What is your name?"

Ilien stared at the little black book in silence. "Tell me where she is!" he cried, pointing his pencil at the NiDemon.

"No, no. Thanks anyhow but I've got my own," said the man, holding up a quill pen for Ilien to see.

Ilien stepped forward, his face twisted in anger. "Tell me!" he shouted.

The man's eyes hardened. His knuckles blanched around the pen. "Listen boy. Forget what those bastards told you, that you're special, you're the one, the only one, only you can save the Nomadin-child. Forget it! They're cowards! Worse than cowards, sending a boy to save the prophesied child. Now give me your name!"

Ilien advanced. "Tell me where she is or I swear I'll—"

The man's hands flew to his mouth. "What? Turn me into a toad?" he mocked. He shook his head and laughed. "Where do they find these kids anyhow?" He placed his palms on the desk in front of him and sighed. He regarded Ilien with the hint of a smile, but beneath the outward expression a dangerous impatience lurked. "Now listen to me very carefully," he said, pinning Ilien with a glare. "You are not a wizard. You are just a boy, probably from a broken home."

Ilien started and the NiDemon raised an eyebrow. "Father left when you were three, I suppose. Believe me, you're nothing special. I've seen a dozen of your kind in my time, each the same, each a cookie-cutter version of the other. All victims, really. Sad, but true. And you're no different. The wizards seem to cling to your kind, as if for the umpteenth time that they fail to destroy Reknamarken they think the umpteenth and one will work. You've been duped, boy. Tricked, brainwashed, programmed. You are no more a wizard than I am a monster. Now give me your name, please!"

Ilien aimed the pencil at the NiDemon, sighting down its length till its tip pointed directly between the man's eyes.

"You're right. I'm not a wizard," he said. "A wizard's power pales to mine. I am Nomadin, like my father. I am the prophesied child and I possess powers beyond any mere wizard."

The NiDemon raised an eyebrow. "You?" he said. "The prophesied child?" He burst into laughter. "Now I've seen it all!" he cried, laying his head on the desk. "The prophesied child! Powers beyond any mere wizard!" He looked up at Ilien. "And he's pointing a pencil at me!" His laughter turned frenzied as he beat his palms on the desk.

"Don't listen to him, Ilien," said the pencil. "Go on. Show him what you can do."

Globe brightened to a shining spark and danced in the air around him.

"My name, sir, is Ilien Woodhill." Ilien squinted down the length of his pencil. "*Mitra mitari mitara miru!*"

A strange hum emanated from the pencil as Ilien kept it aimed at the NiDemon's head. He'd never heard that noise before. The hum turned to clicks, the clicks to knocks. Finally the pencil made a sound like a mouse passing gas and a tiny puff of smoke issued from its tip, a perfect white ring. The NiDemon watched the advancing smoke ring, his eyes wide. It broke and faded to nothing in front of his nose.

More laughter. "Mitra mitari mitara miru. Mitra mitari mitara miru." The NiDemon chanted the spell over and over like a schoolyard bully. "Mitra mitari mitara miru." But each time he did so an object in the room turned into a toad. The feather, the lightstone, the key, the pictures on the desk, even the pictures on the wall. Globe raced forward, a blazing star swirling around the NiDemon's head. The NiDemon raised a finger and she froze in the air. She fell to the ground, a phosphorescent toad.

Toads hung everywhere, bleating and croaking, draped on the desk, hopping across the floor, stuck to the walls. Finally, the only things not turned to toads were the NiDemon, the desk and chair, and Ilien, still holding his pencil in shaking hands.

The NiDemon fell silent. His eyes flashed red in the gloom—most of the lights had been turned to toads as well—and he rose from his chair, advancing on Ilien.

"I tried to tell you. I did," he said. Ilien retreated toward the vanished door. The NiDemon's eyes glowed brighter, like two stoked stoves. "But you just don't listen. You are nothing. You never were. That's why they chose you in the first place." As he drew closer, a pair of shadowy humps rose from his shoulders. "You are just a boy, a lost and lonely boy looking for the father he never knew. Powerless."

Don't listen to him, thought his pencil. *It's not true. He's trying to break you down.*

"Powerless," said the NiDemon again. "Frightened and nothing. Your pencil means well, but it's true. You are nothing. Not a wizard. Not even a man. And most definitely not the prophesied child. You're just a boy, a boy without a home, a boy who's been used by the Nomadin he so looks up to, but a boy nonetheless. A boy! And that is why I know you are

265

nothing. The only Nomadin-child in all Nadae is a girl, my boy. A girl!"

Ilien backed into the wall where the door had been. His pencil, held at his side, was silent. "That's not true. I'm the one," he whispered.

The NiDemon walked closer, growing taller, eyes ablaze. "It is true. I was there. I brought her before the Swan with the others. Gallund and Gilindilin, both so hopeful, so sure in their belief that the Swan could help, could make it all go away. I was there. The Nomadin-child was a girl."

He stopped a step from Ilien. The shadowy humps on his shoulders stretched into wings as black as night. "She is a girl, and you are nothing!"

"It's not true," said Ilien, pressing himself against the wall. "I'm the one." He seemed to fold in on himself, arms wrapped tightly around his shoulders, head turned down, shoulders slumped. "It's not true."

But it was. It had to be. The Swan's words came back to him. *You were brought to me by three Nomadin. One was Gilindilin, the wizardess. The other two were wizards. Yes, one was Gallund. But the other was . . .*

Genten! The NiDemon was Genten! But how? How was that possible? It just couldn't be.

Ilien stood against the wall, a small boy, lost and frightened, who only wanted his mother.

"Look at you!" said Genten, taking a final step forward. "Just look at you." The glow in his eyes retreated, faded away, till what remained were the eyes of a man, soft and blue. The shadow of his wings disappeared and he laid gentle hands on Ilien's shoulders. "It's okay, Ilien. I'm not going to hurt you. I'm not like them. I only want you to know the truth."

He turned and strode back to his desk. "Come. Sit. You will see. I am civilized, not a monster as they would have you believe. And they would, you know." He sat in his chair, leaning back to take a look at the boy before him like a professor studying a potential applicant to college. "We're not monsters at all. It is they who are the monsters. The Nomadin. Not us. We follow the ways of Reknamarken." He saw the look in Ilien's eyes. "There's no reason to fear Reknamarken," he said, sitting forward in his chair. "He's not a monster either, though I'm sure that's another lie they've fed you. He's far from it. He is the Creator, after all."

Again Genten read Ilien's face. "Yes, yes I know. Disconcerting, isn't it, to be told that God is the boogie man. But it's true. What is it they call him? The Necromancer?" Genten shook his head and frowned. "The Nomadin are masters at bending the truth, greying black and white until both look the same, or reversed. Just look at the name they chose for us. NiDemon. So sinister. So evil sounding. It's nothing more than Nomadin in reverse. A child's trick. They've been that way since time immeasurable. Freedom seekers they call themselves. Freedom at the price of truth maybe. Freedom for freedom's sake. That sort of freedom is worthless. Evil thrives on that sort of freedom. And if it wasn't for the Nomadin, evil wouldn't exist at all."

Genten's hands clenched into fists. "They're the ones who rose up against the Creator to fight for their twisted sense of freedom. They destroyed the Eden that was once Nadae. And they're the ones who locked Reknamarken away!"

Ilien remained silent, fear and doubt turning circles in his mind.

Genten raised a hand. "I know what you're going to say," he said, lowering his voice. "That I was once with them. That I too was a Nomadin. That may well be true, but I have since made amends for my foolishness. I have endured their company for three hundred years, always seeking release for my banished brothers. You see, I might have come late to the call, but not too late."

He leaned back in his chair again. "How many wasted centuries have I studied nothing but what they fed me? The True Language they call it. As true as the eye on a butterfly's wings, and as fragile, I might add." He swiveled his chair in a gentle circle, finally coming to rest facing Ilien again.

"But I have since seen the light," he said, his face stretched by a wide smile. "And what a glorious light it is. I have studied the secret power of Nihilic, the secret power the Nomadin have denied the world. I have endured their company, always loath to do so, always waiting for the chance to free my brothers from Loehs Sedah. And now a crossing has been unearthed. The Child has been brought before me, and the key as well. How delightful. How truly delightful. Now the world will see that evil is their doing, not ours."

Ilien shook his head, and pressed himself against the wall.

Genten fell silent, his brow furrowing in anger. "Need proof?" he spat. "Who else would send a Groll to kill one of their own?"

Ilien gathered himself up. "Now I know you lie," he said. "Gallund would never send that monster after me."

The NiDemon steepled his hands behind his desk and smiled. "You're right. He didn't send it after you. He sent it after her. After all, you're nothing but a worthless, little boy."

The tips of Ilien's ears began to burn. His heart raced. The wall at his back felt like fists beating against him. It wasn't true. Lies! All of it lies! He possessed powers. He was the one. They told him. He'd seen it with his own eyes. Powers beyond any mere wizard. He was being tricked, and he suddenly didn't like being tricked. Genten was wrong. He was a Nomadin through and through. Not a worthless, little boy. A Nomadin.

Genten smiled, reading his thoughts. "Will you never learn? You can't save her. You haven't any magic and the sooner you get that through your head the better it'll be for you in the end. I have her. And I have the key."

Ilien's mind raced. The NiDemon was wrong. He did have magic. He'd show him just how wrong he was.

"We have the Book too, you know." The glow in Genten's eyes returned. He seemed pleased with the effect his words had on Ilien. "Yes. The Book. It's right in here." He stroked the open drawer beside him. "Would you like to see it?" He reached a hand forward.

Ilien felt the hairs on the back of his neck crawl into the air.

Genten drew out a lock box and placed it on the desk before of him. "You're witnessing history in the making, my boy. In fact, you'll be the last living soul to see the Book before it's opened. The last person in all Nadae to see God imprisoned."

He fumbled with the lock on the box until it sprang open with a click. He looked up with a smile, his eyes ablaze. "Of course, we'll have to get that girlfriend of yours to do the actual deed. But behold, it's right in here, the Book. The end of evil. The beginning of—"

The NiDemon's wings flew up like window shades.

The Book was already open.

The wall behind Ilien jumped and a crack spread across its clean white surface like a split across a frozen lake. Another blow and the wall exploded, chunks of wood and plaster showering past Ilien, across the desk, knocking the lock box to the floor. A black barbed tail snaked through the hole in the wall, followed by the limping form of the Groll.

Its mouth, once a curve of gleaming fangs, gaped open, its lower jaw missing, its razor-sharp teeth reduced to a mangle of bloody, jagged edges. One eye stared forth, an oozing white orb surrounded by puffy, red flesh, the other eye a swollen slit. Its right hind leg dragged upon the floor, broken and useless. Its human-like hands hung loose at its sides, chafed raw from its battle to climb from the raging river. Only its tail remained unharmed, black barb gleaming with oily venom.

Ilien jumped back. The Groll shuffled forward with amazing

269

speed, its tail lancing out, streaking across the space between it and Ilien with an audible hiss. Ilien threw his hands up, a silent scream caught in his throat.

The air in the room exploded. The thunder-shock threw Genten from his chair. White hot fire raced from Ilien's pencil, striking the hurtling tail, igniting it into a flaming torch. The Groll jerked back and fell to the floor as magic surged through its body, worms of fire burrowing into its flesh. It writhed and screamed, its burning tail stabbing at the floor in agony. The force of Ilien's unsummoned spell flung him across the room. He struck the wall behind Genten's desk, knocked senseless.

Genten rose from the floor. A shroud of smoke hung in the air, tinged with the bitter odor of burnt flesh. The Groll lay in a heap, unmoving. Curls of steam rose from the barb of its tail. Vitreous fluid seeped from its ruined eye. Ilien moaned and Genten spun around. On the floor beside Ilien lay the Book, torn in two.

Genten sat heavily on the edge of his desk. "How could I have been so blind?" he said, his eyes falling on Ilien.

Ilien crawled to the wall, still clutching his pencil, his lungs fighting for air. He coughed and gagged, aware that he was being watched but helpless to do anything else. When he finally caught his breath he gazed up at Genten, dazed.

The NiDemon sat staring at him, the glow in his eyes gone, his wings vanished. A look of awe spread across his worried features and he covered his mouth with a bloody hand.

"Forgive me Master," he whispered. "Forgive me. I never saw it. Your final prophesy, so simple, so brilliant. A Nomadin-child would set you free."

He rubbed at his eyes, then looked at Ilien again. "It's you. You're him. You've been free all along. Reborn! Reborn as a Nomadin-child! Brilliant master! How truly brilliant!" He rose from the desk.

For a moment, Ilien thought that Genten meant to help him

up, but the NiDemon froze, hands outstretched, mouth wide open. A trickle of blood slipped from his lower lip.

Genten's chest exploded in a spray of crimson as a long black spike jutted from between his ribs. He rose in the air, impaled upon the Groll's tail while the beast's ruined body still cowered on the floor. Genten released a silent scream, arms spread wide. His wings flew up to beat the air. A brilliant flash lit the room and Groll and NiDemon disappeared without a sound.

Chapter XXIII

Nomadin

Ilien sat with his back against the far wall and watched the smoke settle, listening to the falling silence. It wasn't until his heart had stopped pounding and his breathing came slow and steady that he noticed the changes in the room since the NiDemon had vanished. The room was bright again, the toads gone, replaced by the lights and pictures they had once been. The door too had reappeared, only now a gaping hole had been blown through it. Globe flew up from the floor to hover over Ilien's head, released from her amphibious prison. Lying at Ilien's feet was the Book, torn neatly in two along its binding.

You're free! He heard Genten's words again, those impossible words. *It's you. You're him. You've been free all along. Reborn! Reborn as a Nomadin-child! Brilliant, Master! How truly brilliant!*

It wasn't true. A demon's trick. All of it lies. It had to be. For if Genten was the NiDemon, present with Gallund and Gilindilin when they brought him before the Swan, then that would make Gallund his father. And if Gallund was his father then how could he be—

Kinil ubid illubid kinar. The words spat from Ilien's mind without a thought. The tattered remains of the Book burst into flames. Lies. All of it lies. He was just a boy. Son of Nomadin wizards, yes, but a boy. Not . . . not . . . he couldn't finish the thought.

"Not what he thinks I am," he said aloud. He kicked the ashes of the smoldering Book away and huddled closer to the wall.

"Ilien!" urged his pencil. "Ilien. Get up! You have to—"

"Wait!" cried Ilien. Scattered around him lay Windy's belongings—the lightstone, the key, the feather. "Windy!"

As he called her name the wall behind him gave out and he fell backwards to the floor, peering once again at more flameless torches hung from the ceiling.

He scrambled to his feet. The wall had been another door, hidden until the NiDemon, until Genten, had vanished. It opened into another small room, this one without desks, without pictures on the walls. This room was empty except for a small figure sitting bound and gagged in a chair by the wall.

Ilien ran and threw his arms around the princess. She screamed through her gag, thrashing, trying to throw him off.

She was blindfolded as well.

Ilien yanked off her blindfold. Windy's eyes grew wide and filled with tears. She said something under her gag and Ilien pulled that off too.

"You came for me," she said. Then she thrashed again. "The NiDemon! He's in the other room!"

"He's gone," said Ilien. "He's gone. You're safe."

"He'll come back!"

Ilien gripped her by the shoulders. "No, he won't. He's dead, Windy. You're safe now."

Windy stopped her struggling and looked at him curiously, her eyes still touched with fear. "You killed the NiDemon?"

"No," he answered. "The Groll did. It's dead too."

The princess looked past Ilien and into the other room. "He thought I was the savior," she said. Her eyes found Ilien's. "I'm supposed to open the Book and release the Necromancer. He said I held the key. He said I was the child of wizards."

Ilien knelt down and started untying her in silence.

273

"He said it was my destiny. And he has the Book!"

The ropes around Windy fell to the floor. "It was a lie, Windy. All of it a lie."

"But the Book! It's here!"

"No. It's not," assured Ilien. "Another lie."

Windy stared at Ilien, dumbfounded.

"Some appearances are not what they seem," said Ilien. "That goes for words as well." Inwardly Ilien winced at the lies he told, lies to cover more lies. "I don't know what his game was, but it's over now," he continued. "The NiDemon is gone. There is no Groll, and there is no Book. You are the princess of Evernden, and I . . ." He paused just long enough to remember that Windy knew nothing of the prophesy, nothing of what the Swan had told him. ". . . I'm just a wizard's apprentice."

Windy hugged him suddenly, and he knelt beside her, feeling her warm embrace, her trust in him. A part of him relaxed, something inside unwinding like a clock that had been keyed too tight. But deeper down he still felt ashamed.

"Let's get out of here," he said. He rose to his feet and pulled the map from his pocket, hoping there was an easier way out than retracing the way he'd come in. As he struggled to open it he heard a familiar, squeaky voice.

"Look. It's him," came a whisper from somewhere in the room.

"Sshh. Sshh," hissed someone else.

"Don't tell me to sshh!"

Ilien looked up and the whispers fell silent. Windy moved closer to Ilien, her eyes darting around the empty room. Globe brightened to a tiny full moon. Ilien smiled and put a finger to his lips, squeezing his pencil tight for good measure. He had a hunch the silence would be unbearable. A moment later he was proved right.

"I told you my intuition would serve us well," came another quiet whisper.

"Blast your intuition! We wouldn't be in this mess if you had just listened to me in the first place."

"What? Am I supposed to—"

"Show yourselves!" called Ilien, stepping forward. "And no tricks! Or there'll be trouble."

The room fell silent and Ilien raised his pencil in the air.

"He knows we're here," came another whisper. "We had better show ourselves."

"Sshh!"

"Don't shush me!"

The room fell silent again.

"I warned you," said Ilien.

He waved his pencil through the air in an intricate pattern. "*Inspiritum callosum*," he intoned. "You'd better show yourselves!" he shouted, and returned to his nonsensical spell. "*Magnesium—*"

"Okay! Okay! We're here! We're here!" cried a high-pitched, frantic voice. "Don't hurt us!"

The two hairless creatures materialized before them. One was covering its large, lidless eyes with its hands. The other stood with its hands on its hips, its eyes shining silver.

"Oh my," said Windy.

"Oh my, oh my," said the strange creatures with the green and silver eyes, ogling Windy up and down.

"Stop it!" said Ilien. "What are you doing here?"

"Trying to escape," said the one covering its eyes.

"Paying the price of intuition," said the other.

Ilien stepped forward and jabbed the creature with his pencil. "Why are you really here?" he said. The creature jumped back and cringed beside its companion, its large almond-shaped eyes turning blue.

"Ilien, you're scaring them," said Windy.

"Remember what I said about appearances," replied Ilien. "Now tell me why you're here. Who sent you?"

275

"We cannot divulge our employers," said the one still covering its eyes.

"Very well," said Ilien, and he began waving his pencil in the air again. "*Inspiritum callosum*—"

"Wait! Wait!" cried the other. "The wizards. The wizards sent us!" And it too covered its eyes in fear.

"You know these two?" asked Windy.

"I've seen them around," said Ilien.

"I told you we should have stayed squelched," said one of the trembling creatures.

So it was true, thought Ilien. *The wizards had sent the Groll! But how could Gallund allow such a thing?* The knowledge of it nearly took his breath away, but he forced a smile for Windy's sake. With all he'd been through, he was far beyond surprises now anyhow.

"Ilien, they can't be all that bad if the wizards sent them," said Windy.

"She's right," said one, peeking out from under its hands. "We can't be all that bad."

If it was true that the wizards did send the Groll, then what else was true? Was the prophesied child really a girl, as Genten had said? Ilien looked at Windy.

Windy moved to the two creatures and put an arm around one. "We're trying to get out of here too," she said. "Don't worry about my friend here. He's had a very bad day, that's all."

The two tiny creatures peered at Ilien in terror. *There's no point pushing the issue,* thought Ilien. The more questions he asked, the more Windy would learn. As it stood, Windy didn't know anything and he preferred to keep it that way.

"She's right," said Ilien, dropping his pencil to his side. "I've had a very bad day. I didn't mean to scare you. We're trying to get out of here too." He turned back to the map, hoping the two creatures would let it drop and seize the opportunity to escape. But blast! The map had reverted to its old, obnoxious self and wouldn't open up.

"Yes, yes," said one, giving its companion a knowing look. "Out of here. Us too."

"Right," said the other, watching as Ilien grew increasingly frustrated with the map.

Ilien felt one of Anselm's tirades coming over him as the map eluded his best efforts to unfold it.

"Never mind that map," said one of the creatures. "My intuition has had plenty of time to determine the best way out. And it's right here." It touched the wall with a long, thin finger.

"You mean to tell me you've known the way out of here all this time?" said the other, its eyes flashing red.

"I tried to tell you several times, but you never listen," replied the first, its own eyes glowing orange as it spoke.

"Well perhaps if you didn't always speak in riddles!"

"But there's no way out that way," said Windy. "It's a solid wall."

The two creatures looked at Windy simultaneously. "A thief never trusts her eyes," they said in unison. At that the intuitive one ran its hands over the wall, its long, thin fingers probing its surface. A moment later a door swung open onto darkness.

"See," it said, turning to give its companion a snide look. "A secret door. My intuition was right as usual."

"But will it get us out of here?" asked Windy, peering through the door and down the dimly lit corridor beyond.

The intuitive one scratched its head. "I'm not sure."

"You're not sure?" echoed Windy.

"Intuition is not a science, you know."

"It'll get us out of here," said Ilien, holding the still struggling map open before him. He released the map and it folded up into a stubborn, little packet. "And it's not far. Come on."

Globe darted forward to lead the way.

Soon they stood blinking in the bright light of mid-afternoon, the mouth of a wide cave behind them. The journey out was quick, without the twists and turns and awful smells of the way in. Stairs led down the mountain in front of them, carved from the rock itself. A heavy mist shrouded the land below. The two hairless creatures bounded toward the stairs and freedom.

"Hold on!" said Ilien. "The last I knew, the Giant's army was camped at the foot of the mountain, preparing for battle. I don't think it's wise to go running down there just yet. Who knows what lies in the mist below?"

The two creatures stood poised on the edge of the stairs, sniffing the air with their button-like noses. "I do not think that's mist down there," said one. The other wrinkled its face.

"I don't care. I still say it's too dangerous to go running into it," said Ilien.

"Um, Ilien?" piped his pencil. "I think they're trying to tell you that the mist isn't mist. It's smoke."

Ilien looked past them at the impenetrable white blanket that hid the plains below. "Then the battle is under way," he said.

"Or it could be over," said Windy.

"And what does your intuition tell you now?" said Ilien, turning to the two small creatures, not really knowing which one was which, and growing annoyed because of it.

The one farthest down the stairs surveyed the haze as if it could see straight through it. "It's over. It's definitely over."

Its companion smiled and gave it a pat on the back. "Come on then," it said, moving past and down the stairs.

"Aren't you forgetting something?" asked Ilien.

The creature stopped and turned back toward Ilien, its eyes flashing green before turning a deep shade of blue. "What now?" it asked.

"If the battle is over as you say it is, aren't you a little curious who won? There's no sense walking down the mountain if it means walking into a victorious Giant army."

SHAWN P. CORMIER

"Ilien's right," said Windy. "Can your intuition tell us who's left down there?"

The intuitive one peered out over the sea of smoke below. "I don't know," it said, its eyes growing large and black. "But I sense many dead." It began to shiver. "Many, many dead. But as to who the victor is, I cannot say for certain."

Ilien too peered out over the thick, white blanket that hid the battle's outcome. "Then I guess the only way to tell is to climb down and find out. If the Giants are the victors, then it's probably best that we try to sneak off the mountain now anyhow, while the smoke is heaviest. Besides, we can't stay here forever."

"Yes, yes," said the creature farthest down the stairs. "Wise words." It resumed its quick descent. Reluctantly, the others followed.

The clear air quickly gave way to a shroud of stinging smoke. Its odor was not the comforting smell of campfires, but the acrid stench of battle and death, tinged with a bitter reek that Ilien could not quite place.

The small company navigated the stone stairs carefully, keeping close not only for fear of losing each other in the smoky haze, but for fear itself. What if the Giants were the victors? Would they be caught? Would they have come all this way just to be killed at the very end? They traveled slowly, methodically, on guard against anything that might jump out at them in the smoke laden mist.

A warm breeze stirred around them, driving away the mountain's chill and swirling the heavy smoke into tiny, white eddies. The stairs finally ended at a small landing of flagstones. Globe's light cast a hazy halo around them, and they could see nothing save for what lay at their feet. The blind, white silence was unnerving. Then suddenly the wind gusted and swept the air clean, and the flagstones they stood upon became a pedestal for the gruesome sight below.

279

The smoking, ruined bodies of Giants and men stretched out before them, crumpled and blackened, strewn across the battlefield like a field of smoldering campfires. Swords and shields littered the ground, sticks and driftwood now, useless without the men and Giants who had wielded them.

"Why are they all burning?" asked Windy, covering her mouth.

"Magic," answered one of the strange creatures. Its eyes were a faded grey, and tears streamed down its leathery cheeks. "Nomadin magic."

The small company stood frozen. No one turned away. No one spoke. Each was lost in their own horror. The silence was broken by a forlorn call for help, weak but urgent.

"Is there anyone there?" The cry came from further ahead, from somewhere amidst the hissing wreckage of burning bodies. "Help me. Please."

Without a thought Ilien ran forward, weaving through the maze of smoking corpses toward the spot the cry had come from. He flung his hand to his mouth to keep from choking on the stench.

"I'm here!" he shouted. "Where are you?"

The voice didn't answer at first, and Ilien thought he'd been too late after all. But then, "Here. Over here," came the call again, quiet now, weaker.

Ilien came upon the man suddenly, nearly stumbling into him among the surrounding bodies. He found him behind the burning remains of a Giant, clutching at the spot where his legs had been, legs seared to ashes now. He knew there would be no helping this man.

"Thank god. Thank god," whispered the soldier. Then noticing the look on Ilien's face he added, "It's not that bad. Help me up. I could walk if only you could help me up."

Ilien stifled a gag with his arm and knelt beside the dying man. "Sshh. Lay still now. Rest."

The soldier grabbed his shield. "Here. Take this. There may be Giants still about." He fell into a fit of coughing.

Ilien grabbed hold of the shield and caught his reflection in its polished surface. He jumped at what he saw and threw the shield aside.

"That's right," said the soldier, studying Ilien as if he'd never seen a twelve-year-old boy before. "You don't need a shield, do you?"

"Don't worry," said Ilien, trying not to look at the man's cremated legs. "The battle is over. Lie still. You'll be okay."

The man's grim smile faded, replaced by a serenity Ilien had never seen before. "I've done well, then," he whispered. And he said no more. Ilien knew then that the man was dead.

The others soon arrived, falling silent as Ilien gently closed the man's eyes.

"Halt!" The sudden shout issued from behind them. Without warning a small company of men approached with weapons drawn, weaving their way through the smoking corpses. "By order of the king of Berkhelven, hold or be killed!" cried the leader. The soldiers, in full battle regalia, chain mail and helms, gauntlets and shields, swords and spears, quickly surrounded them.

"I am Ilien Woodhill, apprentice to Gallund the wizard!" cried Ilien, his throat tight and dry, tears finally springing to his eyes. "I have with me the princess of Evernden. We need your help." He turned to identify the two strange creatures, but they were gone.

"Ilien Woodhill?" asked the leader, a man with a very long spear pointed directly at him. "We've been searching for you. Come with us at once."

For the second time in a day, Ilien found himself sitting in a tent in the middle of the Giant's encampment. Except this time he wasn't tied to a post, and he wasn't alone. The encampment was no longer occupied by Giants either. The army of Berkhelven had commandeered the camp, moving the dead to burial pits and ushering the wounded to makeshift hospitals.

Ilien sat at a table that boasted a large basket of fruit and several pitches of water. Beside him, Windy attacked an apple as if she hadn't eaten in days. He studied her for a moment and realized she probably hadn't eaten in days. He noticed then how awful she looked, her hair matted and disheveled, her face streaked with stains, clothes torn. What had she undergone while a prisoner of the NiDemon? He had, up until then, thought only of himself. But she had no doubt suffered trials of her own, and he suddenly saw her with new eyes. No longer did she seem the haughty princess of Evernden who always looked for attention. She was transformed somehow. Changed.

"Ilien."

The voice caught Ilien off guard and he jumped. He wasn't surprised so much by the suddenness of the greeting as by the familiar voice that had spoken it. He turned to see Thessien standing near the entrance, twice brought back from the dead as far as Ilien was concerned. Poking through the tent flap behind him came the stonewall face of Anselm.

Ilien would have jumped from his chair and ran to them. His friends were alive, his friends who had suffered so much, who had come all this way, who had risked their lives for him! But he sat stiffly in his chair, gripping the table with both hands.

"Thessien! Anselm!" As he spoke their names he began to unravel and tears streamed down his cheeks. But the tangled knot inside him that the NiDemon had tied so tight remained. He stared down at his hands, calloused, cut, dirty, man's hands now.

Anselm rushed past Thessien, nearly knocking the prince of Ashevery to the ground. He scooped up Ilien, chair and all, in his trunk-like arms.

"Ilien, my boy! You're alright!" The chair creaked and

groaned as the Giant squeezed Ilien in a crushing embrace.

"Careful, Anselm," said Thessien as he approached, an equally wide smile across his face. "He's only just escaped being killed, I'm sure. Gentle. Gentle." He looked up at Ilien. "I'm glad to see you well, Ilien." He turned to Windy. "And you also, Princess Windy. Your father's heart will be lifted to learn you are safe. He has feared the worse these last several days."

Windy looked up from her apple.

"Yes," said Thessien. "Your father is safe, though his castle has seen better days."

Windy smiled wearily in relief, but when she saw the Giant her smile fell away. The apple slipped from her hand, rolled across the table and dropped to the ground.

"Don't worry," said Ilien from his perch high up in the Giant's arms. "He's with us now." He looked sideways at Anselm, his brow wrinkled in confusion. "How is that anyhow? How did you escape?"

"The armies of Berkhelven and Evendolen arrived just in time," said Anselm, setting Ilien and his chair back down.

"It seems the presence of a Giant army was enough to settle their dispute," said Thessien, coming to stand by Ilien. "Their combined strength proved a formidable force against the Giants. But even still they might have lost if it wasn't for the timely arrival of the wizards."

Ilien nodded his understanding but remained seated. His body felt drained, empty, and he wasn't sure he could stand just yet. Happiness and relief washed over him and he smiled up at the towering form of Anselm, whose forehead was creased with worry.

"Then it's true," said Windy, still eyeing the Giant nervously. "All the burned bodies. It was their doing."

"Yes," said Thessien. "And thankfully so."

"Thankfully so?" said Ilien. The prince's words had struck

283

a chord within him, and he suddenly didn't feel tired any longer. "Men as well as Giants were burned. I've seen the battlefield with my own eyes."

Anselm suddenly bent over him, smiling sadly. "Yes, it's true, Ilien. Many of my people were killed. But if war is never the best solution, it is often the only one available."

Ilien looked away, ashamed by Anselm's words. "So the wizards are here?" he asked.

"Yes. All of them," said Thessien. "Except Gallund, of course."

"And the wizardess Gilindilin?" asked Ilien, looking up hopefully.

"No," answered Thessien. "Only the wizards came. And they urgently want to speak with you."

I'm sure they do, thought Ilien. There was much they would want to know. He wasn't so sure they'd accept simple answers, either. And lying was out of the question. Wizards had ways of telling fact from fiction. Not for the last time he wished Gallund was there. Though Thessien and Anselm stood by his side, he suddenly felt in danger.

"And they insist on questioning you alone," said Thessien.

"Yes. What of the Book?" asked Anselm. "Did you find it? Is it safe?"

"No!" said Ilien, his mind gripped by panic. This couldn't be happening! After all he'd been through, he wasn't safe even here, surrounded by friends. The wizards had tried to kill him once and failed. Now they had come to finish the job. And what could anyone do to stop them? Just look at what they had done on the battlefield. Who there could stand against such power? He had to leave! He had to flee! He looked to the tent entrance.

"What of the NiDemon?" asked Anselm.

Thessien raised an eyebrow at Ilien's silence.

A commotion rose outside the tent, shouts and the running

of booted feet. The tent flap flew open and a young soldier, out of breath and looking worried, raced in.

"You'd better come quick," he said. "We have a visitor—a very strange visitor."

Thessien sighed and followed the man out. Anselm trailed after him. Windy and Ilien sat looking at each other. Windy was just reaching for a plum when Ilien heard a loud honking, followed by shouts and laughter from the men outside.

"It sounds like a gaggle of geese," said Windy, her plum poised in mid-air.

"It isn't a goose," said Ilien, jumping to his feet. "It's a swan. Come on!"

Once outside, they pushed their way through the throng of sweaty and bloody men that had gathered around the source of the honking. As they drew nearer the commotion, Ilien saw a group of robed men who weren't laughing, but rather staring grimly at the scene before them.

Nearly a dozen strong, the wizards stood apart from the crowd. Tall, clothed in black, grim-faced, with their long, silver beards braided and set with polished, silver beads, the wizards exuded an air of power, and none ventured too close.

The Swan stood in the center of a small clearing surrounded by the rowdy faces of laughing and jeering men. She ruffled her feathers and beat her wings when any tried to approach, including Anselm and Thessien. As Ilien and Windy broke through the crowd, a shout went up from the company of wizards. The Swan turned and honked in Ilien's direction.

Ilien stopped. *Why was she honking? Why wasn't she speaking?*

The Swan honked again, louder this time.

Ilien sensed eyes hardening upon him, and with no effort at all he heard the thoughts of those who stood robed behind him. *It is the child! It is the child! He lives! He lives!*

Ilien pulled Windy forward. The Swan's black eyes flicked

past him at the wizards, even as she beat her wings to keep Anselm and Thessien away.

"What's wrong?" asked Anselm. "I've never seen you like this before. Is it something I've done?"

Ilien moved quickly past Anselm and Thessien, dragging Windy with him. When he drew near the Swan, she said, "Quick! Climb on my back! I have to get you out of here!"

Ilien hesitated. The thoughts of the wizards had fallen silent, but Ilien felt the strike of their eyes on his back like a volley of thrown daggers.

"Gallund's in danger," said the Swan. "You have to rescue him. Now get on!"

The crowd closed in. The wizards broke ranks and ran forward.

"Get on!" cried the Swan.

Ilien turned to Windy. "You have to trust me," he said. "Climb on and hold tight."

"What are you doing?" shouted Anselm as Ilien and Windy clambered upon the Swan's back.

The crowd rushed forward, shouting and jeering. The wizards tried to fight their way through.

"Hold tight!" cried the Swan, and she beat her wings in the air. The crowd fell back, shielding their eyes from the blowing sand and flying debris as the great bird rose from the ground.

"Wait!" called Anselm. "Don't go! Don't leave without me!"

Ilien felt Windy's arms squeeze tightly around him. The earth lurched and fell away. The men below crashed together, engulfing the wizards in a sea of sweaty bodies. But as Ilien watched the scene with more than a little amusement, he saw a lone figure break from the crowd and follow them, bounding over the ground like a ten-ton gazelle.

"Wait for me!" shouted Anselm. "Wait for me!"

THANK YOU!

I hope you've enjoyed reading Nomadin: Book One. Yes! The tale continues in Book Two!

Though I wrote Nomadin from start to finish in exactly thirteen months, the tale itself was over sixteen years in the making. I began writing about Ilien and his adventure in 1987, during my sophomore year of college. Through many fits and starts, marriage, two children, buying my first house, becoming firmly entrenched in a family business, I managed to eke it out one word at a time, writing at night when the house was still and all my other obligations were "responsibly" handled. This will come as no surprise to anyone who aspires to write a book. A writer is compelled to write. I am compelled to write *this* tale, that's all. And a responsible writer will write when he or she can. What *does* surprise a writer is knowing that someone actually took the time to read their book. So **Thank You** for finding and reading Nomadin: Book One. Please tell me what you think of it. I can be reached at www.pineviewpress.com, or feel free to write:

Shawn Cormier
42 Central Street
Southbridge, Ma 01550
USA

And please spread the word about Nomadin. Tell friends and family! Submit your review online at amazon.com and barnesandnoble.com! Ask for it at your local bookstore! And please visit my website, www.pineviewpress.com, for more information on the continuing adventure. Once again . . .

THANK YOU!

ABOUT THE AUTHOR

Shawn Cormier was born in 1967 and grew up in the small town of Southbridge, Massachusetts. He has been scribbling down stories since the fifth grade, and earned his degree in creative writing from Long Island University, Southampton Campus. When not writing, he can be found in his family's jewelry store, repairing jewelry and studying gems. He currently resides in southern Massachusetts with his wife and two children.